JAMES CALDER

ABOUT THE AUTHOR

AMY STOLLS's young adult novel *Palms to the Ground* was published in 2005 to critical acclaim and was a Parents' Choice Gold Award winner. A former environmental journalist who covered the Exxon Valdez oil spill in Alaska, she is currently a literature program officer for the National Endowment for the Arts. She lives in Washington, DC, with her husband and son.

THE

NINTH

WIFE

THE
NINTH
WIFE

a novel

AMY STOLLS

HARPER

NEW YORK . LONDON . TORONTO . SYDNEY

HARPER

FIRST EDITION

Library of Congress Cataloging-in-Publication Data

Stolls, Amy.
    The ninth wife : a novel / Amy Stolls. — 1st ed.
      p. cm.
    ISBN 978-0-06-185189-6
     1. Single women—Fiction. 2. Irish—United States—Fiction.
3. Divorced women—Fiction. I. Title.

PS3619.T65625N56 2011
813'.6—dc22

                                    2010034617

11 12 13 14 15 OV/RRD 10 9 8 7 6 5 4 3 2 1

FOR CLIFF

Rowing with just one oar
I lost that oar

For the first time I looked round at the wide stretch of water

· ⊂━━━━⊃ ·

Look, that dandelion drenched by a shower
is making the best of it, pursing its lips

Stand firm, little girl

—KO UN, FROM *Flowers of a Moment*

PART I

CHAPTER ONE

March 2005, Washington, D.C.

Pick a partner," says Bess's karate teacher, "and get a tomb-stone." As Bess learned nine months ago when she began her schooling in Tae Kwon Do, a tombstone is a black rectangular punching bag that you hold against your torso as a target for someone to kick you repeatedly in the stomach. Or, ideally, your solar plexus, your *myung chi*, the soft spot at the top of the rib cage that if kicked directly with a powerful *eap chagi*, say, by a one-hundred-ninety-pound software engineer from Bethesda, can knock the breath out of you and send you flying across the room into a pile of smelly sparring gear. Tombstones, Bess has come to realize, are a good thing. Tombstones can save lives.

The dojo where they practice karate and self-defense twice a week is an old elementary school gymnasium in the heart of a Latino community. It smells of sweat and mildew. The white ceiling, veined with cracks and water stains, sheds paint chips onto the buckled wooden floor where the occasional cockroach scurries from the dark corners behind the mats. Only two of the tall windows open, but to lift the industrial-strength glass is to risk dropping it and smashing a finger. Bess looks around at the other students in their white *gi*s cinched with belts in white, yellow, green, and blue. She sees pairs make eye contact, bow to each other, get ready for the next drill, and she realizes she is the only one left holding up her hand, signaling her availability.

"Watch this time," says her sensei. He is a sexy second-degree black belt with the body of a gladiator, a man who knows how to swing his nunchucks. He points her off to the side. "Come in next round."

In elementary school Bess was an A-for-effort player, not the last teammate to be picked but never the first. What she lacked in grace and coordination she made up for with good sportsmanship, happy to be one of the ducks who clapped for the goose. It's possible her tendency to flinch at anything thrown at her could be traced to a year of red rubber balls flung meanly (though, in retrospect, perhaps flirtatiously) at her nose by one greasy-haired, hygiene-challenged Douglas Lillicrop in the third grade. Regardless, she didn't see herself scoring points or winning races or really venturing beyond the fitness trends of the decades—aerobics, Jazzercise, Pilates, yoga—until she saw an ad for the D.C. Karate Association.

The first time she wore her *gi* she also mistakenly wore her lucky Valentine's Day panties that showed through where she sweated like a boiled lobster in gauze. And last week in the turtle tot class where she loves to volunteer she bopped one of the cutest tots on the noggin with a foam noodle to get his guards up and he responded by throwing up on her feet. So there were setbacks. Still, working out at the dojo usually makes her feel upbeat and alive, and a force to be reckoned with. In the girls' bathroom one time, an eight-year-old in the ninja class caught her confronting her own reflection in the mirror above the thigh-high sink, saying, *You talking to me? You talking to ME?* The little girl wanted to know why she was saying that. Bess laughed and said she was just practicing looking tough. *Well then sorry, but it's not working,* the girl told her. *I see you around. You're too nice.* She suggested Bess get a gold front tooth, tattoo her knuckles, and stop smiling so much. *Then you be badass,* she said. Bess thanked her for the advice.

So Bess might not appear badass but she *feels* that way sometimes and loves it. She loves the power in thinking of herself in simple warfare terms: you kick, punch, strike; you block, protect, defend. An ebb and flow of pure primal instincts, the body an arsenal of weapons—forehead, back of the head, knees, elbows, feet, fists in various formations, fingers for grabbing and jabbing. For the first time in a long time, she's in good shape and feels confident in her physical self.

Her emotional self, on the other hand, is another story.

"Switch," says her sensei, and Bess bows to a thick, squat man with a hairline that begins on the top of his head. He begins kicking. Bess tightens her stomach behind the tombstone to absorb the blows, keenly aware that today is her thirty-fifth birthday and here she is getting kicked in the gut. Which, in a sense, is a manifestation of how her birthday began this morning when she saw Sonny.

She was getting into the car of her close friend, Cricket—a sixty-six-year-old retired mortgage broker who lives on the first floor of her building. Cricket cooks her casseroles, pulls dead leaves off her plants, and brags about his Shar-Pei, Stella, named after his favorite character in *A Streetcar Named Desire*. He is celibate and gay, and gossip is to him as gasoline is to his black Buick LeSabre. He began visiting Bess often and unannounced two years ago after she organized a community support effort on his behalf. Before that she had only exchanged cordial hellos in the corridor with him and his flamboyant partner and, if there was time, commented on the weather and scratched his pooch's ears. But the news of his partner's death from a sudden staph infection hit her hard for reasons she couldn't explain. She'd see Cricket sitting at his window, alone, lonely, sad, and distant. One morning, she posted notices on her neighbors' doors and coordinated a schedule of dinners, errands, and, if he desired, company to help him cope. To everyone else he posted a notice in the lobby of sincere gratitude. To Bess he bowed, introduced himself anew with his hand over his heart, and said he would be forever grateful for such kindness. Bess has thrived on his friendship ever since.

"Hey, Bess," she heard from across the street. She had just opened the car door. "Bess, it's Sonny."

"Oh my God, this is going to be good," murmured Cricket from the driver's seat, peeking over his sunglasses. They watched Sonny tug a pregnant woman toward them like a suitcase on wheels.

Bess had no time to block and defend. "Sonny," she said,

more as an identifier than a greeting. Sonny was a beautiful thirty-year-old Asian-American Southerner, and that mix alone had been enough to get her attention three years ago when he pulled his supermarket cart up behind hers and said she had *nahce-lookin' onyens*. He was a graphic designer who worked at home and had time to woo her. Over the six months they dated he was full of surprises, and she loved that. He played the harmonica, quoted Chomsky, and meditated each morning to try to cure his sciatica. He was strange, but she was strangely drawn to him, and when he ended it, it was not because she wasn't strange enough for him (as she suspected) but because—and he was brutally frank about this—her age scared him. He didn't want to think at all about marriage and especially not about kids.

"You look good, Bess," he said. "You change your hair?"

"My hair? Probably not." Rebuking every suggestion any hairdresser had ever given her to branch out, Bess's straight, thick, dark brown hair has always stopped above, at, or just below her shoulders, depending on her mood and the season. Often she defaults to putting it up loosely in a clip, always making sure she has a lock of it handy to fidget with the way she used to do in adolescence—twirling it around her finger and clamping it between her lips.

Sonny looked the same: goatee, black hair hanging in his eyes, runner's physique, flip-flops, hemp necklace, thick knuckles.

"What have you been up to, Sonny?" said Bess, looking down at the pregnant girl's protrusion.

The girl looked at Sonny, then smiled at Bess. "Sonnyboy's

always up to something," she said, patting the large bulge under her peasant shirt. She had long soft red hair and a scattering of freckles on her cheeks. "I'm Gaia," she said, pronouncing it *Gay-a*. Bess nodded hello.

"So where you headed?" asked Sonny.

"Karate."

"No kidding." Sonny made a few karate chops as seen on TV. "I bet you can beat me up now." He leaned into Gaia. "Baby, she can kick *mah ay-ass*."

Cricket, observing all this from inside the car, choked down a laugh.

"What's that?" asked Gaia, pointing to the seat.

"My old belt."

"How come it's not black?" said Sonny, tossing a few fake punches to her shoulder.

"It's a pearl belt. From when I first started. I'm a white belt now."

"Pearl? For real? What's next, lavender?"

Bess contemplated a demonstration: a palm thrust to the nose, a kick to the groin. "Pearl," said Gaia, like an interruption, something she pulled from the air.

"What, honey?"

"Pearl," she repeated, dreamily. "That's it, Sonny. That's the name for our baby."

"Pearl," he said. "Yeah, yeah. It's *al-raht*." They rocked their foreheads together.

"Well, if you'll excuse me," said Bess, getting into the car, "I have to go."

"Yes," said Cricket, "we do have to go. It's Bess's birthday today, after all."

Bess shot him a look.

"No way. Happy birthday," said Sonny. "You celebrating this evening?"

Cricket started to say, "She's having a huge blowout par—" but Bess interrupted. "I'm not a big birthday person. I like staying home alone."

Gaia looked like she accumulated the world's grief. "That's so sad," she said.

Bess glared at her through a long silence until Cricket finally ended the encounter. "Okay then. Off we go. Enjoy your day, you two." Bess waved good-bye and got into the car.

"He's having a baby," she said after two stop signs.

"Technically," said Cricket, "she's having the baby and he was probably as yillied as you when he first heard the news."

"What is *yillied*? That's not a word."

"Darling, who knows the Queen's English better, you or me?" He pointed a manicured finger at her, then picked a crumb off his V-necked shirt, which hung loosely over his large belly.

"Good point. He doesn't look yillied now, though. He looks happy."

"For how long? You know as well as I do reality's a mean ol' nasty pit bull gonna bite him right in that cute little ass of his, bite him hard, bite a big chunk offa that—"

"I got it, thank you."

Cricket stopped abruptly at a yellow light and Bess's head

lurched forward, then hit the neck rest behind her. "All I'm saying is," he went on, "he wasn't for you."

"You always say that."

They drove past an outdoor flea market, a police station, an apartment building under renovation. Pedestrians weaved in and out of the slow-moving traffic. For much of her adult life, Bess has carried on through ups and downs with an even-keeled contentment and indulgence in daily comforts: NPR *Morning Edition*, her travel mug of Good Earth tea, her half-mile walk to work, mid-afternoon squares of dark chocolate, an evening shower, Jon Stewart, her crossword puzzle, and her down comforter. She's never been one for drama or complaints, knowing very well how lucky she is to have an income, relative safety, and more freedoms than most. But she also happens to be a thirty-something living in a city, with an ache for companionship and kids, and bad luck in the dating realm. Even though she pays little attention to fashion trends, prefers film fests to cocktail parties, and has only one or two close girlfriends, she knows she fits the stereotype. Case in point: Blissful Ex-Boyfriend has glowing New Pregnant Girlfriend while Still-Single Ex-Girlfriend, who discovers said Ex-Boyfriend with Pregnant Girlfriend, spirals downward into a Super Crabby Mood.

"All of this," said Cricket, looking at her. "It's about tonight, isn't it?"

"All of what?"

"All of this," he repeated, gesturing as if wiping his palm on the invisible shell of her negativity.

Bess looked away. "No, it's fine."

"That's very convincing. Honey, you're going to meet the man of your steamy dreams tonight, I'm telling you. What about that fiddle player Gabrielle met at a bar last week? You told me she invited him. What was his name, Patrick Sean Finnegan O'Shaughnessy . . ."

"His name's Rory."

"So there you go." Cricket pulled up in front of the school. "Listen. Sweetheart. Try to put the *happy* in *happy birthday* today, okay? And don't talk to me about being too old. I have hemorrhoids on my hemorrhoids. But you . . . you look ten years younger than you are, you sexy little Tinker Bell . . . no wrinkles, perky breasts, girlish figure . . ."

"Hairy arms, hook nose, fat ass."

"Your ass is not fat. It's . . . grabbable."

"Great." Actually, she had managed to stave off the saddlebags she often acquires during winter thanks to karate and a near-religious adherence to a daily workout DVD she got at a yard sale, with a woman on the cover so buff she looked bionic. "Say good-bye to your jiggly thighs and watch your rear disappear!" it said on the cover. *Well all right*, she had said.

"Bess, seriously," said Cricket, gently. "Today, let your friends do nice things for you. You deserve to be happy today of all days."

"Thanks, Cricket. I'll try." She smiled for him, though she knew it would take more than anyone could muster today to get her out of the doldrums. This morning she actually woke up wondering what would happen if she ceased to exist, how her sudden absence might make the sound of a tiny ping after which the world would go on with its jackhammers and jet engines and boisterous dinner parties. *Why is this birthday making you so down?* her young assistant at work had asked last week. She didn't know precisely, but she had a few guesses. For example, Bess had said, thirty-five is the age they start checking for birth defects. Her assistant had looked puzzled. *Shouldn't they know by now if you have birth defects?* Bess stared at the innocent tilt of her head. *I mean the birth defects of a fetus. It's not so easy for me to have a healthy baby anymore*, Bess said. *Oh, right*, her assistant had said, and then didn't seem to know what else to say.

Bess shut the door behind her and walked around to Cricket's window. "Thanks for driving me. How about you? You doing okay?"

"Me? Yes, of course. Why wouldn't I be?" Despite his wit and outward nonchalance, there is a fog of sorrow about his person that Bess both identifies with and longs to fully understand.

"We'll talk later?"

"I insist."

Stop. *Kyunyeh*. Put the target away and find a new partner."

Bess doesn't hear her teacher at first. She is kicking hard, breathing heavily, sweaty and determined.

"Hey," says her partner, putting his hand up and pulling the target behind him.

"Oh, sorry," she says. He leaves her to put the target in the corner, and she watches him bow to a new partner. Just like that.

Bess shifts her weight from foot to foot, giving her adrenaline time to adjust. She bows to a nearby student, a strong, bearded father of little ones in the karate school. "Defensive releases," her teacher announces, which means one person grabs hold while the other practices self-defense and escape techniques. Her new partner motions for her to ward off his attacks, so Bess stands and waits. He chooses a bear hug from behind. She has learned to yell *no!*; to try and hit his face with the back of her head; to grab his pants and kick his knee, scrape his shin, stomp on his foot, turn and knee him in the groin and in the face when he doubles over; to push him and run, but at the moment she has forgotten what to do. She can feel his breath on her cheek. His big frame is wrapped around her torso and she feels . . . what, exactly? Comforted? Secure? Turned on? She wants to lean her head back into the crease of his neck, push her hips up slightly into his crotch. It has been so long since she has truly spooned with someone, horizontal or vertical. This partner of hers with his arms wrapped around her has the sweetest hum of a breath, and all she can do is close her eyes. And then he lets go and coughs.

"I'm really sorry," she says for the second time today. "I spaced out there for a second." She turns toward him and quickly looks into his eyes, then down at her feet.

"Start again?"

"Sure," she says, feeling wholly unsure about so much at the moment. *Tonight there will be seventy people in my apartment*, she wants to scream. *Most of them are strangers to me, and if that isn't excruciating enough, thirty-five of them are SINGLE MEN! So sure, attack away!*

This time he chooses a mugger's hold. He wraps his right arm around her neck from behind, grabs her left wrist, and stretches it back behind her.

"No!" she yells. She digs her chin into his elbow, play-kicks him in the shin, stomps on his foot, twists her body under and away from his arm, kicks him again in the knee, yells, "No!" more loudly this time, and runs away to safety.

CHAPTER TWO

I was just a boy the first time I got married, barely eighteen and just out of school. This was back in Ireland, in a suburb of Dublin. That's where I grew up, I mean. My mother wanted me to go to university straight away, but she had my sister still in school and I knew that would be tough enough. My parents weren't rich—far from it. My father was a credit officer, worked long evenings and worked hard, but he was an honest man. My older brother, Eamonn, helped out some, but we couldn't count on him. He was a rough one and it 'bout near broke my parents' hearts.

My mother was traditional. She didn't care for the new social changes afoot and she for sure didn't like the violence up north. My father, he believed in their cause, I think he did anyway, but he was a peaceful man and not one to stir the sea. They knew how close me and Eamonn were and they knew, too, if they didn't intervene I'd get caught up in whatever he was caught up in. He'd come home to take me out and they'd yell all the way to Belfast. "Jaysus," Eamonn'd yell back, "let the boy live a little!" But they'd have none of it.

I'm telling you all this by way of explaining the start of my marriage to Maggie McCabe in 1978 and our trip to America. I loved Eamonn, you know, but his lifestyle wasn't for me. I was kind of happy-go-lucky you might say, playing my fiddle and pulling off the occasional prank. One day my mother saw me hanging about the house and gave me a swift kick out the door. "Go find y'self a job, Rory," she said, and so I did.

With the help of a school chum, I got work at a television studio, running errands mostly. It didn't pay much but it was thrilling, and not just because I was working the set and sharing pints with the camera crew. It's where I first saw Maggie. She was the daughter of a producer and the same age as me, a little wisp of a thing, but the brightest, prettiest green eyes and straight, thick black hair that would sway just top of her short skirt when she walked away. She could be as crazy and blinding as the sun direct, hamming it up and getting the laughs, or like a little firefly, moving about stealthily behind the scenes, flickering her charm here and there until you wanted to follow her anywhere. I thought I was the luckiest guy alive to be the one she took a shine to. It wasn't long before we were passing each other love notes and stealing kisses in the dark.

I knew right away I wanted to marry Maggie. We talked about it, would dream about where we'd live and what we'd do. Her father, though, wasn't all that happy about her being with a poor, uneducated punk like me. So we started talking about running away together, but then something happened. The television show we were working on was suddenly plucked off the air in mid-run in a storm of controversy, which, much to her father's chagrin, was all about Maggie.

The show was called *The Spark*. It was, I should say, a pretty bad drama all things considered, but it had a way of stirring things up. Maggie appeared in episodes on occasion. She was an aspiring actress and her father let her play bit parts. One week, they were filming a scene with a nude model in an art class who comes on to her teacher. The woman who was supposed to do it got the chicken pox, and no makeup was enough to erase the red marks. So Maggie lobbied to do the scene instead. I say lobbied because there was her father to contend with, of course, and no one wanted to step on the toes of a producer. But then he'd been out of town and hard to reach, they couldn't find another actress in time, and Maggie was pretty persuasive when she wanted to be. Plus her father was a forward thinker all things considered, an outspoken advocate of women's rights and free expression.

So she does the scene—tastefully, I might add—and the episode runs and suddenly the public—everyone!—is up in arms. And I mean everyone, not just the Church and the government wankers. I didn't realize this until the whole thing blew up, but it was apparently the first nude scene in an Irish television show. Jesus, it caused such an uproar, you should have seen the letters in the papers. Seriously. It was unbelievable. You'd walk into any pub in the city and they'd be talking about it so much the story grew until it was almost farcical. And Maggie's dad—he was furious. At his daughter, sure, but he'd made peace with that by the time the show aired. No, it was his show, see, and he was livid at the prudish, almost hysterical censorship. And it was that, really. Like it was okay for foreigners to bare skin on screen, but our own kind? Never. And poor Maggie, she took it the hardest. She could hardly leave home without all the taunting. And it was supposed to be her big break.

So that's how we got married and why we left the country. Maggie's father, now having serious money problems because of the canceled season, was all too happy to marry his daughter off to a nice respectable chap and send her to America, the land of free expression. And my parents—happy, too, that I was marrying up and eager to save me from Eamonn—sent me off with their blessing. Her father used his connections to get us visas. We had a small wedding and took off the next day. My father hugged me good-bye and whispered in my ear, "I know y'won't come back to live here, son, and that's okay. You'll have a good life in America and I'll see you again."

And just so you know, my brother made it through his rough years and died of pneumonia six years later. My mother passed on, too. But my father and my sisters, they're doing all right. My dad and one of my sisters have been out to visit.

Anyway, I left, with Maggie on my arm. We arrived into Boston and tell the truth, I was scared to death. We went to Boston because it was thick with the Irish and we figured that's a good place to start, but I'll never forget standing out in the street in the South End, just off the bus from the airport with our suitcases, dirty snow in the curbs and steam coming up from the roofs of the brick row houses, a fat black woman in rags walking past talking to herself, and I just remember getting this wave of

panic and thinking, *What have I done?* I had never been out of
Ireland. The city looked and felt like Dublin in the way one industrial city can feel like another, you know what I mean, gray
and cold and always simmering under the surface. Plus Boston
wears its history like a fur coat, rich and proud, and while it's a
history I didn't know a whole lot about, I knew some of it was
against the English and that put me at ease. But beyond that,
everything new came at me at once and all I could do was retreat. I think what struck me most, and Maggie, too, was the
sheer variety of people: the color of their skin, their languages,
their foods, their faiths, their mannerisms. You didn't see a lot
of that back home. It's not that I wasn't interested in it all, it's
just that it seemed to me, at the time anyway, that everyone kept
to their own kind and no one got along all that well. The Ital-
ians, the Jews, the blacks, even the Irish had their own neigh-
borhoods, their own hangouts. So I guess I just followed their
lead. I got a gig playing the fiddle a few nights at an Irish bar in
Quincy Market and the rest of the time got hooked up doing construction with other Irish ex-pats. I spent my off time watching
American television in our small studio apartment, or at the bar
where I worked, drinking watered-down beer and missing my
family.

But Maggie? She hit the ground running. Everything
was exciting, everything was *absolutely ahmazin', Rory, truly
ahmazin'*. She lived in a constant state of awe, her lovely little
mouth and her green eyes wide open, that's how I picture her.
Over here, Rory, she'd say, pulling my arm toward a store window or a street performer or a boys' fight. We were in love still

and had grand moments of passion in this mesmerizing new world, but she couldn't relate to my periods of melancholy, or didn't want to, I suppose. And she didn't want to spend time with other Irish people, neither. She didn't see the point when there were so many more interesting people to meet. She'd say if she wanted to be with Irish people she wouldn't have left home.

Believe me, I saw her point. I did. And I didn't want to lose her. I felt like she was drifting away from me and I wanted this to work with Maggie, I really did. We were husband and wife and I loved her, but there was just too much working against us, I guess. It wasn't long before she said she was leaving me. We were sitting in a diner sharing French fries, and I felt like I was going to die of loneliness right then and there. But what she said next by way of an explanation was not what I expected. She held my hand and said, "Rory, I love you. I will always love you. But we have to be practical." Then she said that she loved America so much she wanted to stay, that she couldn't see herself going back to Ireland, not after what happened. And for that reason, she needed an immediate divorce from me to marry another man, an American man, who would help her stay and thrive in the country. She said she had found someone, a Jew, a lawyer, who loved her and wanted to marry her and would even bring her to New York and help her start an acting career and that I should know she did not love him the way she loved me, but it was the right course of action. That's what she said: *course of action.*

And off she went. A year and three months to the day. I saw

her after that, kept up with her for a while, and then we lost touch. I called her once years ago, and it was a nice conversation. She got married again, but I didn't hold it against her, especially since I then went off and did the same thing. In a way.

CHAPTER THREE

Bess enjoys a steady stream of visitors at work—Ukrainian wood carvers, Ghanaian drummers, Cherokee potters, Khmer court dancers, Cajun guitarists. During the folk festivals she helps organize, they come in and out of her office, these talented makers of masks and beadwork, players of xylophones and dulcimers and accordions. They leave her with gifts that fill her walls and sing from her speakers.

For six years she's coordinated national multiethnic events for a large nonprofit. She landed this dream job shortly after she received her Ph.D. in folklore from the University of Pennsylvania. It allows her to be part researcher, part community organizer, part curator, but mostly an advocate for the traditional arts, many of which were once across the seas, but because their practitioners were kicked out or escaped or were enslaved by foreigners, or left in search of a better life or maybe just a different life, have traveled to America and—for one reason or another—decided to stay.

For this, Bess loves America. She doesn't buy American products just because they're American. She's never stepped foot in a McDonald's. She doesn't know all the words to the "Battle Hymn of the Republic" or the "Star-Spangled Banner" or, if you get right down to it, the Pledge of Allegiance, except for the reference to God, which she wouldn't say out loud anyway as a matter of principle, preferring the phrase *one nation, under Canada*. Rather, the America Bess loves is a beautiful quilt of cultures and art forms, sewn together with the threads of rich histories, and a new sense of place, of home. She's seen a Japanese calligrapher clap to the rhythms of gospel, a mariachi vocalist marvel at Tibetan sand paintings, a Greek bouzouki player fall in love with a Midwestern decoy carver. Things like that stir her heart, giving her some of her greatest pleasures in life.

And so after karate, she went to her office to pick up a plate for her party, but she knows deep down that was an excuse, one of many she's used to come back to her office during off hours to feel grounded. She needs this grounding today especially. Thirty-five years seems insignificant in the midst of such ancient traditions; in her office, her own story is dwarfed by the quills and feathers, the trills and echoes of other people's ancestors who, she imagines, stand regally on the tops of mountains, along riverbanks, in sexy sweaty jook joints at the edge of wide open fields.

Bess knows too little about her own ancestry to feel connected to a past. Her father—an amateur folksinger and folklorist in his own right—died in a car accident when she was eight. He was a troubled teenager who ran away from a broken home to unlisted numbers and a new identity. Why he chose the name Gray, Bess couldn't say. Weeks of research turned up little about his original name or past history, other than he was three-quarters Polish, one-quarter German. By the time Bess located her paternal grandparents, one was gone and the other was mean with Alzheimer's, living in a nursing home in Georgia with white walls and rented furniture.

Carol, her mother, who was taken by cancer when Bess was in college, was adopted. She was darker in complexion and ethnic-looking, and, despite Bess's questioning on the facts of her adoption and her biological makeup, Carol repeatedly said she cared not a bit about the people who gave her up and to leave it alone. Ethnic-looking, therefore, was as far as one got in description, hypotheses running the gamut from Mexican to Middle Eastern. The only hope Bess has of attaching herself to a culture is her grandparents on her mother's side, who adopted Carol and raised her Jewish, encouraging her to do the same with Bess.

Millie and Irv Steinbloom—the most important people in Bess's life—are a feisty, shrunken couple married sixty-five years. Though they are intensely private about their marriage and how or why they adopted a baby girl, they love telling stories about their own childhoods and how they met, which Bess captured one time on tape for a high school project. She asked them what their families were like in the Old Country. Their answers astounded her. There were brothers who were bootleggers, cousins who were escape artists, wealthy uncles and aunts who were robbed blind by the system but sure to have hidden away treasures, don't you worry.

Bess told it all to her mother. "It's unbelievable what they're saying, Mom. Did you know Gram's father was a spy?"

"Nonsense," she had answered. "My grandfather was a night watchman with a couple of daytime mistresses."

Bess gave up. If only she was half this, half that, quartered, portioned, and percentaged neatly to give the census takers a run for their money. Instead she was blended into something so vague as to be called, finally, a Caucasian-American female with a history best fictionalized to be interesting. So she turned to the stories and crafts of others.

Bess gets the most interview assignments at her organization because her boss claims she can open doors with her warm eyes and sweet smile. Maybe, Bess had said, but she's always thought her subjects open up to her because they can sense her sincerity. Though the world has its share of assholes (Exhibit A: Certain Ex-Boyfriends from Bess Gray's Past), Bess believes people are inherently good and by sheer endurance through life have interesting, or at the very least different and therefore edifying stories to tell. This is particularly true when they're from other cultures. And they're telling the truth.

So turning to the stories of others has always been easy. Turning to the crafts of others proved more difficult. Her fingers bled learning the mandolin; the mound of clay in her pottery class had a habit of spinning bits of itself off the wheel and into the ponytail of the very angry, very large bearded biker in front of her; and no amount of lighting could help her thread a needle. But she didn't give up, for a good way to truly understand the traditions of other cultures—and, if she was being honest with herself, to maybe find her own place in the world—is to experience them. Thus another reason that she loves karate. Part of her study of karate, of Tae Kwon Do in particular, is to learn Korean words and the historical basis for the movements, about the villagers who were forbidden to carry actual weapons and thus developed their bodies as weapons to protect against marauders.

And in turning to the histories of others, she finds herself attracted to certain types of men: foreign ones, or if not foreign then first-generation Americans with ties to their parents' homelands, their accents, their foods and fairy tales. And if not once removed, then halved and quartered in curious ways, like Sonny the Asian-American Southerner.

But most of the dozen or so relationships she's had since college sadly fizzled after a few months. Before she was thirty, she could usually pinpoint the reasons—the South African was an insatiable flirt; the Panamanian had a gorgeous, perfect mother with whom no woman could compete; and the adjunct physics professor from grad school couldn't handle the distraction from his research, which he assured her would one day win him a Nobel. But in the last five years, it seems fear of commitment was the refrain, as with Sonny. Either that or they simply ended it with an acceptance of blame and an inarticulate apology, and then they were gone. When it came to dating, she used to feel too young and naïve until this morning, when she suddenly felt awfully old.

The party is a few hours away. Bess zips up her knapsack and locks the door to her office. On her way home she drops off a handful of bilingual books at a nearby health clinic, offering a friendly hello to the security guard.

"Hot out today," he says, holding the door for her. "Spring's finally come 'round."

"Yeah, it has. My allergies are already kicking in."

"Gotta stock up on them tissues and pills."

"Done and done. Bring it on!" She waves good-bye and for the rest of the walk home, weighs the pros and cons of taking her allergy meds. Big Pro: No itchy runny nose. Big Con: She can't drink. The one time she mixed her allergy pills with alcohol she fell asleep under a bench at a dog park and woke to a giant schnauzer peeing on her thigh. The con in this case seemed like a bigger deal, as making it through this whole evening without a drink was not appealing.

When Bess's assistant, who was new to the area, first posed the idea of a singles party, Bess said absolutely not. *But your apartment is centrally located.* Nope. *It's roomy.* Not a chance. *You know people.* NEIN! *C'mon, Bess, don't be boring.* Boring? she thought. *Boring?* Okay, she had said, thinking of her upcoming birthday, why not? It would be on her own turf, she reasoned, and she could take the focus off herself and adopt the altruistic role of the city's matchmaker. Her assistant clapped with the top half of her fingers and talked of heart-shaped name tags and party games. Bess looked at her and thought maybe she would take matters into her own hands.

That night she spent hours drafting an invitation and by midnight had one wholly unlike her in tone, but perhaps breezy enough to attract single men who might need extra nudging:

So you're temporarily unattached, between relationships, living the carpe diem life. You're painting towns red and peeing on mountains. You're shedding the exes, asking the big whys. You're slated to win the gold for emotional independence.

But suddenly you realize you're tired. You go back to
staring at abbreviated technogadgets—TVs, PCs, DVDs.
When you come home after a long day at the office and
yell, "Hi honey, I'm home," into the echoing silence, your
Chihuahua gets excited and poops on your shoe. Your tropical
fish with whom you've shared intimate thoughts about who
should win Survivor *is now floating sideways at the top*
of your tank. You've metamorphosed, Kafka-style, into a
freakish loner.

Two words, folks: It's time.

She added the where and when (purposely not mentioning
that it's her birthday), explained the rules—you had to bring
someone of the opposite gender with whom you've had no dating history—ran the whole thing by a friend, and the next night
pressed "send" and waited while it sprayed to e-mail in-boxes
across D.C. Then she felt nauseated. There was something unnerving about the silence of such an act, like watching a horrific
death scene in a movie with the sound off. Worse was the ensuing
silence, which she filled with temple-throbbing self-doubt. What
if the invite is too off-putting? What if only ten people respond,
all of whom already know each other? She typed the word *crap*
and e-mailed it to herself.

It didn't help that her longtime friend from middle school had
just lost her job and wrote back that she didn't want to come. Gabrielle Puryear—a fickle, outspoken black rights activist—said
that at a party like this, people are always asking, *So what do you
do?* and as a new member of the unemployed she didn't think she

could hear a question like that without exploding. *On this inter-view I had yesterday*, she e-mailed Bess, *they asked me where I see myself in five years*. They still ask that? *Yeah*, she wrote, *as if I was a twenty-something white chick with the luxury of career planning*. Give me a break, you went to Yale. *On a scholarship, and I'm talk-ing about the principle of it. Why can't I say I want to be right where I got to before I got laid off, you sons of bitches?* As an only child in a quiet home without so much as a pet or an imaginary friend, Bess would jump at any opportunity to spend time at Gabrielle's house with her siblings, all of whom shared a passion for justice. An evening with her family was almost like being in a TV studio audience at one of those reality vent fests.

In the end, Gabrielle decided to come and initiate among their friends a citywide search for single men to bring to the party in honor of Bess's birthday. Gabrielle, in fact, found one quickly— a guy at a bar ordering a drink with a sexy accent. She found out he was a fiddler, which she knew Bess would love, then told him about the party, and *Voilà*, she had said, *he thinks it's a great idea and wants to come*. It was then that Bess allowed herself to get excited. She remained excited until one A.M. this morning, when she woke with her stomach in knots from a party-gone-terribly-wrong nightmare.

To calm her nerves, she got out of bed and made pies, one for her party and one for her grandparents. A pie was Bess's signa-ture dish, as it was for her mom, who taught herself how to make them well and then taught Bess. It wasn't a tradition that came down through generations, but at least it was a shared endeavor, a way for them to connect. Even before she knew how to make them herself, Bess recalls the comforting smell of one baking in the oven. She recalls rushing home with her dad to a warm piece à la mode. Her mom would have made her an apple pie for her birthday. It was her favorite.

Bess arrives home to find her phone's message light is blinking like a silent alarm. She's exhausted. She takes off her coat and stands in a corner to imagine the party in action. Should she run her small, plug-in rock fountain? Should she put salsa on the stereo, or zydeco or opera? Maybe the blues. She has to make the dip. She has to decide what to wear and then allow time to rehang all the articles of clothing she will end up trying on and nixing.

Her phone rings just as she is getting out of the shower. "What are you wearing?" says Cricket in a breathy voice.

"Pervert," she says, dripping onto her Zapotec rug.

"I was thinking your corduroy miniskirt to show off those muscular legs."

"Can't. Varicose veins."

"What about that black halter top, it'll show off your sexy forearms."

"Flab."

"Hair up in a twist, of course."

"Neck zit."

"What is this, nonfat English? I'm coming up. You're having a brevity crisis."

Bess sneezes, then sits down on the toilet lid and hangs her head. "Cricket," she says, her voice cracking. "I'm really nervous."

"Honey, hold back those puffy red eyes, I'm coming right up."

A minute later, she moves toward the knocking on the door and accidentally rams her pinky toe into the foot of her antique desk. She cries out from the sudden sharp pain. She greets Cricket standing on her good foot, wiping a runny nose and wet eyes with the back of her hand.

Cricket envelops her with a hug. "No really, you're gorgeous. Sort of a Mommie Dearest look, I like it."

Over the last two years, Cricket has developed into a germaphobe. Bess has a theory that it is somehow tied to unresolved feelings over the death of his partner. But Cricket views his lifestyle as part of a higher truth: the world is dirty with its hidden microbes and bacteria and viruses, and humans are at the top of the food chain for one reason and one reason only: Lysol.

"Cricket, you're hugging me."

"True, but you've just showered and I'm banking on the fact that you used soap."

Bess hobbles with him over to the couch. She accepts a tissue and follows his advice to breathe deeply. "Cricket, I wish you could be a little bug in my ear, telling me what to say tonight. You're so good at clever banter. Tell me how you do it." Cricket's bulbous nose and ears that he had surgically pinned back as a retirement gift to himself look sunburned, as if they had been scrubbed long and hard.

"It's the gay shtick," he says, "the badminton of racquet sports. Nothing to hurt you, nobody sweats, lots of prancing around the subject. They should teach it in school. Gaybonics, they can call it. Lord knows there'd be fewer wars, more costume parties." Cricket goes to the kitchen to rinse two wineglasses. He opens a Shiraz and smells the cork. "Here," he says, handing her a glass, "this is the other secret of the gay shtick."

Bess begins to sip, proclaiming her final ruling on the allergy predicament.

Cricket wags his finger at her as she lowers her glass. "Not yet. Let it breathe, Bess dear. Sometimes you need to let things breathe. Here, I have something for you." He pulls a small box from his shirt pocket. "Happy birthday." Inside the box is a necklace with a silver pendant etched with a spiral design. "Do you know what that symbol means?"

Bess recognizes the spiral as Native American. "It's a petroglyph, isn't it? From ancient Southwestern cultures."

"Listen to you. So you didn't sleep with someone to get your doctorate. Congratulations. But what does it *mean*?"

Bess is familiar with the symbol and has heard the theories of its possible meaning. The most likely explanation is that it is simply decorative, the thirteenth-century doodling of dawdlers. A Navajo colleague once told her it was a symbol for the walk home after a bachelor party, after which he laughed heartily. But she can tell Cricket is bursting with a different answer. She feels such genuine love for him at this moment. "I don't know," she says. "What does it mean?"

Cricket looks pleased. "It symbolizes the inward and outward journey of life."

Bess nods in recognition. Maybe it did mean life's journey long ago. And if it didn't, so what? She stands and kisses his forehead. "I love it. Thank you, Cricket."

"Ech," he says, making a show of scrubbing his forehead.

"Darren would have been proud. You picked the perfect gift." She says this with immediate regret when he casts his eyes downward. Sometimes, on her way home from work, she catches sight of Cricket staring out his window, a wistful look to him like a wheelchair-bound patient watching kids on a swing set. Sometimes her heart sinks to see the pain in his stare. She has given him four names of therapists specializing in grief, three books on losing a partner, countless links to Web sites for the body and soul. But neither her outreach efforts nor her listening abilities have worked with him. He might have talked to someone else, but he hasn't opened up to her. She wishes he would. "What I mean to say is, thanks for being such a good friend. You mean a lot to me."

"You're welcome," he says simply, genuinely. He holds up his glass. "To tonight."

The phone rings and rings again, as it is connected to the buzzer downstairs. People arrive and introduce themselves, then quickly make their way to the wine. The ones who know it's her birthday come with little gifts, even though she had insisted otherwise. In a short time there are pockets of lively conversations around her apartment, and Bess can no longer hear whom she is buzzing up. The space of her home fills up with smiles and voices until it feels crowded and she has to graze the forearms of her guests as she squeezes past them to replenish the ice, change the CD, explain the origins of her unusual taste in art—a silk smock, a carved gourd, a wooden chicken given to her by a one-armed Santero from Santa Fe. She finds that if she busies herself with hostess duties, she doesn't have to talk to anyone at length, though her friends tell her to slow down.

"Bess, leave the quiche. It's fine. Come meet Harry. Harry works with me at the firm. Harry, this is Bess."

"So you're the brave party host." Harry swaggers before he holds out his hand. "Great idea. I've never been to something like this."

"Harry's recently divorced."

"That sounds so negative," says Harry. "We divorcés say we're *newly available*." His laugh dies down as quickly as it had erupted. He leans in toward Bess. "I'll tell you, though, it's nice not to have to spend the first twenty minutes of conversation figuring out if a woman's available and I'm wasting my time, know what I'm saying?"

"Will you excuse me?" says Bess, already backing into her kitchen. "I just remembered the dip."

She stands on a stool and surveys the talking heads in her home. People seem to be mingling and having a good time, though she notices the food has hardly been touched. Of course, what an obvious mistake. This is a singles party, where there is a collective consciousness of the inelegance of chewing, of getting something lodged in one's teeth.

She hears a crash and a sudden hush in conversation. A sheepish man standing by her hutch says *oops* and bends to pick up the pieces of a small vase. He meets her gaze across the room and mouths, *I'm sorry*. "Don't worry," she calls out and smiles, and the buzz of conversation resumes. She carries a full garbage bag past her guests and out to the relative silence of the trash dump in back of her building. She takes a deep breath to relax, but that's a bad idea at the side of a bin of the week's rancid leftovers. So she goes back inside to the first floor and knocks on Cricket's door.

"What happened? What's the matter?" Cricket stands in his doorway in a terry-cloth robe, holding a handkerchief and a candelabra.

"I came to borrow a pint of blood and some harpsichord music," says Bess, eyeing the candelabra. She sneezes three times in a row.

"Funny," says Cricket, getting her a tissue. "I'm polishing. What's with the party escape?"

Bess hears choral music behind him, possibly from the Gay Men's Chorus of Washington, of which he and Darren used to be members. She slips off one of her strappy, kitten-heeled thong sandals that Cricket made her buy online and stretches her banged toe. "I just came to tell you it's going okay."

He leans into the hallway to hear the unmistakable rumblings of happy partygoers upstairs. "Thank you for the timely update. Fix your strap." Bess untwists the strap of her off-white camisole. After twenty minutes of outfit changes, she overruled Cricket and went for what was most comfortable—jeans and a simple black cardigan. She let Cricket choose the shoes and is starting to regret it.

"Stella!" he yells. Cricket's Shar-Pei bolts past Bess and into the foyer. "STE-LLA!" He sounds like a drunken Marlon Brando. Bess tries to help. "No. You go back to your party. Hurry now. Go, go, go."

At the entrance to her own place she hesitates once again.

"Excuse me," she hears behind her, "are you going in?" It is a maple-syrup voice, a slow-pouring purr that gives her a quick shiver.

"Me?" she says, turning up toward this handsome man's puckish smile. He looks straight out of the Dust Bowl, lean but strong, a narrow face, thin lips, weathered skin that hints of bold adventures. He runs his hand through his thick, wavy, salt-and-pepper hair and it falls back defiantly to his brow. His sharp nose slopes off to the right, his two front teeth are slightly askew, as if they know they take center stage and are too mischievous to line up at attention. What strikes her most, though, are his beautiful green eyes under tufted peppery eyebrows, as animated and lucid as carbonated limeade.

Someone she doesn't know opens her door and beckons, "C'mon in, it's a party!" Together they step into her bare, narrow hallway.

"Do you know the hostess?" he asks. He is rolling up the sleeves of his white button-down shirt, and Bess finds herself mesmerized by his hand movements as she would a magician's. She has an urge to touch his knuckles. They are mountain ranges to her knuckle hills.

Do I know the hostess? "Truthfully," she says, "I really don't think I do." They are far from a window with its gift of an evening breeze and Bess's upper lip is now glistening, which, added to her runny, itchy nose, must be very attractive.

"Well, she's clever."

"She is?" Rather than pull out the crumpled, dirty tissue from her pants pocket, Bess disguises a quick two-finger wipe-down of her nose and upper lip by pretending to scratch her cheek.

"The invitation to this party. It was clever, don't you think?"
He moves like a soccer player, slightly bowlegged, comfortable at
a slant. And is that an accent she detects? A faint lilt here, a skipped
beat there, syllables stressed or glossed over in unusual ways?

"I guess," she says.

"But then I have to say, it was definitely hiding something."

Oh God, shoot me now. "What do you mean?"

"I mean there was an undercurrent of real angst, sadness,
fear, a visceral desire for truths coupled with an overpowering
exhaustion at having eluded those truths for years."

He's psychoanalyzing with an accent. This can't be good. "Really.
All that."

"Absolutely. It made me want to rifle through her drawers,
check out her medicine cabinet, look for her journals. That's
what I always do first at parties."

She is too shocked to respond.

He laughs. "I'm kidding." He holds out his hand. "You're
Bess Gray. My name's Rory. Rory McMillan."

"You're the fiddler?"

"That's me."

"How did you know who I was?"

"I was here earlier. Gabrielle pointed you out. I was just suddenly really sick from something I ate that I had to run outside
for some fresh air."

"Oh no. I—" and then she sees his face. "You're kidding
again."

"Sorry. I actually saw you leave your own party so I walked
out to find you."

"I see."

"Now you don't know what to believe. Sorry about that. I did like your invite. It made me want to meet you. That's the truth."

A high-pitched cackle and a drunken snort erupt nearby. Bess uses the interruption to put the focus back on him. "You're Irish."

"Now wait. Is that my lying that gave it away, or my accent? Careful now."

"Your accent."

"Then you're good. I haven't lived in Ireland for almost thirty years."

"I hear a lot of accents in my line of work. Plus Gabrielle told me."

As if summoned, Gabrielle appears around the bend behind two other women. She seems drunk and unsteady.

"Gabrielle!" Bess calls out. "Gabrielle, report to me please."

"Hey!" she says, seeing Rory as she approaches. She kisses him on the cheek. "Glad you could come. You two have met?" She exaggerates a wink to Bess. Her hoop earring is caught in the long end of a brightly colored silk scarf wrapped stylishly around her Afro puff. Bess fixes it for her. "Rory, my new friend," Gabrielle continues, "did I tell you what I do for a living?"

"Say you don't want to know," says Bess.

"No," says Rory with a grin. "And I absolutely don't want to know."

Bess sneezes loudly into her hands, hyper aware that every box of tissue she owns is on the other side of her apartment. "Will you excuse me?" she says.

She collects herself and drinks, and now that she and Rory

are both mixed in with the crowd in her living room, she watches him from afar.

"He's got a great ass, doesn't he?" whispers Gabrielle behind her. She must have seen Bess looking. "Go talk to him." She slaps Bess's ass and saunters off.

Rory is talking to three women who are pressing their hands to their chests, laughing a little too widely, keeping their eyes on him when they sip from their drinks. She can't walk into that. But he sees her looking and smiles and motions for her to come over. He makes room for her in their circle.

"That's funny," he says to her, pointing to a framed cartoon on her shelf. "I like your sense of humor." It shows two frogs on lily pads in a scenic pond beneath a pedestrian bridge. One of the frogs is looking straight ahead, smiling, posing seductively; the other one is looking at the poser with tired, bored eyes. "You're wasting your time," the caption reads. "Monet only paints the lilies."

"My dad gave me that," Bess says. "He used to leave me funny cartoons on my pillow before I went to sleep so I'd have good dreams." The frog cartoon was one of the last things he gave her before he died.

"So," says one of the more inebriated women among them. "Rory was just telling us about his grandmother who saw the Virgin Mary in a bowl of her own gazpacho."

"Really," says Bess, turning to Rory. Her voice sounds sprightly now that it's emanating from a smile. "Gazpacho? That's not Irish."

"Which is why no one in the history of Ireland had ever discovered the Virgin before. They'd been so focused on potatoes."

"So potatoes don't excite virgins, I take it?"

"'Tis a known fact."

She's doing it! She's engaging in repartee with a handsome straight man and she isn't terrified of what to say next. In fact, she feels elated, buoyant even. She takes a quick calculation of how much she has had to drink and suspects that has something to do with it.

"Lights," she hears someone yell from the kitchen. The lights go off and a candlelit cake floats toward her while voices in surround sound sing "Happy Birthday."

"May I?" Rory whispers, pointing to a short-necked banjo hanging on the wall.

Bess nods, and he has them sing to her again with his flowery accompaniment. Her father's old banjo is somewhat out of tune, but it sounds appropriate for the occasion and the less-than-virtuoso party singers.

She thanks everyone and blows out the flames. They clap and joke about what she might wish for.

"So what have you gotten for your birthday, Bess?" one of her friends asks.

"Well," she says, wiping her nose with a tissue. "This necklace." She holds it out from her neck.

"It's nice," says another friend. "Knowing you it means something."

"It doesn't mean anything."

"C'mon, Bess. Everything has history and meaning, that's your mantra, isn't it?"

"Okay, okay. It can mean a journey."

Rory, who has been listening to the conversation behind them while strumming soft background tunes on the banjo, suddenly plucks a one-note-at-a-time version of "Don't Stop Believing." Bess laughs.

"What is that?" someone asks.

"It's Journey, the band Journey," says Bess.

"White people's music," says Gabrielle.

"Stop, please stop," says a guest. "You can't do justice to Journey on the banjo. That's like Ethel Merman singing 'Amazing Grace.'"

Rory shifts to a bluegrass rendition of "Amazing Grace." There is laughter and booing and someone throws a balled-up napkin at him.

Bess smiles along with her guests, all the while thinking: *This is bad.* He's the center of attention, and the attention centers rarely notice her in the end. But then, it *is* her party and he's looking at her every now and again, even when he plays. Would he want to go out sometime? How would she ask? Maybe she should wait for him to ask. Maybe she should relax, there's still time, the party is in full force. Most of the guests have stayed and she gets busy again distributing pieces of the cake and her apple pie.

"Great party," says a passerby.

"Thanks," she says, beaming.

And then a cool breeze rustles the leaves outside the front window.

"Bess, can you come here please?" her assistant calls out from the entranceway.

Bess makes her way through the L-shaped hallway and as she

is saying, "What is it?" she stops abruptly. There in the doorway are Sonny and Gaia.

"I told them they probably had the wrong place," she says, motioning with her eyes to Gaia's belly, "but they said they knew you."

"Sonny, what are you doing here?"

Sonny is fidgety. He is bopping and tapping his chest with his pinkies and thumbs to the beat of something he's humming. "Bessie, hey." He slow-punches the air off her shoulder. "Gaia here felt so bad that you were gonna be alone on your birthday. She insisted on keeping you comp'ny." He smiles and stretches to see past Bess. "But you always knew how to par-*tay*, girl. Didn't I tell you, Geisha baby?"

"Did you just call her Geisha?" says Bess's assistant with her hand on her hip.

"It's Gaia," says Gaia pleasantly as if she were saying, *There there* to a crying child. She's wearing a tie-dyed sundress that accents the leafy tattoo above her left breast. Her eyelids sparkle, her long orange wavy hair is tangled in the sunglasses atop her head, her wrists are covered with dozens of green rubber bands. She holds out a potted plant wrapped in red ribbon. "Happy birthday, Bess."

"Thank you." Bess rotates the pot as if by turning it she can figure out if it's anything more than what it looks like: a tiny tree.

"It's a fir tree," says Gaia. "Fir trees have powerful restorative qualities, but this . . . this one's just a baby." She reaches out and tickles the pines with her fingers. "It needs your help to grow now and when you're ready, you can choose its home outside and plant it in the ground."

Didn't she mean when *it's* ready? Like when it grows out of its pot or something? Should she mention that if it weren't for Cricket, her green plants would be crackly brown and poking out of garbage bags?

There is something about Gaia that makes it difficult for Bess to break eye contact with her, something mesmerizing and calming, but now that the plant is no longer blocking her belly, her pregnancy is in full view. "This is very nice of you and I'm sorry for the miscommunication about my birthday. I just didn't want to make it a big deal, you know?"

"It's okay," says Gaia. Her slow breathing makes her breasts and shoulders rise and fall as gently as the undulating waves of an ocean's cove, her skin as smooth and white as fine sand.

"*Way*-ell, as long as we're here," says Sonny, slipping past Bess.

"Wait," says Bess, trying to grab his arm, "you can't." But it's too late, as the last flap of his bowling shirt disappears into her apartment. Her assistant shakes her head, takes Bess's tree for her, and follows him to the kitchen. Bess is now alone with Gaia, who is rubbing her belly and leaning against the door frame. Bess contemplates telling Gaia it's a singles party, but she's not sure she has the nerve. A pregnant woman at a singles party, that's a good one. The pregnant girlfriend of her ex-boyfriend at her singles party, even better.

"You know it's funny," begins Bess, "this is kind of a—"

"Ow," yelps Gaia, cringing and reaching out for Bess's shoulder.

"What? What is it? Are you okay?"

"Wow." Gaia sounds like she's under water. "That was heavy."

Bess doesn't want to know what *heavy* means. "Listen, forget it. Here," she says to Gaia, cupping her elbow, "why don't you come in and lie down."

Gaia nods and takes her hand. Bess hadn't offered her hand, but Gaia takes it anyway and Bess thinks, as she leads Gaia to her bedroom, what an odd feeling it is to hold a woman's hand. She doesn't think she's ever done that before, other than holding her mom's hand to cross streets. She's seen little girls hold hands, and young twins, and women from Europe and South America, and every time she sees it she is wistful that such affection and intimacy were not part of her American upbringing. Her female friends hug, that's what they do. Weak hugs with a few generic pats on the back as thank-yous after a dinner party. They don't really touch. It's one of the things Bess misses most being single, that sense of touch. She helps Gaia onto her bed and props her up with extra pillows.

"Thank you," says Gaia. She settles in and begins to survey her surroundings, which makes Bess nervous.

"I'll get you a glass of water," says Bess. In the living room the music is still playing, people are still drinking and talking. Sonny is in a corner talking to two women and Bess has half a mind to pull him away by the ear and thrust him into her bedroom to be with Gaia. But then there are memories of Sonny in that bedroom, and better not add to the weirdness of the circumstances. So she takes her filtered water from the fridge and as she pours a glass she looks around for Rory. *Where is he?* "Gabrielle," she calls out. "Where's Rory?"

Gabrielle sees Bess's disappointment and puts on a serious face. "I'm sorry, sweetie. I think he left."

Bess feels irritated. "He didn't even say good-bye." As she carries the glass of water toward her bedroom, she thinks: *Who cares, it doesn't matter. He's too old anyway, too flirty, too cocky, too . . . unibrowed.* Bess's buzz is wearing off and her toe is throbbing again. She wants the night to end, to get everyone out of her apartment; for God's sake, this has gone on too long. *Good night, people, good night, get out. You get my hopes up and you crush them like ants underfoot. This night couldn't have ended any worse.*

"Oh God, um . . . Bess?" she hears from her bedroom. A guy with a scared look on his face beckons her from the bedroom doorway. She rushes into the room to see Gaia sitting up on the side of her bed, wringing out the bottom edge of her sundress. Water has spread out from Gaia to darken Bess's baby alpaca blanket and her Egyptian cotton weave sheets and is now dripping down Gaia's pale legs toward Bess's antique Turkish rug. "Oh God," the guy repeats, pacing back and forth from the bed to the door. "Is there a *doctor here?*" he yells into the living room. People are now coming into the bedroom to see what's going on.

Bess chides herself for thinking of her personal belongings and tries to think straight. The glass of water she poured for Gaia feels ridiculous in her hand, as if she could just as well dump it onto her bed as watch someone drink it. "I'll get a towel," she announces. She hides for a moment in her bathroom, checking herself out in the mirror. Sometimes people think she's Italian—the near olive skin, the dark eyes, the dark hair that falls just below her neckline. Her nose is slightly hooked, but not too bad. She'd trade in her large ears if she could, but not her long eyelashes nor, if truth be told, her B-cup boobs. She fixes her bra straps, which frequently slip down over her narrow shoulders. Then she takes an allergy pill.

So Gaia's water broke, that's no big deal, right? It doesn't mean she's going to have the baby right then and there. But then there have been stories. She read about that woman on the subway in Boston whose water broke and out popped a baby a minute later. That seems like a Monty Python skit but it can happen, other women go through forty-two hours of labor and some drop in minutes and what if Gaia had to give birth right there in her own bed? She can just see it: the blood, the head, the fingers, the tiny feet, the writhing, crying kidney bean of life right there in her own bed on the very spot where some mornings she stays under the covers and presses the snooze alarm seven times because she is dreaming of a day when she doesn't have dreams of the things she wants because the things she wants she has, tiny fingers and feet to call her own.

In her bedroom she sees towels everywhere, strangers leaning on her dresser, and a woman she just met a few hours ago in her bed with her legs spread open.

"What are we going to do?" says a guy in a high puppet voice, his hand maneuvering one of Bess's sock monkey slippers that she must have forgotten to hide.

Bess looks around for Sonny. He's not in the bedroom. He's not in the living room or the kitchen or the hallway or outside the building. She can't believe he's gone. "You've got to be shitting me!" she cries out to the street. *Is there some sort of black hole in my place?* She doesn't know what to do or what to tell Gaia. The girlfriend of her ex-boyfriend (a label she keeps repeating in her head) is about to give birth, and the only people around to help are a bunch of drunken singles. She needs to call an ambulance.

Everyone in her bedroom, it seems, is offering opinions from *Relax* to *Do something!* The ones in the *relax* camp are amused, have found reasons to pour more drinks. "Hey Bess, looks like someone else is going to have the same birthday as you," calls out a man over the din.

Others are bouncing around words like *doctor* and *breathe* and *ambulance* and Bess finds she is more in this camp, but she can't get a read on Gaia. Gaia is sitting quietly, watching, until she sees Bess and motions for her to approach. Bess kneels at her side.

"It's okay, Bess," Gaia almost whispers, so that only Bess can hear. Her hand is on Bess's shoulder. "He'll be back."

Bess nearly jumps back as if avoiding a punch. *How did she know? Did someone see her walk in with Sonny and tell her? And why is it all right? Sonny should be here. He should fucking be here.* But Gaia is calm, almost smiling reassuringly. It makes Bess wonder if she's talking about Rory, too.

"Yes," says Gaia, as if an answer to an unsaid question. "We'll be just fine."

We? Why *we?* We, as if they were in this together, as if they've known each other all their lives and can feel each other's pain. Bess backs out of the room, picks up the phone in her living room and dials 911.

"Metropolitan Police Department, your name please?"

"Bess Gray," she says. "We . . ."—that word channeling through her as if coming from some ancient place, flying through the ages from long-ago war widows and cocooned queens and poor orphaned girls to all the women now who know, too, the pain of loneliness. "We," she repeats, "we need help."

CHAPTER FOUR

Maggie had made sense with all that talk of immigration. I'd been listening to the boys at the construction site where I was picking up some quick cash off the books, so I knew I had to do something if I wanted to stay, and doing it through part-time jobs was proving difficult. I stayed in bed with my head-splitting pity for the next week until my landlord came crashing in and knocked me up some sense. I thought about going back to Ireland, I'll admit, but I didn't want to go back without Maggie. I was ashamed, but I also wanted to stay closer to her in case she took me back. So I married Carol Pendleton and at the same time worked my way through college.

Apparently there was a whole underground network for this sort of thing, American girls willing to marry immigrant boys like me and all I had to do was know the right people, which turned out to be a friend of the bartender's sister where I played fiddle once in a while. He slipped me her number and said here, call her, she likes Irish boys. I didn't know what to make of it all, I really didn't, but I called. We met out at a candlelit restaurant in Cambridge that she suggested where she ordered lobster and a bottle of French wine and then cappuccino and crêpes suzette and I tell you all these things specifically because I had never had lobster or French wine or cappuccino or crêpes suzette and my knees were shaking under the table the whole time with both excitement and utter terror. Carol was a bold woman, like Maggie, but bigger with curves in all the right places and short blond hair that curled into her chin. She had a lazy eye that took to roving independently every now and again, and that was disconcerting, but she also had the most perfectly straight, shiniest white teeth I'd ever seen and that's what I kept staring at mostly. And she was sexy, too, in her designer jeans and flarey blouse that showed ample cleavage. She was smart and self-assured, that's for sure. She talked about her classes at Harvard and her volunteering for Jimmy Carter, but mostly about the hatred she felt for her ill-informed, narrow-minded, bourgeois parents— that's what she called them, *bourgeois*—and all I was trying to figure out the whole time, sitting there like an idiot in my bib, was how to get the meat out of a claw without flinging it across the room. That's what it came down to really: I was trying to pull meat from a claw and she was sniffing the cork, deciding whether to send the wine back or drink it, have her fun and throw the bottle away; that's what I was thinking and feeling like by the end of the night and I was going to walk right out of that restaurant and say forget it, I can't do this, when she up and paid the check and asked me if I wanted to marry her. Just like that.

She said she was a history major and knew all about Northern Ireland's fight against the British imperialists and the way she was talking, I thought she might know more than I ever did. She said she would have stayed and helped had it been her cause, but she understood my need for a better life and immigration laws being what they were, she wanted to do her part. I didn't tell her I wasn't from the North; I just let her talk until what she was saying sounded fishy to me and I told her as much, to which she admitted that, additionally, her parents had been trying to marry her off to their neighbor's son and she wanted them off her back once and for all. Still, you're only in your second year of study, says I to her, wouldn't they wait until you graduate? Let them get used to it, she says. Won't they be mad? They'll get over it, she says. She had an answer like that for everything and a way of making you feel like she was fully in control and you needn't worry your not-so-clever brain about it any further. And anyway, she said if we were married she could move out of the dorm and we could split the rent on an apartment.

So really, it was all sounding good, but even so I said I had to think about it and she reminded me that I didn't have a lot of time, and what time we did have we should spend getting to know each other, taking photographs by way of documenting our courtship so as not to raise any eyebrows at the immigration offices. She approached our impending marriage like a class, asking me questions, taking notes, studying and memorizing. I tried to keep up, but she liked to smoke dope while we studied and it just always made me forgetful and sleepy. But not Carol, she could multitask. I can picture her even now, leaning against her big red satin pillows on the floor blowing smoke, repeating back to me the names of my teachers.

And yet we pulled it off, the whole thing. We got married by a local justice of the peace and she told her parents over the phone. I didn't hear their initial reaction, but weeks later they came for dinner at our new empty, echoing apartment in Somerville and they were actually pleasant to me. That Carol invited them in the first place was a surprise given how much she said she hated them. They were uptight and snooty, that was all true—you couldn't get more awkward-looking than they did sitting on the floor eating stir-fry with chopsticks—but they never complained and when they left they hugged me and said welcome to the family, we're glad to have you. I asked Carol about it later, but she dismissed me, saying it was my charm that won them over, but I'll tell you the truth, I hadn't developed any charm yet, not at all.

Anyway, I let it be and Carol and I slipped into a routine. She had the bedroom because she paid more of the rent. I slept in the living room on the sofa. She continued her classes and even went away for some volunteer job in South America much of the summer. I took out a loan with her help and enrolled in classes at a community college, though I continued to work construction and play at the bar for cash. Given our schedules that first year, we hardly saw each other, and if I did see her at home she was with her friends who were a motley group, I'll tell you. Nice people, if eccentric. Seemed like the guys wore the girls' clothes and vice versa, her girlfriends all in baggy pants and tweed jackets and ties. But her friends didn't bother me and I didn't bother them.

Now I know you're wondering: Did we ever sleep together? I tell you no, we didn't. Carol didn't flirt with me. She teased me like I was her little brother, and in the way of teenage siblings she was careful never to let me see her nude. So you're wondering again: Did I sleep with other girls during my marriage to Carol? Yes. Can you blame me? I didn't do it all the time and I didn't flaunt it. I can say it was the age and place for sexual freedom and see if you know what I mean, but it wasn't that. I was lonely. Carol and I hardly ever touched, not even a hug or a pat on the back, and I missed Maggie. I didn't even want just sex from these girls, I wanted to stay and talk and do things but they always found out I was married and I couldn't tell them it was a sham marriage for fear they'd go to the authorities.

But then there was a thawing between me and Carol, sometime after the first Christmas we spent with her family, playacting like a married couple. I suppose we had gotten so good at playacting it started to feel natural. We actually became good friends. We liked to do schoolwork together at the café down the street or stay at home and get stoned and watch *M*A*S*H* on TV. Her friends weren't coming around as much and I thought maybe she had been seeing some guy discreetly and they split up or something. Whatever the reason, I liked it. I liked that Carol was beginning to trust me. She and I hopped in her Ford Pinto and went to rally after rally and I tell you, it was invigorating. I got to thinking how much I enjoyed being with her and I wasn't missing Maggie so much and I was trying to make sense of my situation, I guess, being married and Carol being my wife and I don't know . . . I wanted her. Can you imagine? Nervous as a schoolboy, I made my first pass at this woman I'd been married to for nine months and she flat-out rejected me. Rory, she said, what are you doing? I started stammering, *I thought, I thought*, but all she did was shake her head, look at me with real pity.

Two weeks later I came home and found her naked on the couch—where I slept, mind you—her body entwined with another woman's naked body. I ran out and got drunk, but when I started to think about it, it made sense. Carol and I talked about it soon after. She apologized for not telling me, for letting me find out that way that she was a lesbian. She was concerned that my Catholic upbringing would play a part, if I'd even marry her knowing the truth or run out and tell the world once I did find out. Her parents did want to marry her off to their neighbor's son, but that's because they had discovered her kissing a girl in the laundry room of their house and threatened to cut her off financially if she ever behaved like that again. She didn't want to leave Harvard, so she married me and her parents were relieved. She figured if I didn't know the truth it would be easier to convince her parents that everything was fine. And then after a while she just assumed I had figured it out.

Frankly, I was relieved, too. I'm not sure why. I guess because I wasn't really in love with her and I didn't have to take it personally and now that I knew the truth, I could focus on my schoolwork and a brighter future. We stayed married until we both graduated, until we could get divorced at a point when it wouldn't hamper my staying in the country (three years, I think, was what it was) and then we went our separate ways, much to her parents' disappointment. I kept in touch with Carol for much longer than I did with Maggie. Carol was good about reaching out, until her efforts dwindled years ago to just a holiday card at the end of each year. The last one, if I remember, had a photo of her and her partner with their little girl and three dogs. She always had a thing for dogs, which also happened to be the case with Lorraine. Lorraine Doyle, she was my wife after Carol. Now there was a poor girl. What I did to her I haven't yet forgiven myself for, let alone what I did to her dogs.

CHAPTER FIVE

The night moved at a feverish pitch—a fusion of blink-ing lights and a screaming siren; the parting of cars; the bumps in the road; the speed of immediacy all the way to the white coats and the shouted commands—*easy now*, *get her in*, *watch it*—the rolling, clanking metal stretcher pushed through the sliding doors; everything, it seems, parting to make way, for she who is scared and sweating and breathing with exag-gerated gasps and who finds herself down the hospital's hall-way, past a plastic water pitcher on a tray, a lit red exit sign, an empty white room, a patient on his side facing the wall with a light blue gown having slipped from his body showing a sliver of skin from his hairy ass to his neck, down another brightly lit hallway with an overpowering smell of rubbing alcohol, into a white and shiny silver room where everything is right-angled and mechanical and beeping and now turning blurry as they try to move her, point her where she has to go, tell her she doesn't look so good, ask if she's okay, tell her *careful now*, hold her up with their hands scooped under her armpits when she looks faint but lose their grip, watch her as she falls, slams her head into the edge of a table and knocks herself out.

Gaia, on the other hand, cool as a cucumber, delivered drug-free her nine-pound baby girl in twenty-eight minutes flat from the time she entered the delivery room, then slid into maternal meditation, pink-cheeked and smiling, holding Pearl to her breast and knowing life can be as sweet as the scent of powder. That, according to the nurse who is standing over Bess and feeling her forehead. "I'm telling you, honey, you sorry you missed the whole thing, she was a doll. An absolute doll, both of them, mother and daughter. She your girlfriend? That's cool. We got another couple of mamas last night, too. Something in the air, gots to be. La-dy *love*." The nurse opens the blinds and untucks the ends of the bedsheets at Bess's feet. She moves and breathes like a grizzly bear.

Bess turns her face to the window to feel the warmth of the morning sunlight. She takes a moment to realize where she is. "What happened to me exactly?"

"You're fine, just fine, sugar. We thought you might've given yourself a concussion, but I think you'll just have a nasty ol' bump on your head. How do you feel?"

"Headachy, like I have a nasty ol' bump on my head," says Bess, feeling the spot above her right eye.

"Why don't you see if you can sit up and I'll get you some aspirin. We'll need to change the sheets and get the room tidied, so when you're ready. Take your time."

"Thanks. I appreciate it." Bess sits up and feels the night before flood her skull and punch at her temples. Too much wine, too much weirdness. She tries to stand. Her knees feel weak, her eyes sting from the brightness of the white room, her mouth is dry. She takes the aspirin and walks slowly in the direction the nurse points, reaching her palm out to the wall until she rounds the corner. In the hallway she is hit with a memory of the last time she was in a hospital during her freshman year of college, when her mother was dying of cancer. Bess had taken off a semester to take care of her. It had been a slow, unpredictable dying with surges of energy and appearances of normalcy. Bess would sit by her bedside and get angry when her mother laid out facts of a grim future. *I'm dying*, she'd say. *Find someone to take care of you.* I can take care of myself. *I know you can, but it's better. Don't be alone.* Her mother was neither the weeping nor the joking type. Nor was she talkative like the other Jewish mothers they knew. Her love wasn't stated as much as it was understood in the details—a blanket lain over stolen naps, a claim to the smaller of the apartment's two bedrooms. That was true until her mother knew it was her time to go and said, *I love you very much.* A part of Bess lifted to enormous heights, then died, too, when her mother finally took her last breath.

The bathroom is next to Gaia's room and after she washes, Bess enters quietly when she sees Gaia is asleep, spread out upon the bed. Her thick, long, wavy orange hair lays about her pillow. Bess moves in close and thinks of holding her hand, but can't muster the nerve. She stands over Gaia and takes inventory: the freckle above her upper lip, the holes at the tops of her ears where earrings once were, the red eyelashes, the blotchy skin a clear giveaway of Scottish ancestry.

She understands what Sonny sees in her. Gaia is that perfect skimming stone one searches for at the edge of a lake, smooth and shapely, unadorned and peaceful among the other stones but capable of soaring out across the surface as if defying the laws of nature. She is beautiful, but then maybe all new mothers are beautiful, or all onlookers in the immediate aftermath of birth see a kind of beauty they didn't see before.

Giggles erupt from behind the curtain on the other side of the room. Bess peeks around the bend and sees two women, one sitting up in bed, one at her side, gently brushing her partner's hair.

"Where is she?" Gaia says, suddenly awake.

Bess is startled. "The baby? I'm sure she's fine. They probably wanted to let you sleep and brought her to the nursery."

Gaia blinks the sleep from her eyes. She sighs deeply and props herself up on her elbows with great effort. "How are you feeling?"

"How are *you*, is the question," says Bess. "I'm so sorry I caused such a commotion last night. Just what you needed, I'm sure. How is the baby? I mean, how did it go?"

Gaia presses a button and the bed buzzes and angles its top end upward. She settles in, takes a sip of water, closes her eyes. "Mm," she purrs, "yes." Then she opens her eyes and smiles at Bess. "My baby girl, Pearl. She's perfect. Have you seen her?"

"No," says Bess, wondering what that *yes* was for. "I will. I heard it went smoothly, though. She's a big girl. Nine pounds! Wow."

Gaia nods. "I was that big, too, my mother tells me."

"Where is your mother? Do you want me to call her?"

"No, she should be on her way."

The couple next to them laughs. Bess and Gaia turn their heads toward the curtain, then Bess looks down at her hands. Should she mention Sonny? What would she say? That she's sorry? That he's really a good guy and don't be mad? That men are— *Stop. Just stop.*

"You're thinking of Sonny," says Gaia. "But you shouldn't think bad thoughts. He'll come back when he's ready."

Bess's mind is a big blowout party of bad thoughts. "Aren't you mad?"

"No," says Gaia, as if followed by *silly*. *No silly, silly Bess, silly girl.*

"You seem so sure he'll come back. How do you know that?"

"I just do."

"Is it faith? Is that it?"

Gaia stretches her neck from side to side, front to back. "It's not faith for me, exactly. More like I can sense it."

"You're psychic or something? Or what do they call it . . . clairvoyant?"

"Something like that. I can't read people's minds, but I can sense things. It's easier to do with plants, they're less complex."

"Plants? Like, you touch a plant and you know what it's thinking?"

"Bess, plants don't think." *Stay with me here*, she seems to communicate with a slow blink and the downward tilt of her head. She looks exhausted. "It's more that I can sense what's wrong, what they need."

Bess rubs her temples. This is like an Alice in Wonderland conversation with its slippery, stealth logic. "Still," she says, "you can't change the fact that Sonny took off at a crucial moment. I can't believe you're not pissed off about that."

Gaia squirts a dollop of lotion into her hands and rubs her palms together. "Think of it this way," she explains in a soft, tired voice. "You have a child who is so upset he won't stop cry-ing, but he's not able to communicate why. His crying is so loud you want it to stop, but you don't know what to do. You can try all sorts of things you've tried before which may or may not work, or you can go on doing what you do, be there for him if he needs you, not with anger but with compassion. He will stop crying. You know that. You know the outcome so you can have more control over the means. I think Sonny left your party so he can have himself a good cry."

How can a person be so calm, thinks Bess. "But what about you? Sonny's not a child. What about your needs?"

Gaia closes her eyes. "I need him to go away every now and again."

A cheery nurse enters and claps in sync with the syllables of "Good morning." She claps three more times when she says, "How. Are. We?" Bess watches her move around the room. What is it with these nurses that they're so happy in the morn-ing? Are they this happy in the proctology ward?

"I'm sorry, mommies, but I'm going to have to ask your visi-tors to step out of the room for just a few minutes, okay? We just want to clean up a bit, okay? Okay."

"Okay," says Bess, with a quick smile to Gaia. She is actually thankful for the interruption.

"Can I see my baby?" Gaia asks the nurse.

"In a few minutes, okay?"

"I'll go check on her, wish her a happy birthday," says Bess. "I'm glad you're doing well. I'll call you later."

Gaia reaches for Bess's hand. "Bess, thank you. Thank you for being here."

Bess holds on to Gaia's hand with both of hers, feeling a sudden powerful mix of emotion take hold and rise into her throat, as if she were holding her mother's hand. "My pleasure," she says, and exits the room.

Just outside the door, Bess hears Gaia ask the nurse once again to see Pearl, this time in a more forceful, less controlled voice. *Now*, says Gaia, *I want to see my baby now. Please don't tell me I can't.*

So she's human after all, thinks Bess.

The newborns are behind a window decorated with cranberry and peach flower decals. There the hair brusher is standing, staring, making little breath marks on the glass. Bess stands next to this tall woman and looks for Pearl. It occurs to her that she doesn't know Gaia's last name and though she searches among the infants, she can't tell one from another. More intriguing is the whole group of them, where they were just twenty-four hours ago, where they will scatter to, and what they will become as they age.

"That one's mine," says the woman, pointing to one corner of the room.

Bess is suddenly overcome with a visceral sadness that she may never be able to say those words herself. She's thought at times of being a single parent, but knows it's ultimately not for her. Being a single woman is hard enough. "Very cute," is all she can think to say.

Her cell phone rings from inside her knapsack. She answers it as she walks to the front exit of the hospital.

"Hey. Where are you?" says Gabrielle.

"Still at the hospital."

"That woman had her baby? She's okay?"

"She's fine. Baby's fine. Me, I need two Valium and a six-hour nap. Did you get everyone out of my place after I left?"

"When the wine ran out. I ended up talking to the guy in the football jersey all night—Paul. Totally hot. And smart. Did you see him?"

"I think so. Did you get his number?"

"Home, work, cell, e-mail, oh yeah. Major chemistry. Think I'll quit looking for a job and get married after all." Gabrielle has told Bess many times she has little interest in marriage, monogamous relationships, or children of her own. She gushes love and energy toward her five nieces and nephews who live nearby and that's enough. Though she listens with attempted empathy, she doesn't understand Bess's needs for those things, so Bess doesn't burden her with those particular longings. Rather, Bess harbors a secret jealousy of Gabrielle's aloofness, which, coupled with her voluptuous physique and dimpled smile, seem to attract droves of eligible bachelors, the way Gabrielle used to attract so many of the boys in high school. "That was a joke," Gabrielle says. "What's with the pregnant pause? Ha, get it?"

Now that Bess is out of the hospital, she finds she can think more clearly and her mind turns to Rory. What's his story? she wonders. What would have happened between them had the whole night continued on as it was? "Gabrielle, remind me . . . how did you meet Rory again?"

"The Irish guy? At a bar last week. I told you."

"I know, but *how*. Did he buy you a drink? Did he come on to you?"

"Okay, stop. Honey, I'm not his type, he's not my type, you know that. I invited him for you."

Bess steps into a cab. She feels like closing her eyes and sleeping right there on the seat. "Sorry. I'm just upset he left. I kind of liked him."

"I know. He'll call. I got the feeling he liked you, too. Let me know if you want help cleaning up, okay? I'm around."

Bess hadn't thought of that, how messy and smelly her apartment would be, post-party. "Right there," she says to the cabdriver, pointing down the block, "where that man is with the dog." Cricket is standing out front of their building in the colorful kitenge shirt Bess had bought him last year from a Kenyan colleague. Stella is on a leash, lying by his side, her head and front paws draped over his right sandal. When Bess steps out of the cab, Cricket peers at her above his sunglasses, then with an exaggerated twist of his neck, looks the other way down the street.

"Morning," says Bess, leaning down to scratch under Stella's chin. Stella sits up and sniffs her wrist. "Are you ignoring me? What did I do this time?"

"Who are you? I don't know you. Stella, bite her ferociously." Stella is distracted by a fly buzzing around her head. Her flabby chins swing as she pants and follows the fly's flight pattern. Her drool drips down onto Cricket's big toe.

"She's a monster," says Bess. "Listen, are you going to tell me what's eating you or do I have to shake it out of you with my dirty germ-ridden hands?"

"What should you have done very first thing this morning?"

"Called you."

"I can't hear you."

"Called you."

"Why?"

"Because you're a nosy son of a bitch."

"Because I helped you plan that party to the very last Kalamata olive, because I caught numerous nasty infections from you sniveling on my shoulder, because you know I'd be waiting by the phone to hear every last detail, but what do you do? You forget me. You stay out all night with some Casanova—whoever he is I don't like him—and you fall out of the cab in the same clothes, in a cab, I say . . . where does he live, in the suburbs? Oh, can this get any worse."

"Are you through, oh Queen for a Day?"

A large yellow bus pulls up beside them and opens its doors. On the side of the bus is a picture of two dogs relaxing on lounge chairs by a pool wearing sunglasses, bikinis, and wide-brimmed hats. A waiter is serving them bones wrapped in red ribbons on a silver tray. Above the picture it reads, "Dogaritaville." Cricket leads Stella onboard, disappears for a moment, then steps back off the bus. Stella's head appears in the last window in the back. Cricket blows her a kiss from below her window. "Bye-bye, beautiful baby girl. Play nicely with your friends. Daddy loves you." Cricket waves to Stella as the bus pulls away.

"Why is Stella going to a kennel?"

"Camp, you philistine. Canine camp, the very best."

Bess is about to say that she would have looked after Stella, but she realizes (and she knows Cricket is thinking this, too) that she was not home this morning for him to ask that of her. "Where are you going that you couldn't bring her with you?"

His voice drops. "Nowhere. Out."

"Now who's the cagey one?"

"I prefer a cloud of mystery about me, it's part of my charm. And don't turn the telescope on me, we were talking about your whereabouts."

"I just came from the hospital. Didn't you hear the ambulance last night?"

Cricket gasps, pressing one hand to his mouth, the other to his chest. He is in and out of his persona so quickly it's hard sometimes for Bess to keep up. He never seemed to be that dramatic when Darren was alive. Darren was clearly the queen in their relationship. "Ambulance? I took an Ambien, I must have slept right through it. What did those single beasts do to you? Germinators, every one of them! Here, sit down, you look feverish. Can I get you a sprig of mint? It's very refreshing. Opens the passages." Cricket is following his own advice, fanning himself and breathing deeply.

"I'm fine."

"You're a liar. What is *that*?" With a dainty finger, Cricket points to the swelling above her eye.

"Nothing. I hit my head. Some woman—" she begins, but stops. It's too much to get into now. "Listen, I have to go. I'll stop by tonight and catch you up on everything you've missed."

"I won't be there."

"Why not?"

"Because I'll be somewhere else."

Bess can't remember the last time Cricket went away overnight. She knows he doesn't like to sleep anywhere other than on his own extra-firm, dust-free mattress, special-ordered from New York's Lower East Side, approved by nine out of ten doctors and twelve rabbis according to the label Cricket won't cut off because it says not to. "Why can't you tell me where you're going?"

"Oh, now suddenly you care about my well-being."

Bess steps up to the front door. "Cricket, I hope it's nothing serious and that you're okay, but I really have to go. I'm supposed to be at my grandparents in half an hour. Call me from the road if you need me and let me know when you're back, okay? I'll be thinking of you."

"Go away then. You're dismissed. But write everything down that you must tell me. You have a terrible memory."

Her apartment smells as musty and fermented as a frat house basement. She opens a window and double checks that her stereo is turned off. Her friends had been kind. They stripped her bed, rinsed and lined up the wine bottles for recycling, and wrapped the cheese in the fridge. There are still crushed chips in her rug and half-full plastic cups abandoned on shelves. She finds someone's black sweater bunched in a corner, and on her pillow a business card that reads: "Harry Selwick, patent attorney." She has to think about this for a minute. Harry Selwick? Oh, right, the divorcé who, toward the end of the night, interrupted a story she was telling to let her know he could see her nipples were hard. On the back of the card, Harry had written, "Call me." Bess calls him several things as she tosses the card into the trash.

She has minutes to jump into the shower, get dressed, and get
over to the lot where she reserved a Zipcar for the day, but she allows herself a moment to strum the strings of her banjo and think
about Rory. Perhaps this is the time to squelch her pride and try
and find him. If she is supposed to be learning anything in karate
it's to have confidence. Confidence, she says aloud, clapping to
the syllables. Con. Fi. Dence.

CHAPTER SIX

I didn't mean to hurt Lorraine. She was such an innocent girl and I was a real ass. But then that's just it, isn't it? Nice and innocent—don't we so often use those words with a tinge of disdain? When there isn't a whole lot of substance there to grab on to? Listen to me, still the ass. But you know what I mean, right? No edge? Maybe she had an edge, I don't know. Maybe at the time I wasn't looking for an edge. I was looking for someone calm and steady, that's what I needed. They say with distance you're supposed to get perspective, but it seems harder to do with Lorraine and the way I was then.

I met her at church. I wanted to leave Boston and get a fresh start with my green card, so I traveled west, found myself in Toledo one day and landed a job at a computer company. This was in, let's see, 1984. I had taken classes on music and literature and even television production, but I ended up with a college degree in computers, mostly because it was a new field back then and it seemed the most practical. *Practical.* Maybe Maggie was still in my head then, I don't know.

I was feeling kind of lost and decided to go to confession

and unload some of the things I'd been thinking about my marriages, you know, to get some grounding. I haven't exactly made religion a part of my life, but I tend to seek it out when I'm down. At least I used to. *Bless me, Father, for I have sinned, it's been five years since my last confession*, I said, and I started to tell my tale, and the priest, you know what he said at the end? *Do the right thing. Always do the right thing.* I tell you I don't think he heard a word I was saying, and probably he said that stock phrase to every sorry soul who came to see him, but for whatever reason, it resonated with me. I thought it was deep and I pondered its meaning and tried to abide by it however I could. And it was under those circumstances that I met Lorraine, because she was watching me from the back of the church when I went to sit in the pews for a while. Then I saw her again out in the parking lot and when I went to get into my car she waved hello and I waved back. Next thing I know I go to pull out and there she is in her Volkswagen and BAM I hit right into her. Not hard, just a tap, but I heard a definite crunching of metal and so I got out and ran over to her car to see if she was okay. I'm fine, she says, and then she fires questions at me, ignoring the fact that we just had an accident. What's my name, where am I from, do I like dogs? Seriously, she asked me that right from the start, about dogs, and I tell you I was a little taken aback. I suppose I like dogs, I said, and then I mentioned a car repair shop around the corner. I offered to follow her there and then give her a lift home, which I did because I'm thinking it's the right thing to do. And when we got to her apartment, a dreary gray building between a construction site and a used car dealership, I walked her to her door and when she invited me up to her place, I went because I thought it was the right thing to do after I just hit her car. Well I'll tell you, seven months later I'm standing at the courthouse with Lorraine, saying our vows, saying those words the priest said to me over and over again like a mantra: *Do the right thing do the right thing*, but everything I ever did with Lorraine couldn't have been more wrong.

Why did I marry her? Well, if you want to get Freudian about it, I'd say she reminded me of my mother. She was of Irish stock, and she was quiet and tidy. You'd take your last sip of coffee and before you could set your mug back down on the table she'd whisk it off to the sink. Now wait, let me explain because I don't want you getting the wrong idea about my mother, God forbid: it wasn't sexual at first with Lorraine. I don't mean to say she was altogether unattractive, just plain. She had meaty thighs, reddish shoulder-length hair she wore back in a headband, and she favored plum-colored outfits with matching socks and sensible shoes. But she also had very large breasts and full lips and the softest pale skin I ever felt, though she was addicted to lip gloss and all types of hand lotion, tubes of which turned up everywhere so that I was always sitting or stepping on them, squirting the lotion onto the furniture or the carpet where her dogs would lick it up and end up vomiting into the wee hours of the night to make matters worse.

Jesus, those bloody dogs. Lorraine had four mutts that she had rescued from the local shelter, all shapes and sizes, all ludicrously named after one of the Seven Dwarfs. I say ludicrous because their dispositions had nothing to do with their names.

Sleepy never stopped barking; Sneezy was aloof, almost cata-tonic; Happy wore a muzzle to stop him from biting people; and I couldn't get Bashful to stop humping my leg. It got damn well crowded in that apartment of hers, and I didn't even mention all the stuffed animals she had piled up on her couch, her bed, her shelves, her counters. You couldn't pee without some wide-eyed, pastel-colored monkey or bear or dinosaur staring you down or threatening to fall into the toilet. Crazy, no? Now you know I'm a storyteller and you probably think I'm making this up, but I swear it's true. She was clean, but my God she liked clutter.

Anyway, like I said, no sex. It wasn't like that at the begin-ning, for me anyway, not with a big cross over her bed and all those animals—real and stuffed—and her seeming young and innocent. She *was* Snow White. When I met her she was twenty-five, a year older than me and living on her own, working as a receptionist in a dentist's office, but she seemed in many ways just like a little girl, a *kid* really, and yet she had a maternal nature and she was kind and I was in need of a friend and that's how we started spending time together. We'd walk her dogs in the park and go to movies and do volunteer work at the local soup kitch-ens through the church. She told me at the outset that she was a virgin and she intended to keep her virtue until she got married and I took that as a warning not to make a move, which was fine because I didn't have designs on her and certainly had no inten-tion of getting married again.

But then, as it happened, my brother Eamonn died.

I got the call from my father. He said Eamonn was sick and they didn't think he was going to make it and maybe I should come home, that they would help me pay for it if they could. The news hit me hard. I took off for Ireland immediately. Eamonn looked so thin, so gaunt there in the hospital. Hearing him say he loved me before he let go was more than I could bear. He passed on three days after I arrived. I stayed for the funeral and a week beyond, helping out around the house and stopping in on my old haunts. It was nice to be home, to sit and have soup with my parents, catch up with my sisters, get drunk with my friends. We all dealt with our grief in our own way. But after a week there I was ready to leave. I don't know how to explain it. It's a powerful thing to go back after a few years to a place where you grew up, but you get to realizing it's not going back exactly as time's moved forward and you feel kind of stuck. Plus I missed America. And I mean just that . . . I didn't miss anything in particular, not my job or Toledo or even Lorraine so much as I missed the whole package. America was an indescribable *feeling*, I guess you could say. I missed the feeling.

Besides, they knew about Maggie and me and that was hard to live with. I didn't tell them about Carol, but in a moment of weakness, when my mother looked like she was on the verge of tears worrying about me so far away, I did tell her about Lorraine, about how she was a nice Irish-American girl who reminded me of her and not to worry. I didn't say we were dating exactly, but I didn't say we weren't. *You goin' t' marry this girl then, Rory?* she asked. My mother wouldn't stop worrying until she knew I was married and cared for, that much I knew. And the poor woman had just lost her eldest son. So I answered yes without thinking. And I went back to America.

Lorraine picked me up from the airport and there were those lips and those breasts and her soft-skin embrace . . . you get what I'm saying? She grabbed hold, hugging me the way she did with such sympathy, and I cried and she cried with me. We went home and made love. *Are you sure*, I said. *I've never been more sure*, she said back.

Two months later we were married. I never bothered to get my marriage to Maggie annulled—she married a Jew and Carol wasn't religious. Lorraine wanted to get married in the Church, so I said I would try to contact Maggie to get an annulment, but I never got around to it. In the end she agreed to just saying our vows at the courthouse. I always suspected she regretted that.

See, I convinced myself Lorraine was the right kind of girl for me. I felt . . . well . . . *comforted* is maybe the word. Each morning she handed me my lunch in a brown bag decorated with a Disney sticker and a quote of inspiration. She baked apricot muffins and gave me answers I couldn't get on my crossword puzzles. She remembered my birthday and handmade me a party hat. Our lives were ordinary lives folding one day into the next. And one of those ordinary days I just cracked.

I didn't do anything but have an epiphany standing in the kitchen, but what happened after I ran out of the apartment is where the story is, the beginning of the end, you could say. My epiphany was this: I was wasting my life. I was in a kind of fairy-tale coma and I needed to get out. I wasn't in love with Lorraine and my God, I had had it with her dogs.

The problem was, Lorraine wasn't home when I got this rush of a feeling that made me grab my coat and make a fast escape. Now you're thinking I left the door open by accident and let all those dogs loose. No, I knew better than that. Lorraine had trained me well, and locking the door behind me was habit by then. No see, Lorraine was up the whole night before baking sugar cookies for the homeless shelter's anniversary celebration. She baked something like twelve dozen cookies. They were stacked on trays on the counter and I was to wrap them up and bring them over to the shelter while she was doing errands, but I didn't. I left them there unwrapped. In the kitchen. While I was gone for hours. Are you getting what I'm saying here? The dogs! I forgot to feed the dogs and them being hungry and curious and typical canine food grabbers, they got ahold of those cookies like there was no tomorrow, ate every last one of them. Well, those dogs got on such a sugar high they went wild! They tore through the apartment like a tornado, chewing through every last stuffed animal so that the living room looked like a battleground in winter, little limbs and heads strewn about in a blanket of cotton. They knocked over lamps and broke her figurines, vomited up the cookies and the cotton and finally passed out on their backs in such deep slumber that when Lorraine came back to this scene— can you imagine?—she thought they were all dead.

I found out about it all the next day when I returned, because I had to come back and end it properly, that was the least I could do. The dogs turned out to be okay, but Lorraine . . . she wouldn't speak to me. The neighbors who were there to help clean up formed a wall between her and me, saying she didn't want to see me and I should go, just go. If I'm going to be completely honest I'll also tell you I cheated on Lorraine that night and one of her neighbors commented on my smelling like perfume. It was just someone I picked up at the bar and I wanted to tell Lorraine it didn't mean anything, that I was sorry, but Lorraine had had enough. She peeked at me from around the bend, looking at me with such sad sad eyes, and then she receded into the other room.

In the days and weeks that followed, I tried to call, but she wouldn't answer. So I had no choice . . . I broke it off in a letter. I wrote her several letters as a matter of fact, but I stopped when one got returned and I found out she moved without a forwarding address. Getting a divorce after that, I can tell you, was no small task. Maggie and Carol made it easy; I had no idea where Lorraine had gone, and I had no money for an attorney. But then one day, about a year later, I received divorce papers in the mail (I hadn't yet left Toledo). According to her attorney, she was eager to marry someone else, so I was happy to oblige.

I hope she's happy. And the truth is, the wrong I did her came back to me tenfold. I'm saying I got what I deserved with my next two wives, who sent me spiraling downward and straight into rehab. My late twenties . . . I call them my dark years.

CHAPTER SEVEN

It's karate that Bess is thinking about as she drives up Wisconsin Avenue toward the Beltway. Her school requires a paper before each test for a new belt, and the one Bess has due tomorrow is on the concepts of yin and yang. She had gerbils once named Yin and Yang, when she was eleven. True to their names, Yin was dark and passive and female, and Yang was a lighter, more aggressive male. They played well together, balanced as they were, and for a time Bess imagined having little Yin and Yang babies, but then Yang escaped the cage one afternoon and was brought back by the neighbor's cat, a prize dropped on the front stoop. Yin wasn't herself after Yang's death. She shed most of her fur and wouldn't eat. Two weeks later, she, too, took her last breath. Bess felt guilty naming them Yin and Yang, as if the labels themselves dictated Yin's fate. Maybe Yin could have survived had she been called Wonder Woman, or Cher, or Mother Teresa.

She would write in her paper that the symbiotic relationship between yin and yang manifests itself in several ways, the artistic (choreographed and beautiful) aspects balancing out the martial (physical and more violent) aspects to create a true martial art. Karate depends on a healthy balance between offensiveness and defensiveness, physical strength and mental acuity, competitiveness and camaraderie, patience and determination, an awareness of details (heel down, elbows in, wrist straight, thumb tucked) and a sense of the fluidity of moving through a whole routine. "We are, each of us, teacher and student always," her instructor had said.

But then in her paper she is also supposed to write about how this particular philosophy—this balance—applies to her life outside of class, and here she is stumped. Like many of her fellow folklorists, she is often in awe of the genuine, unassuming, talented craftspeople and folk musicians she meets through her work. She has spent her career increasing, or in some cases creating audiences for them, but is that a fair exchange for all they've taught her? She finished graduate school with a near-perfect GPA and yet what does she know of the world?

And what of a balance in her personal life? Do the things she enjoys doing compensate for the things she doesn't enjoy doing, or hates doing, or fears doing, like, say, dating? This week, the answer is a no-brainer. In this first week of her thirty-sixth year she feels like a big yin-yang failure.

She crosses into Maryland where the large houses on hills sit atop hoop skirts of perfectly mowed lawns. She is headed to Rockville where her grandparents—Millie and Irv—moved more than twenty years ago. Over the decades they'd migrated steadily northward and westward through the district, up from their first years of marriage in the 1940s at Q and Sixteenth

Streets, to Cleveland Park where they adopted and raised Bess's mother in the '50s and '60s, and on into Bethesda when Bess's mother moved in with Bess's dad on Capitol Hill at the start of the 1970s. In the '80s, when Bess was in her early teens and living with her mom back in Bethesda, her grandparents made their final move farther out to the Maryland suburbs.

This was a common route for Jews in Washington, D.C., the first of whom migrated from Baltimore in the mid-1800s. Irv claimed that his great-great-great-grandfather was among those who fled persecution in Germany and came to the New World, to Baltimore, in 1848—the year a sawmill worker discovered gold and sparked a mass exodus to the west, also the year they broke ground in the District of Columbia to build the Washington Monument. "*Nu?*" he'd say. "My ancestors come and suddenly they either run for the hills or build a big *schmeckle*." Bess tried but failed to verify his assertion. Still, she liked his stories.

"My family was in the dress business," Irv had told her. "Why? Probably my great-grandfather liked to know what touched his hands would also touch the naked bodies of the dames in town. But that's it. End of story."

"What's with you, no story," Millie chimed in. "Always with the no story, he's got nothing to say your grandfather, you believe that one? Don't listen to him." She looked like she was about to tell a secret.

"What's with the face?" he said. "We Steinblooms are normal law-abiding people. Well, except for Uncle Abe, this is true."

"See, there he goes."

"Uncle Abe, boy. He used to play fiddle down at the movie

houses. I was too young to go into those places, but I could hear him from the street. He drank too much, but he was a good musician, and you know what? They asked him to be part of this new orchestra they were putting together back then, and you know what I'm talking about, Bessie? It was the National Symphony Orchestra!"

Bess noticed when it came to talking about the past, Millie and Irv liked to expose each other's faults and failures in a competition of superiority. She liked to tell about the time he hired the wrong man to run his shop in Baltimore—*He was a nice boy, what are you talking about?*—who took to wearing the flapper dresses he was supposed to be selling—*I said there was a dress code, so he took me literally*—and because Irv hardly ever visited the store like a good manager should—*It was so far away*—this man in a dress scared women out of the store telling them things like if only they weren't so fat they'd look as good in the dress as he did—*Well, someone should tell it like it is*. It's stories like that, said Millie, that show you just how soon he'd have been out of business had she not been there to knock some sense into him.

Oh yeah, he'd say. He'd say he'd like to see where she'd be if it weren't for him—*With Melvin Finkelstein, that doctor from Harvard, that's where I'd be, I should have married Melvin when I had the chance.* Yeah, he'd say, the poor Russian Jewish girl who didn't even have a penny in her pocket—*I had everything I needed thank you very much*—who walked into his shop and rang his bell in her torn pedal pushers—*Torn, my tuchas*—whom he took pity on and hired as a salesgirl—*I was your best salesgirl*—who all day long punched clack-clack-clack-ka*ching* at the heavy black cash register—*I always paid you back whatever I borrowed*—and holy mackerel if someone could just have told him what he was getting into, boy oh boy.

Sometimes it's in fun, their bantering. But often it turns to bickering that turns to vicious verbal attacks. "Nobody cares, Irving," she'd say, or "Shut your mouth," he'd say, as if the anger inside them—an anger so deep that it is before Bess's time and beyond her comprehension—has no choice but to bubble to the surface in small explosions of hostility. The tension, like smoke, makes anyone else in the room cough and leave. Bess has tried to tease out the roots of their anger to no avail. She thinks maybe it stems from their inability to have children of their own, genetically speaking, for it is one topic they won't talk about. But then it could be anything, for what does Bess know about keeping a marriage afloat for sixty-five years? What does she know about marriage, period? She would like to believe that her grandparents loved each other once, deeply and passionately, to know they were happy in their lives as a whole, but then what does that say about marriage, that the descent into misery is directly related to the number of years a couple spends together, the accumulated anger and grief winning out in the end? Where is the yin and yang in old age? It's as if Millie and Irv's imbalanced inner state manifests itself on the outside, the way they walk slowly and diagonally, bumping into things and losing their footing.

And still, despite all their fighting, Bess feels lucky to have them in her life. They shower her with all the love they withhold from each other, it seems. How important it is to have family nearby, thinks Bess, as she turns onto their street. She loves the moment when they open the door, smiling and aching to hug her, saying, *Come, come, dear* as she walks into their embrace.

"How's my birthday girl!" Irv yells out, beaming, squeezing her shoulders. "It's good to see you, sweetheart. We haven't seen you for ages."

"For God's sake," says Millie. "You just saw her last week. What's wrong with you?" She knocks his chest with the back of her hand and shoos him aside. "Bess dear, you made good time. Was there traffic?" Millie grabs Bess's face in a tight grip and gives her cheek an exaggerated kiss. Whereas Irv is slow, soft, and gentle, Millie is strong and hard-angled.

"No, not really. I'm sorry I'm late." Bess rotates her jaw and rubs her cheek where Millie has pressed on it. She wipes her shoes on a doormat that has ducks around its perimeter. "For you," she says, handing Millie a homemade caramelized pear pie. "I haven't made this in a while but I seem to remember you liking it, Gramp."

"You know it!" He beams, bopping her playfully on the nose.

Bess feels like a giant standing next to her grandparents. She figures they must be down to under five feet by now, and they can't weigh more than a hundred pounds each. They were never big people, but lately they seem particularly small and getting smaller, like thawing snowmen: their wrists thin as twigs, their clothes too big for their frames, their round faces now sallow and sagging so their crooked noses stick farther out. She can look down and see the brown sun spots on Irv's scalp through thin rows of gray hair and the bits of dandruff stuck to the outside folds of his big ears, wrinkled like dried apricots. Millie's silver hair is thinning, too, but she has it styled and sprayed into place each week, preserving its pouf by sleeping on a special moon-shaped pillow. At eighty-six, Irv couldn't give two farts what he looked like, his white dress shirt hanging haphazardly over his belt, his fly undone. But the day Millie, who is four years younger, gives up on her appearance is the day she gives up on life, she likes to say. The women's fashion magazines still pile up at her bedside, her closets are still full of seasonal ensembles. She dons her pantsuits for appointments in the city and her jogging suits for her morning walks around the neighborhood or, when it's too cold out, around the top floor of the mall before it opens. Today she has on a black sweater, pearls, and gray slacks with a perfect crease down the front and back of each leg. "I like your sweater," says Bess, making conversation. "Where'd you get it?"

Millie places the pie on the kitchen counter. "You like it? I don't remember where I got it. You want to try it on?"

"No, that's okay. It looks good on you." Bess has to be careful distributing compliments in their house, for they will offer her anything they own if she shows interest.

"So tell us," says Irv, leading her into the living room, "how does it feel to be sixteen?"

Bess chuckles. "I'll always be sixteen to you, is that it, Gramp?"

"Sweet, Bessie. You'll always be my sweet little girl."

"Big charmer over there," Millie calls out from the kitchen. "He's forgotten how old you are, don't let him fool you. He's terrible. Only has one grandchild you'd think he'd remember how old she is."

"Of course I remember how old my sweet granddaughter is, what are you talking about?" Irv yells this out, then leans in toward Bess with raised eyebrows. *Thirty-five*, she whispers. "Thirty-five!" he yells, triumphantly. "Twice as sweet! A very grown-up, accomplished young lady."

"Ech," groans Millie.

"Bessie, come see my latest acquisition. Come." He takes a book from the shelf and motions for her to follow him. "Mildred," he yells, flicking on the light at the top of a dank staircase. "We're going downstairs, we'll be right back."

The spiral wooden stairway to the basement creaks with each step. The walls are cement and the air is considerably cooler. Irv pulls a string from a bulb in the middle of the room and the harsh light shines on dozens of pairs of eyes surrounding them, staring blankly in their direction—an eerie, unsmiling audience of stiff anorexic bodies, some pointing their accusatory fingers at Bess, some looking upward as if in contemplation, some about to take a step, a few missing an arm, one in the corner disturbingly headless, all upright and female and frightening in their thinness, their nakedness, their having been crowded into this cell like prisoners of war. "Your mannequins freak me out every time, Gramp. I don't understand why you still keep them."

"They keep me company, these ladies. And they keep quiet." He smiles and winks at Bess. He must have about thirty or forty of them, Bess figures. He started bringing them home from his dress shop when they got scuffed or broken and had to be replaced. There would be five or six mannequins at a time on display in the shop's front windows, each with its own distinct wig and dress and maybe a shawl or handbag. He liked seeing them each morning. *Hello girls*, he'd say, *keeping an eye on the store, are you?* He grew attached to them and felt in some odd way it was his duty to bring them home after they'd served their purpose. But after a while, he started to buy them quicker than he needed them, looking for unique ones with distinct markings or more movable parts. Once he retired, he slowed his purchases down considerably, mostly because he was running out of room and Millie was on his case about it to no end. Bess had the feeling he spent a lot of time down here among his harem.

"Look," he says, pulling one out from behind a box in the corner. "I just got her from a store in Northeast." She is dark brown with long thin fingers and—as her grandfather proceeds to point out—movable at the wrists, elbows, shoulders, neck, waist, and knees. She has full lips and black, painted-on eyebrows, but her most noticeable feature is her Afro, as she is one of the few mannequins in the room with hair.

"How old is she?"

"Probably a '70s model. She's scuffed at the joints, but other than that she's in perfect shape. Look, someone drew a peace sign around her belly button."

"But she's supposed to wear clothes. What's she doing with a belly button?"

"That's the beauty of it. They probably needed the belly button to show off low miniskirts or high halter tops. Remember halter tops? I'm going to name her Peace."

Bess stares at her eyes, which are gazing confidently toward a corner of the ceiling. Her stillness is spooky, as if when the lights go out and the humans leave she might come alive and incite her fellow mannequins to revolt.

Irv leaves the room for a moment and returns with a cassette player. He plugs it in and presses "play," and the room suddenly sounds like a smoky bar. "T-Bone Walker," says Irv. "Best blues player there ever was. Peace, would you like to dance?" He positions her arms—one around his waist, the other around his neck—picks her up, and with closed eyes dances her around to the old scratchy recording of Walker's "Hypin' Woman Blues."

Bess watches him. The reasons for her grandfather's fondness for female mannequins is probably not all that difficult to figure out, she thinks. Students in a Psych 101 class might comment on his loneliness, his need for ownership and control, to savor the past and forget about aging, to create a safe haven among friends, not to mention any sexual overtones Bess doesn't want to contemplate. But what's puzzling is his interest in this particular mannequin, this African-American '70s beauty, which makes Bess think she really doesn't know her grandfather well, or at least the man he was in his younger days. Maybe he was a swinger. Maybe he dated women like Peace before he married Millie. Maybe he didn't do a whole lot of what he really wanted to do in the eighty-six years he's been on this earth, which is why he's dancing around his basement with a mannequin in his arms, humming, swaying, smiling, imagining.

Bess taps him on the shoulder, feeling a sudden urge to be part of this imaginary world that makes him smile so broadly. "May I cut in?" She means could she dance with him, but he nods and hands her the mannequin, stepping back to clap to the rhythm. "Oh," says Bess, face-to-face with the woman's perfect plastic cheeks. "Okay then." She grabs on to the figure's tiny waist and slowly twirls her around like a schoolboy at his first social. "Look, Gramp," she says. "I'm giving Peace a chance." Either he doesn't hear her or he doesn't get it, for his gaze is elsewhere and Bess can tell he is alone somewhere, out there.

"Hello down there! Where are you two? Come back up and let's go outside."

Millie's yelling from the top of the stairs brings Irv back to reality. "We're coming," he yells back.

Bess follows him upstairs to find Millie in front of the back door, holding a tray of fruit and rugelach.

"Bess dear, will you bring the tea out?"

Bess holds the screen door for her and comes back with the tea tray. Bess likes their home, their property. The house is a large, two-story mock English Tudor made of brick with stone around the front entrance and wooden shutters painted dark brown. It has a magnificent maple in front and a trellis off to the side with lilacs that will soon bloom in late spring. In the back where they go to sit is a small goldfish pond, now filled with weeds instead of fish; four ornate iron chairs too uncomfortable to actually sit on; and a stone bench pressed up against the trunk of an old cherry tree. Their property would be lovely and colorful had they kept up the landscaping like they used to, but they let it age the way Irv was aging: naturally, nonchalantly, hinting of happier times.

"So how was your day yesterday, birthday girl? What did you do?" Irv unfolds the chairs and places them around Millie's portable bridge table as she folds the napkins and distributes the cups and saucers.

"Not much. Some friends made me a cake and sang 'Happy Birthday.' "

"That's nice," says Millie. "I'm glad to hear you didn't stay at the office."

"You work too hard, Bessie. You need to have more fun." Irv tosses up a raspberry and catches it in his mouth.

"Leave the berries alone, Irving, and don't tell her what she needs. She knows what she needs, look at her. She's all grown up. Aren't you, dear." Was that really a question? "Eat," says Millie, pushing the plate over to Bess. "You love rugelach."

"Thanks." It's actually Bess's mom who used to love rugelach, but Bess doesn't correct her. "Gram, did you need help with something in the attic?"

"No dear, that's all right. Gerald already carried some things down." Gerald is a middle-aged, autistic man who lives nearby with his mother, Vivian—a longtime friend of Millie and Irv's. He is like a son to them, and was always hanging around their house, wherever that happened to be. Bess's mom had a particular fondness for Gerald, too; to Bess he was like the older cousin she tried to ignore in private but vehemently defended against bullies in public. Deep down she has always had a soft spot for his harmless, endearing ways.

"How is Gerald?" Bess asks.

"He's doing fine. If he knew you'd be here he'd have come, you know that."

"Hey, Bessie," says Irv brightly. "Why don't you come down to the store this week. We just hired a new manager. You'll like him, he's a nice boy. Jewish, good business sense." Irv is retired but he sold his store to his cousin's boy to keep it in the family, plus it allows him to stop in and give advice every now and again.

"What are you talking about?" says Millie, gesturing high above her head with a dismissive flip of her hand. "He's too young. And his feet smell."

"What do you know about his feet?"

"I know about his feet."

"You know nothing."

"I know he takes his shoes off in your old office, sitting there behind the desk and it's enough to make you go *meshuggener* with no windows and your air-conditioning never worked anyway."

Irv swirls his finger in the air as if to say, *Big deal*, and leans in toward Bess. "Don't listen to her. Feet you can wash."

"How young is he, Gramp?"

"I don't know. Twenty-something. But he's wiser than his years, I can tell you that."

"Gramp, that's too young."

"I told you," says Millie, wiping the table around her cup with a flowery cloth napkin. "You don't listen."

"What's too young? I should find you an old man?"

"You don't have to find me anything."

"All that matters is he's ready to settle down, have children, I can see it in his eyes."

"You can't see a damn thing through those glasses," says Millie, which was true. His glasses were filthy, but he didn't seem to mind. Irv must have learned over the years how to refocus past the bad spots.

"What do you know."

"What do I know?" she yells, her raspy voice flaring up like a bucking horse. "Why don't you leave your granddaughter alone? Why do you have to make her feel bad talking of children, eh? What's with you?" Millie is slumped a little too low for the table, the edge of which comes up to her ribs. Where she gets the chest power to yell so loudly, Bess can't figure out. Talk of children always seems to rile her.

"I'm looking out for my granddaughter, what's your problem?"

"You're my problem!"

"Okay, that's enough," interrupts Bess, looking back and forth between the two of them. "This is supposed to be my birthday celebration."

"Speaking of your birthday, dear," Millie says quietly, regaining her composure. "Irving, please go get her gifts on the dining room table, will you?"

"Of course, seeing as you asked so nicely." Irv disappears inside the house. A squirrel darts up a tree. A lawnmower erupts in the distance. Bess rolls her neck and pours herself more tea. Her grandmother is pensive, running her fingertips along the table's edge.

"Here we are," says Irv, placing before Bess a wrapped box and a colorful bag.

"How pretty." Bess opens the bag first, finding a nice card with their signatures below a line of X's and O's. She unwraps each gift inside—a pair of black leggings, tangerine-scented lotion, fancy Hanukkah candles—and rattles off sentiments of appreciation.

"Good, dear, I'm glad you like the gifts. They're just tokens."

"Open the box, Bessie. But be careful, it's fragile." He pushes it a few inches in her direction. She unfolds the bow and loosens the box from its wrapping. What's beneath the tissue paper shocks her. It's a Chinese porcelain vase, white with blue markings, about six inches tall, delicate and lovely. It has been on display in her grandparents' various homes for as long as she can remember, a gift from a young Irv to his new bride, a gift Millie polishes with her sleeve sometimes when she's on the phone. Bess had asked a colleague about it once, a Chinese-American woman who paints porcelain pieces in the old tradition with a goat's-hair brush. The woman said if it was an authentic ginger jar from the eighteenth century, it could be worth about fifteen hundred dollars.

"I don't understand," says Bess, holding it out in her palm. "Why are you giving this to me?"

"We know how much you love it, dear."

She carefully places it back in the box. "Listen, just because I admire something doesn't mean I need to possess it. It's yours."

"It was your mother's favorite piece. She'd want you to have it."

"Don't get me wrong. It's beautiful. But I can't accept this. Thank you very much for the gesture, but really . . . no. It should stay right here."

Irv and Millie exchange glances, then they look down at their hands.

"What's going on? Gramp?" But he couldn't look at her.

"Bess, honey," says Millie hesitantly. "We, that is your grandfather and I, we can't keep everything anymore and this is a little thing, it's true, but it's so fragile and could break if you don't take it and take care of it."

"Not following here. What do you mean you can't keep everything?"

Millie takes a deep breath. "We had a hard winter this one past, Bessie. We're not getting any younger, you know. My arthritis gets so bad sometimes I can't button my own shirts and your grandfather forgot and left the burner on last night after he made his hot cocoa and something started to smoke and he didn't ever hear the alarm. I had to shout at him to turn it off."

"Like you need a reason to shout," says Irv, hunched in his chair.

"Never mind, I got plenty."

"Gramp, is that true? You left the burner on?"

"Maybe I did. Turned out okay in the end, didn't it?"

"The two of us are taking so many pills we can hardly keep track," Millie continues. "And it's impossible to get around anymore. You know how bad your grandfather's eyesight is, and they think I need cataract surgery. We hardly know anyone on the block anymore so we just keep to ourselves and, well, it can get lonely, can you understand that?"

"Yeah," Bess whispers. The synapses of her brain, clotted with denial and incomprehensibility, are not letting this new information get in. But loneliness she can understand. She has only to hear the word and her mind envelops it, no questions asked.

"So your grandfather and I think it's a good idea for us to move to a smaller place and someplace warmer."

An ant crawling up the stem of Bess's spoon feels like her

worst enemy. She wants to squash it with her thumb. "Where are you going?"

"We're moving to Tucson near my sister, Shirley. They have a nice place there, she sent us pictures. Two-bedroom apartments where there is a nurse on duty twenty-four hours and shuttle buses to the market and places of interest, and other people like us, Bess."

Bess's foot is tapping uncontrollably. "How come nobody told me this before?"

"Sweetheart, we didn't want to concern you with this until we had to."

Bess looks at her grandfather, who has remained quiet. She implores him with her eyes to say something. He tries to avoid her stare but he can't. "Bessie, we don't like to bother you. But you've seemed kind of down lately." *Has it been so apparent that an old man nearing senility with poor eyesight and dirty glasses can see that?*

"I'm fine. I've just had a lot of work to do, but I'm not as busy now. Really. I'm fine." She stops herself for fear she will say, *I'm fine* too many times until the meaning of the phrase reverses itself.

Millie gets a little popped bubble of energy and pokes Irv's shoulder. "You—don't just sit there. Say something else. Don't make me the bad one here."

"What do you want from me?" he yells back, straightening his back, confronting her. But then he retreats back into his shell, hunched quietly in his chair. "I never said I was fully sold on the idea," he says softly.

"Don't you dare do that. We've talked about this."

"You talked about this," says Irv, more loudly, gaining steam. "You and Shirley. I never said I wanted to live around a bunch of old farts."

"Don't give me that. I got news for you, you *are* an old fart."

"I can run circles around anyone my age and you know it."

"Yeah, because you'd be *lost*, you and your circles!"

"Shut your trap, Millie!"

"Stop!" yells Bess.

Irv stands up so he can look down at Millie and raise his fist in the air. "I'm perfectly capable . . ." he is saying when he knocks his cup of tea into her lap.

"*Idiot!*" Millie jumps up and wipes her pants down furiously with her napkin. "What is wrong with you? Are you blind? Are you blind and deaf and stupid, old man?"

"I said shut your trap, Mildred! Just shut it!"

"Go to hell."

"Stop it, both of you," yells Bess again. They are all standing now, the two of them screaming with pointed fingers and heaving chests, two cocks in a pit and Bess in the middle with both her hands out when suddenly her cell phone rings from inside her knapsack. She could ignore it, but she doesn't know how to stop the ring. *Shit*, she hisses as she flips it on.

"Bess. It's Gabrielle."

"Hey. Listen. Can I call you—"

"So I'm at the Social Safeway," Gabrielle starts in, "I'm in the detergent section, minding my own business, and guess who I bump into?"

Millie in mid-scream heads into the house and slams the

screen door behind her. "Gabrielle," says Bess, pacing. "I really can't—"

"C'mon, Bess. Guess."

Irv screams something to the door and throws his hands up in the air. He screams again and his voice is hoarse. "Gramp," says Bess with her phone away from her ear, but he doesn't listen. Instead, he storms into the house after Millie and leaves Bess standing over her birthday gifts.

"Okay, I'll tell you," Gabrielle is saying. "You're no fun today. He hasn't stopped asking me questions about you so I said I'd call you right now on my cell."

"What?" Bess says, halfheartedly. She feels defeated. She takes a seat at the table. It sounds like her grandparents are still fighting in the kitchen, though she can only make out a word here and there.

"Hang on," says Gabrielle, and then Bess swears she hears Millie bark out, *Fuck you!* But that couldn't be. Millie? This tiny old Jewish woman saying, *Fuck you?* You've got to be kidding. But then as if to confirm her suspicions she distinctly hears Irv scream it back. *Fuck you, too, you fucking bitch.* Bess is *whoosh*, back up on her feet. Where did they get that from? Never once has either of them cursed in front of her; Bess is sure of it. She half laughs. They sound so ludicrous, like children trying out the nasty bits their parents have forbidden them to say. But her amusement is short-lived while she realizes what has happened for their fights to have escalated to such a degree. "Fuck," she says. "Fucking unbelievable," she now yells so they might hear her. "*Do you hear what that sounds like? Fuck!*" she screams.

"Hello, Bess?"

It's a male's voice. *Oh God, it isn't.* "Yes," whispers Bess.

"It's Rory. From last night?"

It is. Fuck. "Hi. Sorry for yelling that in your ear."

"You wouldn't be the first. You're quite charming, you Americans."

"Thanks. I don't usually start up phone conversations like that."

"Well, you should. I think you're on to something. The whole hi, hello, how are you bit can become a thing of the past. Shall I try it?"

"I think you should," she says, sitting back down. Her grandparents must have stopped arguing, since she can't hear anything from inside the house.

Suddenly he screams *FUCK* so loudly into the phone she jumps back. She hears some other voices in the background, and then Rory sounds like he's talking to someone else. "I just can't be*lieve* the price of these Snuggles," he is saying. "Can't a guy soften his fabric without going broke?"

"Making new friends at the supermarket?" says Bess. She thinks she can hear Gabrielle's distinctive laugh.

"You should have seen that woman's face," says Rory. "I think I really just scared her half to death."

"We'll have to fine-tune our new greeting."

"Yes, let's work on that."

The sound of Rory's masculine voice ignites a small electrical storm of desire inside her, but she is uneasy. The house is too quiet. She picks up the fallen cup and saucer and uses her cloth napkin to wipe the spilled tea on the table. "Listen," she says, "can I call you back? I'm with my grandparents and I really should go."

"Of course. Right. I think your friend wants her phone back, too. I just wanted to say I'm sorry I didn't get a chance to say good-bye last night. I had to run off to a gig."

"That's okay. You missed all the excitement."

"So I hear. And I missed your pie, which Gabrielle tells me is to die for."

"I pay her to say that."

"I doubt that. Listen, can I make it up to you? Would you like to get together?"

Bess smiles and mouths, *Thank you* up to the heavens. "Sure."

"I'm playing fiddle Tuesday night at the Four P's in Cleveland Park. I was thinking you could come by. I'm on at eight, but come by anytime."

"Okay. Sure. I'll see you then." She hangs up before Gabrielle gets back on and says something embarrassing that he could hear. She feels giddy. *He asked me out! Hallelujah!*

She's in the shade now that it's spread across the table and she shivers from a slight breeze. She holds the Chinese ginger jar and traces its design with her fingertip. How will she protect this delicate vase? It looks too easy to drop or crush. She's already seeing it in pieces on the table, sharp-edged and dusty. She leaves it for the moment and enters the house. "Hello?" she calls out. She makes her way to the kitchen. Her grandfather is standing by the back window looking out with his hands clasped behind him. He is wearing a threadbare undershirt. The old wrinkled skin on his arms like that of rotten apples hangs on his bones, soft and easily bruised. She could cry for him he looks so vulnerable. "Gramp. You okay?" He looks at her as if he doesn't recognize her. "Gramp?"

"Oh, Bessie dear," he says with little breath behind it.

"Gramp, where's Gram? Where's your shirt?"

"I don't know."

Bess notices black and blue marks on his arms now that she is standing next to him. Maybe he really is losing his balance and bumping into things. Maybe he needs help, more help than she can give. She turns to look out the window with him, at the old cherry tree and the empty pond. "What are you going to do with all your mannequins?" she asks. But he doesn't answer. He looks so old, and so lovable. "It'll be all right," she says, and reaches out to hold his hand.

CHAPTER EIGHT

I carry around the weight and shame of those years after Lorraine like a hunchback. Sometimes the shame is all I have. My memories are foggy at best. My downward spiral started slow: one drink here, another there to drown out the loneliness. Beer turns to hard liquor, and liquor empties the pockets so you find yourself in seedier places where the local barflies gather around you like fresh dung. Twenty-four years old and three failed marriages, for Christ's sake. Not to mention my brother dead and gone and me missing the last six years of his life.

So predictably, I lost my job. I packed up my things and thought it was high time I saw America, for real this time . . . the whole big expanse of it. I hitchhiked from one place to the next, playing my fiddle for handouts and sleeping in two-bit motels, you know the kind that advertise "No Pests," and you know if they're advertising that, that's the least of your worries. I had some skirmishes, but mostly I was okay and after about six months this one trucker said, *You like drinking? Gambling? You should go to Vegas*, and that's just what I did.

I don't like talking about my year there. It's hard to be filled with so much regret, and it was regret galore even then, immediate regret, which is the only way I know to talk about my drunken mistake of a marriage to Fawn Gilman.

Let me tell you straight out that Fawn was twice my age: I was twenty-six, she was fifty-two, and she found that hilarious. In fact, just about everything was hilarious to Fawn. She was hyped up on you-name-it most of the time, coke and martinis mostly, and everything about me—and me and her together—was just too damn funny to her. We met at a bar, got drunk, went back to her place, met at the same bar the next night, and so on and so forth. I don't think I ever saw her in the middle of the afternoon, come to think of it. I was either sleeping or playing blackjack at the Venetian—my luck wasn't so bad, it got me free drinks, but I always played until my money ran out. But then what did I care? I was a kept man. Fawn always paid for my meals and we always went back to her place, which wasn't a bad gig for a guy like me, seeing as her condo was large and luxurious. She had two bars and a marble bathroom with a Jacuzzi and a TV set into the wall. It was pretty incredible.

And Fawn was a good-looking fifty-two-year-old, I'll tell you. Her skin could look kind of green and her eyes deep in their sockets were a little worse for wear, but you could tell she was gorgeous once, there were still remnants. She had long shapely legs, in fact a great figure all around that she loved to show off in tight, sexy outfits. She was a dancer in her past and kept a dancer's posture. I admired the way she stood and sat up straight, or the way she attempted to sit up straight anyway when she was two sheets to the wind.

And that laugh of hers! Like I said, she found everything hilarious and every few minutes she'd let out a long, robust laugh with her mouth wide open, her hand smacking the nearest shoulder. It was so catchy everyone around us would be laughing, too, though they wouldn't know at what. She'd gasp for air and laugh some more, laugh, gasp, laugh, gasp, until she'd have a coughing fit and have to drink a shot to soothe her throat.

That's how we got married one night, laughing, gasping, on the verge of passing out.

It started because someone at the bar brought up the issue of marriages in the plural and I, too drunk for self-censorship, confessed that I had three under my belt. Three what, they wanted to know. Three marriages, says I. There was a pause, and then an explosion of laughter, initiated by you-know-who. One of those damn laughing fools wanted to know if I was going for four before I reached puberty, which caused a whole new wave of laughter. Fawn's laughing, in particular, went on longer than usual and made her eyes drip big, black mascara—filled tears down her cheek. What's so funny, someone asked her, as if she needed a reason more specific than life itself. She'd been married *five* times, she blurted out when she could finally catch her breath, *Isn't that a howler?* She liked that word *howler*, which always struck me funny seeing as she came alive at night and looked sort of wolfish with her big pointed nose and red fingernails like claws. Another sloppy buffoon yelled out that if we married each other, we'd have an even ten between us and that was apparently the howler to beat all howlers. It gave Fawn the hiccups. It made her snort out of her nose and rise up from her seat, fall to the ground, get up again and declare that a dare's a dare: she and I would get married that night. No one had mentioned a dare, but that didn't stop the crowd from cheering us on.

It being Vegas there was a twenty-four-hour chapel of the famous something-or-other across the street and the crowd of drunks followed us down the red plush carpeting to the altar of white pillars and potted geraniums and there an enormous man with sideburns down to his chin and a mustache thicker than I'd ever seen in my life—that's what I remember most about him, his facial hair—this man asked me if I'd take this woman to be my lawfully wedded wife and I yelled out, *I'll take them all!* or something to that effect, and then I threw up on his cowboy boots. Fawn yells out, *See? He loves me!* and everyone is now doubled over with laughter. That's the last thing I remember of the night: a crowd of drunks bending over their knees trying to breathe because they're laughing so hard.

I woke up the next morning, or afternoon I should say, feeling horrendous, and seeing that there was no ring on my finger, I was thankful that whatever it was I did the night before, I didn't do the worst possible thing, which was get married again. Fawn wasn't there, so I let myself out of her place and went back to my apartment to sleep some more. It wasn't until I went back to the bar that night that I was delivered the blow. It was the bartender who told me by way of congratulating me. *Congratulate me for what*, I said, and he started laughing. I wanted to punch his face in, I was so sick of laughter. Fawn came in then, and I said to her, *Is it true? It's true*, she said, but thankfully she wasn't laughing. Maybe she saw the look on my face. *It's not so bad, honey*, she said, *we'll have a grand ol' time, one howler after another*. She said that, but I don't think she really meant it. I think she was as regretful as I was, only she'd done so many regretful things in her life she learned to take them in stride. I stood up and kissed her cheek. She looked really sad, not just down-and-out sad but to-the-core sad, it's hard to explain, like there were things in her past I didn't know and wouldn't understand if I did, but it was too late anyway. *You'll give me a divorce*, I said quietly. It wasn't a question. She wouldn't look at me. She stared at her drink. *Good-bye, Rory*, she said just as softly, *it's been fun*. And I left. I never saw her again. I filed the divorce papers right away and she obliged.

Don't you think a marriage like that shouldn't count? I mean, if your country declares war and it's over in one day, that's different than, say, a war that lasts a year or five years. Consider the casualties, the lasting effects. Nobody will even remember when that one-day war happened or which country it was against, will they? Will it be listed in the history books because someone called it a war? I don't know what I'm trying to say. I guess I just get angry that people can have lots of relationships that no one would blink an eye at, but because mine have formal labels they get listed against me somehow, and they get lumped together as if they're all equal, but they're not. I've been married eight times, this is true, but Fawn shouldn't count. She just shouldn't. It was an evening that got out of hand. No casualties, which is more than I can say for my marriage to Olive Ann. Olive Ann Fennelly had a daughter, Cici.

I loved Cici more than words can say.

CHAPTER NINE

Following a full workout, Bess and her fellow karate students stand at attention and recite the student creed, beginning with *I intend to develop myself in a positive manner.* When they are told *shio, shake it out, good class,* Bess jogs to the back of the dojo, wipes her neck down with her towel, and glances at her watch. She has an hour to get home, shower, and catch the Metro up to the bar if she wants to see Rory's first set, but she needs the full first date prep time, so she gulps her water and with a wave and a quick *Have a nice evening everyone!* she bows and rushes out.

By the back door, she sees the mother of one of the teenage students rocking an infant and her mind starts to wander, first to Gaia and her baby whom Bess makes a mental note to check up on, and then to Rory. Is he good with children? Does he want children? Does he have children? He must be in his mid-forties, she figures. That could mean a lot of things. He could be a father, divorced, widowed. Maybe he has an ex-wife who never leaves him alone. Maybe he really is just single, never married, in which case what's wrong with him? Is he a player, a commitment-phobe, a closeted gay? *Oh, just stop*, she can hear Cricket say. *Is there something wrong with you that you're still single? Nice positive manner you got there.* She wishes she knew where Cricket was. She could use his sage counsel tonight.

At home, she primps and parades in front of her mirror in her new boho chic, earth-colored ensemble, feeling like an actress playing a part, albeit a more feminine, sexier part than her usual persona. Yesterday she didn't know what *boho chic* meant, and is still not sure, though she was educated on the subject for an entire lunch break by her assistant and an equally young salesgirl whose style Bess admired. *The first date!* her assistant had exclaimed. *You know what that means . . . shopping spree!* Now she's looking at her gladiator sandals and mid-length peasant skirt and form-fitting white T-shirt and wondering if she should give it up and throw on jeans. She grabs a light sweater and runs out the door before she loses her nerve.

It is quarter to ten when she finally arrives. The bouncer surprises her by asking for her photo ID with a flirtatious body scan. Bess surprises herself by reacting with a giggle. *A giggle*, for God's sake. She blames the skirt.

The bar is crowded and boisterous with red-faced twenty-somethings not at all interested in their environment outside pheromone range. They're not listening to the lively music emanating from Rory's fiddle and another man's guitar up on the small stage. Bess sits at a dark table in the corner and tries to block out the bar din. It sounds like they're playing a jig, the rhythm bouncing off the fiddle in cheery refrains. He's having a good time up there. He holds the neck of the fiddle low and uses the full bow, end to end, rocking back and forth, tapping his foot. He cradles the other end of the fiddle in the crook of his neck affectionately, like he's hugging a cat, and Bess imagines resting her head under his chin, his arms wrapped around her. He looks handsome in his black T-shirt, jeans, and black boots, his gray-flecked dark hair dangling seductively over one eye.

"Thanks very much," he says at the tune's end to the few who notice the sudden silence and clap. Bess claps the longest, which is when he sees her. She waves, he smiles, she blushes.

"Now if you'll indulge us," says Rory, leaning into his microphone while his partner frets his guitar. He has placed his fiddle behind him on a table and has his hands in his front pockets like a little boy who has gotten into trouble. Bess feels something like a craving for him, he's so damn cute, and blushes again when, as she stares at his hands in his pockets, an image of unzipping his pants runs through her, brain to crotch and back again. "We're going to do a well-known tune for you now by our boy Thomas Moore from the early part of the nineteenth century." Bess feels like the only one listening. Rory continues: "'Twas a time when the people of Ireland were in the poorest of spirits, had lost the last glimpses of liberty and brotherhood in their fight against the British Empire, and this is a sad song indeed, but also a hopeful one, if you're one to see things that way. You ready, Sean?" *Am*, says Sean with a strum of his strings. "Right, then," says Rory, and clears his throat. "Here is 'The Harp That Once.'" And he sings with his eyes shut, dark and heartfelt, his voice up the octave in cries of passion and down again at the end of each stanza to lay grounded in the doleful resting place of Irish history.

Bess is transported. The beauty and sadness of the song lift her out of the bar across an ocean to an echoing empty castle where flags are flapping on their poles and bodies in rags are crouched in corners and a bell tolls far away and sends a dove back to circle the cemetery's dead and a cherub with his harp is too far away to touch. When the song ends and the voices of the philistine frat boys at the bar filter back into her consciousness, Bess realizes she has tears in her eyes for Millie and Irv and her parents long gone.

The next piece lifts her out of the darkness. She taps her toes in rhythm with the lively reel and sips the beer the waiter has brought over, compliments of the "act." *The act?* The waiter gives a nod to Rory. Bess holds her glass up in a toast of thanks and Rory winks at her.

"Ready for a break, Sean?" asks Rory, as if reading her mind. She sees that Rory has pointed her out to Sean, who nods a hello to her, too. He whispers something to Rory. Rory laughs and rubs his eyes. "You know," says Sean into the microphone, "we don't always mean to pick on Mother England."

"If it weren't for England, we wouldn't have our Irish rebel songs," says Rory.

"There's that," says Sean. "But they also have their share of characters, wouldn't you say, Rory? Take ol' King Henry."

"To King Henry," yells the bartender, suddenly. Bess glances his way and sees his glass raised, his broad smile, his eyes to the stage aglow with what appears as an inside joke.

"Yes, take King Henry," Rory says back to the bartender, shaking his head, grinning the way someone would who's being teased. He cups his hand over the microphone and says something to Sean, who laughs and looks at Bess, and then begins to strum and sing.

The song about King Henry and his wives is lighthearted, and when it ends, others finally clap along with Bess, though she isn't sure whether it's for the King Henry antics or because Rory and Sean are stepping off the stage, as if it had been too much effort for the frat boys and barflies to clap after each song and instead had saved it up for the end.

"You made it," says Rory as he sits opposite her.

Bess repositions herself to face him. "You're really good."

"Thanks. We usually get standing ovations, I don't know what's going on tonight." Bess is learning to read the sparkle in his eyes when he's joking.

"I threw my bra on stage, didn't you see it?"

"That was you? I thought it was Sean's—his always slips off his bosom when he hits a low C."

Bess laughs. "Bosom?"

"Well, I can't very well say *tits* in the presence of one who has them, can I?"

"Absolutely not. I'm leaving."

"Please stay. I'm trying to make my first dates last more than three minutes and you're my last hope."

"Fine, but one more slip-up and these bosoms are out the door."

"I promise," he says, and winks. How sexy a wink is. All this talk of tits has her turned on, fully aware of the nerve endings of her nipples against fabric, the floating particles of air in her cleavage.

"So what were you guys laughing about?" Bess asks, looking at Sean at the bar.

"Nothing." For a moment Rory looks down at the floor. "The boys get a bit soggy into the evening. So you found this place okay?"

"I've been here before. They have good potato soup and corned beef sandwiches."

"That they do, though corned beef is an American thing, we never ate that in Ireland. The best is their soda bread. Perfection. The owner uses his grandmother's recipe with real buttermilk and raisins, the crust is so hard it can make a man homesick." Van Morrison bursts from a lit jukebox. A waitress carries a pungent waft of sauerkraut past them on a plate. "You hungry?"

"No, thanks," she lied. She ate only a PowerBar and a chunk of cheddar cheese after karate; she is too butterfly-stomached to eat anything else. "That reminds me, I brought you something." She reaches into her bag and retrieves an item wrapped in tin foil. She hadn't planned on bringing him a piece of pie, thinking it might be too much on a first date, but she had leftovers that Millie insisted she take home and decided as she was running out the door that it was best to part with the calories. She hoped he would see it as a nice gesture.

"Ah! You read my mind. I've been craving this since I saw it at your party. It was a true work of art, that pie of yours."

Bess blushes. "Thanks."

He retrieves a fork and digs in, closing his eyes as he chews. "Pure heaven. Where did you learn to make such a master-piece?"

"My mom taught me. She was amazing in the kitchen."

"Was?"

"She passed away when I was in college."

"I'm sorry."

Bess takes a quick look around the bar, takes a deep breath. "So, do you get homesick?"

Rory leans back and wipes his chin. "For Ireland? No. I mean, sometimes sure. It's not like I've made such a success of my life here." He looks down at his glass. "I'll tell you it's mostly when I see Americans who fancy themselves Irish, the ones who barf up green beer every St. Paddy's Day. And they look at me as if I'm just like them only more so."

"I think I know what you mean. I hate when someone claims a heritage he knows little about out of some fake sense of pride or, I don't know . . . to join the party. But then we're talking about Irish Americans, and you have to admit not all of them are like that."

"No?"

"What I mean is, the term Irish American has a different meaning than Irish. It's easy to see the former as a dilution of the latter, but at some point the new group takes on its own shape so focusing solely on its derivation isn't enough."

Rory puts down his fork and leans back in his chair, flashing his dimpled, boyish grin.

"What?" says Bess, sheepishly.

"Tell me, Bess Gray, what do you do for a living?"

Bess tries to conjure up a clever answer, but that banter train has already derailed and fallen into the ravine of work-speak. "Sorry. I'm a folklorist."

"That explains the decor of your apartment, which I loved, by the way. You travel a lot?"

"Some. But mostly I've collected stuff from artists here."

"Your African masks are amazing, but I must say, you're the first woman I've met with a banjo on her wall. I saw that and my heart did a little leap." Rory flutters his hand over his heart.

Bess's heart responds with a little leap of her own. "I loved that you took it down to play."

"Do you play?"

"No. It was my dad's. I remember him being really good actually."

"Was? You lost your dad, too?"

Bess nods. "When I was eight. He died in a car crash."

"I'm sorry. That's awful."

Rory's gaze turns sympathetic. Bess takes a sip of her beer and looks away.

"So!" says Rory in a clear attempt to brighten the mood. "Let me ask you. I've been here for almost thirty years, nearly twice as long as I lived in Ireland. My friends back home make fun of my American ways. Would you call me an Irish American then?"

"Is your vomit green?"

"Yes. But I'm a bulimic on a strict grass diet."

Bess's laugh turns her sip of beer into a snort out her nose. Mortified, she reaches for the nearest napkin. "That was bad."

"What, my bulimic reference or your very dainty spray of snot?" Rory finishes his beer and stops the waitress to order another.

Bess politely declines. She took an allergy pill today and doesn't want to push it. "Identity is such a hard thing. Painful sometimes, for me anyway. I don't know much about my family background. Maybe that's why I do what I do."

"Do you have any siblings?"

"No. Not even any aunts or uncles or cousins, that I know of anyway. I have my grandparents, and I love them dearly, they're so good to me, but they adopted my mom and are pretty private about that. What about your family?"

"I have my dad and two sisters. My mother and brother have passed on. My brother I was quite close to. That was hard. I'll tell you, I still think of all of them, of Ireland, as home, even though I don't want to go back. I'm Irish through and through. I was practically born with a Guinness in my hand. I feel most comfortable in a pub. I follow soccer and boxing. I sing a mean 'Danny Boy' and I don't go to church unless someone makes me. I'm a damn cliché, is what I am."

"I feel like a cliché, too."

"You? Yes, of course, there must be thousands of beautiful brown-haired folklorists in this country."

He said I was beautiful. "No, I mean . . ." and here Bess hesitates. "I'm a single thirty-something woman living in the city. It's such a boring story by now." She can't look at him. How could she have said that to a near stranger on a first date when she won't even bring this subject up with her closest friends? She is suddenly aware that under the table she is pulling a scab off her knee and now it will scar. She at least stops herself from saying what she's thinking next: that the friend she most talks to is gay. (Where could Cricket be? she wonders. He's not answering his cell phone. She should check up on Stella in Dogaritaville.)

"Are you saying you have a cat?"

"No, I'm allergic, but see? You know just the stereotype I'm talking about."

Rory reaches out and brushes her forearm. "I understand. It's not my choice to be alone, either."

Bess looks at his fingers on her arm and shivers with desire. How did their conversation get so intense so quickly? "Let's get out of here," she says, and then cringes at the sound of it aloud.

"A girl after my own heart!" says Sean, bursting onto the scene with beer in hand. He grabs a chair and sidles up to their table. "I like my women to take charge, right, McMillan?" His smile at Bess is wide and mischievous. Bess blushes.

"Bess, this is Sean, the smoothest-talking scoundrel in the District."

"Aw, go on. Don't listen to him," says Sean. "It's a pleasure to meet you." He extends his hand. When Bess offers hers, he holds on to it, massaging the back of her hand with his thumb. "Sweet Jesus, your skin's like silk. McMillan, you old, pale, hairy son of a bitch, what'd you do to land such a dark-haired, young beauty?"

"I'm not sure," says Rory.

"Darling, you'd be better off with someone like me, trust me.

I'm richer, I'm better-looking, I'm much more talented, musically and otherwise, if you get my drift."

They are both looking at Bess, and Bess, for her part, is feeling looked at, feeling desired, feeling pretty and sexy and almost unbearably desirous of Rory as she enjoys Sean's caresses that are now along the inside of her wrist. She pulls her hand away when she realizes this and drinks her beer. "I'm enjoying your performance," she says to Sean, though she says it with enough of a pause before the last word that Sean and Rory laugh.

"Okay, seriously," says Sean. "Rory here is a simple guy. No, no," he says as Rory tries to push him away, jokingly. "I'm telling you the truth. He likes a good beer, an exciting game, good music . . ."

"And a lovely woman to come home to," says Rory, winking at Bess.

"Interesting," says Bess. "Why not a woman to *share* the beer, the game, and the music *with*?" She's surprised she said this aloud and feels a little burst of heat in her cheeks, but Rory's grin widens into something different this time, something less impish and more tender.

"Oh, I like this woman," says Sean. "I think she's got your number, McMillan."

"That she does," says Rory.

Rory finishes another short set, says his good-byes, and with his palm in the center of Bess's back escorts her toward the door. "You look amazing, by the way," he whispers into her ear as they wait for the bouncer to let them pass.

Bess smiles as if with her whole body. "Do you have a car?" she asks. He nods. "C'mon then. I want to show you something."

She had brainstormed during his second set where they might go after he was done working. Someplace romantic and nearby, she thought. Throw illustrious, gothic, and D.C. into the mix and she had the perfect place: the grounds of the National Cathedral.

"Let's park here," she says as they approach the winding road around the property.

The cathedral is lit up gloriously against a black sky. It's a commanding structure of limestone blocks and spires; the center tower rises thirty stories high, one of the tallest points in the city. The Bishop's Garden just next to the cathedral is rumored to be one of the best make-out locales in the district. Couples ignore the "Closed After Dark" sign and slip through the arched wooden doorway.

Rory cuts the engine. "You're taking me to church? That's not a good sign."

"No, I'm taking you here."

He follows her into the garden. Without lamplight, it's eerily dark for a city spot. Bess has been through the garden enough to know which way the stone pathways curve.

She hears the crickets and water trickling from a spigot and if she listens closely she can hear the heavy breathing of other couples around the bends of stone walls and on benches behind long branches.

The prime real estate for groping before God is the stone

gazebo in the center of the garden and as luck would have it, Bess and Rory find it empty.

"This is amazing," Rory whispers, looking up at the cathedral from inside the gazebo.

"Isn't it?" Bess whispers back. They have to stand close to each other to make their whispering as quiet as they can. "What I love about the cathedral is its gargoyles. It has over one hundred, including one of Darth Vader."

"Really," whispers Rory. A sigh that sounds female escapes from the darkness to their left and Bess and Rory chuckle quietly. Rory takes Bess's hands; she looks down at his hands cupping hers. Did he notice she was a nail-biter?

"I love your knuckles," she whispers. When he laughs a quick laugh, Bess realizes how ridiculous that sounds. "I always notice a guy's knuckles, I don't know why. I like masculine knuckles, I guess."

"I can honestly say I never heard that before."

"Well," whispers Bess, somewhat embarrassed, "what did you notice about me?"

"Your tits."

Bess's laugh is another snort.

"See, there it is . . . that smile of yours. I love when it's so wide it makes your eyes all squinched. It's adorable. It makes me want to be funny all the time so I can see it. Unless . . ." and here he pauses, waiting for her to look back at him. "Unless I can get your lips to do something else?"

And then he kisses her.

They caress and kiss and add to the collective heavy breathing of the garden and when they disengage Bess whispers *wow* with her eyes shut, because though the entry into the kiss may have been corny and contrived, the kiss itself—long, luscious, addiction-sweet—*the kiss* is to die for.

And because the kiss is to die for and their hands are exploring with increasing urgency the curves of their bodies, now pressed together, and their breathing is spilling over into the realm of gasping, they don't hear the patrolman approach until his flashlight is shining directly at them. "The gardens are closed," he says, sounding like Eeyore. He doesn't bother to whisper. "You'll move on now."

Bess and Rory collect themselves and try to focus once the flashlight is pointed down at their shoes. Where did this guy come from? It's as if the cathedral itself, sensing sin from its flying buttresses, sent out one of its openmouthed gargoyles to eradicate the enemy by motioning with his light the path to salvation. "This way, if you please," he says, and Bess and Rory follow his light like kids caught stealing candy.

In the parking lot they see other disheveled couples walking to their cars.

"Sorry about that," says Bess, getting into Rory's car.

"But that was great. It's a good first date story for you."

With all those couples there, though, were the gardens just another first date cliché? Is there anything that wouldn't feel cliché short of getting mugged by Nepalese drag queens and dragged to Wichita on the back of a camel?

Rory leans over and kisses her neck. "What should we do now?"

Bess can't think straight, so she stares straight ahead and tries to think straight; *Think straight*, she says to herself. "Well, it *is* a work night. And it's late. I should really head home." She comments on the way about the parking problems near her apartment, thankful that she won't have to deal with the dilemma of inviting him up. "Thanks for the ride," she says as the car idles in her alleyway. "I had a great time."

"Me, too. And thanks for the pie. May I have another piece sometime?" She nods and he kisses her again.

When she is inside the lobby of her building, she stage-whispers, "*YES!*" and smiles all the way down the hall. There she sees Stella guarding Cricket's door like a gargoyle.

"Stella, what are you doing here?" She leans down to pet Stella's head and knocks. "Cricket!" she calls out. "Cricket, are you in there?" She puts her ear to the door. "That's the oddest thing, you here like this." Stella looks sad, but then she always looks sad with her droopy eyes. "C'mon, then."

Bess leads Stella up to her place and pours a bowl of water. She finds the number for the kennel, but gets an answering machine. She calls Cricket's cell and gets his voice mail, too. "I found Stella in front of your place, so now I'm worried. Call me first thing when you get this message. I'll keep her with me until you do."

She lies down on the floor and rubs Stella's belly. "I hope Cricket's okay." Stella lies down next to Bess and drapes her head over her front paws. "You're right, he's probably fine. He'll call soon." She takes off her sweater and bunches it under her head. "You know what, Stella? I had a great date tonight. It was only a first date, but I feel like I know him somehow, you know? He's a nice, straightforward kind of guy. A *nice* boy." Bess touches her nose to Stella's nose and whispers, "Do you think he's the one, Stella?" Stella backs away and sneezes. Bess rolls to her back. "You're right again," she says. "Absolutely right. It's been such an emotional week, but Stella . . . I think things are looking up," and within minutes the two of them are sound asleep.

CHAPTER TEN

You'd think that as grand a mistake as I'd made with Fawn, I'd have gotten myself cleaned up and straightened out, but it wasn't easy. I tried. The first thing I did was leave Vegas. I knew a guy who'd moved to Denver and said he had an extra room and could use the help on rent, so that's where I headed. He fixed me up with a job at a music store, just to tide me over. I didn't have experience in retail, but the owner heard me play fiddle and I think I impressed him, so he gave me a chance. I played for cash some evenings at a local pub, and managed to get computer consulting work on the side from my roommate's father.

In other words, I was getting by. I weaned myself off gambling, which wasn't too difficult seeing as I was never really a gambler deep down. What I should have done is wean myself off hard liquor, too, but moving cities didn't get rid of the self-hatred, it only buried it for a bit and old habits die hard, right?

Anyway, I wasn't out of control or anything like I was in Vegas, just keeping it all at a minimum and functioning as best I could when I met Cici. It was at a Laundromat around the corner from my apartment. She liked to hang around there rather than at home with her mom, she said, where it was cold and not all that quiet because her mom liked to sing at the top of her lungs to Tammy Wynette records.

I'd see her sitting in the corner with a book—this knock-kneed girl of about nine, hiding under the hood of her gray sweatshirt. She said she liked the quiet of the Laundromat and the fresh smell of the detergent and especially the heat, which felt good rising out of the dryer. She didn't tell me all this at first, though. In fact, she didn't say much of anything at first because her mom told her not to talk to strangers and she didn't know to trust someone like me until she saw me breaking up a fight over some accusation of stolen quarters and I figure she thought I was a good guy after that. And then when she did talk I could hardly understand her on account of her stutter, and I knew that was the real reason she didn't say much. Poor girl, I'm telling you my heart ached for her. I could tell people would give up trying to listen to what she had to say and she was as lonely as I was and could really use a friend.

So once or twice a week we'd meet at the Laundromat and she'd tell me about school, and we played checkers, lots of check-ers. *You l-l-l-l-lose*, she'd yell out with such delight—not malice mind you, just pure delight and abandon, which you didn't see in Cici often—and it so cheered me that I'd lose on purpose. I caught on to her way of speaking before long, meaning I was al-ways patient with Cici, and in return she made me feel . . . well, like I belonged. Here was someone who gave me a tissue when I sneezed, you know?

But I was leery of what our friendship might look like on the outside and so it wasn't long before I was encouraging Cici to bring her mom around just so she would know I was an okay guy, too, and nothing to worry about. I could tell Cici wanted to keep her mom out of our friendship, but I insisted and so one day she brought her to the Laundromat and I just about dropped my jaw to the floor she was so pretty. I mean, like a model from bottom to top: long legs, small waist, almond eyes, long, thick dark hair like Maggie's, and beautifully shaped . . . you get the idea. *So you're Rory*, she said. *You like to pick up little girls in Laundromats?* That's the first thing she said to me. I couldn't answer. She was chewing gum and all I could focus on was her lovely jaw moving up and down. Well anyway, Cici came to my defense and I did my share of fumbling an introduction until she softened and invited me back to their place for afternoon tea.

I soon found out that "afternoon tea" was Olive Ann's euphemism for the evening's first vodka and cranberry. She was an artist, an abstract painter, and her work was all throughout the apartment: on large canvases, but also on every wall and stairwell, sometimes on the ceiling and on appliances. I could understand why Cici described her place and her mom the way she did. They had hardly enough money to pay the heating bills, so yeah, it was cold. And with all those swirling colors around, it seemed loud, too. But most of all it was Olive Ann who drew me in. She was a presence, the way she occupied space and made you watch her all the time. Or I watched her . . . I couldn't take my eyes off her. The first time she sang out like Tammy Wynette, standing on her couch, I fell in love.

And that's how it went. Olive Ann, alive and crazy in everything she did, grabbed my attention and never let go. She'd cook spaghetti and you never knew whether you were going to eat it or wear it or hang it from the lamps or draw with it on the walls. I lusted after her, I *craved* her. I started spending all my time at Olive Ann's place just to be near her, and after a while she let me stay.

Now, I'm not forgetting about Cici. I'll admit I got wrapped up in my desire for Olive Ann, but something told me Cici was used to that with the men her mom dated. I guess I snapped out of it when one time Olive Ann returned from a shopping spree with kimonos for us to wear that evening. Where she got the money for these sprees, I don't know. She had us put them on and paint our faces and she and I were laughing and drinking our vodka cranberries and getting into the spirit, but not Cici. Cici didn't want any part of it. *C'mon, sweetie,* said her mother, *geishas don't have to speak, isn't that perfect?*

At the moment her mother said that, poor Cici started to hyperventilate and I knew she was on her way to one of her panic attacks. She'd been getting them more frequently and I got good at talking her down from them, but I couldn't this time. She ran out of the apartment. I took everything off as best I could and ran after her, knowing I'd find her at the Laundromat. *I'm so sorry,* I said. She wasn't panicking anymore, but she looked pretty sad. I got her to talk after a while until we were laughing at the lipstick I still had on my cheeks. I hugged her and then I walked her home.

I so loved Cici, you know? Maybe it was the first time I felt the feelings a father might feel, that kind of love. (Cici's own father was up in Alaska and pretty much out of the picture.) I think back on it now and I'm not sure I'd say the same about my feelings for Olive Ann. I was enraptured with Olive Ann, lustful. But is that love? At the time I thought it was. But there was something else . . . I wanted to protect them both. I thought maybe I had finally matured in the love department.

I say all this as an introduction to what happened next, which is to say Cici and I returned home and found Olive Ann in the bedroom with the door locked. We cleaned up and I fell asleep on the couch. In fact, I slept on the couch for the next three nights because Olive Ann wouldn't come out of the bedroom and when she finally did, she looked awful and had terrible body odor. I coaxed her into a bath and made her some dinner. She got herself up and around after that, but still . . . she wasn't the same. She was lethargic and depressed. Cici and I spent a lot of time together, at the local diner or bowling alley, and Olive Ann would get jealous and storm into her bedroom and I'd be sleeping on the couch again. I'd try to find out what was the matter, but Olive Ann wouldn't say.

One night, though, when she let me back in her bed, she told me that it was time Cici had a father again. *What are you saying*, I said. *I'm saying I think we should be a family*, she said. *But we are a family*, I said. *No*, she said, *a real family. You're the one*, she said, *the right one*. Well, I sat up and rubbed my head. I told her all about being married before and I wasn't about to do that again, and she told me she didn't care about my past mistakes. That's the word she used, *mistakes* instead of *marriages*. She said we all had our pasts to contend with, but we're in the here and now. By now I had stood up and was pacing the room, saying, *Olive Ann, I'm sorry but I can't*, to which she delivered this blow, slow and succinct, so it would sink in: *Rory, I'm pregnant*.

Pregnant! I thought we had been so careful. Well, I'll tell you I got drunk that night. By myself. And not on vodka cranberries; I needed my Guinness and lots of it. I remember telling the whole saga to a large, bald bartender who listened well enough and told me, if you can believe this, that I didn't have any choice but to marry her for that was the right thing to do. The right thing to do! That's what he said, and there was Lorraine and the priest all over again. I said thank you very much to the bartender, you said just the right words, and I walked out of that bar thinking I had my answer sure enough. I had followed that advice once before and look where it got me and no way in bloody hell was I going to follow that advice again and I was feeling light in my step as I walked back to the apartment to say all this to Olive Ann and who did I see but Cici sitting on the front step. Shouldn't you be in bed? I said. But she wouldn't answer. *She wouldn't answer*, do you get what I'm saying? All that work she did to open up to me, to gain confidence in herself despite her stutter, all for nothing. I asked her question after question, I pleaded with her to speak but she sat there silent, as silent as she'd been most of her life. My God, it just about killed me.

I finally got her to sleep and crawled into bed next to Olive Ann. She nestled into me without waking. I lay awake with her in my arms thinking what I was feeling for her was surely love. And a baby! My baby. I'm sure some other men my age would have wanted to run, but I liked the idea of being a daddy. All the men in my family back home were young when they had children. I was about to turn thirty and what had I accomplished? I suddenly felt as if I'd been so selfish in my life and it was time to give back. Olive Ann and Cici needed me and I really thought I could help them. And maybe Olive Ann getting pregnant was a sign from God, that's what I was thinking, that I could be happy again.

So in the morning I asked Olive Ann to marry me and she started to seem like her old self. She jumped on Cici's bed to tell her and then took us both out for pancakes. Two months later we were married in a small ceremony with just Cici and one of our neighbors as witnesses and off she and I went to ski the slopes near Boulder for a honeymoon, leaving Cici with a friend. Neither Olive Ann nor I knew how to ski, mind you, we might have been the only people living in Colorado who could have said that, but it didn't matter. Olive Ann wanted to ski and said she could pay for it, too, so I didn't argue. She was alive and wild again and every fall she or I took on the bunny slope just made us horny.

Of course, I was always nervous about the baby. What would a fall do to the baby, I thought. What about too much sex? And Olive Ann promised she'd stop drinking, but she didn't. She just hid it from me, but back home I'd find half-empty bottles tucked in corners and I think it was then that I started to wonder. I tried to go to the doctor with her, but she didn't want me there. I was reading up on how to have a healthy pregnancy and tried to suggest things she should eat, but she'd have none of it. Cici and I would have long conversations about what it would be like to have a baby around to play with, but Olive Ann mostly ignored us. And then one day, when she was supposed to be about four and a half months pregnant though she wasn't showing, I saw something in the trash—a feminine product, I'll say, and leave it at that.

What you're thinking is right, I'll just tell you now: She was never pregnant. Unbelievable that a woman would lie about something like that, no? She tried to tell me she miscarried, but the truth came out soon enough and I don't know how anyone can bounce back from a deception like that. I certainly couldn't. Not even for Cici.

You understand why I had to leave, don't you? I tried to be sympathetic, to be there for Cici. I tried to tell myself that we could just have a baby for real now and everything would be okay, but I knew it wouldn't. I couldn't forgive her. Not when she knew how difficult a decision it was for me to marry again.

Cici took it hard, but I told her I wouldn't leave her. I moved into another flat nearby and took her out whenever I could. Olive Ann didn't want her to see me so we had to be secretive and that was unfortunate, but we managed. On the last night of 1989, just before it was to turn into a new decade, I took Cici out for a fancy dinner and I clinked my wine to her soda and toasted to new beginnings. Three days later Olive Ann was taken away in an ambulance after she tried to kill herself by slitting her wrists.

I guess I didn't really know what *bipolar* meant when we were together, though I could always sense something was off. The state took Cici away from her. It was so sad, for both Olive Ann and Cici. I tried to get custody, but it proved too difficult when her real father was willing to take her, and in the end her father wasn't such a bad guy. But it meant Cici had to move up to Alaska and we had to say our good-byes. That was one of the hardest things I've ever had to do.

I'm happy to say, though, that Cici and I managed to stay in touch. We both liked to write letters, so much so that I feel as if I was a small part of her growing up. She's been to visit me on and off over the years, and now I'll tell you, she matured into one hell of a woman. She beat her stutter and got herself into Oberlin College. She's going to grad school now in California for her MBA. Olive Ann stayed in Denver, got on medication and steadied herself, sometimes for long stretches, but she was never really okay. About every six months, or so Cici told me, she'd refuse to take her medication and they'd find her out on the street doing crazy stuff. I visited her once, but it was too painful for me to see her like that, so I didn't go back.

But backing up to when Cici left for Alaska . . . that's when I finally hit bottom with my drinking. The loneliness just came back full force. I'd rather not go into details on this leg of the journey, seeing as it's outside of the story I'm trying to tell. I'll save it for another time if you like. Suffice it to say rock bottom, if it doesn't land you in the grave, can be a good thing in the long run. It got me into rehab and that's where I took responsibility for my life.

And that's how I came to marry Pamela Crane in the spring of 1994. I have no regrets about marrying Pam. I gave her a gift and she gave me the same gift back tenfold. What was it we gave each other? Peace. We gave the gift of peace.

CHAPTER ELEVEN

Bess opens Rory's fridge and pours filtered water into her Nalgene bottle, taking a sip before closing the lid. She tiptoes to his front door and slips the bottle into her knapsack, trying not to wake him this Sunday morning. She has seen him almost every night since they met four weeks ago and as a result, she's been unfocused at work, unfazed by annoyances— sighs, *Oh well* when she misses a bus, laughs when she steps in a puddle, presses the wrong button on the elevator and is confused when she enters the wrong office. Each day she replays in her mind their encounter from the day or night before and is afflicted with sudden hot flashes and smile bursts in sober places, like last week at her boss's mother's funeral. *About time you're happy*, Gabrielle had e-mailed. *You deserve it, girl. I thought we were waiting for goddamn Godot.*

Rory's apartment is clean, but cluttered, and masculine in that much of its contents feel more useful than aesthetic— computers and computer gadgets, music magazines, a soccer ball and other sports equipment, clothes piled up in the closet. She likes that he has family photos on his desk, a star chart on his wall, and mugs, calendars, carry bags from charities he'd supported that help reduce world hunger, protect the environment, bring music to at-risk kids. And, of course, musical instruments—fiddle, guitar, keyboard, harmonica. His apartment turns her on, and in that department he has proven deliciously skilled. The fact that she is having sex again is enough to catapult her into blissfulness, but that it is hot and heavy, varied and frequent, and in the last few days particularly tender . . . well, it's enough to send her over the edge.

"Hey," he yawns, appearing in the doorway to his bedroom in his gray boxer briefs, still looking half asleep. He rubs his face, scratches his disheveled hair, yawns again. "Where you off to?" He has the hoarse, scratchy voice of someone uttering his first morning words after a late night.

"I'm meeting Cricket for brunch. Sorry I woke you." Bess takes in his long legs, his not insignificant biceps, his broad chest with just enough hair to feel texture with her fingertips, the shadow of scruff on his cheeks, the whole picture of this man of hers—*of hers!*—standing half naked before her. The word *lucky* comes to mind: lucky that she is the one who gets to watch him sleep, to wake up feeling his naked skin next to hers, to know him in a way that not many have. Or maybe many have. She wishes she knew. Despite her vault-opening admissions of past relationship blunders, he hasn't shared all that much about his own, nor could she find much evidence of past relationships in his place except for two photos of a young girl named Cici who he said was the daughter of an ex-girlfriend. He talked about Cici as if she were his own daughter, Bess noticed, but said very little about

Cici's mother. She lives out West so he doesn't get to see her often, but they try to talk once a month.

Rory shuffles into the bathroom to pee. She loves that he keeps the door open, even though she doesn't feel comfortable doing it. She loves watching him pee, how he arches his back slightly, how he holds his "Vincent." (*Vincent?* she had asked when they were first formally introduced. He told her an older boy in primary school named everyone's pecker and it just stuck. Considering his mates' were labeled Digger and Sister Mary, he considered himself lucky.)

He flushes and saunters over to her. She kisses him good morning. He kisses her with the hope of an even better morning, slipping his hand under her shirt. "Do you have to go right now?"

She lingers and sighs, then pulls away. His growing erection: sweet. His morning breath: not so sweet. "Sorry, I gotta go. I'm already late. We're still on for tonight?"

"Tonight?"

"The concert."

"Oh, right."

"You can go, yes?"

"Not sure. Maybe. I'll have to see. I'll call you." He says this as he heads into the kitchen.

Bess suddenly feels deflated. "Oh, okay," she says. "Later, then." What runs through her mind is that she bought concert tickets three weeks ago because he said he would go. But she doesn't want to sound naggy. Is he a commitment-phobe like so many of her past boyfriends? Is this a bad omen? Though they've hinted at exclusivity, talk of a future together, *anything* in their future, it seems, feels too emotionally risky. Maybe if he doesn't end up going, she tells herself on the walk to the Metro, she'll get the nerve up to say something. Until then, *stay positive!* she reminds herself.

Stella is sitting and panting in front of Tryst, a neighborhood café along the Eighteenth Street strip of Adams Morgan in Northwest D.C. Her leash hangs from a polka dot collar under her triple chins and loops around the leg of the table where, at the edge of the café whose floor-to-ceiling windows open to the sidewalk, Cricket is basking in the sun shining down on his double latte. He has on his black sunglasses, which he uses to surreptitiously check out the bulge of the muscular cyclist who bends down to pet Stella before he enters the café. Bess watches Cricket lift his sunglasses to better glimpse the cyclist's behind when he walks away.

"Sorry I'm late," says Bess, sliding into her chair. "Thanks for getting the table."

"Look stately, Stella darling," says Cricket, rubbing her belly. "Be regal for Daddy." Stella yawns and lies down. "You're smiling eerily," he says to Bess without looking up. "Stop that."

Cricket rarely says hello. Bess often feels like she fades into his scene, as if onlookers who thought he had been talking to himself will see that he'd been speaking to someone all along.

"Can't help it," she says, grinning even wider. "I'm glad to see you."

Cricket looks to be the largest man in the crowded café, and possibly the oldest, definitely the most flaming, for he likes to turn it up when they go out together. His white silk shirt hangs loose over his gut. His silver pinky ring glistens like a beacon when he pats his wide and shiny face with his napkin. A sun visor covers his large skull and rests on sun-reddened ears, the right one pierced with the tiniest of diamonds. "What did Daddy tell you about licking your loo-loo?" he says to Stella. "We don't lick our privates in public, my angel."

"Speak for yourself," says Bess.

The young tattooed waitress comes to stand at their table so they are eye-level with her pierced midriff. She says she's sorry, but they don't have asparagus on the menu, healthy or not, and no she's afraid they don't have Brussels sprouts, either, and c'mon Gramps, you got the menu right in front of you, to which Cricket places his hand on his heart and orders a plain bagel. Bess orders a waffle with strawberries and Nutella.

"Cricket, really," says Bess. "She wasn't exactly Miss Congeniality, but you don't have to be so difficult, either."

According to certain friends of his, there was a time years ago when Cricket wore jeans and tees and a baseball hat and wouldn't admit it aloud but liked to watch the Super Bowl. That was when Darren was alive. They lived together for years and it was always Darren who was the dainty one. He was an interior designer, and sometimes shared clients with Cricket: Cricket, the mortgage broker, helped young couples purchase a house; Darren helped the couple make it a home. But after Darren died, Cricket started walking his walk and talking his talk, even wearing his clothes. He used to oscillate more between his two personas—old and new, gay and flaming—but now he's almost *become* Darren, and Bess is beginning to question his stability.

Cricket ignores her comment and turns his attention back to Stella, his neck ballooning like a bullfrog's when he looks down. "Poor thing, look at her. I don't know what's bothering her." He holds up Stella's paw, then rubs her belly. "Have I been neglecting my canine princess, have I? Yes, I have; yes, I have." He sits back up and leans in toward Bess. "I think she's still traumatized from that time she had to wait all alone for my return," he says, glancing at Stella and holding his finger up to his lips. "Shh, poor dear. She idolizes Lassie, you know, *idolizes* her, practically begs me to put the old movies on. She likes it when I pretend to be a teenage Elizabeth Taylor, calling out to her to come home." He takes a sip of his latte with puckered lips.

"She doesn't seem traumatized," says Bess, remembering the evening over a month ago she found Stella at Cricket's door. "And she was with me, remember? But I still don't understand why someone would just leave her at your door."

"That's Claus. He'd leave his mother at a whorehouse to finish a game of pool, the lecherous louse." Stella, who's been watching Cricket, returns to licking her loo-loo.

Bess leans back in her chair. "Who's Claus again?"

"Childhood acquaintance. I was running late; he was the only one who would pick her up from the kennel with such short notice." He looks askance at Bess, laying on the guilt.

"Hey, don't give me a hard time," says Bess. "I'd just met Rory then."

Cricket nibbles on the animal cracker that came with his coffee. "So how is the lucky leprechaun?"

"Good. Great. He's great." She brushes her forefinger over her lips. "You know that's the first time you've asked me about him in a long time, since you came back from your trip, that mysterious trip you won't talk about."

Cricket turns his head to the street. Bess can't tell where he's looking because of his sunglasses, but she suspects he's not looking at anything, more that he's looking away from some unwanted thought or emotion, and if she didn't know Cricket as well as she does, his looking away might go unnoticed, but she does know him well, knows there is a vast world behind his shtick.

"You're delusional," he says. "I know everything there is to know about your blip boys." Cricket came up with the phrase *blip boy* a while ago to describe the men who come and go in Bess's life, like blips on her life's radar.

"Rory is *not* a blip boy," she says. "Is that why you've been afraid to ask?"

"I assure you the only thing I fear are gay Republicans." The waitress serves their waffle and bagel and refills their water. "So, all right," says Cricket, giving her his full attention. "I've bought my movie ticket. Let's roll the film. *Montage* me," he says, fanning his fingers out around his face.

She spreads Nutella on her waffle. "Let's see," she says, swallowing a mouthful. "There would have to be Irish music in the background. And then you'd see us, maybe playing a game of darts, and mine hits the wall next to the board, and he makes a show of whistling and looking around, you know, so that no one will notice when he moves my dart to the bull's-eye and we start laughing and then . . . we're at a soccer game and we pop up out of our seats to cheer when D.C. United scores their only goal and he gives me a big bear hug that makes us both pause and look into each other's eyes and kiss even though everyone else has sat back down . . ."

"Enough!" Cricket makes a grand gesture of covering his ears. "Please stop. I need a vomitorium immediately."

"I told you I'm not as good at montaging as you are."

"Clearly. Honey, your movie's going straight to video." He extends his chubby paw to Bess's plate and steals a strawberry. "And since when do you like soccer?"

"I like soccer. I mean, it's okay. He likes it. And I'm open to new things." She licks Nutella off her fork. "I was just trying to show that we've been having fun, getting to know each other. I can skip to the sex if you want."

"*LA LA LA*, I can't hear you suddenly. Terrible traffic noise." He takes off his sunglasses. "Bess," he says more quietly, looking at her under the shadow of his curled lashes. "Have you two done anything that *you've* suggested? What's *your* music playing in the background?"

"My music?" Bess pushes away her plate. A polished black sports car with a fat elbow resting out the side window blares loud hip-hop and succeeds in turning heads as it drives past. Bess asks the waitress for the bill. "We've done stuff I like. He's going to a concert with me tonight, Bolivian music, at the Kennedy Center."

"Well, good then. I'm very happy for you. You deserve it, enjoy it while——" and here he stops.

"While it lasts? Is that what you were going to say?"

"While the big asteroid headed for earth is still far, far away." He pulls from his carry bag a small plastic bag of cheddar cheese Goldfish and proceeds to eat them one at a time. "Look, Bess darling, what do you really know about this man?"

"I know he's forty-six, single, no kids, and is one of the most romantic guys I have ever met." Bess recognizes by the way Cricket pulls back that she has raised her voice, that her neck is stretched high, her hands clenched into fists. She leans back and breathes deeply. "Okay, so we don't know everything about each other, but it's only been a month and we're not in our twenties, you know?" Bess puts her napkin down over her plate. "There's still a lot to learn about him, but I will. I'm not worried."

Cricket finishes eating his cheese fish and wipes his fingertips with his napkin. He opens a tiny hand-held mirror and checks his teeth. The basic contents of Cricket's man purse hardly ever change: mirror, tushy wipes, cheese Goldfish, playing cards, dog treats, poop bags, travel-sized Lysol, cell phone if he remembers. Things like keys and a wallet don't seem high on his priority list, as he often forgets them.

"His friends tease him about wanting to be married and he just takes it in stride. That's a good sign, don't you think?"

"I do. I do, I do, I do," Cricket intones, putting his sunglasses back on. "Oh, the life-sucking sounds of wedding vows."

There is something in his delivery that betrays a certain sadness or fatigue—an extra exhalation maybe, the dropped shoulders, a slight head shake, a look-down-admit-defeat frown—that makes Bess think it is not of the moment but of the memory. The orchestra of his humor is slightly flat sometimes and she often wonders: Does he speak more often from experience than from mere observation and cantankerous opinions? Aren't old queens supposed to be gushing and maudlin about their past? How is it she ended up with one as tight-lipped as a CIA agent?

"Hi," says a little boy who has approached their table. He stands in place fiddling with the metal buttons of his red overalls, his eyes roving the nooks and crannies of Cricket's exterior.

Cricket notices the boy's curiosity and places his hand on his heart. "How unnerving," he says, pulling Stella closer to his side.

The boy presses his forefinger to his teeth and sways. "Is that your dog?"

"Yes. He bites, you don't want to touch him."

The boy points to Cricket's belly. "What do you have in there?"

"Small children. I ate two this morning with a side of bacon and I'm suddenly very hungry again."

The boy stares into Cricket's eyes and takes a small step back. He puts his arms inside his overalls and sways again. "My mother says being fat is bad for your heart."

"Yes, well," says Cricket, looking away, "mine's already broken, so what."

The boy takes his hands out of his overalls and places them on his hips with his thumbs in front like an old man. "If you laugh a lot," he says, "it's like exercising, and you'd forget about eating and you wouldn't be so fat."

"Very enlightening. Now run along to your mama and throw a tantrum or whatever you beasts do to pass the time."

The boy stays where he is. Bess laughs. "He's a smart kid."

"Listen," he says to the boy, pointing to Bess, "go pick on her. She's very lonely, you know."

The boy turns his face first, then his eyes, which have been glued to Cricket all this time. Now he stares at Bess. He pokes his tongue into his cheek. "Why are you lonely?"

"I'm not," she says. It *is* unnerving how long a child can stare into your eyes.

He thinks for a moment. "My mom has a camera. She can take a picture of you after she says cheese and after you smile and then, and then you could keep the picture, and then you could look at the picture and not be lonely."

Wow, thinks Bess.

"Luis!" yells a woman with a black ponytail like a horse's mane and large hoop earrings. She bends down to grab the boy's hand and pull him away. "I'm sorry if he was bothering you," she says. "Luis, come eat your bagel."

"That's okay, he's very cute," says Bess, as she waves good-bye to the boy.

"Adorable," says Cricket, spraying Lysol in the space the boy was occupying.

"C'mon," says Bess. "Let's go."

The sun feels hot without the late morning breeze. Bess loves springtime in D.C., though it is fleeting and always defeated by the insipid sauna of summer. "Come with me to Eastern Market," she says to Cricket as they leave the café and cross the street. "I'm meeting Gaia."

"Who's Gaia?"

"The woman whose water broke in my bed. Remember?" She'd seen Gaia a few times over the last month, though finding her to begin with was nearly impossible. The hospital had no record of a "Gaia," as she must have used a different name, and the administrator at the front desk would not give out any personal information though Bess described Gaia down to the last freckle. It was finally the nice mama-bear nurse who succumbed to the sad story of Gaia's boyfriend leaving her at the critical moment and how women like them should stick together.

"Why do I need to go to Eastern Market?" says Cricket, unlocking his car door. "I'm very busy."

"Because you need fresh produce. Just come."

Stella revels in the wind, her rubbery cheeks flapping out the back window as Cricket drives them down through the city to Capitol Hill. On a warm spring weekend Eastern Market is abuzz with shoppers. Outside near the main building, local farmers slice off pieces of pears, holding them out for passersby. Farther down are local artisans selling jewelry, vintage maps, light switch plates, handmade paper.

Bess wouldn't say she and Gaia are bonding like fast friends, but Bess enjoys her company. Gaia's strange ideas and calm ways are sometimes infuriating, but mostly cathartic to Bess, who feels a sense of responsibility to check up on her and baby Pearl.

She usually meets Gaia and the baby for a walk in Rock Creek Park. This time, Bess had suggested to Gaia that they meet at the market instead; the park had become too distracting. Bess would try to be in tune to the rustling of leaves, the texture of bark, the feel of roots on the arch of her foot. But that's as far as she'd get. Rats, dog piss, teenage couples' carvings of declarations—they are what drew Gaia's comforting arms to their trunks. *You're like the ultimate tree hugger*, Bess once joked, but Gaia had no humor in the shade.

"Listen," says Bess, as Cricket attempts to parallel park, "don't mention Sonny when you see Gaia. She still hasn't heard from him so . . . bad subject, okay?"

Cricket is breathing heavily from his parking efforts. "Not a word, I promise."

"I'm serious, Cricket . . . I know you. No *It's so SUNNY out* or *I love your SUNNY disposition*. Don't be clever, okay?"

"I don't know why you're saying that, I'm a gentleman to the core. Where is she living now?"

"With her mom in Leesburg."

"Poor girl. I told you he was yillied."

They find Gaia on a park bench, humming, gently rolling the stroller back and forth. She has on jeans and a peasant shirt, her long red hair pulled back in twine. She's lost much of her weight from pregnancy, but is still curved and voluptuous. She hugs Bess hello, rubs her shoulders, fingers Bess's ponytail. She smells vaguely of Patchouli. "I like when you have your hair away from your face, Bess. You have such pretty eyes and cheekbones."

"Thanks," says Bess, never sure how to react to Gaia's compliments. Bess adjusts her knapsack so it rests on both shoulders. "Gaia, you remember Cricket, don't you? And this is Stella."

"Nice to see you both," says Gaia warmly, but she reaches out only to the dog. Does she instinctively know that Cricket wouldn't shake hands?

Bess leans over the stroller to examine the cherubic Pearl. Pearl stares at her the way the little boy did in the café, wide and unflinchingly. Bess smiles and strokes the feathery hairs on Pearl's head. "How's my happy little girl today?" She addresses Gaia as the three of them stroll toward the market. "So how is she really? She was a little colicky last week."

"She's fine now. Sleeping well, has a hearty appetite. She's my angel."

Gaia stops at several small leafy plants arranged in a patch of dirt at the edge of the sidewalk, a block from the market. She bends down and touches their stems, then pulls from the bottom part of her stroller a pair of scissors and a full watering can. She attends to the plants with surprising efficiency.

"Doesn't the city or these stores take care of that or something?" Bess asks.

"I don't know," says Gaia, returning her equipment to the stroller. "I like taking care of them. Keeps me out of my mother's house." Bess asks how it's going, living with her mom with Pearl there, and Gaia tells her it's okay for now, though she can do without the constant Dustbusting of curtains, fluffing of pillows, and polishing of countertops, not to mention the shouts of her mother's private trainer who comes to the house every other morning and circles around her and her Nautilus machine like a buzzard, then joins her for chocolate martinis. Daughters are either just like their mothers or completely opposite, Bess once concluded. It's not hard to see which way Gaia went. "Let's go this way," says Gaia, touching Cricket's elbow to emphasize the direction. It's interesting that Cricket doesn't flinch at the touch.

Suddenly a man calls out to Cricket from the corner where the market begins. He is hard to see through the crowd, but he's loud and getting louder as he approaches. Once in view, he appears short and squat and so pale as to look albino. "Cricket!" he is yelling. "Cricket!"

"Oh my God!" Cricket screeches. He does an about-face and quickly pulls Stella around the corner, up a set of stairs, and into the Wife of Bath's apparel shop.

"Cricket, stop!" yells the man. "Call my sister, will you? For Christ's sake, just call her!" He slows and then stops, shrugs and shakes his head, and gives up, swallowed by the undertow of market browsers who crisscross in front of him and carry him back into the depths of consumer shopping.

"Welcome to Cricket's world," Bess says to Gaia. "Will you excuse me for a moment? I'll go retrieve him." Bess follows Cricket into the store, leaving Gaia and her stroller outside by a mound of organic tomatoes. Cricket is sitting in a chair in the corner of the store, swathed in a wide woven scarf like a burqa.

"Are you going to pay for that scarf?" drawls a dreary saleswoman.

"Of course not, it's hideous," replies Cricket. "Bess, is he coming?"

"I don't see him," she says, peeking out the door. "You're clear. Who is he?"

Cricket lets his burqa slip down to his shoulders. "No one. Stella, come here. Daddy's all right."

"Cricket, tell me. I'll make a scene."

"That was Claus, for heaven's sake."

Bess searches her memory. "The guy who left Stella at your door?"

"Yes, the very same. You can see why I wanted to run from him."

"Excuse me, miss," says the scowling saleslady, buttoning a blouse on a hanger. "Is there something I can help you with?"

"No, thank you," says Bess. "Cricket, I don't understand. Who's his sister?"

"I don't know. The man is obviously delirious, pure insane asylum material."

"Cricket!"

"All right! My God, woman." Cricket sighs deeply. There are lit candles flickering nearby, sending out the scent of honeysuckle and lavender. "She's my ex-wife."

Bess tries to speak but she has lost her voice.

"What?" he spits out like an insult. "Yes, I was married. A very long time ago in another life."

Scenarios are flipping through her mind—Cricket as a young, 1960s businessman, polite and evasive . . . and sexless? How does that work? "All this time I've known you and you never told me," Bess says when she finally finds her voice.

"Don't look at me like that. It's not something I like to talk about."

"What was she like? How old were you? Why didn't it

work?" Cricket furrows his brow at this last question. "Right," she says. "Why does Claus want you to call her?"

Before Cricket can answer, Bess's cell phone rings. She finds it in her pocket and flips it open. "Hello?"

"Hi, gorgeous," says Rory. "Where are you?"

"I'm at Eastern Market. It's hard to hear you. Where are you?" She glances at Cricket, then turns her back to him and curls into her phone.

"I'm with Sean." Rory says something else after that she can't quite understand.

"Rory? Are you there?" She cups her hand over her other ear.

"Bess?" she hears. "Listen, I can't make the concert tonight. I'll make it up to you."

"Rory?" She thought she heard him say he couldn't make it tonight, but she isn't sure. "Rory, you're breaking up. I can't hear you."

"Tonight," she hears, ". . . call you." And then the connection ends abruptly.

Her hands are in fists now around her phone. She turns back to Cricket, who is untangling himself from the scarf. "He can't make the concert tonight," she says. Cricket looks at her with more wisdom than sympathy, which annoys Bess.

"Look," says the shopkeeper, grabbing the scarf from Cricket. "If you two are not going to buy anything, I'd appreciate it if you'd take your conversation and your dog back outside."

"Sorry," says Bess. "We'll go." They find Gaia perched on the edge of a pickup truck nursing, the top of her rounded breast exposed to passersby. Gaia looks as peaceful as the Virgin Mary with sun-kissed cheeks and the tips of her lips tilted slightly upward in a vague, directionless smile showing utter comfort and contentment.

"Hi," she says to Gaia. "Sorry to leave you like that." The cool metal seat of the truck bed is covered in spinach leaves and smells of diesel and dirt. The owner of the truck tips his hat to Gaia and Bess, then turns his attention back to his customers.

Cricket turns his back to the breastfeeding activity. He tells Stella to sit while he rifles through his bag. Then Gaia's cell phone rings from the stroller. Bess hands her the phone. With one arm around Pearl and her other hand holding the phone up to her ear, Gaia answers, and then with such excitement that her breast breaks free of Pearl's lips she yells, "*Sonny!*"

Bess can't believe it. *Sonny?* Calling after all this time in the middle of the afternoon? And Gaia without a trace of anger in her voice? *Seriously?!* "Give me that!" Bess cries out, grabbing the phone out of Gaia's hand.

And then she stops. *Gaia, honey?* she hears Sonny say. But Gaia is looking at her with such pity and Cricket is shaking his head and Pearl is noisily sucking the air looking for more milk that Bess realizes what she just did and lowers her arm. Her frustration feels misplaced, but in the swirling energy of its onslaught it seems impossible to work out its origins and all she can do is realize its harm and hang her head. "I'm so sorry," she says to Gaia, handing her back the phone.

Gaia's gaze is forgiving. "Will you take her?" She holds Pearl out to Bess while she takes the phone. "Sonny," she says. "Hi, baby."

Bess accepts Pearl into her arms, coos to her until she smiles and wraps her tiny hand around Bess's finger. Bess can't help smiling back, even as her eyes moisten. "She really is the sweetest thing, isn't she?"

Cricket looks over her shoulder. "She is," he says softly.

CHAPTER TWELVE

S eattle attracted people like me, especially in the early '90s. I suppose I just followed the crowd to the edge of the country until I couldn't go any further. I checked into a clinic, and got cleaned up. Then I got a job again in computers and for the first six months I went to a support group—every night. And since I can see the worry in your eyes I'll tell you right now I haven't touched an ounce of hard liquor in fourteen years. I've been through tough times in those years, too, I'm coming to that, but I never went back. I know, you see me drinking beer. Well, *good* beer anyway. That's what I did before the problems started and that's what I do now, and I've never had a problem since, knock on wood.

So anyway, my support group. It was just what I needed to realize I wasn't alone and I had the rest of my life to turn things around. The therapist who led the group, his name was Steven, he was so kind and encouraging you wanted to be around him all the time. He was an ex-biker with a long silver beard that tapered off at his big belly, and when he spoke, he spoke gently. He'd cross his legs, stroke his beard, and say words of ancient wisdom in such a soothing tone you'd almost want to close your eyes and let your imagination wander. Tell you the truth, I still conjure up his voice in my head every now and again when I need it.

I made friends in the group, too, friends I could see a movie with or shoot hoops with or just meet at a café. Cafés are perfect when you don't want to go to bars. I learned to love reading the newspaper on gray drizzly days, which is to say I found the weather amenable to self-reflection. Which is also to say I often sat in cafés by myself, and that was new for me. I had to learn that being alone didn't have to mean being lonely, that solitude can be purifying and restorative. Those were Steven's words, *purifying* and *restorative*, and I liked the way they sounded.

Anyway, like I said, I made friends and my best friend—I suppose you could call him my best friend—was a guy named Vijay. He was from Sri Lanka: short, dark, and skinny, you know? You'd never guess he was an ex-coke addict. He was the kind of guy who buttoned his perfectly pressed dress shirt all the way to his neck even without a tie and never rolled up his sleeves, but he'd dirty up that shirt if it meant helping a friend out of trouble. He liked to hang out under bridges. Seattle had a fair share of them if I remember and Vijay was fascinated with the way they were built. Under one of the bridges a group of art students had constructed a troll. It was made out of cement and had a Volkswagen Beetle under its arm, that's how big it was. We spent a lot of time there, sitting on the troll's arm, helping tourists take photos.

Now I'm taking the long way around to get to Pamela, but

I'm getting there because Vijay, you see, was the one who introduced me. He was always doing some sort of volunteer work in the hospitals and I'd join him on occasion. Sometimes I played the fiddle for older folks or sang for the kids in the cancer ward. Vijay, though, he had certain people he'd visit, people who'd been in for a while and needed some company. Pamela, he said, was his favorite. *I think she is no different than you and me,* he'd say. *She is just sick, that is all, and it is most unfortunate.*

And it was true. Pam was a lovely woman. She was thirty-nine when I met her and full of hope. She was witty and smart and playful, all that, but she also had ovarian cancer and she was in and out of the hospital so often the staff knew her well. When Vijay introduced me, she was recuperating after her third surgery. Vijay said she didn't have many visitors when she was in. Her parents had passed away and she was estranged from her brother. A couple of friends stopped in, but they were hardly regular, and Pam, not wanting to deal with their pity and polite optimism, would often turn them away.

We took to each other immediately. I was shy at first, not knowing exactly how to be around her, all things considered, but Pam told me right off under no circumstances was I to pussyfoot about or she would send me away, too. *Stomp, don't tiptoe, is that it?* I said. *Exactly,* she said. *Belly laugh, don't giggle.* And from that moment I was hooked on Pamela Crane.

When she had to be at the hospital, I'd sit by her side and we'd talk about everything there was to talk about. Everything going on in the world was of interest to Pam, she was a real newshound, especially science stuff, like new inventions and discoveries in space and climate changes. She asked Vijay about bridges and me about Irish music and the three of us would play Boggle for hours making them feel like minutes.

And sometimes, between hospital visits, I'd meet her out at the lake or at the mall. She'd get tired easily but she'd never say so. She'd just sit somewhere as if she simply wanted to slow down and take in the scenery.

And then one day, Vijay called me and said I should meet him at the hospital, that he had something to tell me. By the way he sounded I was too worried to wait and made him tell me right away what it was. He said Pam had been admitted to the hospice wing. I said I didn't understand what that meant. He said it meant she had decided to forgo any more medical tests or treatments and it was now a matter of time. He hesitated before he said that last bit and I could tell he was fighting back tears. I wanted to know how much time. I may have even said this too loudly, for I had tears in me, too. He said he didn't know, but patients admitted to hospice usually don't have more than six months. But then he said she seemed strong, able to walk about still, so maybe . . . but he didn't finish his thought. *What do we do?* I asked. *We be there for her*, he said. He said they'd help control her pain and make her as comfortable as possible and all we could do was be supportive.

This is hard for me to talk about. I used to have to collect myself each time I visited because Pam didn't like tears. I'd stand outside her door, take a deep breath, and try and clear my head. At the beginning, it was okay. We continued talking and playing

games and watching TV together like we did before, and if she
was short of breath I called the nurse and if she was tired I'd read
while she took a nap. The first time she woke up and found me
still there she chastised me, saying surely I had better things to
do than hang around while she slept, but I could see how happy
it made her and from then on I wanted to be there every time she
woke. I wanted to see her happy.

Sometimes Vijay would bring his new girlfriend, Yasmin, by
so the four of us could play bridge. She was a petite Jamaican
woman. They joked that they were the most unlikely couple and
I think maybe they were. Pam liked being with the three of us.
She liked our different accents, she said, it was like her own private little UN.

And that's how it went until one Sunday afternoon Vijay
and Yasmin came by to tell us they had just gotten engaged. We
were elated and toasted to their happiness and heard the whole
story of the proposal and whatnot and at some point we qui-
eted down and Pam had a lost look about her. I asked what was
the matter and she said nothing at first, and then, almost as an
aside to no one in particular, she said the one thing in her life
she would regret is not having a wedding, that she had always
envisioned herself married with children at the age of forty. And
before anyone could say anything else I cried out to Pam, *Marry
me*. She just shook her head vehemently. I leaned down on one
knee beside her bed. *Will you marry me*, I said. She said, *Stop,
be serious*. I said, *I have never been more serious in my life*, and I
meant it.

It's a complicated thing, what was going on in my head. I

suppose part of it was that asking for Pam's hand in marriage didn't seem as significant a request as it might have to others. I had made such a mess of the institution that it felt as if I had rendered it meaningless. I thought I would never seriously marry again. But then I thought, if marriage can mean so much to this woman I care for who's dying, why not? I can do this for her. I wanted so desperately to do this for her, to give her this gift.

Well, Pam knew all about my marriages and she was a smart woman. *Thank you for asking*, she said, *but I told you . . . no pity*. I said pity had nothing to do with it. I said I'd been roaming around for years looking for contentment and I finally found it right here by her side. *Please*, I said, *I love you*. And I did love her, though I knew by then that love was complicated and I hadn't yet found the kind of love that is jam-packed with all the meanings it could contain, but I had said it before and felt comfortable saying it again. Vijay then came up with the idea of having a double wedding and when the excitement of such an idea took off among the three of us, Pam allowed herself to be swept up in our joy. When Vijay and Yasmin left and Pam and I had a moment alone, Pam finally said her official yes, she would marry me. *But promise me*, she said, *after I'm gone you won't settle for mere contentment. You deserve more from life, Rory*. I thought about that for a long time.

Anyway, I won't dwell on what you can already assume. The four of us had a beautiful wedding under the Fremont Bridge, in front of the troll, married by Steven, our counselor from the support group who was also a justice of the peace. It was drizzling, it being April in Seattle, but that didn't sour the mood. Pam was in a wheelchair by then, but she looked lovely in a white dress Yasmin had picked out for her and flowers I'd bought her that morning. We celebrated with poached salmon and Chardonnay overlooking the bay and we were happy.

And then . . . well, and then she was gone. That's what I'll say because the last undignified days of cancer are not ones to remember, though I'll tell you that on the day it happened, the very day she slipped away two months after our wedding—that's what it seemed like, slipping away, for there was no fight left in her—I was dozing in a corner chair and when the nurse woke me and told me, I felt like someone had taken all the bones out of my body. What I remember is not being able to stand. What I remember is the feeling of staring at the TV like I used to do for hours back in Ireland when I was young, utterly mesmerized. It was around the time of the O.J. murders, and they kept playing that intolerably slow car chase. I remember watching the Bronco in the hospital that day and thinking that at the moment of Pam's death the world must have turned into a funny place. Murder and car chases and cops, it should all be fast and furious the way it usually is, but there he was going thirty miles an hour on the highway. Was he really going that slow? I thought. Did this woman I love really just die? And then it was strange but sitting there in the chair next to Pam's bed, the nurses moving about, taking care of things, touching my shoulder with their sympathies, I felt a profound sense of peace. I don't know how else to describe it. I watched the Bronco pull into a driveway and stop—*he was giving up*—and with that I held Pam's cool hand

and cried and thanked her, my Pam, my wife, who showed me what it was to love again, God rest her soul.

And I did. Love again, that is, deeply and passionately in a way I hadn't yet experienced. My marriage to Pam taught me how.

CHAPTER THIRTEEN

With her new karate belt, Bess has stepped up to a new class, and now each week whips into play with a hundred *kima* punches. To get into position, she takes a big step sideways and squats with her butt out and her knees directly over her ankles. If she holds this stance long enough her thigh muscles start to burn, reminding her that sometimes the more difficult things in life come from trying to stay still.

From there, she twists her hips into alternating jabs, *hana, dool, set, net, dasut*, and with each count she keeps her eyes up, aims to the middle, squares off her shoulders, keeps her wrists straight, and—because she is concentrating hard—she throws in a childhood habit and lets slip from out the side of her mouth the tip of her tongue. When her teacher walks in front of them, telling this one *power*, this one *speed it up*, this one *good intensity*, he gets to Bess, points to her tongue, and shakes his head. It is in one of those moments of lost dignity that she has this thought: If she wants to be taken seriously, she should keep her mouth shut.

"It's funny almost, but true. I really should just keep my

mouth shut." Bess is talking to Rory as he drives them north into Rockville where he will meet Millie and Irv for the first time. He has agreed to spend this Sunday afternoon helping them pack for their move. It is part of his reparations for missing the concert a few weeks ago. He had a gig he'd forgotten about, he told her, so she brought her assistant and was glad she went, but nevertheless, she told him it wasn't considerate what he did. He assured her that it was not, as she'd put it, a "foreshadowing." He apologized, she forgave him, he apologized again, she kissed him so he'd shut up, then they had satisfying makeup sex. Still, it reminded her to tread cautiously where future plans were concerned.

"Bess, seriously," he says, "your teacher wasn't telling you you talk too much. It's kind of cute the way you read into things." There is a rattling in his old Corolla. He presses down at points on his dashboard to find the culprit, then gives up and searches instead for a music tape, several of which he is sitting on.

"Looking for this?" says Bess, holding one up. His car is so musty and messy it makes Bess cough. There is dust on the dashboard, crumbs in the cracks of the threadbare seats, coffee stains on the carpet below his bare feet. It doesn't seem to bother him. He must be the only person she knows whose car still plays cassette tapes.

"That's the one." He pops it in the player and taps his fingers on the wheel to the Chieftains' "Changing Your Demeanour." "You know my grandmother used to scold us for getting words wrong. Before she passed, God rest her soul, she would sit in our kitchen and say, 'Boys, don't mince your words, don't mumble your sentences!' She said it so often we'd make fun of her for it. Then one day in winter she had a stroke, poor thing, and lost her ability to differentiate between her S's and her SH's. 'Come boysh,' she'd say, pointing to the chairs, 'shit, shit, and have shome tea."

Bess laughs. "True story?"

"True story."

Bess never knows whether to believe him. In the beginning, he rarely relented on his "true story" defense and Bess would get frustrated. But since then she's taught herself to not care about believing, to feel lucky that she's with a man who can make her laugh. Now, when he tells a story of lady luck or the girl next door, of boyhood bullies and devilish shenanigans, she asks, *True story?*, he says, *True story*, and they leave it at that.

"My grandmother isn't the stuff of legend, but she can be a character," says Bess. "She's very nice, you'll see. Or maybe you won't. She and my grandfather fight a lot and haven't been hiding it lately, so who knows if they'll hide it from you."

"It's got to be stressful for them, a big move like this. Are you sure they're okay with me helping them pack? It won't be awkward?"

"No, they've heard all about you. Besides, they don't have a choice. They sold the house; the closing's next month and there's so much to do to get ready." Bess is touched by Rory's sensitivity. She is touched by the way he grabs on to his chin with the V of his thumb and forefinger as if stroking an imaginary beard, how his fingers stay there to pinch his ruddy cheeks and scratch below his ear. She loves the relaxed way he sits behind the wheel, his legs spread open, the thick material of his jeans peaked below his belt like an erection. She reaches out to touch him.

"Bess, c'mon now, I'm driving." He is smiling, warding off her advances.

She retracts her hand, gazing out the window and surveying the passing houses, thinking of her grandparents leaving their home. She's been over to see them often in the last month and each time is more difficult than the last. One more box packed, one more carload to Goodwill. They are disappearing one bubble-wrapped bowl at a time. She's glad Rory is coming with her today. "Have I told you how long my grandparents have been married?"

Rory glances at her and doesn't answer.

"Yeah okay, I've told you. But it *is* amazing, isn't it? Sixty-five years? Unbelievable."

"Unbelievable," Rory mumbles.

How long does she have to wait to ask if marriage is a future consideration? Bess wonders. Did Millie experience this with Irv sixty-five years ago? Probably not. They probably both day-dreamed of growing old together as young lovers and now here they are, old and together.

"I can't imagine what it would be like to be alone again after sixty-five years," says Bess. "Maybe that's why my grandmother wants to move. I think she's thinking how she'll cope when my grandfather's gone." Bess leans her head against her headrest, enervated by the sadness of these thoughts, seeming more por-tentous said aloud.

"It is sad," says Rory, pensive and distant. "I don't think it matters how long you've been married, it's hard to lose someone you love, to see death come and take her away."

Bess turns to him. "You said her."

"What?"

"You said take *her* away."

They come to the end of the road and he has to ask which way to go. She tells him to turn here, fifth house on the right, but her words are on autopilot, separate from the shock that's locked her mind on to a million new questions. "Rory," she finds the strength to say, "were you married to someone who passed away? True story?"

He pulls up to the house, looks at her and then down at his lap. "True story. Bess," he says hesitantly, "we should talk . . ." and before he can say anything else, before he even turns off the engine, Millie and Irv are at the edge of the curb, knocking on her car window, smiling, waving, bending over to see past her to the nice boy she has brought for them to meet. *Hello*, they cheer, *hello young man, we've heard so much about you, come in, come in.*

When it comes to how they feel about their impending move, Millie and Irv are polar opposites. Millie, for whom packing is akin to spring cleaning, sings and flits about and wonders out loud how nice the weather will be out West, how many of her new neighbors will like to play bridge, what activities she and her sister can do together, and Bess, too, when she comes to visit. Irv, on the other hand, slogs and slumps and bumps into boxes. He curses their contents, empties them faster than he fills them looking for something that he's forgotten. He doesn't want to talk about Tucson or the move or the damn bridge players, and in his saddest moments, he says good-bye to Bess as if he'll never see her again, an old elephant going off to die.

"You seem like a very nice man," he says solemnly to Rory. "You take good care of my granddaughter. She has meant the world to me."

"Oh, for God's sake, Irving!" yells Millie. "Enough with the past tense. Do you see what I have to put up with?" They are all standing in the kitchen keeping Millie company as she does some early preparation for dinner. She refuses to let anyone help, but Bess knows she likes to talk when she cooks. The kitchen is yellow and bright and where there used to be photos posted on the cabinets of Bess and her mom and her grandparents' siblings' grandkids, there are now Post-it notes in Millie's frilly handwriting about utility bills and change of address forms.

"Smells good in here," says Bess. The kitchen has the scent of citrus and rosemary, remnants of which are stuck to Millie's white apron.

"Thank you, dear." With the wooden spoon Millie slaps the rump of a capon as if sending it on its merry way and slips the dish into the oven. The slapping of poultry is part of Millie's superstitions about cooking. Pat the rear end of a bird and it'll be tasty and moist. Toss a matzo ball in the air and it'll cook through to perfection. Say a prayer over a brisket and there will always be food on your table.

"Gramp, listen to your wife, will you? I'm still going to mean the world to you tomorrow, right?"

"Ech, tomorrow," says Irv, wiping his brow with his monogrammed handkerchief and placing it back in his pocket. "Who can think about tomorrow."

"Well you get back to me then, okay?" Bess rubs his back.

"Rory dear," says Millie, "pass me that bowl behind you, will you?" The name Rory sounds odd coming from Millie's lips, as if it's some slang she overheard and is trying out. He looks like a giant next to them.

"Bess tells me you've been married sixty-five years," Rory says to Millie.

"I'm afraid so."

"What's your secret?"

Millie runs her hands under the sink and turns off the faucet with her elbow. She looks at Rory over the rim of her glasses. "Inertia."

From the time they entered the house, Bess has been mostly quiet, mulling over their conversation in the car. She let Millie and Irv do the talking through the tour of the main floor and out behind the house. They told him of that stone wall over there—*See it?*—and this entryway—*Look at the detail*—and oh, how many times they caught Bess's parents kissing under the old cherry tree—*Don't get any ideas you two*, which Bess took to be approval of her new nice young man. At this last comment before they walked into the kitchen, Rory squeezed Bess's shoulder and she took a deep breath and tried to shake off her funk.

So what if he didn't tell her about his wife? He'll share in time, and that can only bring them closer together, like it did with Cricket. In the quiet of a recent pajama-clad night, when Cricket seemed more like his old self—subdued and reflective—he had poured Bess a cup of jasmine tea and told her a few stories of his nine-year marriage to a young typist from his hometown of Louisville, Kentucky, named Isabella. He and Isabella were close childhood friends whose parents practically arranged their marriage when they were in preschool. Cricket was in sales and hardly home; she tended the garden, folded sheets, twirled the phone cord around her pink-frosted fingernails when she gossiped with girlfriends. He regretted putting her at the center of that gossip when he left her. Bess had more questions, but she was sleepy and had to ask for a rain check to hear more, and somehow that seemed okay with Cricket. It was the not knowing that had hurt. With a good friend, the knowing has time and space to grow and take root. It should be no different with Rory.

But then there was something still niggling at Bess: *We should talk*. Every person who has ever been dumped knows those words, like the poised palms right before they push you off the cliff.

While Millie sets the oven timer and Rory steps out to use the bathroom, Irv leans in to Bess and mimics her countenance with a frown. "Have a nut," he says, reaching out to her with a bowl of salted cashews. Despite his sight impediments, his memory loss, and his own grievances, Irv can sometimes be very perceptive of Bess's moods. He doesn't usually come out and ask her what she's thinking; instead, he offers her something to chew on like a mother offering her crying infant a pacifier. When Bess says, "No thanks," he moves the bowl closer to her and says, "You like cashews." He says it as if she may have forgotten who she is and he is there to help her remember. She takes a few nuts. He smiles approvingly and reaches up to gently pinch her cheek. "You're young. What could be so bad in your life that you can't enjoy a nut, eh?"

"Nothing," says Bess, "you're right, nothing's so bad for *either* of us, Gramp."

Suddenly, a loud male voice squawks from the entryway. "Hi, Mrs. Steinbloom, it's Gerald!" For his fortieth birthday last year, Millie and Irv gave Gerald—the middle-aged son of their best friends—a key to their house. He uses it on average once a week. "Mrs. Steinbloom, are you home?"

"We're in the kitchen, Gerald," Millie answers.

Gerald continues to yell from the hall. "Mrs. Steinbloom, I ran here in 7.28 minutes from my house! It's my fastest time. I think it's because I didn't clench my teeth. Is Mr. Steinbloom home? Mr. Steinbloom, are you home? It's Gerald."

"Gerald, slow down," Irv calls out. "You'll hurt yourself."

Gerald is all movement as he zips into the kitchen and over to the sink to help himself to water. He is a small man about six inches taller than Millie and Irv, with knobby knees and scrunched shoulders and a slight paunch. He has on running shoes, shorts, and a white T-shirt soaked through with sweat. His dark hair looks like a layer of fur on his head, arms, legs, and back of his neck. He gulps his drink and wipes his mouth with the back of his hand. He reaches behind and pinches his underwear out from the crack of his buttocks.

"Hello, Gerald," says Bess.

Gerald whips around. "Oh, hi, Bess. I didn't see you." He is still yelling. He has only one volume of speech and that's as if the person he's conversing with is down the street. "Did you come to say good-bye to Mr. and Mrs. Steinbloom?"

"Well, they're not leaving just yet, Gerald. I came to visit and help them pack."

Gerald's fingers are splayed and moving about like bugs' antennae. "They're flying on an American Airlines jet in nineteen days."

"That's right," says Millie, removing her apron. "We're flying out to Tucson."

Gerald holds his face in a constant look of confusion or pain. His eyebrows are angled down and his mouth is spread wide so that his cheeks jut up and form a resting barrier for his thick black glasses. "Bess, do you think they should fly?" he yells, rocking back and forth. "I don't think they should fly. There could be a terrorist attack or a crash or e-quip-ment mal-func-tion, but also diseases like air-borne in-fec-tions from re- . . . re-circ-u-la-ted air and exposure to cosmic ra-diation and prolonged in-act-i-vi-ty which can lead to—" and here he stops for a moment, looking at the ceiling. "It can lead to deep vein throm-throm-bo-sis."

"Gerald, really," says Millie, removing her apron. "I know you don't want us to go, but that's not nice, all that talk about bad things."

"Gramp, you all right?" asks Bess. Irv's face looks pained suddenly. He eases into a seat, lost in thought. These conversations must be hard for him, thinks Bess. "I'm sure Gerald is just sad like I am that you two are leaving, isn't that right, Gerald? Are you sad?"

"I'm sad they're leaving, yes." He nods vigorously.

"Oh, but you'll come visit us, won't you?" Millie takes a paper towel from a kitchen closet and hands it to Gerald. "Dry your face dear, you're dripping onto the tile."

He wipes under his chin first, slowly, craning his neck. "Maybe Bess and I will come visit together," he says.

Rory comes back from the bathroom at that moment and stands in the doorway of the kitchen. "Well, hello," he says to Gerald.

"Gerald," says Bess, eyeing Rory, though she isn't sure just what she means to communicate. "This is my friend, Rory."

Gerald's movements get smaller, slower, closer in. "You're Bess's friend?" he asks, still with a raised voice but slightly softer than before. "I'm Bess's friend, too."

"Nice to meet you," says Rory. He keeps his hands in his pockets and bows.

"We were just talking about—"

"How long have you been Bess's friend?" Gerald interrupts. "I've been Bess's friend for thirty-five years and in less than five years we can get mar-ried."

"Oh, really," says Rory. He looks at Bess, amused.

"You have to know someone for forty years before you can get married."

"Who told you that, Gerald?" says Millie. She has taken a seat at the table with Irv and is picking dead leaves from the table's centerpiece.

"I think it's a good idea," says Irv, half to himself.

Bess sighs. "I'm sure I told him that at one point as a joke," she says to the side, as if everyone but Gerald could hear her at a lower frequency. "But Gerald," she now says openly, "you know I took that back. Didn't I? What did I say?"

Gerald looks down at his knees. "That you're never going to get married."

"Now this is getting interesting," says Rory.

"Yes," says Bess, "I'm sure I said that at some point, too, but *after* that. What did I say after that and have stuck to ever since?"

"I don't know."

"You know, Gerald. I told you that I'm not the girl for you because there's another girl for you somewhere and she's going to find you someday. She'll be a very *lucky* girl."

Gerald isn't listening. He is looking at Rory through his thick glasses. "Bess, is your friend Jewish?"

Bess looks at her grandparents, for this question has caught her off-guard and has garnered their attention.

"No, he's not, Gerald."

Rory is leaning against the wall, keeping quiet.

"Because," says Gerald, "I'm Jewish. You have to marry someone Jewish."

"Oh, for God's sake," says Bess.

"Bess," says Millie as a warning. In her look is a reminder that Gerald's mother, Vivian, is strict on interfaith marriages and has taught him what he believes to be true. Millie attempts to change the subject. "Bess, have you heard that Philip Perilman's daughter just got married last week? Big ceremony, the whole *chazerai*. I heard it was expensive."

"Did she keep her name?" asks Bess.

"Would you change your name if you got married?" asks Rory.

Now why would he ask me that? "I think I'd keep my own name," she says. "I've gotten used to being Gray."

Gerald raises his hand as if to be called upon. "You don't have to be gray," he says. This time everyone in the room looks his way, for there is something different in his voice, something gentle. "You could be any color, any color in the whole rainbow, Bess."

All in the kitchen are silent. Gerald is rocking back and forth.

"That's lovely," says Rory, looking at Gerald and then at Bess.

"Yes, it is," says Bess. She is overwhelmed with emotion. "Thank you, Gerald."

"Gerald, you're quite the romantic," says Irv. "I gotta give you credit."

"Yes, I'm a romantic," says Gerald, pushing up his glasses, "a ro-man-tic."

There is a warm afternoon thunderstorm that keeps Gerald inside the Steinblooms' house where they task him with putting a completed jigsaw puzzle back in its box. He is content and very careful to break apart every piece. Millie tells him he's such a big help he should stay for dinner.

Irv sets up camp in the corner of the kitchen to pack one box, looking around the house for each object that would fit perfectly shape-wise into the box's particular spaces. He wraps each item carefully and stands it up, lays it down, angles it, stands it up again until he puts it aside to start the next box where it will have a greater chance for a perfect fit. Soon there are more items on the table and on the floor than in the boxes.

Once he comes to Bess and Rory who are working in the family room and says, "This isn't right," and then moves back to the kitchen. Bess follows after him. "Gramp?" she says.

"I'm okay," he answers. "It's just difficult, leaving this house after twenty-two years."

This house, thinks Bess. Over the years a house becomes a vault for the most intimate thoughts and acts. Its floors know the secrets of Irv's sleepless nights when he shuffles to the kitchen in his wool socks. Its basement holds the key to his ballroom dances of salvation. The walls hear his prayers each night by the side of his bed before he tosses his yarmulke (used just for prayers) into his nightstand, pulls the chain on his table lamp to darkness, and slips his withered feet between the sheets next to Millie's, the house standing guard, protecting them while they are dreaming and most vulnerable.

And for Bess, too—who was thirteen when they moved in— this house represents so much. There in the driveway is the first time she got behind the wheel of a car and ran over a flower pot. There in the guest room is where she fell asleep crying over a botched clarinet performance and woke with a teddy bear next to her. How many times she did laundry here, ate home-cooked meals, thought of it as her home base when she had loud fights with her mother as a stubborn teenager or during school breaks after her mother passed away. A house long lived in represents a lifetime of achieving, accumulating, defining who its occupants are by what they choose to surround themselves with inside that house. All this only to be reduced to the essentials that favor pill bottles and handrails and alarm clocks with four-inch numbers over the delicate and decorative and hard to see. "I love this house, too, Gramp," she says, and sits with him a moment before he heads to his study.

Bess and Rory fill giveaway boxes with books and board games Bess played as a child, *Sorry!* being one of her favorites. Millie comes to them with old photographs Bess might want of her mother as a child, standing by a tricycle, frosting a cake, sitting curbside by their old synagogue. In all of them her mother looks reserved and posed, not a dark hair out of place in her pixie cut or a wrinkle in her dress, no abandon in her stare. "Who's this?" she asks Millie, pointing to an older photo of a man next to a young Irv.

Millie glances at it and swipes it away. "How did that get there?" She looks behind her as if looking for Gerald. "His name is Samuel, an old friend of your grandfather's." She frowns. "Not a very nice man."

"Why not?"

"Never mind," she says, and departs abruptly.

Bess looks at Rory. "There's a story there," he says.

When Bess and Rory finish what they can in the family room, they go searching for Millie or Irv. They find Irv curled into his armchair, sleeping and snoring with his mouth open, a book in his lap. Bess closes the door and leads Rory to a guest room where Millie is showing Gerald her hatboxes. Bess holds her finger to her mouth, backs up, and whispers, "Let's go downstairs. I want to show you something."

Down in the dank basement, Bess flicks a switch and illuminates for Rory the room of mannequins. It is at first glance a sweeping shock of hard flesh under piercing fluorescent bulbs like a modern art museum's installation. On second look it is more the parts, the sheer number of breasts and asses and smooth, hairless crotches, the slender ankles and waists, the smooth one-colored skin tone, their perfectly positioned and sustained postures, the way models stand for photographs. They are women, they are naked, and they are eerily still: Bess can tell that's how Rory sees them by the way he moves around them, reaching out to touch one after the other, moving their parts, running his fingers over their private parts and smiling like a little boy. "Wow," is all he can say.

"Careful," says Bess. "These mean a lot to my grandfather."

"Ah, right. I remember you telling me. 'Tis a little strange though, no?" He asks this while mischievously tickling one's crotch.

"It is, yeah," says Bess, ignoring his gesture. In many ways Irv's mannequins have ceased to feel human to her, or represent anything female. There is no slouching among them, no furrowed brows or crossed arms, no blemishes or bulges or scars. They don't exist in relation to one another the way a woman would if she found herself in a room with twenty-odd other women. Either consciously or unconsciously, Bess knows women react to the vibes or energy from others, but these ladies have the energy of coatracks. And it would almost feel like a room full of coatracks by now, Bess thinks, if it weren't for one thing: their eyes. Their vacant, no-blinking stares are the eyes of dolls and clowns and windup toys in horror films that come to life with a bloody vengeance.

"What's your grandfather going to do with them all?" says Rory.

"I don't know." Bess moves one to make it more visible. "I like this one, though. Her name is Peace. He has a particular fondness for her."

"She's very attractive. And she has hair. I always like hair on a woman."

He doesn't say anything more and the ensuing silence feels uncomfortable to Bess. "You've been kind of quiet today," she says.

He joins her in the corner and kisses her. "I'm just enjoying learning more about you. I love watching you with your grandparents, you're very patient. And I love watching your face when you get nostalgic. It's nice to be with a woman who values her family."

She relaxes into his embrace. "My grandparents aren't arguing, at least. That's good. Must be because you're here."

"Well, they seem to like Gerald."

"He's good for them, too. They're good for each other."

"We're good for each other." His hands are cupped around the curve of her waist.

She pulls away from him a bit and looks down. "Rory, I'm sorry you lost your wife. That must have been very difficult."

Rory gently caresses her arm.

"But you don't have to tell me about it until you're ready. Really. It's okay."

"Thank you for understanding."

That's it? "You know I have a million questions."

"Bess, I have a million things to share with you. I don't want there to be secrets between us. But it's difficult." He pauses before he says *difficult* and she can see it is. "I'll tell you what, let's go away for a weekend."

He's making a future plan! Hallelujah! "Okay," she says quickly. She is about to say something else but loses her train of thought amid the zing of endorphins now that he's nibbling her ear and squeezing her ass and pressing in close. "Someplace romantic?" she asks in breathy syllables.

"Absolutely," he says between kisses. "A cabin by a lake where we can skinny-dip and walk around nude, like our friends here. I think these girls have the right idea."

And now she can feel the heat of him on her skin. His hands are roaming under her shirt with more determination, one pressing in on the small of her back, the other cupping her breast and they are both breathing hard, grabbing at hair and unbuttoning buttons, loosening a belt, unsnapping a bra, pushing into each other until a plastic body tumbles over and they both look and laugh. He pushes her up against the wall and when her shirt falls to the floor and their skin is hot and moist and their breathing has almost turned to moaning, his tongue wanders down to her nipple and she thinks she could explode right then and there. *Wait*, she mouths, unsure if she has said it aloud, and for a brief moment while she speaks, she opens her eyes and looks around at the eerie eyes of the women, witnesses to her exploits. She reaches out for his erection but for now he wards her off, whispering into her ear, "I love you, Bess Gray." It sounds far away in a rush of wind, like a shout from an open airplane, but it registers and with a high-pitched yelp she grabs on to his shoulders when suddenly someone yells her name from the top of the stairs. "Shit," she says, catching her breath. She identifies the voice as Gerald's and can tell it is one of alarm.

"I'm here, Gerald!" she yells, "I'm coming up." She knows neither Gerald nor Millie will come down among the mannequins, but she wonders if Gerald heard anything. She quickly zips up her pants and buttons her shirt. "Sorry," is all she can think to say, eyeing his erection. "To be continued?"

"Absolutely," he says, placing a kiss in her palm. "You better go see what it is. Give me a minute and I'll be right behind you."

Gerald is at the top of the stairs to the basement. He is rocking back and forth, clearly agitated.

"Mr. Steinbloom, he can't breathe, he's having trouble breathing," he yells.

"Where is he?"

"Upstairs."

With Gerald in tow, Bess runs up the stairs and into the study where Irv is sitting on the floor, curled into himself. His breathing is erratic.

"Irving, what's wrong with you?" Millie is bent over him with a towel over her shoulder and her hands on her knees, yelling into his ear. "Irving, you're scaring me."

Bess rushes to him on the floor, afraid he is having a heart attack. "Gramp, what's the matter, can you talk? Can you breathe?" She tries to see his face. He is clenching something in his left hand. He won't look at her. She looks up at Millie and then over at Gerald standing in the corner. "What happened to him?"

Gerald doesn't say anything, so Millie speaks up. "I came in here and like you, I see him on the floor like this, I don't know what's going on."

"Gram, call 911," Bess says loudly. "Now! Please!"

"Yes, okay. I'm calling." Millie turns quickly and hustles over to the oak desk.

"No," Irv responds between labored breaths. He tries to hold up his hand, but he is too weak. His shoulders move up and down. His brow is damp.

Bess is starting to hyperventilate herself as Rory enters the room. "He can't breathe," she tells him. "I think he's having a heart attack." She looks back at Millie and tries to discern what her grandmother is saying into the phone. "Gram?" she calls out. "Tell them he can't breathe."

Rory kneels beside Irv. "Mr. Steinbloom," he says, trying to make eye contact. "Do you think you're having a heart attack?"

Irv shakes his head.

Bess is annoyed. "What kind of a question is that? Look at him."

"I *am* looking at him," says Rory, squeezing her shoulder, trying to keep her calm. "I'm just wondering if he's, in fact, having a panic attack."

"What are you talking about? How do you know?"

"Cici used to get them. Mr. Steinbloom," he says steadily, "look at me. That's right, now do just as I do, we're going to breathe in slowly through the nose, hold our breath, then let it out through the mouth." He shows Irv what he means. Irv's first few attempts are futile.

"This is ludicrous," says Bess. "Gram? Are they sending an ambulance?"

But Rory doesn't give up and after a few tries Irv is able to keep better time with Rory's breathing and soon he's no longer hyperventilating.

"Gramp?" Bess can see by his rising chest and upturned face that he is taking in big expanses of air and feeling calmer. She keeps her hand on his forearm.

"Okay," Millie calls out, no longer on the phone. "They're sending an ambulance." She joins them again and looks down at Irv with her hand on her heart. "Irving! You're breathing normal. You're not having a heart attack?"

"I'm all right," Irv says, holding his hand up. "Thank you, young man."

"Not a problem," says Rory. "I'm glad it wasn't more serious."

Millie hands Irv the towel from her shoulder. "Irving, you're going to be the death of me, you know that? Scaring us half to oblivion. Why do you do this to me?"

"Criminy, Mildred," says Irv with slightly more spunk, "it's a wonder I'm still breathing around all your hot air."

Each of them says *feh* and waves the other away with a back sweep of the hand.

"I think he's feeling better," Rory says quietly to Bess.

"Are you feeling better, Mr. Steinbloom?" yells Gerald.

"I'm fine, Gerald. You've been a very big help. Good boy. Now can someone please help me up? I need to use the toilet."

Bess supports his elbow as he rises and makes his way out toward the hall.

"So can anyone explain to me what just happened?" says Bess. "Gram? Why did Gramp just have a panic attack?"

Millie sits by the bay window and looks out at the drizzle dripping down the glass. She looks scared and worn out. "I know what it is. He doesn't want to go."

Bess looks down at something crumpled on the floor. She recognizes it as the item Irv was clutching in his hand during his attack. "What's that?"

Rory picks it up and inspects it. "It's just a bag." He hands it to Bess.

At the top she reads, "For motion sickness and refuse." "It's a barf bag. Maybe he found this in a book or something?" Suddenly she understands. "Gram, when was the last time Gramp flew in an airplane?"

Millie rubs her neck. "I don't know. He likes road trips better, you know we go up to Newport or Cape Cod to visit Gertie and Sid."

"Think, Gram. Did anything happen the last time he flew?"

"I'm thinking. It must have been five years ago, for Samuel's funeral in Toronto."

"Samuel. Is that the guy in the photo, the one you don't like?"

"That's him. I didn't go, just your grandfather. But I remember him saying it was a miserable trip. Flight was delayed, bad turbulence, you name it. He was sick for a week."

So he doesn't like to fly. How come she didn't know this? "Gram, you didn't know Gramp has a fear of flying?" says Bess, taking a seat by the window next to Millie.

"How would I know? I just know he doesn't like to do it, so we don't do it."

The room takes on a library's silence in the darkening of a day coming to an end. Bess turns on a lamp. Shouldn't married people know these things about their partners? Especially two people who have been married for sixty-five years? Isn't that what marriage is, Bess wonders, that you know everything about your spouse, almost to the point of being able to read his or her mind? Isn't that what you look forward to in a relationship? Isn't that how you know you're not alone? Or is it that you don't want to know a person like that so you tune out? Maybe it's a way to make sure there will always be surprises. Maybe if there are no surprises left, all you have to look forward to is death.

"What are we going to do if we can't fly to Tucson?" says Millie.

"There are other options," Bess answers. "Train, bus, car, we'll figure something out." Bess looks at Rory. She's not at all sure she likes the idea of surprises in a relationship, but looking at him in the glow of the soft lamplight, she is moved. She remembers what he whispered to her downstairs and knows that she loves him, too.

"Enough already," says Millie, standing up. "I'm going down to the kitchen. Dinner should be ready soon."

Thirty seconds later they hear the commotion of the ambulance. Irv agrees to let the paramedics check him over, but he tells them he won't leave the house. It is the last time he will say that resolutely, the last time anyone will listen and let him be.

CHAPTER FOURTEEN

I met Dao Jones at an oil spill off the Oregon coast in the summer of 1995. That was her name, Dao Jones, and I know how it sounds. Believe me, she lived with the jokes her whole life. Her mother was from Saigon, her dad an American soldier. Dao was one of those children brought to the States during the war and taken to an orphanage when her mother passed away. She was lucky, adopted by a nice middle-class family in Sacramento who thought she should keep her name as a reminder of her dual identity.

Dao was twenty-eight when we met, eight years younger than me, but she was already successful in her career as an oil spill expert. She was a freelance consultant on everything from preventing big spills to cleaning them up, but her specialty was protecting wildlife. That's what she was doing in Oregon, washing crude oil off gulls in a sink full of dishwater detergent when I wandered up to see if I could help. I was on vacation from my job at Microsoft in Seattle (after two promotions in five years, I could finally call myself a full-time software development engineer, no more of these consulting or temp gigs). I was working hard and needed a break, but I didn't exactly have anyone to travel with so I got in my car and drove down the coast and there I found myself, walking along the beach when I saw all the commotion. Dao tied me in an apron and showed me what to do.

One week later, the intoxication of our flirting gave me the courage to kiss her, and that kept both of us in Oregon longer than either of us had planned. She lived in San Francisco. We managed a long-distance love affair until something had to budge one way or another, so I moved down there. My job had me just sitting in front of a computer, so my boss at Microsoft let me stay on at the company and work from home.

This was the kind of love I'd been searching for all those years. We cozied in to domestic life. When I say *domestic* I mean the kind of bliss they talk about in the mundane. We'd read the newspaper in bed. We'd take long walks to the local farmers' market on weekends and carry home organic produce so that we could cook these delicious vegetarian dinners together. We got a cat.

Dao was petite and had long black hair like Maggie, but while Maggie was quick-witted and energetic, Dao was calm and contemplative. She tended toward the spiritual side, so she meditated each morning. I'd pretend to meditate, but usually I'd keep one eye open and watch her. Dao was hard to read sometimes. She kept her facial expressions to a minimum so it became a hobby of mine, you could say, to figure out what she was thinking.

On our two-year anniversary, I remember thinking I could spend the rest of my life with this woman, listening to her sing in the shower, touching toes with her when we'd curl up in the corners of the couch to read. And the funny thing is, up until then we never talked about the two of us getting married. Dao knew about my past, and never pushed it. Me, I thought about it because I still say it feels right to call the woman I love my wife. But it had gone wrong so often I thought better of it.

Until, that is, Dao turned thirty and said she wanted a baby. I thought of Olive Ann and Cici and knew that was wrong and this was right and so we started trying. Well, in the midst of trying, that's when we started talking about getting married. We'd been together long enough that her mother started buying her bridal magazines. But understandably we were both ambivalent, so Dao found a marriage counselor. We saw him once a week for five months and got to talking about our fears of failure and what marriage meant to us. Now I know that's a hard question and I can tell you I'm still trying to figure it out, but sitting there in therapy all I can tell you is that I wanted to stand up and vow to the world that I would commit to this woman for the rest of my life, that I loved her that deeply and completely. Dao hadn't been married before and didn't see it quite the same way. Her birth parents never got married and her adopted parents had recently separated, so she was sorting out her feelings on that. What convinced her, I think, was the role marriage played in having a family. I don't think either one of us thought it was necessary. I'm as open as the next guy when it comes to family combinations, but for me and Dao it felt right. It felt like it was a way that our love could conquer our fears, that this marriage would be true and long-lasting and would show up my past marriages as discarded attempts in the process of trial and error.

And then also, Dao got pregnant. We were unbelievably excited and so, caught up in that excitement, we eloped to a beach in Baja and spent some of the best days of our relationship swimming and lying about. Dao taught me how to kayak, and I remember the warmth of the sun on my back as we glided along the coast, thinking it didn't get any better than this.

But then three weeks after we got back, Dao had a miscarriage. That's when I learned how painful miscarriages can be, physically and emotionally. I say miscarriages because—I might as well just say this all at once—Dao, over the course of the following year and a half, had three. I don't think she ever fully recovered.

It was rough going after that: Dao didn't want to do much away from home. She became even quieter than usual, more withdrawn. When she stopped meditating and started eating fast food, I knew it was serious, and in our counseling sessions I started to bring up the issue of adopting a baby.

It took Dao a while to sort out her feelings on that issue, too, seeing as she was adopted herself, but we made slow progress and Dao eventually came around to the idea. I was glad to see her getting back to her old self, humming as she watered her potted herbs, that sort of thing. But there was something different, too. She became interested in her Vietnamese heritage in a way she'd never been before. Maybe it was all that thinking of adopting and about her own childhood, I don't know, but *interested* isn't the right word: *obsessed*, I would say. She spent hours at the library, poring through books and old documentaries on the American war there. She found Vietnamese refugees in the city and interviewed them. She learned to cook Vietnamese food and took classes in the language. All that and then one day she announced she wanted to adopt a Vietnamese baby. Her mother loved the idea, said she'd even pay for us to go there and get our family started.

Now don't get me wrong, I didn't mind adopting a little one from Vietnam, but when I say Dao announced such a thing, I mean she didn't ask me what I thought like she had always done. She said it like it was a fact closed to discussion. I should have recognized then the change in our marriage, that feeling of being shut out, but I was too eager to please. She said she wanted to visit the country to start the whole adoption process, and so off we went.

We flew to Saigon and Dao immediately started looking for her uncle. We never did find him, but while we were looking we saw a good cross-section of life there and it was like being with Maggie all over again in a new country. I was overwhelmed and didn't much like the heat or the noise of the traffic or the constant throngs of people. I towered over most, my sunburned cheeks floating like balloons over a river of black hair and bobbing conical hats flowing through a stinking alleyway. That's what it felt like in the sweltering humidity anyway. Everywhere I turned it seemed someone was trying to pickpocket me or sell me something and the exhaust fumes were just too much to bear, I thought for sure Dao would be the first to complain about the pollution. I'm sorry to sound so negative, maybe the whole experience there with Dao is clouding my memory, but I think of Vietnam and I shudder. I mean, I remember some of the food was good—some sticky rice dishes and dumplings, but I had some fish dish that had me vomiting for two days straight. And some of the people we met were quite nice, but they all looked so much like Dao—their petite frames, their skin tones, their round faces and flat noses. These people, they swallowed up my Dao. They took her away and made a red-faced stranger of me.

In my dreams, that's how I remember it. In my waking hours I know it was all Dao's doing. She told me she felt like she didn't have enough sensory perceptors to take it all in. She needed three ears to hear the nuances in their speech, two tongues to taste and remember the things her birth mother used to cook, five eyes to see the place she had left behind. But she didn't hold my hand or grab my sleeve to show me things the way Maggie used to do. She shut me out. Not meanly or maybe even consciously, she just did it, separated me from who she'd been, who she was discovering she was and wanted to be.

When it came time to speak with an adoption counselor we'd been in contact with, Dao had made up her mind. This was in Hue, a city north of Saigon. I remember we were standing at the corner of a big open lot. It had some grass but mostly dirt, and small children on their rickety bikes riding circles around piles of garbage. That's when Dao told me she wasn't going back. I pleaded with her, but she was adamant and I knew in the end she meant she wasn't going back to our home, our marriage. I could have stayed, but I didn't want to, frankly. I was angry and I didn't think that my staying would have saved my marriage. I thought going home and waiting for her was my best chance. I assumed she'd get to missing me and get this all out of her system and she'd write and say finally that she was ready to adopt a little baby and bring that child back to our life in America.

It was a very teary good-bye, for both of us I might add, and I took that as a good sign, but I never saw her again. I waited for her for the better part of a year. I wrote her every day at the beginning, then every week, every month, and then I stopped. She wrote me, too, but her letters weren't filled with longing as mine were, they were filled with observations and conversations she'd had and they read like letters to an editor. Then one day I got a letter that burned my palm. It said she had met someone else, a Vietnamese guy. She said, "There's so much to clean up here, Rory," and I didn't know whether that referred to the environment, her past, or the debris of our marriage. She could have meant all three, I don't know, I didn't care. This was the marriage that was supposed to last, you see?

And yet, that was the thing. I got to thinking that Dao wouldn't have given up on me had I not been married so many times before. I think she assumed it was never going to last. I think if I hadn't been married before she would have seen marriage the way I had come to see it, vows for a lifetime.

I'll tell you something: I still believe in marriage. I changed back in Seattle. I wish everyone could just believe me when I say I'm sincere.

But there is one more, it's true. I hate to say it. I really do,

because I think this is the one you're going to have the tough-
est time understanding. It's going to sound like I regressed, went
back to my old mistakes after Dao, but you've stayed with me
until now and if you'll stay with me a little more I swear I'll show
you how it really was: two innocent and lonely people thinking
the world was coming to an end.

CHAPTER FIFTEEN

As she squats over a pretty patch of the Shenandoah National Forest in Virginia, her shorts at her knees and her bare ass dipped into the glossy leaves of what she will later discover is poison ivy, Bess catches a glimpse of Rory standing watch and thinks about love. Sometimes she gets an image in her head of Rory sitting on her couch, fidgeting, getting ready to dump her, saying, *We have to talk*. Usually she can get rid of it with images of the couch collapsing or her living room whirling up to the sky in a tornado, *Wizard of Oz*–like. But sometimes she can't get rid of it, as hard as she tries. She wonders if this is the reason she's developed a nervous stomach, why this is the second time on their hike that she has asked Rory to keep an eye out for hikers as she squats in the great outdoors.

"You okay?" Rory asks when she rejoins him on the trail. He offers her his walking stick.

"I'm okay."

Rory throws a rock. "Want to turn around? The path down below isn't as hilly."

"Sure." Bess reaches out to the nearest tree to steady herself.

"It feels good to be out here in fresh air, you know?" says Rory. "I like how it's so quiet you can hear the chipmunks scurrying around."

With hardly a fork in the winding dirt path and Rory in front leading the way, Bess can let her mind surf more positive images in the hopes of soothing her nerves. The last several weeks have been chock full of them. Her grandparents have been upbeat on the phone for a change. Gabrielle landed freelance work she actually enjoys with a nonprofit. Cricket has been more talkative than usual about his past, and Rory has been more affectionate, more passionate than ever. In fact, something had changed in him the day they spent at her grandparents. He said he was touched by how close she was to her family, how nurturing she could be. He said he can't believe how sexy she is and how turned on he can get thinking about doing it with her amid her grandfather's mannequins. And he said he loved her, this time voiced, not whispered, eye to eye and unmistakable and she had responded in kind, barking it out on the subway platform like a hiccup.

"Bess, look," Rory says. He is bent over the trail, his hands on his knees and his lovely ass raised in greeting.

"I'm looking, I'm liking," Bess says as she reaches him, checking out his behind.

He points to the ground. "It's a praying mantis. And there's another one, over there. Ever see one?"

Bess leans over to look. "Not outside of a book, I don't think. I know the female eats her mate after sex, though, right?"

"I've heard that." He studies the insects patiently, allowing them to do what they do in the woods: remain immobile, rub their tiny front legs together, twitch their wings. "You don't see these often. They blend so well with their environment. And I don't think I've ever seen two together. They could be the only two here and they found each other."

Bess feels a swift seizure of shuddering love for this man. Enough with the doubts. "I love you," she says. "It's a miracle we found each other."

You said that?" Cricket says, sounding tinny on Bess's cell phone. "You said, 'It's a miracle we found each other'?"

"What's wrong with that?"

"It's sappy."

"People in love are sappy." Bess is leaning against the car at a rest stop, waiting for Rory. "You know, you don't have to be critical. You can just be psyched for me that I'm happy."

"I *am* happy for you, you know that. I think it's superb that he planned this whole romantic weekend away, just the two of you."

"Thanks. I thought it was sweet, too." Bess watches a family emerge from an SUV. "It's just . . . I don't know."

"Talk to me. What's going on?"

"I seriously don't know. Maybe I just don't know how to be in love."

There is silence on Cricket's end.

"Cricket?"

"Sorry, darling. I'm not sure I'm the one to give you advice on that."

Bess sees Rory exit the building and walk to the vending machine for a soda.

"Listen," says Cricket, "you don't know what's going to happen, so stop worrying. Concentrate on the present, that's what I do."

"You're right." In karate, Bess is reminded often to stay in the present. Any drifting to the past or future and your present face is likely to get punched. "Actually, what I really called you about is my grandparents. I'm worried about them."

"Why? Are they okay?"

"My grandfather has a fear of flying, so he won't fly to Tucson. My grandmother, well you know how she can be. The whole thing's a mess."

"Why don't you drive them? You have enough vacation time. It would be cathartic. I've always wanted to take a cross-country road trip."

"Yeah, me, too. I thought of that. I'll run it by them, see what they think." Bess smiles at Rory as he approaches the car. "Thanks for listening, Cricket. I'll talk to you on Monday."

Seventy-five miles west of Washington, D.C., there is one of the most scenic byways in the country, so people say. Called Skyline Drive, it curves along the crest of the Blue Ridge Mountains and slices through fairy-tale forests with deep rocky ravines, waterfalls, and the promise of something ancient and healing. In autumn this part of Virginia is most spectacular, but spring is lush and beautiful, too. Down below Skyline Drive is the Shenandoah Valley, one of the most fought-over battlegrounds of the

Civil War. Bess and Rory drive past the valley's horse farms and apple orchards and onto the dirt road leading up to their B&B. The sun's brilliance is stronger than its heat. Still, the breeze is welcoming.

Bess feels good. It's lovely, this baby blue B&B with its white Adirondack chairs and potted geraniums. Rory parks and shuts off the engine. They walk toward the front porch.

"Well, hello," says a short, older woman come to greet them, peeking out from behind the front screen door. "Welcome."

"Hi," says Bess.

"You have a nice place here," says Rory, placing their bags in the foyer, which smells faintly of roses. "Pretty drive in."

"Thanks. We think so," she says, walking behind a desk. Gold-rimmed glasses hang from a chain around her neck. With both hands she raises them to her face and hooks them onto each ear. She leans in close to a folder. "You must be the McMillan party," she reads, then looks up, taking her glasses off and letting them hang once again.

Rory nods. "I'm Rory. This is Bess."

"Bess Gray," says Bess, not sure why she feels the need to clarify that.

The woman seems to take it in stride. "You're from D.C.? We get a lot of folks from there. My husband and I are from Baltimore. We left seventeen years ago and never went back."

"You and your husband must be very happy," says Bess, almost like a question.

"Yes," is all she replies. "Here's a key to your room. Number four, top of the stairs. It's the one with its own bathroom. I think you'll like it."

"I'm sure we'll love it," says Rory. "We love it already." He flashes a winning smile. "Tell me, do you have a dinner recommendation? Someplace you and your husband like to go on special occasions?"

"Of course." The woman opens a drawer and presents a handful of menus. "Here's the Copper Kettle, a local favorite. The Marsh is pricier, but wonderful. We like Rosie's—we think she has the best cherry pie in the state."

"Couldn't be better than Bess's homemade pies," says Rory, winking at Bess. "One bite can make a man fall in love."

Bess kisses Rory's cheek, then lets the two of them charm and be charmed while she meanders out to the common room. There are quilts spread across the tops of the couches and baskets with old *Town & Country* magazines on the end tables. The bookshelves on either side of the fireplace smell like wood polish and hold interesting selections of titles about the history and geography of the valley. Bess sits down on one of the couches and notices the B&B's guestbook on the coffee table. She flips through it. The handwriting in each entry looks almost exclusively feminine, rounded and legible. The messages are mostly generic: thanks for the hospitality, lovely weather, nice to get away, God bless. Only two of the entries make an impression. The first has this curious sentence: "It's very white here." There is little indication of what the *it* refers to, or what the person meant by *white*. Did it mean the interior design of the B&B? The landscape of Virginia? Was it snowing then? Or is it what Bess first thought of, that one doesn't see many nonwhite people in this area?

The second entry is the most intriguing. It seems to be one of the only ones written by a man. It reads: "How come you don't have a working TV with more than two channels? They get satellite dishes here, don't they? What do you do here all day? My wife said it would be good for us to get away. I don't see how it was going to work anyhow."

"What's that?" asks Rory, looking over her shoulder.

"Look at what this guy wrote."

Rory reads and chuckles. "Fish out of water, sounds like."

"But it's more than that. There's a whole story here. You can tell a lot about their relationship, even about his wife just from these few sentences."

"Oh yeah? Like what?"

"That she's the one trying to hold them together. That she can more easily find fulfillment in her life. That she needs to dump him."

"But he could have felt that way writing that and then five minutes later maybe he felt completely different."

"I doubt it."

"Why? Because people don't change? Bess, really." He pokes her in the ribs.

"Things like this can be very revealing."

"Let's go upstairs," says Rory, leading the way.

They make love in the shower. They soap each other's backs and buttocks and kiss with the water pouring down the sides of their faces. They lie naked under the top blanket and take a nap.

Bess wakes to a lovely melody. Rory is sitting in a big chair in his jeans, softly playing his guitar.

"That's beautiful," she sighs, rolling to her side.

He puts down his guitar and comes to lie next to her. He kisses her cheek and places a piece of hair behind her ear.

They are facing each other on their sides, caressing. "So this is what one of those perfect happy moments feels like," says Bess. "I've read about them."

"It's superb, isn't it?" Rory whispers.

"I wish it wouldn't go away."

"It doesn't have to. We don't have to go to dinner. We'll order in. Pizza. Anything. We'll eat lying down, just like this. We won't move."

Bess tries to look at ease, but already the idea of pizza and the passage of time is making her stomach flutter. That, and knowing she has to muster the nerve to ask him about his wife who passed away. Neither of them has yet brought it up. What if he says he doesn't want to marry again? "Hold that thought," she says.

She sits on the toilet for dreadfully long minutes. Can there be anything more uncomfortable than having to spend time in the bathroom on the first romantic weekend away with a lover?

"Bess?" Rory is pacing in front of the bathroom door and finally gets the nerve to knock. "Bess love, are you okay?"

She feels like an idiot. "My stomach is just off, that's all. Must be something I ate."

"Can I get you something?"

"No, I'll be fine."

He hesitates. "Bess, are you nervous about something?"

"No, of course not." She cringes when she says this. "I do my best thinking in the bathroom, that's all. I'm solving complex mathematical problems. Very important work."

"Ah, I see." She hears a thump and guesses he has taken a seat on the floor on the other side of the door. "My Uncle Johnny did a whole crossword puzzle each time he sat on the can," he says. "When he got tired of that he took work in with him. He was an important man, often called on to write historical agreements between heads of state, that sort of thing. Then after a time he found he could only summon his brilliance while sitting on the can. The rest of the time he was a bumbling buffoon."

Bess appreciates the levity. She rests her chin in her hands, her elbows on her knees. "So what did he do?"

"What else could he do? He set up an office in there. He put the phone in the sink and built a desk over his lap. It worked fine until my cousin Jimmy got drunk one night, went in, got turned around wouldn't you know, what with all the machinery in there . . . ended up pissing all over a new Middle East peace accord and that was the end of that!"

Bess laughs. "True story?"

"True story."

They stay silent for a moment, thinking. A door closes somewhere in the inn. "Are you feeling better then?" he says.

"Yeah. Sort of. I'm sorry. I feel ridiculous."

"No, none of that now," he says through the door. "I want

you to feel comfortable with me. Tell me I'm scaring you. Tell me I'm moving too quickly. Tell me to bugger off."

"No, you're not. I mean you're doing everything right. It's just . . ." Her voice trails off. "It's just that the relationships I've had . . . they haven't, or I haven't—" She stops, and takes a deep breath. "It's been so long since someone has said *I love you* to me." There, she said it. She's tried hard to bury this pain, this unspoken truth out of embarrassment and fear that she'd continue to be alone, unloved in that way, year after year. But here it is, the truth sliced open and wobbling soft-side up. She hangs her head and feels like crying.

"That's sad," Rory says softly. At least that's what she thinks he says, his voice sounding like it's part of another hushed conversation. And his saying it's sad makes it seem even sadder. This exchange would be so much harder face-to-face, she thinks.

"Bess, what can I do to prove that I'm serious about you? That I truly love you?"

She rips off a square of toilet paper to wipe her eyes. "You don't have to."

"I know!" he interrupts, sounding elated. She can hear him standing up, getting excited. "Bess, I . . ."

"Rory . . ."

"Marry me!" he cries out, and in his enthusiasm he punches the bathroom door and before she can stop it, before she can reach her arm out to brace it shut, the door accidentally swings open.

Rory looks at her.

Bess is conscious of the skin of her thighs against the white porcelain seat, her feet facing forward like a schoolgirl's, her naked, enervated body curved into a question mark.

"Oops," he says quietly. But he doesn't move.

Why doesn't he shut the door? She's too far away from it or she would do it herself. "Can you . . ."

"You're adorable," he interrupts.

"I'm on the toilet."

"You're adorable on the toilet."

"And sexy. Don't forget sexy."

"And very sexy."

She can only look at him quickly, then look away. "Feel free to close the door anytime, you know. I'm not embarrassed at all. Really."

"Right," he says, turning away. He closes the door and she sighs with relief, but she can hear him breathing just on the other side and can sense his hesitation, his desire to say more. "Rory, can you give me a second?"

"Of course," he says, his steps retreating into the bedroom.

Bess looks to the floor, the ceiling, the walls, trying to make sense of what just happened. *Marry me*, he said. *Was he kidding?* Everything in the bathroom, she notices, looks so white: the shower curtain, the hand towels, the plastic bag in the wicker basket and the tissues, the shelf where there are seashells and a bottle of bubble bath. *It's so white here.* Is this what that other guest saw? Did he have a reason to notice, too?

This is *the* moment she has dreamed of her whole life, the very moment a man she loves asks her this question, pops it like the cork from champagne, and yet, look where she is. Did she bring this moment on herself? Maybe he's going for a good story. She wants to ask him why: Why me, why now, why in the bathroom? But in her fantasy it doesn't go like that, either. In her fantasy, the nuances of his voice and expression aren't blocked behind a bathroom door. In her fantasy, she screams *yes!* and wraps her arms around her new husband-to-be. Boy, he screwed this up. She reaches behind her and flushes.

She washes her hands and checks her appearance in the mirror, running her fingers through her hair, and makes her way back to the bedroom. She slips on her underwear, T-shirt, and shorts and sits on the edge of the bed.

Rory is standing by the window, looking out. "That was awkward," he says. Now it's his turn to sound nervous. "I'm sorry. I don't always think things through. Obviously."

Bess catches her body in the act of relaxing. She can feel her shoulders drop slightly, her breathing decelerate. She rises to stand next to him. "Remember when we first met?" she says. "You were weird then, too . . . about going through my drawers at the party and then getting sick from something you ate. Remember?"

He nods. No longer confident and charming, he looks like a little boy who might hide under a chair with a toy truck.

"Well, I didn't hold that against you."

He turns to embrace her. "I'm grateful that you're so forgiving."

"I don't forgive you for proposing in the bathroom. That was terrible." She feels something like joy sprouting from deep within, and this is curious to her. Could it be that the question itself has begun to sink in? Despite the horrendous way he asked, she thinks, he asked. *He wants to marry me. He loves me that much.* "I do love you, you know," she says. She rubs her fingertips over the smooth skin of his muscular back.

"Bess," says Rory, looking down again. "You don't have to answer. I just want you to know that the idea of proposing . . . it didn't just come on suddenly. I'd been thinking about it. I was going to broach the subject this weekend, see how you felt."

Wow, she thinks. *Future galore*. "Let's stay in tonight," she says, taking his hand. "Let's just talk. I think we need to talk before we, you know . . ."

His head is hanging low. He is pulling at a hangnail.

"That's what I thought this trip was all about," she continues. "To get to know each other. I mean, we really do hardly know each other."

He looks to the window, then back at his hands. "I don't need to know anything you don't want to tell me."

Bess stops his fidgeting by holding his hands in hers. "But I *want* to tell you. I want us to share things." Where did this sudden strength come from? she wonders. Is it just merely the switching of roles that brings it out?

"See," says Rory, "this isn't going to help my cause."

"Your cause?"

"Talking about my past is not going to help me prove to you how serious I am, Bess. Trust me. It's going to muddle things. It always does. Please promise me you won't let it."

A familiar wave of panic returns to her stomach. "I don't get it. Did you murder someone? How serious are we talking?"

"Nothing like that."

"Well then, whatever it is, I'm sure we'll get through it."

Dusk has set in and the sheer white curtains on the window look ghostly.

Bess rises and turns on one of the lamps by the bed. "How about you tell me about your wife. I'd like to hear about her."

Rory runs his hands down his face and slips limply to the floor. "Wives," he mumbles.

"What?" she says, standing above him.

"Wives," he says again. He is cringing as if about to get hit.

Bess takes a moment. "Wives?" she cries. "*Plural?*" She starts to pace. "So you were married more than once. Okay. When were you going to tell me this?"

"This weekend. I was. Look . . . five minutes ago you were in the bathroom because you yourself couldn't talk about . . . things."

"Not true, and we're not talking about things; we're talking about wives, Rory. And what does that mean, anyway? Two? Two wives? Please tell me it's not more than that."

Rory doesn't answer.

"Rory? How many?"

"Eight."

"JESUS CHRIST!" Her fingers are pressed to her temples. "You've been married *eight times*?"

"Bess, I can explain."

Now she's hyperventilating. The room is spinning. She has to sit down. "Eight times," she breathes.

"It sounds worse—"

"Eight times you were married. And you're what . . . forty-five?"

"Bess . . ."

"Eight wives."

"Technically . . ."

"Technically? Technically, you were married to eight different women before you met me."

"I know this sounds off."

"No, not at all, it sounds perfectly normal. I just want to be sure I get this right: I'd be your *ninth* wife. Technically, I mean, I'd be your ninth, that's all I'm asking!" She takes a deep breath in the space of his no response. What is she supposed to do now? Run out? Wouldn't any sane woman do that? Cricket was right to caution her. She should have known. *The toilet, of all places. How fitting.* She looks at Rory on the floor, his face in his hands. He suddenly seems like such a stranger. And yet, not a bad stranger or a scary one, just a stranger.

"This is a big deal," she says.

"I know."

"I don't know how I'm supposed to believe you when you say you're serious about marriage." Now she looks at him and sees his eyes are glassy.

"Whatever I could say, I'd say, Bess. Whatever I could do, I'd do. I love you. Maybe I'm a hopeless romantic, but I do. I want to be with you."

"You've said that now eight, no—nine times."

"Not exactly, but yes, that's too many times, I agree, and I'll be paying for it for the rest of my life, but can you honestly tell me that's worse than not saying it enough? I never lied, Bess. My crime is that I love with too much hope."

Was that rehearsed? "But why get married each time? Why not just live together?"

"Because, despite what it looks like, I actually believe in the institution."

"I need some air," she says, and leaves the room.

The woman who checked them in is sitting in the living room with a book in her lap. Her curious countenance tells Bess that the walls of the B&B are far from soundproof. "Is everything all right?" she asks.

"Fine," says Bess, curtly. She's in no mood for this woman who's been married seventeen years to one man and brags about it to every guest who walks through the door. "I just left something in the car." Bess hurries outside. The trees are rustling from a slow breeze, fading under the darkening sky. She feels lost and unsteady. Her stomach, though, is not forcing her back into the bathroom. But why? Was her body trying to tell her something? Did she know deep down to expect something like this? Maybe now the knowing is better than the not knowing, even though the knowing is pretty damn lousy. And now what is she supposed to do? Call a cab and get out of here? Ask him to take her home? She looks up and sees Rory in the window, looking down at her. She just told this man she loves him; maybe she owes it to him to hear him out. And frankly, she's curious . . . how does somebody pull off having eight wives?

Slowly, she retreats inside, and stands in front of their bedroom door. Rory opens it, though she hadn't knocked. "We'll go," he says. "I can take you home."

"I don't want to go home," she says, quietly, not meeting his eyes. She crosses the room and sits on the bed. He closes the door and sits by her. He waits for her to speak.

She lies down on the bed in a fetal position, slides a pillow under her head, and holds her stomach. "You're a storyteller. Tell me the story of your married life."

"Are you sure you want to hear?" He touches her leg. She doesn't recoil.

"Yes, I want to hear."

"Okay," he says, and sits next to her. And he begins.

CHAPTER SIXTEEN

I moved out of the flat I shared with Dao because I couldn't afford the rent. Then I couldn't afford to stay in San Francisco, either, and besides, the city held too many memories. I liked my job, but I was ready for a new adventure. I thought maybe it was time to focus on my music for a change. I packed up my old banger and drove back East and I tell you it was only at the last minute that I decided to go to Washington. It was literally a sudden turn off a highway. I was on my way north to Boston, but I was thinking a lot about Dublin, and it being the capital of my country, I thought it was high time I saw the capital of yours.

I leased a room in Mount Pleasant for two months with money I'd saved up. Then I got a map of the city and did a little sightseeing, spending the better part of my afternoons sitting in Dupont Circle playing for handouts.

One morning, a few weeks after I arrived, I noticed that everything seemed to be off somehow, like the sun was shining a little too brightly and the pedestrians were moving more quickly than usual. I walked over to the circle with my fiddle case in one hand and coffee in the other when a skateboarder ran right into me and knocked my coffee all down my shirt. This is a kid I'd seen several times there, and he was good, the best skateboarder among the whole tattooed lot of them weaving in and out of the people and up and down curbs. It was hard to believe he'd suddenly become so clumsy. *Sorry*, he said, as if he, too, was surprised he knocked into me. *It's all right*, I said, *just be careful*, and that, too, was surprising because usually I'd be royally pissed off at something like that but I rather felt fatherly at that moment, I don't know why. The kid picked up his skateboard and took a seat by the fountain. His friends skated past, coaxed him to get up, but he just sat there, slumped over his knees, rolling the wheels of his upturned board.

I took a seat on a bench and watched the people walking past. They all seemed to be in such a hurry. I know, it's a city and people are always late for work or wherever it is they've got to be, but I mean that morning everyone seemed to be rushing somewhere, the suits and the students and the dogwalkers. *Something's not right*, I heard a soft voice say. I'd been in a daze and hadn't noticed this woman sit down at the other end of the bench. She wore a smart beige pantsuit and sat poised and still on the edge of the bench. I remember she had a silk green scarf around her neck that billowed in the breeze. She was maybe twenty-five, I guessed, a young professional with beautiful red hair to her shoulders and curled in at the ends like single quotes around her lovely round face. She had notes to herself in ink on her palm and carried a leather satchel.

Excuse me? I said, and she said it again in an eerie lowness:

Something's not right, like she was picking up some extrasensory static. *I'm thinking the very same thing*, I said back, finding it uncanny that this young woman said exactly what I was thinking.

And that's how I met Gloria. Her name was Gloria K. Jones and I can tell you it was no small discomfort that she had the same last name as Dao, even if it was common. But she didn't look like a Jones, though that's hard to explain, and she didn't look like a Gloria, either, so maybe names sometimes have a way of misleading us.

But anyway, I moved closer to her on the bench and we started talking. She was late for work at an architectural firm downtown, but on her way to the Metro she had noticed that none of the dogs in the circle were barking. The Jack Russell always barked at her, she said. *Do you have a cell phone?* I remember she asked me. *No, why?* I said. *I have to call my brother*, she said. It was her twin brother she had to call and you know how they say twins are psychically connected somehow? Well maybe I've got the sequencing of events all wrong, but the way I remember it, she asked about her brother before we found out the news, before a guy in a janitor's uniform stopped right in front of us and started shouting into the phone and then, when pressed to tell us what was the matter, told us to get out of town as fast as we could. He said two planes had just crashed into the Twin Towers in New York and another plane had hit the Pentagon and still another one was headed for the White House or the Capitol and who knows what else and then the panic on people's faces and in their quickened strides in the circle were no longer subtle signs of a day gone strange but hints of Armageddon. That's how it felt to me initially, like here we were in the nation's capital and under attack and this was it, the end of the road. I was panicked, more panicked than I had ever been in my life I'd say, at least for those initial minutes.

We should get away from here, I said to Gloria. *My brother*, she said. I said: *We should hurry, find a TV or radio to let us know what's going on*. Again she said: *My brother*. It was so sad the way she said it with her head bowed and her eyes closed. Her twin brother, Ray, see, was a musician who worked part-time as a coffee vendor in one of the Towers. For the life of her, Gloria couldn't remember which days he worked and that haunted her. She borrowed the janitor's phone and tried to call her brother but there was no answer.

So I gently urged her to walk with me and the two of us walked silently up Connecticut Avenue, watching police cars whiz by with their sirens blaring. We must have walked a mile or two until we were tired and stopped in some restaurant's bar. Gloria was dazed. I feared something was really wrong with her, and I wasn't about to leave her in her time of need. And really, it was my time of need, too, it was for all of us.

The bar had a few patrons on stools and a television high up in the corner and for the first time we saw the crashing down of those Towers. What a horrific sight, all those people covered in white, panicked themselves, and my God, the thought of those people jumping . . . well, you know. You lived through it, too, so I don't have to tell you. I was choked up but it was Gloria who was shedding the tears and shivering and I put my arm around her and we watched the TV together for hours. She tried to call her brother throughout the day but couldn't get through. Her mother lived out in the suburbs—had moved there a few years back from Kansas, where Gloria and her brother grew up—but she was on vacation in Hawaii, so Gloria couldn't get through to her, either. I tried to get her to eat, but she had no appetite and when the sun eventually went down she looked exhausted. *You should rest*, I said. She said she didn't want to be alone, that she had just moved to the city from Maine—on a whim, like me— and was crashing temporarily at her mother's place an hour away and that she didn't know anyone else in town except for the architects she worked for, answering their phones and filing their paperwork, and she didn't really like their shallow ways, truth be told. *Can I stay with you?* she asked.

I took her back to my room and laid her down, covering her with a blanket and as I turned to go she said, *No don't*. So I stayed until she fell asleep and then lay down on the floor myself to get some shut-eye.

Well sometime in the middle of the night, I woke to find Gloria beside me on the floor. She was facing me in a fetal position and I just looked at her. She was beautiful, even in pain. She wasn't the professional D.C. woman anymore, she was an innocent little girl with pink cheeks and long eyelashes and freckles just over the bridge of her nose. I knew she was seeing me that night as her guardian angel, but I tell you it felt like the other way around, like she had floated down from the heavens to calm my wandering soul in the chaos. I didn't know anything about her except for what I was feeling, but it was the feeling I had about America the first time I went back to Ireland, that indescribable nearness to truth, a powerful sense of what it must feel like to be home. Believe me, I was missing Ireland at that moment.

I stirred and she opened her eyes. *What time is it?* she whispered. *Two A.M.*, I said. She looked out the window and a tear rolled down her soft cheek. *My brother is dead*, she said. *Shh*, I said, *you don't know that*. I hugged her and then she asked if anyone close to me had ever died. I told her about my own brother, Eamonn, and about Pam. She told me her father had died when she was a baby, that her mother was always traveling around looking for her fountain of youth and how she had always been closest with her brother, Ray, that he was a good musician and how she felt she wanted to make money to support him any way she could.

We talked about feeling vulnerable, how we could never be sure that we were really safe, that it was a miracle that we hadn't died already, like in a car accident or from disease. We talked about the meaninglessness of our lives and clung to each other like frightened children in the creaking dark. We nodded off again and by morning the one prevailing sentiment that stayed with us for the rest of the day and into the year we spent together was that whatever we wanted to do we had to do it quickly for we had precious little time left.

And I'll tell you before I say anything else that Gloria's brother, Ray, did die that day in the second Tower. Her mother wailed at his funeral into her black velvet gloves, dripping big tears down her face, her surgically lifted face (a mother-in-law to beat all mothers-in-law, I'll tell you), but Gloria was silent during the ceremony and into the dark days following.

I accompanied her to the funeral and stayed by her side as she walked the streets of downtown New York. I held her hand when she had to stop packing up Ray's apartment and sit down on his bed, taking a moment to study some photo she found on his desk or keepsake he had from their childhood. And when we finally drove back to D.C. with a trunk full of Ray's things, Gloria in one sudden moment put her hand on her heart and looked at me strangely. *Rory. Ray. Rory. Ray*, she said, bouncing the words with her chin. *Do you see?* I didn't see, I told her, and she explained that we shared the same first initial, Ray and me, and that I came into her life at the exact moment Ray passed away (how she figured that I couldn't tell you) and what's more, we were both musicians.

Now I know what you're thinking. If there was ever a red flag flapping in the wind this was surely one of the biggest. She was looking at me with such love and longing, I should have known not to trust it. I should have known that a romance formed in the passionate wake of a disaster had nowhere to go but to subside when the uneventful days of real life inevitably surfaced. True enough.

Or maybe you're saying: *Rory, how could you? Taking advantage of a poor, vulnerable girl like that in her time of need, someone so much younger than you. You should be ashamed of yourself.* True enough again.

I suppose if you are on one side or the other, you'd be right either way, but what you need to know before you hand in your verdict is that I was mad about Gloria from the moment I laid eyes on her, and whatever spell she was under, I was under, too.

When she cried it seemed like she was crying for the whole hu-man race. She would lean into me and I'd hold her in my arms, smelling the green apple of her hair, feeling the soft flesh of her upper back beneath her fleece. Strange details to share, maybe, but that's what being with Gloria was like, you were hyper aware of her, of your own senses and the presence of unexplainable forces. When Gloria said it was no coincidence that we met, that it was fate, part of a divine plan, she there and I there on that bench, I believed her. And when she said there's no telling how much time we have left on this earth, I believed her, too.

Maybe you're saying I was too quick to believe, but let me complete the picture here and you'll understand the power of all I'm telling you: there was a rainbow. What I mean is, we were in the car coming back from New York when it rained for a bit, then stopped and Gloria said pull over and I did, and we got out, and there over the trees was the most vibrant rainbow I'd ever seen, full from end to end. *My God, it's glorious*, I said. That was the word I used, *glorious*, I swear it just came to me, and when I said it, Gloria looked at me as if I had called her name. And what did she say back to me? *It's Ray.* I thought she was referencing the initials again, Rory, Ray, rainbow. No, she said. She said Ray loved rainbows, that he used to call them raybows and when they were little, Ray used to tell her he could make raybows anytime he wanted. *It's from Ray*, she said again. *It's for us.*

Now you tell me, if you were me looking at that rainbow and that sad, beautiful woman beside you and thinking of people jumping from buildings, I mean, wouldn't you have believed? Can't you imagine that you might have been swept up in that moment and convinced that you two were meant to be with each other, that the past was nothing more than a prelude to this moment and this moment was a prelude to an uncertain future? Mightn't you have cried a little and taken her hand in yours and told her you loved her with all your heart and asked if she would marry you?

Well, I didn't. Of course I didn't. I'm aware of who I am.

But the fact is, I still want to be married. Always have. I like the version of me as someone's husband better than the version of me alone and single. Plain and simple.

Which is why I said yes when Gloria asked me to marry her. God's honest truth, she asked me. Not that day when we saw the rainbow, but three weeks later in a barn on a friend's farm, surrounded by deer and rabbits. We got married, Gloria quit her job, we moved out of the city after one too many "code orange" terror-alert days, rented a cabin in Virginia, and mostly lived in isolation. She did some freelance work on the Internet and I taught a computer class or two at Shepherdstown College, played my fiddle some evenings, and was a substitute teacher at the local high school. Gloria painted and had her garden.

It was nice at the beginning, but then after six months we found we didn't have much to say to each other. We started to fight. She hung Ray's things all around the cabin and started getting into this new age stuff: astrology, tarot cards, crystals. When one day she said she was thinking of making a pilgrimage to India, I had visions of the downfall with Dao and I knew I had once again made a terrible mistake.

I didn't leave her; she left me. She met up with Ray's best

friend and called me from a pueblo in New Mexico. The only time I heard from Gloria after that was on September eleventh the following year. She touched base, talked of rainbows and Ray and fear and death, and then she was gone, almost as if she hadn't ever been there to begin with.

I don't know. Maybe I'm not telling any of this the way I should. Maybe I shouldn't be telling it to you at all. I'm leaving things out, but it's been a long night already.

I'm tired. I so desperately want to stop fucking up, do you see? I want it all to stop. I want the bloody story to end.

People say I don't have to rush into marriage. But the way I see it, why prolong? Dao and I waited more than three years and she still left me. And it's true, Gloria left me after a short marriage, but there were reasons I'm aware of now that I should have been aware of then, even from the first moment. I still imagine myself with a woman I can grow old with. I want to be able to look back on my life and see how much we shared. It's what my parents had and I think I've always been searching for that. But already more than half my life is over. That's a sobering thought. You understand, don't you? If I meet the right woman I don't want to wait. I want to start the rest of my life now.

I'm not the type to be with one woman and go on to the next. I hope you can see that. I'm the type of person who means well and knows only what he thinks is right and finds out later it was all terribly wrong. But that all has to change. It has to. I dream of everlasting love. I dream of that with you.

PART II

CHAPTER SEVENTEEN

Place: a big, flat, empty parking lot. Temperature: sizzling hot. A plastic bag rolls by, a hawk squawks in the distance. A line of black dots snakes toward her, crystallizes into hearses and, behind them, a Toyota Corolla. The vehicles approach, peel off left and right, continue on. The Corolla stops, makes her move aside, parks neatly between white lines. She approaches tentatively. A window rolls down. She sees bodies stuffed in every which way like a clown car.

Hi, says a sideways head.

Ow! yells another head from somewhere near the dashboard. There is unintelligible chatter, occasional whoops of laughter, sighs. A forearm pops out of the window and dangles its fingers toward the ground. Limbs shoved into corners look unnaturally bent and absent of ownership. She stretches to see in the car.

Are you all women? she asks.

All women, says the first head.

She tries to count the different sets of hair: straight

blond, curly red, pulled-back black. Eight? Nine? This is ludicrous, she says. How can you breathe?

Easy, I'll show you: give me your hand.

She extends her hand.

No, GIVE it to me.

Oh, she says, and with her other hand she breaks her arm at the wrist like a loaf of bread. Here, she says, handing her hand to the head.

Down there, says the head, pointing with her eyes to another hand ready to grip and shove. She sees her hand disappear into the bodies. Now give me your leg.

She detaches her leg, and two right hands slide it onto the floor.

Now your arm.

She breaks off her arm and with her remaining leg pushes her torso into the backseat. Flesh against sticky flesh. I can't breathe, she says.

Don't panic, we're going to the mall.

Her head is elbowed off her torso and wedged into the neck of the driver. She recognizes this neck.

Hi, says Rory, looking ahead, two hands on the steering wheel.

The car is now weaving between recreational vehicles. She can see his face in the mirror. She can kiss his neck. She can whisper in his ear and he could hear. It's a good position to be in, she thinks.

I'm glad you came, he says, leaning on her a bit.

Where are we going?

It's a secret.

Oh please, says a mouth under the dashboard.

Stop pussyfooting around and tell her the truth, two say together.

He pulls up and parks in front of a suburban mall. I'll be right back, he says.

Sure you will, says a head from the backseat.

Rory? Rory? she yells.

What's the matter, honey? Tell us and we'll help. They are suddenly giggling.

I . . . she says, but her mouth is dry, feels full of pebbles. She can't find her hands to empty her mouth. She can't breathe. She tries to spit out the pebbles. Rory! she hears someone call. Rory, stop that! Stop that right now!

"Sit DOWN!"

The freckled face of a little boy comes into focus above the seatback in front of Bess. He has a baggie of sunflower seeds and a few in his poised right hand that he tries to hide when she opens her eyes and she makes the connection: woman falls asleep with mouth open, makes good target for fidgety kid on long train ride to Boston. She spits two seeds out of her mouth, shakes them from her shirt, untangles them from her hair. She hears what must be his mother in the next seat scold him.

"I'm sorry he bothered you," she says to Bess, leaning around her seat.

Bess wakes up her tired body in sequence, stretching her fingers, rolling her neck and shoulders, yawning. She takes out her journal to record this dream, as strange as the others she's been having.

Her ass itches. Thirty-six hours after she sat in poison ivy, she dropped her drawers in front of a mirror and saw a pink rash spread across her cheeks like dabs of strawberry jam on a split biscuit. The itch was agonizing. She tried to sleep on her stomach with her ass covered in medicated cream and when that wasn't enough, she secured ice packs to her skin and for hours watched the glamorous Eva Gabor act the hillbilly on cable TV. Now two weeks later, the rash is mostly gone, though she'll get an occasional itch so potent she has devised ways to get at it in public: the seat squirm or the hand in the back pocket.

"Your son's name is Rory?" Bess asks the woman, her voice deflated.

She nods. "Lord knows I call him something else when I'm at the end of my rope."

Bess looks at her watch and surmises her train from New York must be a half hour away from South Boston, where she will transfer to the subway and head out to the suburb of Newton. Carol had said she'd be there to pick her up. When Bess had Googled her and the other ex-wives, Carol Pendleton—the second one, who kept Rory in the country—was the easiest to find as she had kept her maiden name, stayed in roughly the same place. There were three Carol Pendletons in the Boston area. Bess got her on the second try and though she had rehearsed, she fumbled for words when she heard the voice.

"Hi. Hello. You don't know me but. Well, I mean. Forgive me. I have an odd question that you'll probably . . ."

"Start again, why don't you." The voice was firm but not un-pleasant.

"Sorry. My name is Bess Gray. Does the name Rory McMil-lan mean anything to you? I'm a friend of his."

There was a pause. "A friend," she said. It wasn't a question so much as an utterance one might make if one's mind were off accessing long-buried recollections.

"Well, more than a friend I guess you could say. He asked me to marry him, but I don't know if I should say yes. I thought maybe you could help. I'm sorry I bothered you."

Carol seemed amused. "You shouldn't be sorry. How is he after all these years? I thought he got married again after we parted." It was that last word—*pahted*—that betrayed her stoic New England grooming. She sounded like a young Katharine Hepburn.

"He did get married again," said Bess.

"And divorced *again*? Now I think I know why you're call-ing. A man's been married three times, it would set my fingers dialing, too."

Bess had played out this conversation in her mind time and again—married, yes; more than once; more than twice; *eight* times!—always building to a crescendo of their shock, her de-spair. Why had she never imagined she would simply say it mat-ter-of-factly? *Not three times, eight times. I'd be the ninth.*

After the weekend with Rory she had told no one. In the space of her phone silences and vague responses about her week-end away, her grandparents told her that she didn't sound well and should go to a doctor. Gabrielle couldn't understand why she was screening her calls and left irritable ultimatums on her voice mail. Cricket baked her mint brownies and monitored her from afar because he assumed—when he saw she had skipped work on that following Monday and stood unshowered and zombielike in front of her mailbox—that Rory must have ended things. *He's a louse*, he wrote in green icing on the brownies and left them at her door. Bess had smeared the icing in an attempt to spell *spouse* instead, then clawed out a chunk from the middle and ate out of her cupped hand.

To Rory she didn't have much to say, either. She stayed at his place a few times to remain connected, but they watched TV until they slipped into bed and each rolled to his or her own side. She found herself looking at his apartment anew, searching for signs of his ex-wives, but she couldn't detect much. Was the coffee grinder in his otherwise poorly equipped kitchen a gift? Was the mountain landscape photo above his computer taken with one of his ex-wives at his side? She didn't feel like asking. What she stared at instead was the photo of Cici on his dresser. It showed a young woman who knew she was being watched. She sits upright, regally, with her legs crossed and her chin high. She is long and lean, with short brown hair, full lips, a long pointed nose, and dark eyes slightly close set under prominent eyebrows. She is resplendent and exotic-looking, a silhouette to be captured in oil-paint portraits. Her hair is held off her tanned face with a blue bandana. She must command any room she enters, Bess thought, feeling a pang of jealousy at remembering how Rory described Olive Ann when he first saw her.

Bess was heartened to know Rory has been there for her all

these years, through all her bouts of depression and aggression during the Alaskan winters and teenage years, and the ongoing saga of her mother in and out of psych wards, as he had described. It says he has the capacity to endure with someone, doesn't it?

In truth, neither Bess nor Rory knew how to bridge the divide left from their private earthquake. Bess was still hovering precariously over the fault line, bracing for aftershocks, and she made that fact known, saying, *Let's not talk about it for a while, okay?* That night he had told her the story of his marriages was one of the longest nights of her life. She had shivered under the covers and listened with a quiet intensity, gripping the edge of her pillow until her fingers cramped. She asked questions for clarification and skipped-over details, but the more significant questions loomed large as storm clouds over the rickety shack of her held-back emotions. A feeble *why?* slipped out once and he gave her answers that she didn't remember in the way answers that don't satisfy don't stick. Too shocked to speak, she had lain still and let the wives in, one by one, until they inhabited the room in the light of dawn with a feminine feng shui that made Rory seem outnumbered and out of place.

They had driven home the next morning amid the deafening sounds of deep sighs and turn signals and tapped knuckles on glass. She had felt heavier than wet sand. He helped her lift her bag out of the trunk and she kissed him quickly, hoping it seemed less like a parting gift than a preoccupied habit in a hurry. She needed to be alone to think.

But thinking gave her vertigo. How does one wrap one's mind around eight wives? *It could have been worse, he could have murdered someone*, her interior voice whispered. If he were a murderer, she answered, she certainly wouldn't be sticking around. But isn't that the response she should have to a serial spouse? To run fast in the other direction? How bad is that in the realm of a lover's baggage? Or maybe she was making a bigger deal out of it than she should. Maybe she could just be with Rory and not get married and then it wouldn't be a problem. *But you want to get married, you've always dreamed of one day being married*. So what, life gives you lemons. And anyway, just because their relationships failed doesn't mean ours would. *I bet they all said that*.

Bess couldn't imagine a response to the story that she hadn't already thought up, so she didn't want to air it, not yet. Especially given that someone would no doubt use it as fodder for gossip or jokes. And yet, she desperately wanted to talk to *someone*. She thought about calling a therapist, and started asking around for recommendations. But then there she was one day, at the supermarket, opening a carton of eggs and nudging each one to check for cracks when it came to her: a visceral desire to talk to the only other women on the planet who might know what she was going through, who could help her through this by giving her insight into a man she suddenly felt she knew little about—the ex-wives.

"I was wondering," she said to Carol, "if you wouldn't mind if I came to see you. I need to meet with an oud maker in Belmont, which I think isn't far from you, right?"

"A what maker?"

"An oud maker, O-U-D. It's a stringed instrument, like a lute."

"I see. Come to my house, yes. We'll go for a bike ride."

A bike ride? "Okay. That sounds nice." In fact it sounded

strange, but she was relieved Carol had agreed to meet. After the particulars of where and when, Bess had hung up and questioned what she had just done. But maybe Carol *would* have some helpful advice about what to do. At the very least, Bess could judge for herself if Rory was truthful in his character descriptions. It would be one more way she could know to trust him.

But should she tell him this trip isn't all work-related? That question plagued Bess the whole week leading up to her departure. If she wanted to establish trust between them, she should set an example by keeping no secrets, she knew that. But he might ask her not to meet Carol, and then what? Doesn't he know she's a researcher at heart? How else could she give him an answer? And then there are the strange dreams that won't go away of these women to whom she suddenly feels connected. Bess decided to tell Rory after her trip. It was his turn to be understanding, wasn't it?

Carol is standing outside the Newton station in the rain under a two-person umbrella. Rory had described her as blond and curvy, stylish and self-assured, and there she is, standing confidently on tanned legs with a steaming traveler's mug in her free hand. She has a round, pale face with big eyes behind rimless glasses. Her hair is still blond, but it's short like a man's, with bangs separated into pieces like the teeth of a comb. She has on khaki shorts and an oversized denim shirt over a white T-shirt. She doesn't look curvy so much as robust, but she carries it well, more like a day laborer than a fast-food binger.

"Hi," says Bess under the hood of her rain jacket, "are you

Carol?" The train has pulled away. They are the only ones left by the track.

"Yes." Carol nods toward a row of stairs. "Let's get out of the rain."

Her Volvo smells like wet dog fur and mildew, despite the rainbow air freshener that swings from the rearview mirror. A soccer ball rolls around the backseat as they turn onto the main road.

"Not exactly the best day for a bike ride," says Bess.

Carol steals a quick glance at Bess. "You're younger than I expected."

"I'm thirty-five. Rory's ten years older than me."

Carol offers a lightning-quick smile, then turns back to the road.

The car turns left and right onto neighborhood streets that dip down and up again past dead ends and fenced-in yards. The car's windshield wipers sound like the short gasps of an asthmatic. They pull into the driveway of a light brown brick house. Carol points to the front door in a bold shade of pink. "My partner, Ina, chose this color scheme. My daughter says it looks like a baboon's ass."

The house is warm and fragrant—of jasmine maybe, or lilacs. To the left is the living room where a wide ceiling fan circulates slowly over high-backed wicker chairs and wall-to-wall bookshelves. In the hallway past the living room is a Cubist collage of a naked woman sliced into odd-angled pieces. "Ina did that," says Carol, noticing that Bess has stopped to stare. "She's the artist in the family."

"It's weird," says Bess. "I mean, it's a lot like these dreams I've been having."

"Ina would insist that you elaborate," says Carol, continuing down the hallway. "Me?" she adds over her shoulder, "I think there's nothing more banal than listening to other people's dreams. No offense."

Whereas the living room feels Southern genteel, the kitchen is urban modern. Copper pots hang over a wide granite island crowded on one side with blocks of expensive-looking knives and clear canisters of flour and sugar. The sleek appliances look state-of-the-art. The white-tiled floor extends out toward two sliding glass doors that open to a teakwood deck with a cushioned lounge chair and a small Zen garden.

Carol dumps her wallet and keys on the table, places her travel mug in the sink, and walks to a floor-standing wine rack filled with twenty-odd bottles. "Glass of wine?"

"Sure," says Bess, settling herself onto a stool. "Nice house."

"Thanks." Carol pours two glasses from a bottle already uncorked. "I should warn you, there's a teenager in our midst. My daughter, Delia, is upstairs in her room. I doubt if she'll come down; she hates people. Fourteen's a tough age, so I forgive her."

Now that Bess is conversing with Carol up close, she notices Carol's lazy eye. She remembers Rory had mentioned that. But Carol's left eye is only slightly off from her right, so that her line of vision seems not split so much as defocused and bulging a bit to incorporate more of the scene.

"Don't you have a dog, too?" Bess asks. "I thought Rory told me that."

"That was a while ago. Ina's allergic. To cats, too, and I had several of those, as well. The sacrifices we make for love, may they be ever so minor." Carol holds up her glass to toast. They clink and drink. Bess wonders why her car smelled like wet dog fur.

"Is that Delia?" Bess nods toward a photo attached to the fridge.

Carol turns around to look. "That's her. You have children?"

"No."

"Does Rory?"

"Not that I know of." It is the way Carol's head tilts that makes Bess aware of how much information that must have imparted. *Trust issues galore*, it screams.

"From what I recall, Rory always wanted kids. A wife and lots of kids to make up for the family he left behind."

The issue of children had come up the night of the telling. Hard as it was to believe Rory had eight wives, it was equally difficult to believe none of these women had had his children. Or rather, it was one more piece of the story that seemed far-fetched but somehow explained. He had wanted kids all along, yes, but there was Olive Ann's fake pregnancy and Dao's miscarriages and a long period in between when he was drinking too much to want to be anyone's father. "Bad luck, I guess," Bess says.

"I see."

Bess watches Carol at the counter now tossing a salad. *What am I doing here?*

"So tell me," says Carol, "how did you . . ."

"Rory's had eight wives," Bess blurts out like a loud belch.

Carol turns slowly from the counter. "What was that?"

"You were his second wife," says Bess more slowly. "There were more, six more to be exact. There was Lorraine in Ohio—Toledo, I think; Fawn in Las Vegas, which was a total mistake—it lasted only a day; Olive Ann in Denver; Pam in Seattle—she died; Dao in California—his longest one; and Gloria in D.C. right after 9/11."

Carol barks out a laugh. "Wow."

Bess leans back in her seat and crosses her arms. "You're the first person I've told."

"Did you just find this out?"

"Two weeks ago, when he was trying to propose."

"My Lord! The man has to work on his timing."

Bess sips her wine.

Carol looks pensively out toward the garden.

"Can I ask what you're thinking?" Bess says quietly.

Carol comes back to sit on her stool. "I don't know what to think, really. It's shocking. Well of course it's shocking. Who in his right mind gets married eight times? But then people in their right minds have always bored me. It's why I was partly drawn to Rory. I'm guessing that's why you were drawn to him, too, no?"

What does that mean, *in his right mind*? "I'm not sure," says Bess. Above the wine rack Bess notices a framed poster of two flapper girls in all their 1920s splendor—the bobbed black hair, the hanging pearl necklaces, the martini glasses, the heads tilted back in hard laughter. Bess feels emboldened looking at the poster, as if the flapper girls themselves—the original sassy singles, saviors from the spinster labels—were giving her advice. *This is life, darling. This is what it's all about. Enjoy every minute.*

"Do you love him?" Carol asks. She is poised on her stool, studying Bess.

"Yes, I love him," Bess says resolutely. This question she had been prepared for. Whether it would be true in future moments or change from moment to moment because love continually unleashes new questions that turn it inside out and make it stronger or weaker or just plain tiresome, this question is not why she came to Boston. The way Bess figures it, you have to start somewhere. If A (love), then B (marriage); and if A and B, then C (happiness). Will A lead to B and will A+B lead to C? This is the formula in question. A is not up for discussion.

"Ina would say: Then what's the problem? With love you can forgive anything." A lawnmower revs in the distance, a screen door squeaks open and shut. "Let's have lunch." Carol sets the table and serves gazpacho and spinach salad and whole wheat bread. They talk about Washington politics and the Middle East, about feminism and books they've read recently. Carol asks for more details on Rory's wives and Bess shares what she knows. They finish a bottle of sauvignon blanc.

"I'm curious," asks Bess, "what was your first impression of Rory?"

"I didn't like him."

"Really?"

"Not at all. If I remember correctly, he showed up to the restaurant late. And drunk. Not sloppy, but slow and overly anxious to impress. His jokes were vulgar. He smelled of cigarettes.

Some of his stories were amusing in an Old World sort of way, I'll give him that, but naïve, too, I thought, in the way he told them."

"So what happened? To make you like him, I mean?"

"He ordered chocolate milk." Carol wipes her lips with her napkin. "There we were at a French restaurant with chandeliers and an exquisite wine list. The chef came out to deliver our entrees and say bon apetit and when he asked if we'd like anything else, Rory, in a luscious moment of pure childlike sincerity, said, *Yes please, I'd love some chocolate milk*. I tell you it was the first time I saw him for who he really was—a poor Irish boy out of his element, working so hard to keep up with all these strange foreigners. The chef smiled wickedly and said, *I'm sorry, monsieur, I cannot serve zuch zings with duck à l'orange*. Poor Rory, his cheeks turned bright red with shame. I couldn't stand it. *Of course you can*, I said to the chef. *If you want our money and our good recommendations.*"

"And did he?"

"Of course he did. He wasn't happy about it, but he did and it was delicious. Rory and I laughed through the rest of dinner. That's all it took."

"You mean, to know you could get married?"

"To know I could deal with this man for the next few years. I saw it like picking a roommate: you don't want to be best friends, but you want to be compatible."

Bess tries to recall the way Rory described his first date with Carol. Wasn't he eating lobster? Wasn't he intimidated and scared? She still sees this quality in Rory, his childlike innocence, or awkwardness almost. It's one of the things she loves most about him.

"I'm glad to say," says Carol, "Rory grew more confident as I got to know him, and more politically minded, that's for sure. He held his picket signs higher than most."

"Rory? I got the impression he didn't really get involved in all that."

"Oh, he did, believe me. He was the one to get the crowds going." Carol rises and opens the door to the deck. "It stopped raining. Do you mind if we continue this outside?"

"Sure," says Bess. She takes her wineglass and follows Carol to the lounge chairs that had been tipped over to avoid getting wet. Carol wipes them with a towel and invites Bess to sit. She lifts a small rake from a corner and begins gliding it over her Zen garden, a four-by-four-foot patch of wet sand surrounded by bamboo stalks and purple lupine.

"This is a ritual for me. I tried various diets over the years and didn't notice much of a difference until I started to rake after each meal. So I don't ask why, I just do it. Ina got me into bike riding, which I try to get excited about, but she's not here. I'd rather rake."

It's interesting, thinks Bess, that Carol had mentioned going for a bike ride, though it was something she didn't really want to do.

"Rory said you married him to hide the truth from your parents, that they had caught you with another woman and had threatened to stop paying for college."

"True," says Carol, putting down her rake. She reclines in the chair next to Bess. "I'll tell you something Rory never knew. I fell in love for the first time that year. Her name was Gretchen. She was a cop at the immigration office. She loved lemon lollipops and swing sets, yet she could disarm hoodlums faster than anyone on the force, slamming them against walls like she was five times their size."

Bess notices movement in the kitchen. She turns to see Delia taking a juice carton from the fridge. Should she say something? She opts not to. Delia must have come down because she heard them go outside. "She didn't turn you in?"

"No." Carol sips her wine. "She cheated on me."

"I'm sorry."

"With Rory."

"Rory?"

"To this day I don't think I fully understand it all, but yes. I saw them in the backseat of her patrol car. I kept thinking: *There's my girlfriend fooling around with my husband*." Carol chuckles. "I was so angry. At both of them. But mostly Gretchen. She knew what she was doing. But I was angry with Rory, too, in some odd way, even though he didn't know about me and Gretchen. I still felt he betrayed me."

"So what did you do?"

"I should have said something then, but I didn't. I picked up some woman in a bar and took her back to Gretchen's place so she'd catch us in the act. Then I did the same to Rory. I mean, I let him catch me with a woman in our apartment. It was time for him to know the truth. I thought he might have suspected by then, but I could tell he didn't by the look on his face."

"Wow." Bess remembers this part of Rory's story. "But then once Rory knew, it got better, didn't it? At least, that's what he said."

"It did. We became good friends, in fact. He helped keep my mind off Gretchen, and I did the same by keeping his mind off Maggie."

"Maggie, his first wife?"

"He pined away for her all throughout our marriage. He would stake out her apartment before she moved to New York, follow her to work, dial her drunk from bars."

"And she never wanted to get back together?"

"I don't think so, no. My memory of Maggie isn't all that clear. I never met her, just heard a lot about her from Rory. When she finally did move, he calmed down, but I wasn't ever convinced he got over her. She was his first love."

Bess hadn't thought of this. Is it possible he has been searching (and failing) all this time to find a likeness of his first love? Bess experienced her first and only love in college and, though it was intense and sincere, they went their separate ways after graduation and grew up and out of what they had together. Each passing year she thought less about him until she thought about him hardly at all, except to wonder if he was married with children. But she could think of two single friends who had never gotten over the pain of a first love's breakup. It can take its toll. Is this what she's facing with Rory?

As if on cue, Carol says: "It was a long time ago and I'm sure he hasn't thought much about her in all these years."

"Will you excuse me?" says Bess, placing her cloth napkin alongside her plate. "I have to use the restroom."

"Upstairs. Second door on the right."

Bess climbs the stairs and peeks into rooms. In one of them, Delia is lying sideways on her bed, reading a book. She doesn't look up, so Bess quietly heads to the bathroom. On her way she notices an empty bag of chips by the top of the stairs. Was this evidence that Delia had been listening in on their conversation? Bess thought she had heard occasional noises from the stairway, like the creaking of wood.

Once out of the bathroom, Bess decides to be friendly. "Hi," she says, standing just outside Delia's bedroom.

"Hi," Delia says back.

Bess glances at the hardback Delia has open in her hand. On the cover is a pair of legs in jeans swinging on a tire. "Good book?"

"It's okay," says Delia. "Harry Potter's better." She seems neither rude nor overly friendly, but sleepy and guarded.

Bess smiles politely. Not knowing what else to say, she starts to make her exit when Delia speaks up.

"If it were me," she says, "I'd dump his ass." She waits a few seconds to gauge Bess's reaction, sees Bess is stumped for words, then goes back to reading her book.

Bess returns to the kitchen, amused. "Your daughter seems like a smart kid."

Carol is washing the lunch dishes and loading the dishwasher. "Top of her class, but you'd never know it by her one-word answers. Would you like some coffee?"

"Thank you, but I should probably head out."

Carol wipes her hands. "Let me run upstairs and then I'll take you to the subway."

Bess retrieves her bag and wanders toward the foyer, coming upon the dining room. It's more ornate than the other rooms: bloodred walls, crystal chandelier, maple wood china cabinet. On a hutch is a row of framed photos. Bess enters the room to get a better look at what appears to be a posed wedding shot amid the full colors of autumn. Carol is facing the photographer in a white suit, holding hands with a petite woman in a wedding dress who is looking lovingly at her. In the photo, Delia is behind them, frowning.

"That's Ina," says Carol, catching Bess leaning into the photo.

So Carol is married to Ina? Why didn't she mention that? "You're married?"

"We got married eight months ago, though we've been together for seven years."

"Six years, eight months!" a voice calls out from the doorway. Bess turns to see a short, thin woman with a broad smile and dark hair swept up in a clip. She is artily dressed in a flowing, Aztec-patterned halter dress. "Hi, I'm Ina," she says, placing her portfolio on the table. Her wide silver bracelets look like handcuffs. She smells like vanilla.

"Nice to meet you," says Bess, accepting her handshake.

"Don't let her fool you," says Carol, looking at Ina. "She's not punctilious, she's superstitious. She thinks the seventh year will bring on some sort of apocalypse."

"Let's hope I'm wrong. It's happened once or twice. Are you having a nice blast from the past, my dear?" she says, bumping hips with Carol.

"I've enjoyed our lunch, yes."

Ina's gaze leaves Carol slowly. "Rory is well?" she asks Bess. "He is. Did you know him?"

Ina flashes a quick, intimate glance at Carol. "Just heard stories."

"Bess wants to know if she should marry Rory," says Carol.

"Do you love him?"

"Yes, I think so," says Bess.

"Then what's the problem?" says Ina, with her hands in the air.

Carol turns to Bess. Her eyebrows leap, as if to say, *See?* "He's already been married eight times, that's the problem."

Ina claps with delight. "How delicious! I love an optimist."

"I knew you'd say that," says Carol. "You love drama. Never mind all the broken hearts along the way."

"Yes," she says, teasingly. "All those risky hearts that for moments on this earth burst with love and joy. No, I applaud him. He sounds romantic."

Carol shakes her head. "Well, then," she says to Bess. "What's the problem?"

Ina leans in and pulls a stray hair off Carol's shirt. "What's this?" she says, flirtatiously. "Have you been cheating on me?" Her body sways as if she's slow-dancing to music in her head.

"I have," says Carol. "He's big and hairy and does all sorts of nasty things with his tongue." Ina laughs. Perhaps this is how Carol flirts, thinks Bess—straight-faced and still as if to balance out Ina's dramatic ebb and flow. They are oddly paired, these two—one black-haired, short, thin, bohemian, the other blond, big-boned, preppy—but there is a warm chemistry between them. Their collective energy feels deep and intimate.

"Carol's in love with our neighbor's Lab," Ina explains.

"Ina thinks he's a walking stink bomb," says Carol. She turns back to Ina. "Kyle asked me to take Cooper to the vet this morning. Poor thing was scared to death, so I let him stomp in the puddles."

So that explains the car smell, concludes Bess.

"I see. Well, I just came back to pick something up. If you'll excuse me," says Ina, exiting the dining room. They hear her singsong voice upstairs in what must be a conversation with Delia.

"Can I ask," says Bess, "how you and Ina decided to get married after all that time?"

Carol looks at the wedding photo. "It was important to Ina."

"Okay, I'm off," Ina cries out, flying back down the stairs.

"That was fast," says Carol.

"I've got to get back to the studio. It was nice to meet you, Bess." She glides out the door with a wave and a bow like a fairy godmother.

Bess wishes she could have talked more with Ina and Carol together. "Are you glad you got married?" she asks.

"I suppose." Carol yells up to Delia that she'll be right back, then resumes her thought. "I didn't want to at first. It wasn't about my commitment to Ina; I just didn't need a legal license or public announcement. I already knew Ina loved me. I knew she wouldn't run at the first argument, that she'd do the work to make it last."

Maybe, it dawns on Bess, after all her heartache, after all

those times guys have broken off relationships, she has come to believe that the only way she can trust a man to commit and do the work it takes to make a relationship last is if he marries her. And maybe—she is formulating this theory on the spot, reeling from its implications—maybe meeting a serial spouse like Rory renders that theory useless, and now what? What trust test can she use anymore? "How did you know you could trust Ina?" says Bess. "I mean, how did you know she would try hard to make it last if you didn't get married?"

"I just knew."

"I don't understand."

"I can't explain it. I just . . . knew."

Bess suddenly feels emotional. "Then why did you agree to get married?"

Carol motions toward the front door. Bess follows Carol to the car. "When it became legal in Massachusetts, Ina felt it was important—especially since we lived here—to make a statement. To say we should have the choice. I've always been antiestablishment. It just so happens that in my world, getting married is antiestablishment."

"So is getting married eight times," says Bess, offhandedly.

"Very true."

The rain has cleared, but the air is still damp and the gutters still pocked with puddles and mud. Delia's silhouette appears in an upstairs window as they pull out to the street. "When I went upstairs, I spoke to your daughter. She told me I should dump him."

Carol laughs. "Sounds like Delia."

"Do you think that's good advice?"

"Well, she's told me at various times to dump Ina. But she loves Ina. My daughter has abandonment issues."

Bess wants to ask why, but there isn't time. Instead, there is the receding landscape of this Massachusetts town she may never see again. She sums up the stone buildings and old willow trees and trolley tracks curving along the street into a melancholy feeling.

"I know you came here hoping for answers," says Carol. "I'm sorry."

"It's okay. I'm glad I came. I think Rory described you well, and that's something. At least his stories aren't all far-fetched."

"Most of them, though, no? He was quite the raconteur."

Carol pulls up in front of the station. A small, faint rainbow arches up from a row of buildings. "Rory proposed to his last wife at the sight of a rainbow," says Bess.

Carol turns off the engine. "May I ask if you told Rory about coming to see me?"

"No, not yet."

They sit in silence for a few moments.

"I read recently," says Carol, "that in Sub-Saharan Africa, girls are used as currency and forced to marry as young as eleven or twelve, before puberty, to men who already have several wives and are three or four decades older."

Bess looks down. She knows of cultures like this, of polygamy and arranged marriages and laws that allow husbands to beat their wives. She has met women from some of these countries whose politeness is eerie and impenetrable. "I should be thankful I have choices," she says, softly.

"Oh, but it can be a curse, too . . . having too many choices." A car pulls up to their side and discharges a gray-haired gentleman with a briefcase. He waves to the woman inside and says he'll be home late, so . . . He ends it there, on *so*.

"Sometimes I wonder why I need a man in my life," says Bess. "It feels weak and embarrassing."

"Don't go there," says Carol, pointing her finger at Bess. "Some of my friends stopped being my friends after I married Rory. They thought I sold out. And now look, decades later and women are still defensive." Carol's cell phone rings. She reaches into her bag in the backseat, looks to see who's calling, then shuts it off. "The easy thing to do, I should think, would be to end it with Rory. But you're not doing that. You're facing your choices. Maybe you're doing that not just for you and Rory, but for reasons you're not even aware of. This is making you face your demons, whatever they are."

"I hadn't thought of it that way."

"It's an interesting idea to try and find Rory's ex-wives. Is that your plan?"

"At the moment, yeah. I'm leaving next week to drive my grandparents across the country to their new home. I thought I'd look along the way for whomever I can find."

Carol helps Bess retrieve her carry-on bag from the trunk. "Well, just be careful to keep your expectations in check."

"I will," Bess says. "Thank you for meeting with me today."

"You're quite welcome."

Bess slings her bag diagonally over her shoulder.

"He's a good guy," Carol says. "I want to say that. Deep down, you know, from what I know . . . he's a good man."

"I know," says Bess. She steps down to the tracks to wait for the train.

An hour later, Bess settles in to a busy woodworking shop not far from the neighborhood known as Little Armenia, a shop well known among Greek, Armenian, and Middle Eastern musicians. She is there to interview an oud maker for a magazine piece on traditional folk music. He is an older man who offers her tea and sweet tahini breads. She presents him with a little gift bag from the Smithsonian museum and while he finishes up with a customer, she asks if she can borrow his computer to check her e-mail. It is an old model, and slow. When her in-box appears, she scans the list of messages and stops at the reply from Dao, Rory's seventh wife. Bess had sent an e-mail days ago to an address she found on an oil pollution site.

dear bess gray,

i believe we were meant to be introduced. in past incarnations, we might have passed as concubines in the curtained halls of some sheik's pleasure palace and locked eyes under our veils, knowing each other intimately in that moment like mirrored images. can you imagine? i am not surprised you found me. i bow before you and say welcome to my sphere.

yes, i live in saigon with my husband and two stepsons, giang and sy. i am sorry we cannot meet. i travel sometimes back to california for work, but i don't like to fly, so i am thankful for the internet. such a toy, isn't it? i love the terms "virtual reality" and "cyberspace." i love their floating, infinite possibilities. we will need possibilities when we complete the destruction of mother earth.

i am glad to hear rory is well. he is a genuine old soul. you may ask me anything about him or about us or anything you want and i will answer with honesty. that was not an easy time. it is never an easy time. as you are and as i was, so shall we come to understand.

peace, dao

CHAPTER EIGHTEEN

Rory surveys the rowdy crowd around him and wonders just what the hell he's doing in Baltimore, four rows up from a flat-track Roller Derby all-female championship game. The better question, as he takes in the raunchy uniforms and gestures of the players, is what Sean is doing here with his eleven-year-old daughter, Katie.

"It's a beautiful Saturday afternoon, for God's sake," he says to Sean. He is sitting between Katie and her dad, shaking his head. "Your daughter should be at the zoo or, I don't know, at a picnic." He has to speak loudly to be heard over Heart's "Barracuda," blaring throughout the arena.

"I would argue this *is* a zoo," says Sean, "and we're having ourselves a fine picnic." He toasts Rory with his plastic beer cup and offers him a nacho. Rory declines. The congealed orange cheese has an unnatural shine.

Rory is often amazed at how little Sean has changed in twenty-five years. Their friendship goes back to their days in Boston when Rory was fresh off the boat. Sean hadn't been in the country much longer, but was a year older and had done some traveling before he settled down. Both fine musicians, they had an easy repartee on stage and off. Sean flirted with Maggie any chance he got until she walked out on Rory; he sided with Rory after that like a true friend and helped him land on his feet. When Rory married Carol, he and Sean slowly drifted apart, and when he left Boston, they lost contact. Many years later, when Rory moved to D.C., he came upon Sean playing at an Irish bar in Virginia. They settled in to an easy back-and-forth, reminiscing and catching up. It wasn't long before they were friends again and musical partners, playing weddings and other gigs when they could get them.

A whistle blows, the announcer says they're ready to rumble, and a pack of women in short skirts and helmets shoves off counterclockwise around the rink.

"Jammer on jammer action!" yells Katie. She's got a skate painted on her cheek and a pom-pom in her hand that she's waving above her head and into the motorcycle jacket of the guy in front of her.

"This isn't right," says Rory. "Does she even know what that means?"

Sean is laughing. "Do you?"

There is shoving and shouting and in seconds the jam is over. A point was scored, though Rory isn't sure how. A skater named All Gore in a ripped tank top and black fishnet stockings skates by and flips up her skirt for the crowd. The number written on her forearm above her elbow pad is "4-Nick-8." It takes Rory a minute to get it. The whistle blows, another jam begins.

"Booty block! Booty block!" yells Katie.

Rory turns to Katie. "Where you getting this stuff?"

"Babs taught me. We've been hanging out." Babs is a recent divorcée who lives three doors down from Sean on Capitol Hill. Sean's been trying to get up her skirt for months. He pointed her out to Rory when they first arrived at the rink—the tall blond with the alias Barbara Butch. Sean said above all else, he comes to watch her stretch at the hips.

"I *do* have other friends, you know," says Katie.

For the last two years, Rory and Katie have had a special relationship. It started when he began hanging around Sean's house, sometimes sleeping on his couch. He tickled her mercilessly, helped her with her math homework, babysat on the days Sean had custody of her but had clients to attend to through his real estate business. She developed a crush. Rory could do no wrong until his visits diminished because he was spending time with Bess. Katie didn't like Bess when they met. *Competition*, Sean pointed out.

"That's it, Babs! Bend your knees! Stay low! Oof!" The whistle blows, Sean jumps up and yells something at the ref, then sits back down. A large woman named Axe Alice gets sent to the penalty box for an illegal block amid a roar of shouting: *Go Axe Alice! Go Axe Alice!* "Female anarchy," says Sean. "Life just doesn't get any better than this. Where's Bess, by the way?"

"In Boston." Rory catches Sean's look. "For work," he adds, defensively.

"Things okay?"

The players are off again. Rory is aware of the sound of rolling skates on a hard floor. "I asked her to marry me."

Sean suddenly turns his body toward Rory, his eyes wide with disbelief. "You didn't."

"I did. Last weekend."

"Bloody hell, McMillan. You're not a hopeless romantic. You're worse, you're an embarrassment to our gender, man." Sean wonks him on the head.

"Thanks." Rory has shared enough details with Sean about his marriage history that Sean feels entitled, so he says, to offer his opinions any time opinions are called for, especially when "Perfectly Normal Guy Rory" has been taken over by "Bleeding Heart Pussy-Whipped Love-Struck Rory."

"So what did she say?"

"She didn't."

"You mean she didn't say no."

"She didn't say yes."

The announcer's voice is quickening and growing louder. *The pack's speeding up. Twat's half a lap behind. Jane's fixin' to score, ducks around Romp, takes on Butch, sneaks by on the outside, Butch down! Twat's in trouble. Jane slams Dish, she hits the ground hard! YOWʒa!* What kind of person says *yowʒa?*

"Well," says Sean, "at least you know it's not because of your history."

Rory stares straight ahead.

"You did tell her about your ex-wives?"

"Yeah, sure."

"On your first date."

"Not exactly then."

"When?"

"After."

"Okay, see that? That look. I know that look. I know your bullshit look, McMillan."

"Yeah, McMillan," says Katie, leaning in. "Even *I* know that look."

"Okay you two, that's enough. Katie, your dad's going to watch his language from now on. Isn't that right, Sean?"

"That's right. Sorry, sweetheart. Yes! Nice work, Butch!" Sean is standing again. A skater falls in front of Babs, and Babs jumps over her in an impressive show of finesse and athleticism. "So," he continues, sitting down in his seat and leaning back so Katie can't hear, "you just told her."

"Right after I proposed."

Sean laughs. "You're a piece of work, you know that? Did she flip out?"

"Not really. I told her the whole sordid story, beginning to end, in more detail, mind you, than I told the others, even to Dao. In fact she reminded me of Dao, the way she just listened, didn't say much, only Dao was hard to read. I could never tell if Dao was listening to me. And she never really told me what she thought of my past. But then I told Dao all of it from the start; that was my mistake with Bess, I know."

"Yes!" Sean yells at the rink. Then he turns back to Rory. "Sorry. Go on."

"I'm just saying, Bess really listened, like she wanted to understand. But I could tell I lost her trust. It's been a tense week." In fact it had been a miserable week, Rory thinks. Bess made it clear she didn't want to talk about it, so he was giving her space.

But then everything within that space felt uncomfortable or forbidden—small talk, intimacy, sex, humor. He was glad she still agreed to see him, but she wasn't the same whenever they got together and he didn't know how to make it better. It was easier to wallow in self-reproach. What did he think was going to happen when he told her? Immediate sympathy and understanding, happy-ever-after? Has it ever been like that?

"Listen," says Sean. "Do you love her?"

Rory has thought a lot about love his whole adult life with the conclusion that he absolutely hates trying to understand it, hates hearing people go on about it because chances are good they're talking out of their asses. After all these years, Rory has learned to simply read the signs: when he needs a drink and/or he's bored and/or he doesn't want to share any stories and/or his right cheek is twitching, it's not love. When he wants to be with her all the time (and not just sexually, though frequent erections are a good sign); when he can't stop putting his foot in his mouth or trying to impress her with his stories; when he likes imagining her as grandma to his grandpa; when he feels deep down somewhat unworthy of her, well . . . that's love in his book, pure and simple. He knows now he was never in love with Lorraine (boredom) or Fawn (alcoholism) or Olive Ann (cheek twitching). But he was in love with Maggie and he was in love with Dao, too.

A skater who looks a little like Bess rolls by and a sudden memory pops into Rory's mind of an evening in Bess's apartment, just before their weekend away. She had made him a delicious chicken dinner. They were drinking grappa, laughing a lot, debating the pros and cons of Porta Potties and waiting for Bess's apple pie to come out of the oven so that the apartment smelled to Rory like home and family. At one point Bess said hold on and went into the bedroom and came out wearing her *gi*. She started performing a form for him in her living room, or at least trying to do the form, but she kept messing up and couldn't keep a serious face, though not for lack of trying. Her beautiful dark hair swung down into her face. When she stuck her butt out to get into a low stance Rory's interest turned from one of delight and a kind of mesmerized adoration of her animated determination to a lustful craving. He jumped up and carried her to the couch. She had nothing on under her *gi*, which was wildly exciting. Her skin was soft, her hair silky smooth, her thrusting a turn-on. Afterward, they ate pie washed down with big glasses of milk, he played the guitar for her, they made love again and then they read to each other in bed. It was, to Rory, as perfect a time as he's ever had. *This*, he had said to her, *this is what I want out of life*.

"McMillan! Where'd you go? I asked you a question."

"Sorry. Yes. I love her."

Sean studies Rory's face for a moment. "Even though you've known her for what, four seconds?"

"Aw, go on. Danny Murphy, you remember him? From Dorchester? He met Meg in February, married her in June and they're about to celebrate their forty-first anniversary. So don't give me that."

"Right, but Danny wasn't divorced before. And he was, what, twenty-five?"

"And I'm forty-five, for God's sake. Bess is thirty-five. Times a-wastin'."

"Well then, why not just move in together?" Sean is raising his voice to be heard over the announcer's play-by-plays.

"That would have gone over well," says Rory. "Bess, I love you, but I've been married eight times already, so sorry, I'll never get married again. But hey, let's live together!"

"There are plenty of women who wouldn't have a problem with that."

"I know, but I'm an old-fashioned guy." Rory looks over at Katie. She is swinging her legs under her seat, looking at the program. Though Sean can seem cavalier about her sometimes, Rory has heard him say that she is the best thing that has ever happened to him.

The announcer calls the end of the first bout. Players skate over to their corner while the DJ plays Joan Jett's "Bad Reputation." The announcer asks everyone to make noise for the winners. Some of the members of the audience are shuffling out of the rows.

"You really want to marry her?" says Sean. "For real?"

"I do."

"No, listen to what I'm asking." He is looking at Rory intently. "Do *you want* to marry her? Not, *should* you marry her or does *she* want you to marry her. You have to want it for the right reasons. If you don't, it's never going to work."

Rory throws up his hands. "What the hell are the right reasons to get married? Tell me that please, would you?"

Sean eases back into his usual relaxed state. "Fuck if I know.

That's what my divorce attorney told me. I figure she must know what she's talking about."

Rory turns to Katie, worried that she's feeling left out. The atmosphere is loud and chaotic and in many ways overwhelming. "How're you doing, penguin?"

"Okay." Katie is braiding pieces of her hair, which is strawberry blond like her dad's and long like her mom's.

"You want something more to eat?"

"No, but can we go look at the merch?"

"The what?"

"The merch. Merchandise. You seriously need to get with it, McMillan." Calling him by his last name the way Sean does is a new thing for Katie. Rory finds it amusing and kind of adorable.

"Ask your dad."

"Go, you two," says Sean. "I'm going to head off to the restroom. I'll see you back here for the next bout."

Katie and Rory take a walk. Katie sips from a water fountain, crossing her long spindly legs and holding her hair back as she drinks. Around the next bend they find the merch table. They crane their necks over and through the people looking at what's for sale—key chains, buttons, bandanas, hats, bumper stickers, and T-shirts in all sizes, including tiny ones that tout "Skater Tots." Finding a clearing, Katie reaches across the table to take one of the water bottles on display and accidentally knocks over twelve other bottles in the process. "Hey," says a fat man behind the table, "careful." Katie blushes and says, "Sorry sorry sorry" with her head way down. She backs up and walks quickly away. Rory runs to catch up to her. "Hey scout," he says, finding her at

a table in the food area, which smells like hot dogs. Katie is leaning over, her elbows on her knees, her fists lightly punching her
cheeks. "I thought you wanted something," he says. "C'mon,
my treat."

"I don't want anything."

Sometimes Katie reminds Rory of Cici. She was about Katie's age when they first met. He has the same visceral feeling he
did with Cici of wanting to protect her from the world. "What's
wrong?" he says.

"I'm a klutz."

"You are not a klutz. The way they had those bottles? They
were asking for it."

"No, I am a klutz. I always have been."

"Who told you that?"

"My mom. And some of the kids at school."

Rory feels a hot flash of anger at Kelly, Katie's mother, for
putting such an idea in Katie's head. Truth be told, Rory never
liked Kelly. He'd met her a few times and always found her rather
cold and stuck up. Someone should give her a talking-to about
the dangers of giving a child a label like that. "Can I tell you
something?" he says. "My father always used to call me a clown
when I was a kid. I hated it. I mean, sure . . . I fooled around now
and again, making people laugh, but I had a serious side, too,
only no one seemed to remember that. I could hardly get anyone
to take me seriously."

"So what happened? What did you do?"

What happened? Rory thinks. *I still can't get people to take me
seriously.* "What happened was," he says to Katie, "I sold my

sense of humor for a buck fifty to a very serious man. Now he's having a grand ol' time, walking around Dublin telling jokes and laughing up a storm. And me? Well, I turned into him, see? I became very serious. I never told another funny story ever again. I never laugh and I never ever tell a joke, *especially* not the one about the two gorillas in tiaras at their high school prom."

"You've told that one to me, like, a million times."

"Nope, you're wrong. It couldn't have been me. I'm very serious, remember?"

Katie smiles. A large man eating a soft pretzel brushes their legs as he walks by. "Come," says Rory. "Let's get a slice of pizza."

Katie follows Rory to the end of the line of people waiting to order. They stand by the gallon of ketchup. Katie unwraps a straw to chew on. "Rory?"

"Yeah?"

"Can I come visit if you and Bess get married?"

"Absolutely. You know what she told me when you two first met? She said you were very pretty. She thought you must be fighting off all the boys at school."

Katie rolls her eyes. "She wouldn't say that if she knew the boys in my school. Most of them smell like barf."

Rory laughs. "I see. Well, maybe they'll smell better in a year or two."

Rory and Katie catch the tail end of a halftime show featuring two belly dancers who provoke whoops and catcalls with their stomping, jiggling finale. Sean is a few rows down, talking to Babs over the divider. Babs blows Katie a kiss; Katie waves.

What must Katie think of her dad and Rory, these two middle-aged, single, divorced men trying to figure out how to win over women? Will she end up marrying for the *right* reasons? Will she want to marry at all? She hasn't exactly had the best role models. Rory wonders what he could say to help her. *Don't be afraid*, is what pops into his mind, though he's not sure what that means.

Sean returns to his seat. "Give her time," he says.

"What's that?"

Sean leans back in his chair with his arms crossed, his gaze out toward the rink. "Bess," he says. "Give her time. She'll come around."

"Thanks," says Rory. Moments later a whistle blows and a new game begins.

CHAPTER NINETEEN

The plans to drive her grandparents to Tucson progressed quickly and now the departure day is upon them. The rental minivan is illegally parked below her bay window. Bess is eager to take a few weeks off from work, D.C., her life. She needs time alone to think about Rory, and to be with Millie and Irv as a family before they move away for good. She hopes the journey will help them talk about aspects of their lives they have kept hidden from her all these years. Maybe, too, being together will calm them through this rough transition, curtailing the recent escalation of their vicious fights.

Bess looks around her living room at what she has packed. Gathered around her suitcase are several bags: one for snacks and bottled water; one for her laptop, iPod, and other gadgets; one for maps, guidebooks, a notebook, books—including one on Zen for the martial artist—and CDs of old radio shows from the library she hopes will get her grandparents in the mood to wax nostalgic.

There is also the box Gaia asked her to transport. Bess hadn't seen Gaia or Pearl since that day at Eastern Market when Sonny called. She didn't want to. She was too mad at Gaia for accepting Sonny back into her life so easily. But when she found out they were flying to California to live with Sonny, she found it hard to say good-bye. It was too much, all this moving away. Gaia asked her to take the box because she didn't want Sonny to ask about it and because what it held—a secret Gaia promised to reveal when it arrived—meant too much to risk shipping. Bess said sure, she'd do it. She had decided to drive the extra miles to California anyway in part to visit a grad school friend who was now teaching in the folklore and mythology department at UCLA, but mostly to have the last day of her cross-country journey to herself. It seemed the right way to end this sort of trip. She'd drop off the rental car there and fly home.

Bess checks her iPod to make sure it is fully charged. She has downloaded a variety of music for the trip, mostly from female folk artists for when she feels mellow, and zydeco and gospel a capella quartets when she needs a boost. She has music she thinks Irv would like, too, blues singers like Henry Gray and Willie Earl King, and still others she wants him to hear: good old-time banjo picking and bluegrass the likes of Dwight Diller, Ralph Stanley, and Doc Watson. Maybe she should bring her banjo and try learning how to play. The instrument always makes her think warmly of her dad, playing her to sleep. And now it makes her think of Rory, too. She takes it off her wall, strums a few chords. And then there's a knock on her door.

"Coming," she sings. "Who is it?"

"Your chauffeur, reporting for duty," shouts Cricket.

Bess opens the door and sees Cricket in brown Bermuda shorts. To his right is a small suitcase with pink ribbon identifiers; on his left is Stella, looking up at Bess and panting noisily, a blue traveling backpack strapped around her torso. Hanging from his neck are sunglasses and a money holder clean enough to look freshly purchased. There is a whiff of grapefruit about his person. "Where are you going?" she asks.

"With you."

"What do you mean *with me*?"

"You can't drive the length of the country by yourself, we both know that. You fall asleep at the wheel, it's not safe." Cricket waves her aside and enters her apartment.

"Cricket," she says, following him. "I appreciate your looking out for me, I really do, but we have everything worked out."

How would she deepen her bond with her grandparents with Cricket there? She packed folk music and R&B for the montages, not show tunes. And how could she look for Rory's ex-wives? She hadn't told Cricket. She had merely said she and Rory had had their first fight, but they were working it out. "Seriously, we don't have enough room."

Cricket pours Stella a bowl of water and stands by the bay window. He peeks down at the van. "You can fit Millie and Irv in the glove compartment of that *monstrosity*."

"It's smaller than it looks. We can't fit any more luggage in there."

Cricket surveys her living room floor.

"Okay look," says Bess. "You can't exactly just come in here five minutes before I'm about to leave and announce you're coming. My grandparents are looking forward to spending time alone with their granddaughter, know what I mean?"

"Touching, but no. They're thrilled I'm joining you. They used the word *thrilled*, I'm almost positive."

Bess stares at him, then drops onto her couch. Stella nudges her for a good chin scratch, then licks Bess's knee just below her denim skirt. "When did you talk to them?"

"Well, I didn't speak to them exactly. I e-mailed Millie—you know I adore her, she's so cute on e-mail. I wanted to wish her the best of luck with her move."

"That's it? And they invited you without asking me?"

"I offered to help with the driving." Cricket is now wiping the counter with a folded paper towel, purposely not looking up. "And I may have mentioned I have a friend in Denver who's dying."

"Oh please, that's low."

Cricket doesn't look up, doesn't snap back a snide remark.

"Cricket? That isn't true, is it?"

Cricket stops moving. "It's Isabella."

Bess thinks for a moment. "Your ex-wife?"

"She needs a lung transplant, but they don't think she's a good candidate for it. She's very sick. That's why Claus wanted me to call her, remember? I haven't seen her for years and—" He stops abruptly. He has his hand over his heart, a gesture that looks wholly unselfconscious.

Bess feels a deep tenderness toward him. Because he only recently mentioned he had an ex-wife, she had assumed that Isabella was a minor player in the sum of what makes Cricket tick. But she understands how certain people from the past can surface at any time and have an effect as powerful as those who are physically present. She has only to think of her mom and dad to know this is true. "I'm sorry," she says.

Outside, Bess hears muffled laughter, the closing of a car door, the revving of an engine. She wonders briefly who belongs to the sounds, what they're talking about, where they're going. It would be nice to have Cricket along for support and comic relief, she admits. Maybe this could work. "For the record, you should have asked me instead of talking to my grandparents first. And you could have given me fair warning instead of springing this on me as I'm leaving."

"You're quite right," he says, gently. "I'm sorry."

She loves this soft side of him. "I guess we could go to Denver and then head south. We're already going north to Chicago for a few days. Millie wants to see her sister."

"Stella loves Chicago."

"When was Stella in Chicago?"

"Well, she wasn't. But she loves the movie. Richard Gere was positively edible."

"And how do you plan on getting home?"

"I'll get home, don't you worry."

"You'd be on your own today. We're staying in Pittsburgh tonight and stopping off first for a tour of Fallingwater, the Frank Lloyd Wright house."

"Yes, Millie told me. I've already seen Fallingwater, thank you very much. I had to pee through the entire tour. I'll read in the van. And I already called a friend in Pittsburgh. She has graciously opened up her home to me and Stella."

"Okay then," says Bess, slapping her thighs and standing up. "It's the four of us. *Five* of us, excuse me," she adds, patting Stella. "It's nine-thirty, we should be on our way to Millie and Irv's. You have more luggage downstairs, I take it?"

"Just a wee thing."

"You don't have anything *wee*," says Bess. "With Gaia's box we're already tight, but we'll make it work." Bess hands Cricket the van keys. "Why don't you put your stuff in the van and I'll meet you down there."

Bess needs to talk to Gabrielle. She chose to tell her about Rory after her trip to Boston mostly because she thought Gabrielle could ask Paul, her new boyfriend at the Social Security Administration, to get information on the whereabouts of the other ex-wives. Paul was the guy Gabrielle met at the singles party; they've been hot and heavy ever since. Gabrielle—after she heard the story and stopped saying *holy shit* and laughing and apologizing for laughing and saying she was ready to get serious, *holy shit*—agreed to help Bess locate these women. After all, Bess pointed out, she was the guilty party who introduced her to Rory in the first place.

"Sorry I woke you," says Bess to Gabrielle's yawn. "I'm leaving soon and you're the only one with a key to my place. Can you water my plants and take in my mail?"

"What happened to Ignatius?"

"Turns out, Cricket's coming. He just told me."

"Quite the party."

"It's fine. Hey, did you ever ask Paul if he could get any information for me?"

"He's not helpful. Even if you could get him their social security numbers, he says he'd get in big trouble if he tried to look them up, something like five years' jail time. I told him he'd look hot in an orange jumpsuit." Gabrielle yawns again, a long, vocal yawn in a high register. "So what's the update? Did you ever hear back from the oil slick chick?"

"Yeah, listen to this." Bess boots up her laptop and reads Dao's e-mail.

"Concubines in a pleasure palace? She's on something."

"She does sound kind of strange. It's like she's some guru who's been alone on top of a mountain too long. But maybe she's really wise."

"Or she might be a fucking lunatic. Did you write her back?"

"I did." Bess had typed several drafts, in fact, before she sent it. There were too many questions—What was Rory like back then? Do you think he would have honored his vows had things been different? What made you want to get married? What made you want a divorce? Is your new husband like Rory?—on and on until she wanted to crawl under her covers and never come out. Dao was the real deal. That was Rory's longest relationship, probably his healthiest one, too. She seems key to understanding Rory. But Bess decided to keep it simple. For now she needs information. *Today I visited Rory's second wife, Carol,* she wrote. *I'm not sure why, and I'm not sure what I got out of it, but I liked her. And I suppose I understand Rory a little better, which is why I'm writing you, and why I'm thinking I might search for Rory's other ex-wives, even though I'm not at all sure it's the right thing to do. Did you ever do that? Might you know where I can find them? I'd very much appreci-*

ate the help if you happen to have information on any of them. Thanks.
She didn't know how to end it. *In solidarity . . . Peace to you, too
. . . Sincerely . . . All best . . . Yours?* Bess had erased all of them and
wrote, simply, *Bess*, as if the word in the end was best left alone.

"What about his first wife?" Gabrielle continues. "Did you
call her?"

"Maggie? Yeah, we've exchanged messages. I found her
through her ad agency in New York. She's some sort of executive
there, travels a lot. She seems eager to hear about Rory. What if
she's still in love with him? Or he with her?"

"Please. Too Hollywood. You're not going to try and conjure
up the one six feet under, are you?"

"Her name was Pam, and no, no séances scheduled in the immediate future."

"So who does that leave? You saw Carol, you're e-mailing
with Dao, and you know how to reach Maggie."

"There's Lorraine, his third wife with the dogs; Fawn, the
one-nighter from Las Vegas; Gloria from 9/11; and Olive Ann,
Cici's mother, but I don't really have the desire to meet her since
she's in some institution somewhere."

"Do your grandparents know you're doing this, by the way?"

"What am I doing? I don't know where anyone else is."

"Okay, I'll do more digging. Good luck with Rory. He's
meeting you at your grandparents' place?"

"He said he'd be there."

"So he'll be there, honey. Call me from the road."

Cricket is arranging the contents of the van when Bess makes her last trip down to join him. She sees a white canvas bag on the sidewalk and is about to thrust it behind the passenger's seat when Cricket yells, "Don't touch that!"

"Jeez," she says. "Touchy." He takes it gingerly from her and places it upright near where his feet will be. She asks him what it holds, but he ignores her, getting Stella set up in her crate.

The roads are clear. Bess is driving; Cricket is filing his nails. To Bess, the scraping of nails on an emery board tops the list of the most excruciating sounds in existence. "Can you stop that, please?"

"What, this?" says Cricket, holding up his fingers. "Fine." He puts the emery board back in his bag. "We're going to have a barrel of laughs, I can tell already."

Bess yawns and turns on the radio low to catch traffic and weather reports. She sees Stella in her rearview mirror, looking out the window. "You didn't want to leave Stella in Dogaritaville?"

"Shh," Cricket says loudly. "I couldn't do that to her again. The schnauzers ganged up on her last time and stole her treats."

This could be the longest few weeks of my life, Bess thinks.

Bess is relieved to find Rory's Corolla parked outside the house. She hadn't seen him since her visit with Carol last week, and she couldn't read his reaction over the phone to this cross-country trip. In fact, she hadn't been able to infer much of anything about him lately and she suspects it is the same for him.

"Hi Gerald," says Bess, getting out of the van. Gerald is peering in Rory's front window. His hands are hidden in the pockets of his hooded sweatshirt, which he wears despite the seventy-five-degree weather. "You remember Cricket, don't you?"

"Yes, I remember Cricket. Cricket has a dog."

"I do indeed," Cricket calls out from the back of the van. He lets Stella out of her crate, clipping on a leash. "Stella, remember Gerald?"

Gerald pats Stella on her head like he's bouncing a basketball.

"Where are my grandparents?"

"They're inside the house," says Gerald. "Your friend is inside the house, too, Bess. This is his car. It's not a nice car. I don't think he's very rich."

"You're probably right about that." She heads to the house. The screen door wheezes and snaps behind her as she enters. "Anyone home?"

"Hi," says Rory, appearing in the foyer. He's holding a Styrofoam cup that smells pleasingly of hot coffee. His smile is friendly but his eyes jitter with restless intensity.

"Hey," says Bess. She reaches up to kiss him. He offers his lips to be kissed, briefly.

"Bess, dear, we're all ready for you," says Millie, coming around the corner. She is wearing comfortable tan slacks and a light yellow sweater, and has tried to camouflage the circles under her bloodshot eyes with makeup that doesn't quite succeed.

Rory peers out the screen door. "Cricket's going with you?"

"Apparently," says Bess. "He sprung that on me this morning. His ex-wife in Denver is really sick."

"I see. And his little dog, too?"

"His little dog, too." Bess says this in a witch's voice, striving for levity.

Rory smiles and turns away. "Let me help you with that, Mrs. Steinbloom," he says, entering the kitchen.

The house echoes in its emptiness. It has reverted to a mere shelter: walls, floors, windows, the skeletal remains of a once bustling hub of activity and emotions. The smells are gone, too, Bess notices as she goes about the house surveying the rooms— no mothballs in the closets, rising yeast in the kitchen, Ben-Gay in the bedroom. It seems bigger, of course, but harder somehow, with too many right angles. And the basement where she finds Irv is painfully bare. He donated his mannequins to a local store and made sure he wasn't home when they were picked up. Bess finds him sitting on a stool in the middle of the room, looking as small and insignificant as a lone pebble in a shoe box.

"Hi, Gramp. You doing okay this morning?"

"Bessie," he says, standing to give her a hug. "I'm fine." He pats her cheek. "You?"

"Good, Gramp." She's been worried about Irv and how he'd take to their final departure. "Are you all set?"

"Let's go!" he says, and leads the way upstairs. Whatever he's been through to say good-bye to the house and the life he's led here, Bess can tell he's done it privately and on his own time. He must have made a pact with himself to make peace with it all— at least outwardly—before she arrived to drive him to his new home. She admires him for that.

"Oh, Bessie," he says, stopping at the top of the stairs. "Is it all right if we take Peace?"

Bess thinks for a moment. "The mannequin? With the Afro?" Irv nods.

"Sure," says Bess, making a quick tally of how little room they have in the van. Hell, they'll make room. "Of course we can." *So he didn't part with all of them after all*, she thinks. But Millie catches this part of the conversation and is suddenly furious.

"You're not bringing her with us!" she screams.

"Yes I am, Mildred! Yes I am!" Irv pulls Peace from the front closet and carries her around the waist out the door. Millie follows indignantly, her hands in tight fists, her cheeks flushed red. Bess half expects her to yell out, *It's her or me!* but Millie collects herself and turns back into the house.

Bess wonders if this is something she should get in the middle of. Is Millie angry over the object itself or what it represents? And what *does* it represent to Irv? To Millie? "Rory," she says, walking out with him, "while they're finishing up, let's talk, okay?"

"Please," he says.

Bess lets Cricket know where they're going and leads Rory to the stone bench in back of the house by the old cherry tree. For a few moments they sit in tense silence. Bess feels afraid. She takes a deep breath and reaches out to play with his fingers. He raises his other hand to her cheek and runs his thumb along her bottom lip. "I've missed you," he whispers. Her eyes well with tears. She has missed talking to him, honestly and openly. She has missed laughing with him, hugging him, making love to him, lying in bed in his arms. He is an attentive lover, the kind to slow the pace and study her with his fingertips. He caresses the inside of her wrists, the soft baby fat around her hips, the rim of her belly button, and by the time he surfaces to kiss between her breasts and finally her lips she is fully present, and she is happy. "I'm so glad you're here," she says, wiping her eyes. "I was scared you wouldn't want to see me off."

He lifts her chin to kiss her. "Bess, please don't shut me out. I know this is going to take time. We don't have to rush into anything, it's just . . . I feel like I might lose you, that you'll pull away from me and I don't want—"

"Stop," she says, softly. "You don't need to. I'm sorry. I didn't think what this must be like for you." She looks down at her lap. "I have to tell you something." She looks back at the house. "I saw Carol."

Rory jerks back as if he just popped a balloon. "Carol who?"

"Carol Pendleton. I called her and she invited me over when I was in Boston."

Rory throws up his hands. "Unbelievable!"

"I wanted to tell you before this. I did. It was hard not telling you. And she was just like you described. She was very nice."

His leg is shaking. He is alternating between flexing his fingers and tightening them into fists. "It's not right that you did that, Bess. It's *my* life."

And it's a free country, the little girl in Bess wants to cry out. "I'm sorry. I didn't tell you because I thought you'd tell me not to go."

"That's exactly what I would have told you."

"But this is how I approach things when I'm confused, Rory. I do research."

"I'm not one of your assignments, Bess."

"No, you're more important than that. You're the one I'm considering marrying for the rest of my life. Please."

Rory glances at her, trying, it seems, to figure her out. His eyes are swimming in anger. It lets her know she can't tell him about Dao's e-mail, or her intention to seek out the others. She will, in time, and hopefully he'll forgive her. After all, he didn't tell her right away about his wives. He of all people should understand how hard the truth can be.

"She's doing well, in case you're interested."

Rory runs his hand down his face. Bess can tell Carol's well-being is not where his head is at the moment. "Bess, why can't you see that it's all just . . . history?"

"What do you mean? It's not worth exploring? Look at what I do for a living."

"But you don't have to know everything about the past to live in the present."

"And you don't have to dismiss it all so easily, either." Bess realizes she has raised her voice, and lowers it. "You can't disconnect from a past just like that, just because you want to. I'm trying to understand you and you're a sum of your experiences. We all are. I need to understand those experiences to understand you."

"But those experiences . . ." Rory searches for words. "I was a different person in each of those experiences."

"You were and you weren't. I need more to go on than that. I had this friend once. She hardly listened to anything I said. I must have told her a million times how much it bothered me, and she would try to listen, but that would last a week and then she'd go back to her old ways. This went on for years until I finally said: *I can't have a friendship like this anymore.* She was not going to change. Do you see what I'm saying?"

"But she could change. She just didn't want to."

"I don't think she could. Or maybe she could, but it was a default mode for her. What's your default mode?"

"What's yours?" Rory cries out. "To distrust? Find fault?"

Bess looks to the house, recalling the fights between her grandparents. Is this what they feel when they argue? Like having a boa constrictor tightening around your chest?

"Bess," Cricket calls out from the kitchen window. "We should get going if you want to make Fallingwater in time."

Bess waves and says she'll be right there. Then she looks at Rory. Her mind is reeling. Is he having second thoughts about his marriage proposal? How long will he wait for an answer before his love wanes and the question is no longer in play? What if he finds out about her quest for his ex-wives and rescinds the offer for good? "Rory, don't give up on me, okay? I need to do this trip."

He sighs deeply.

In twenty minutes they are set to go. Stella's in her crate in the back next to Peace, her right arm bent upright in a permanent wave. Bess positioned her behind Millie so she wouldn't see Peace easily, and put a T-shirt and a pair of her shorts on her. Irv and Millie are in the second row of seats, waving to Gerald through the window. Millie's eyes are glassy. "I hope Gerald will be okay," she says. "I so worry about him."

Bess reaches through the open window and squeezes Millie's

hand. She knows how fond Millie and Gerald are of each other. But she suspects Millie's sadness goes deeper than that, tied up in the feelings of more permanent good-byes, of change, of letting go. She can't imagine what her grandparents must be going through right now. She looks over at Irv. He is fiddling with the map.

"So long," Cricket yells to Rory from the passenger seat. Bess had been cagey explaining to Cricket why she had been in a bad mood after her weekend away with Rory. Ever since, Cricket has been acting as if Bess is keeping secrets and Rory is surely to blame for something.

"G'bye yourself," Rory calls out. "Have a safe trip." And then it's Bess and Rory's turn to say good-bye. He leans on the van and looks at the ground. She wipes her sunglasses on her cotton shirt. *I'll miss you*, she says. *I'll miss you, too*, he says.

Bess drives out onto the suburban street. In the mirror she can see Gerald and Rory waving good-bye. Poor Gerald. She is touched by the poignancy of their image together.

"Look at Rory's cup. He's going to drive away with it still on his roof," says Cricket.

"Oh, I think you're right," says Millie. "People do that all the time, don't they now." She tries to sound airy, but her scratchy voice betrays her dolor.

"Mildred, you're sitting on my hat," says Irv. "Move your tuchas."

"America," says Cricket, "here we come."

Bess catches Millie and Irv looking back at their diminishing house. They turn back around and she sees in their faces the depth of their sadness.

CHAPTER TWENTY

Rory watches the van turn the corner and feels the emptiness of a long day ahead. There is a silence particular to the suburbs that makes him feel sleepy. It's a silence of distant noises—the tiny cries of birds and insects, the low hum of a car or plane or lawnmower as if everything interesting is happening far away. He remembers this feeling from his teenage years, lying on the front lawn of his post-WWII tract home, the other members of his family out somewhere: at school, church, the pub, playing football. He'd daydream of hopping a bus to Dublin, though he rarely acted on his escape impulses until his mother kicked him out of the house to get a job. Then, it seems, his impulses went into overdrive and have been strong ever since. At one point during this week a deep-rooted desire to escape his relationship with Bess and even the city took hold the way it used to in his twenties, that desire to say to hell with it and move on in the hopes it would all get easier if he left the hardships behind. But thankfully it was a fleeting thought, recognizable to him now as a puerile cop-out. Still, as he leans against his car under a warm sun in the heart of Rockville, he can't help feeling left behind and out of control.

He looks over at Gerald. Gerald is standing on the sidewalk, slightly hunched, rocking back and forth with his hands cupped around his eyes as if he's blocking out light while gazing in a window. Rory suspects he is crying. "You all right there, Gerald?"

Gerald suddenly takes off, walking quickly at a slant as if he's heading determinedly into a strong wind.

"Shit," says Rory under his breath. He gets into his car and turns on the engine. He has no idea what to say to Gerald, or even how to talk to him, but he suspects the right thing to do is to keep an eye on him for now. He follows behind Gerald, driving slowly while his mind wanders. *So*, he thinks, *Carol Pendleton*. He still feels angry at Bess for going behind his back to find her, though he supposes he understands why she did that. What's getting at him, at least in part, is that it made Carol real again. Like old scars from a childhood accident, his past marriages are inescapable, they are a part of who he is, but he's gotten good at hiding them from view and ignoring them or transferring them to the realm of a good yarn as if they happened to someone else. He even felt this way retelling the whole story to Bess as he did telling it before to others, like he was playing a part in someone else's play. Maybe that's why he's always a little surprised when his listeners are shocked. Don't they see it's just a story after all? But then Bess actually saw Carol. Carol is twenty-five years older, living (not surprisingly) in the Boston area. Rory imagines what their conversation was like. Did Carol frame him in a positive light? How much did she elaborate on the crazy, drug-induced shenanigans they found themselves in—the raucous party-crashing, cop-bashing, peace-disturbing tribulations of twenty-year-olds on the fringe? Rory is sure he alluded to it all with Bess, though perhaps not to the degree Carol might have. Though if she's anything like she was, she'd have the discretion not to go into details, especially not about his promiscuity. He was sure Carol knew how much he slept around, even though they never talked about it.

Oh God. Rory is suddenly bombarded with a jarring memory of one of the girls he had sex with back then who, he discovered too late, was a junior in high school. When he tried to end their trysts, she threatened to divulge the details of said trysts to the police, but somehow Carol had stepped in and saved his ass. Was it a phone call she answered, threats made in return? Rory can't fully recall. All he knew was, Carol made her go away. What would Bess say if she knew?

Gerald stops abruptly. Rory, lost in thought, finds he is looking at Gerald directly through his open passenger side window. "Gerald," he calls out, "can I give you a ride?"

Gerald doesn't answer right away. He just stands there, moving his fingers around. Then he walks around to Rory's side. "Is this yours?" he says, handing Rory a coffee cup from the roof.

"Ah, how stupid of me," says Rory, chuckling. "Kind of amazing it didn't spill."

"No, it isn't. You were only driving the speed of walking." Gerald walks back to the passenger side and leans into the window. "Do you want to see my beetle collection?"

Rory is taken by surprise. He feels sad for Gerald, which at the moment is a welcome distraction from his own self-pity. "Sure," he says. He puts the car in park, expecting Gerald to get in, but Gerald takes off again, walking more slowly this time. Rory follows him for three more blocks. Gerald turns into the driveway of a brick house that's smaller than its neighbors. Rory parks on the street. The lawn looks to be several days' overgrown, but the general appearance is not without its charm. Though the shades are drawn, the potted hydrangeas are as welcoming as the flowery doormat and the ornamental bunny on the front step. Gerald's bike (Rory assumes it's Gerald's) is leaning against the garage. There is a rusted rake on the ground and an unraveled hose pointing toward a pile of stones and four cut-off gallon milk containers filled with muddy water. Rory picks up a newspaper still in its plastic bag. "This is your house?"

"Yes," says Gerald, examining his milk cartons.

"What ya got there?"

"Nothing. Follow me please." Gerald picks up two stones and walks to his front door. He rings the bell three times. "That's a mezuzah," he says, pointing to what looks to Rory like a pack of gum stuck diagonally to the door frame. "It protects us because we're Jewish."

"I see." The door opens to a dark interior. Gerald goes in and the door closes behind him. Rory finds himself standing on the stoop in front of the closed door, wondering if he should knock or turn around and go home. Before he can decide, the door opens again to a short, plump woman in sneakers, hospital pants, and a cardigan. Her frizzy gray hair frames her round face and a particularly shiny forehead. She smiles up at him.

"Hello," she says.

"Hi there." He hands her the bagged newspaper. "My name is Rory."

"Nice to meet you." Despite her warm countenance, she doesn't invite him in. It seems like she's waiting to hear what he's selling. Should he say he's Gerald's friend?

"Excuse me, Mom," says Gerald. "He's here to visit me."

"Gerald, don't push." She points a doughy finger his way and shakes her head.

"Ma'am," says Rory, "Gerald and I met last week at Mr. and Mrs. Steinbloom's home. I was there with Bess."

"Oh! Forgive me, I know just who you are, Millie told me. Please come in. I'm Vivian, Gerald's mom. Very nice to meet you. You're from England."

"Ireland, actually."

Vivian studies him, head to toe, like she's gathering information for a gossipy phone call to Millie. "They got on the road all right? Millie was a wreck this morning."

"They seemed okay. Just sad."

The foyer is cluttered with coats, hats, umbrellas, a bike helmet, and other outdoor paraphernalia. On the wall next to a glued puzzle of a rabbi is a note reminding Gerald to take off his shoes and wash his hands. Rory can see the living and dining rooms from where he stands: the plush, baby blue carpeting, the sectional black leather sofa, the glass coffee table trimmed in gold. There are at least a dozen wooden boxes with compartments the size of ice cubes, each housing a little glass animal or figurine. "Can I get you something to drink?" says Vivian.

"No, thank you."

"I would like a glass of cream soda," says Gerald.

"You have too much soda."

"I would like a glass of cream soda, *please*."

"Gerald, how about drinking some water? Remember what the doctor said? Eight glasses a day."

"Your shoes," says Gerald, pointing to Rory. "After you take them off you can come up to my room. It's to the right." He disappears into his room.

"*Oy gutenu*," says Vivian, closing the door. "You're a very nice man to come visit my son."

"Oh, my pleasure," says Rory, bending over to untie his sneakers. "I think this morning was a bit rough on him."

"Yes, yes it was. Millie and Irv are very special to him. To both of us. And poor Bess, I think she'll feel their absence most of all. It's a good thing she has you." She says this last bit as if baiting him for an interesting response, but he simply stands and smiles down at her. He suddenly recalls Maggie's dad asking him what his intentions were with his daughter. The man scared him half to death just by looking his way so when he pulled Rory aside and asked him this question, Rory nearly vomited on the spot. *I intend to marry her, sir*, he had said, sounding prepubescent, and the man laughed. It occurs to him that people like Sean still laugh when he utters those words.

"How long have you two been together?" she asks.

"A few months now."

Vivian is standing with her hands on her hips with her thumbs forward, the way he's seen Gerald stand. Her eyes are still roaming Rory's surface: his hair, his arms, his jeans, his white gym socks.

"Bess is very special," says Rory to fill the uncomfortable silence.

Vivian goes into the kitchen and comes back with a large jar of salsa. "You're a lucky man to snatch her up," she continues. "I never understood why a bright, pretty girl like Bess never settled down. Can you explain it? Will you open this for me?"

Rory opens the jar and hands it back. He should be going up to see Gerald now before he says something gossip-worthy. "Please excuse me, but I don't want to keep Gerald waiting too long. Up that way?"

"Yes. You sure I can't get you something to drink? Something to eat?"

"No, thank you. You're very kind, but I don't think I can stay long."

"All right then."

Gerald's room is marked "Private Property" on the door and warns against trespassing. Rory finds him sitting at his desk playing chess on his computer. Rory clears his throat. Gerald doesn't react. "Hey, Gerald," he says.

"I have three minutes and twenty seconds left," says Gerald without turning around.

"Okay." Rory takes the time to look around the room. There is a mound of clothes on an unmade twin bed next to a tall dresser with a fish tank, various canisters of fish food, and what looks like four different types of deodorant. The posters on the walls are either in Hebrew or astrological or botanical in nature, showing solar systems and plant life and insects. A mobile of planets twirls languidly above a coatrack in the corner where a gray, janitorial-type uniform is slung—at least Rory assumes it's a uniform. Does Gerald work? he wonders. He had never thought about that until now. Also on the coatrack is a kitchen strainer attached to the end of a long cane. On his desk next to his computer are two stacks of books and several framed photos.

Gerald gets up from his desk and without looking at Rory walks around him to his closet. He reaches up to a top shelf and pulls down two wooden boxes and places them in the middle of his floor. Then he retrieves two more, and two more after that. He carefully arranges them in a semicircle and sits down on the floor in front of them. Rory can see now they are display frames, each about eighteen by twenty-four inches, each with dozens of beetles pinned in neat columns. Up close they look both prehistoric and futuristic with their tiny eyes and antennae, their armor and claws.

"This is a mega-ce-phala caro-li-na," says Gerald, pointing to one of the larger and more colorful ones in his collection. "It has seven abdomen segments because it's a male. I didn't catch this but I could have, I could have easily caught one even bigger if I lived in Georgia, USA."

"Impressive," says Rory, referring more to the sheer number of beetles and the care with which they've been organized and labeled. He follows Gerald's lead and sits down on the floor, too. "What's that one?" he says, pointing to a large beetle almost three inches in length with long mandibles like the horns of a male deer.

"That's a giant stag beetle. There are one thousand two hundred species of stag beetles in the world. It can't turn over very easily if you put it on its back."

"It's like me with a backpack," jokes Rory.

Gerald ignores him. He takes off his sweatshirt and throws it onto his bed. "I have one hundred sixty-two beetles," he says. "No, one hundred sixty-three."

"Did you catch them all?"

"No way." He shakes his head. "I saved up and bought these ones on Beetlesforsale.com. It's a company in Taiwan. The rest my father gave me. He's dead."

Now that Rory is on the floor and leaning against Gerald's desk he can more easily see Gerald's photos. One is of a man with a fedora, his hands in his trouser pockets, a cigar between his lips, his expression tough and impenetrable. It is the same man whom Bess saw in a photo and asked Millie about. Millie had said he was a bad man.

"I'm sorry to hear he passed away," Rory says. "Is that him?"

"Yes." Rory wants to ask more but is afraid of how Gerald might react. Was he really a bad man? How bad is bad?

Gerald puts his face close to one of the boxes as if he is studying the details of his insects. "Kenneth Gray is dead, too," he says.

Rory thinks for a moment. *Kenneth Gray?* Oh right, Bess's father. "Did you know him well?"

Gerald is now examining the side of one of his boxes, moving his head up and down while keeping the box still. "He let Bessie Girl jump on the sofa."

"I'm sorry?"

Gerald makes a fist and winds it up over his head like he's going to throw a lasso. "Kenneth Gray let Bessie Girl jump on the sofa. JUMP, JUMP, JUMP!" he suddenly yells with his chin in the air, frustrated with Rory, it seems, for not understanding. Then he goes back to studying his beetles.

Rory just watches him, wishing he knew what was going on in that head of his.

A long minute or two of silence ensues until Gerald says more quietly, "Bess didn't jump on the sofa anymore after Kenneth Gray died."

Rory knew Bess grew up without a father for most of her formative years, but he never really thought more of it than the fact itself. Now he finds himself imagining Bess at nine, ten, and in her teenage years. Was she lonely? Who taught her about boys? About men? Her mom? Might this have anything to do with why she never married? No one could live up to the memory of her father, sort of thing? *Aw go on*, he can hear the devil on his shoulder say. *Piss off with your psychobabble.*

Gerald reaches over to his desk, grabs one of the other photos and thrusts it at Rory. "That's me and Bess and Carol Gray in Montauk, Long Island, New York, on July eighteenth, 1976, eleven A.M. My mother took the picture."

Bess with her little pink bathing suit and pigtails looks to be about six years old. Gerald must be twice her age but looks younger. They are sitting next to each other and hugging, eagerly and genuinely hugging each other, arms wrapped tight, cheek to cheek. Bess is smiling widely; Gerald is not exactly smiling—his lips are puckered—but his eyes are engaged with the camera. Bess's mom is smartly dressed in blue shorts, halter top, and wide-brimmed hat. She has an arm around them both though she's not looking at the camera. She's looking at them the way Rory has seen moms look at their young children: full of pride and poised to protect. They all look so happy.

"You seem like you were having a good time there."

"Yes. Carol was my favorite person. Now Bess is my favorite. Mr. and Mrs. Steinbloom are my second and third favorites, but only because they're old, like my mother."

"Your mother's not old, Gerald," says Rory, though he is a terrible judge of age. Maybe she is as old as Bess's grandparents but doesn't look it.

Gerald pokes at his temples. "She's always saying she's *getting* old and if you keep *getting* old you have to *be* old soon. Also she snores."

Gerald sounds almost logical, though how did snoring get to be his threshold for old age? Should he tell Gerald that he snores? Even Bess snores—or at least breathes heavily—when she's on her back. It's kind of cute.

Poor Gerald. With only his mom left to take care of him, maybe he's angry at her for getting older. Rory is starting to feel a fatherly protectiveness for this boy-man. And he suddenly misses his own dad, picturing him either asleep on his threadbare couch or behind the wheel of his Volkswagen Golf. Rory's older brother, Eamonn, had been his father's favorite, that was clear in his father's nostalgic and often drunken indulgences whenever Rory lent him an ear. Not surprisingly, Rory grew up looking for ways to gain his favor. But that didn't mean his father didn't love him. Rory knew better. His father was a quiet, thoughtful, well-meaning man. Since his mother passed away fifteen years ago (*God rest her warm and loving soul*), he and his dad talk on the phone at least once a month and have managed to see each other every three or four years, the last time in Disney World in Orlando, one of his father's dream destinations. He suspects his dad would love Bess. As would his sisters, though he speaks to them much less often.

"I think your mom will be around for a good long time, Gerald," says Rory. "And I know Bess will always be there for you."

Gerald sits up straight and slaps the carpet three times. Then he reaches over for the farthest box. "This," he says, pointing to a shiny beetle about an inch and a half long. "This is my Bess beetle."

Rory leans in to look. It's not one of the more interesting beetles in the collection, but it's the only one that has a little smiley face sticker next to its label. The sticker is faded and peeling at the edges. "That's nice that you named a beetle after Bess, Gerald."

Gerald erupts, pounding the carpet with his fists, yelling, "NO NO NO NO NO!"

Rory holds out his hands, careful not to touch him. "It's okay, Gerald. Calm down. It's okay. I'm sorry. I take it back."

"Everything okay in here?" says Vivian, poking her head in.

Gerald quiets down, rubs his hair. "We're fine, Mom."

Rory gives her a reassuring nod.

"All right, Gerald. I see you have your bugs out."

"Beetles, Mom, they're beetles. *You're* a bug. *You* bug me."

Was that a joke? Did Gerald just say something funny? Rory laughs out loud, mostly to let Gerald know he got it. Vivian gives Rory a knowing look, then withdraws. They hear her footsteps down the stairs.

"Good one, Gerald," says Rory.

Gerald doesn't smile or look up from his beetles, but he says, "Thank you." He pops up and darts to his desk. He brings back a large book, sits back down on the floor, and opens to a page marked with a yellow sticky note. "Read! Read now!"

Rory takes the book and reads the paragraph under a photo of the beetle that looks like the one they're talking about. "Odontotaenius disjunctus," he says, "also known as the Bess beetle or Bess bug." He looks up at Gerald. "I'm sorry, Gerald. I stand corrected." He reads more—about how they are usually found in the woods in decaying logs and stumps, that they don't bite, and most interestingly, they like to live together and form small colonies showing social behavior, a rare trait among beetles. "This is very special."

Gerald is sitting quietly, fidgeting with his hands, looking out his window.

Rory looks at Gerald and thinks of his lifelong friendship with Bess. He is moved by their affection for each other, their bigheartedness, by Bess's kindness toward Gerald over the years. "Gerald," he says, "do you have a dream?"

"Everyone dreams four to six times per night during R-E-M sleep. R-E-M stands for rapid eye movements."

"No, I mean something you would love to do someday before you yourself get old."

Gerald tilts his head. He pushes down on his bottom teeth with his knuckles. He hums.

"Gerald?"

Gerald gets up and from under his mattress pulls out a February 2001 issue of *National Geographic* with a large red and yellow beetle on the cover. He hands it to Rory. The beetle, says the title, is called a jewel scarab. "You want one of these?"

"Yes," says Gerald. "But I would like to collect it myself."

Rory skims the article. The jewel scarab is a particularly colorful beetle found only in the cloud forests of Honduras's Cusuco National Park. Maybe, thinks Rory, he and Bess can take Gerald to Honduras some day. That would be lovely. "I hope someday you get to go," he says, feeling the sincerity of his statement deep in his gut. Then he stands. "And now, I'm afraid, I have to go." Rory takes pen and paper from Gerald's desk and writes down his phone number. "I don't have a cell phone, but here's my home phone. Give me a call if you ever want to catch a ball game or something."

Gerald holds the paper, pointing to each number Rory wrote like he's counting to make sure there are the correct number of digits. Then he writes down his phone number and hands it to Rory. "Here's my phone number. Don't call after nine P.M. Or before eight A.M."

"Okay. And hey, thanks for showing me your collection."

"You're welcome."

Rory reaches out to shake hands. Gerald hesitates, staring at Rory's hand, then obliges with a weak, quick-second gesture. He leads Rory to the front door. Vivian seems to be somewhere else.

"Say good-bye to your mom for me, won't you?" says Rory, as he puts on his sneakers.

"Yes. When is Bess coming back?"

"Not soon enough. But I'll make sure she visits you as soon as she does."

"Okay." Gerald and Rory walk out to the driveway. The midday sun is hot, the air thick with moisture, the sky threatening to storm. Gerald kicks the hose. "You can come with Bess when she visits."

Rory smiles. "Thanks, Gerald. I look forward to seeing you again."

CHAPTER TWENTY-ONE

Ever since Bess was little, she has dreamed of driving across America. She never thought about the particulars, the long hours of numbing boredom, the flat roads with nothing but gas stations and billboards, the neck aches from sitting upright too long. To a five-year-old in the 1970s, a car was an amusement ride with rock-and-roll radio stations. Highways had other cars with passengers to wave the peace sign at and license plates to spark letter games. She remembered trips like that from D.C. to upstate New York and if the short ones were fun, she could only imagine how exciting the longer rides would be.

But she never did drive across the country. Her father's car accident left her mother fearful of automobiles, angry at all drivers, and so sad as to become mildly agoraphobic. And that ruined the dream for Bess, too, for a time, seeing her mom like that and understanding at the age of eight only that her dad was laughing with her one day and gone every day after, evaporating from their home over time until he became, not a separate entity, but a part of her like an occasional ache.

But in her late teens the dream returned and took on mythical proportions. Her eleventh grade teacher assigned Kerouac's *On the Road*, and Bess reread it until the pages were frayed and fanned out from overuse. When she got her driver's license, she wanted nothing more than to *use* it, to search out her Holy Grail, her Shangri-La, her El Dorado. But then over the years, the idea of a cross-country drive for Bess reemerged as a quiet meditation, a desire to escape the blinders of daily life and see life anew.

She has therefore concluded that the emphasis for the next couple of weeks should be on the journey itself, and as such has let go of any strong desire to see a particular place. A few ex-wives perhaps, if she could find them, but not a place. This isn't, ultimately, about her, she told herself. It is about spending time with her grandparents and making sure that they see what *they* want to see, if indeed it is to be a last hurrah. But when asked, Millie and Irv weren't all that obliging. Millie wanted to spend time in Chicago to see her sister, and beyond that, she said, maybe it would be nice to see the galleries in Santa Fe. Irv said he wanted to see Alaska and Tahiti. Millie didn't think that was funny. Bess told them about the kitschy, manmade, usually large-sized pop art across the plains, but Millie and Irv didn't get kitsch. *What do I need with a seventy-foot ketchup bottle?* said Millie. And for once Irv agreed.

Bess was able to make a few suggestions that stuck: Fallingwater, the house built by Frank Lloyd Wright, was on the way to Chicago and an hour south of Pittsburgh, where they could spend their first night. The following day they would drive direct to Chicago. Beyond that, they'd decide later which way they

wanted to head first, south or west. And now with Cricket pointing them toward Denver, they had more of a plan.

"Talk to me, Thelma, I'm bored," says Cricket, pulling down
the car's visor against the bright sun. They've been driving west
for two hours with little more to look at than fallow fields and
silos and black cows. Occasionally, their ears pop. Smaller signs
on the side of the highway beckon them to the Waffle House and
Bob Evans Restaurant and Sheetz gas station and convenience
stores, while larger green signs overhead let them know which
Maryland towns they're passing by—Frederick, Boonsboro,
Hagerstown. The route flirts with the Pennsylvania border
all the way. It's the part of Maryland that makes the state look
greedy, the long thin beak of the bird nudging out a slice of West
Virginia. Bess takes a quick look behind her in the van. Millie and Irv, and Stella she assumes, have been lulled into sleep.
Peace, on the other hand, is still wide awake and waving to passersby. "What do you want to talk about?" she says.

"I hate when people ask that, so unimaginative. Tell me what
you're thinking."

Bess yawns. "I was thinking I was tired, actually. I got
up early this morning." She's had the AC on in the van to keep
down the noise, but she feels the need for some fresh air. She
cracks open her window. "And I guess I was thinking about my
dad."

Cricket is polite in his silence, giving her space to elaborate.

"You know he died in a car accident. It's probably why I never
got my own car."

"Remind me what happened."

"A Mack truck moved into his lane. Smashed him up against a cement barrier."

"And your mother sued the bastard."

"She won a suit. We basically lived off the settlement for a long time. That and whatever my grandparents gave us." She pauses, then continues. "I mean, I don't mind driving. But it sometimes makes me think about him, what he must have been feeling. He was dead when they found him, but none of us ever knew if he died on impact."

Millie stirs audibly in her sleep. Bess looks in the mirror to see her roll her head to the other side of the seatback. She had always gotten the feeling that Millie didn't think much of her dad. It was a comment here and there that made Bess defensive. "You know," she says, "my dad used to wake me up for school every morning with a shout song."

"What's a shout song, it sounds awful." Cricket uses a yellow handkerchief to adjust the vent on the dashboard, then folds it into fours.

"It's what shack rousters used to sing. The guys hired to wake up the work camps." Bess sings: "Wake up, Jacob. Day's a-breakin', peas in the pot and hoe cake's bakin'. Early in the mornin', almost day, if you don't come soon, gonna throw it all away."

"Charming," says Cricket. "Dare I ask what a hoe cake is?"

"I don't really know. He'd finish singing and I'd ask him to come back in an hour. He'd say no. I'd say, a half hour? He'd say no, all the time taking a step closer to my bed. Ten minutes? Nope. One minute? One minute, he'd say, and sit at the edge of my bed, rub my legs, and whisper the shout song until I sat up."

Cricket, uncharacteristically without some kind of movement about his person, sits quietly. "He sounds like a nice father. You must miss him."

"I do miss him sometimes. When I think of him, it's usually in the morning, maybe because of that memory. It's one of my favorites. And because he was often cheerful in the morning. He'd wake up in a good mood and then all the problems of the world would get to him and he'd be sullen by evening."

"I know the type."

"Was your father like that?"

"My father was never cheerful. His shouts, unfortunately, never turned into songs."

Right, thinks Bess. She had forgotten what Cricket's father was like: a traveling salesman who *drank his shame and hit to blame*, he had told her.

A few green signs pass overhead. "So how come I hardly know anything about your father?" says Cricket. "Shame on you."

Bess looks at Cricket. "I probably never told you I was married before, either, did I," she teases. "In fact," she says, amusing herself, "I've been married eight times."

"All right, now."

"Actually . . ." she says, sinking into a more serious mood. Now might be a perfect time to tell Cricket about Rory's ex-wives, she thinks. She should have told him days ago; as it is he'll be hurt that she waited this long. "I need to tell you some—" she begins, but is interrupted by her cell phone ringing from inside her purse.

Cricket looks to see if he can make out a number or caller. "Should I answer this?"

"No, give it here."

"That's not safe while you're driving."

"Cricket!" Cricket hands it to her and she flips it open, but misses the call. She checks the number. It's a New York area code, which reminds her of Maggie.

"Who was that?"

"I don't know. Can you take over the driving? I'll pull over at the next exit."

They stop at the Hancock Truck Plaza and Little Sandy's Restaurant. It has a 1950s-style general store that smells of motor oil and creaks like a haunted house. Irv stands at a wall display of baseball hats and tries on a black Harley-Davidson one with orange flames. "Take that off," says Millie.

Bess peeks in at the adjoining restaurant with its salad bar in a covered wagon. To the right, a plump waitress behind a counter pours coffee for the trucker hunched on his stool who sees something in the waitress's eyes and slowly turns to look over at Cricket.

"Good afternoon," Cricket says, approaching the counter. "Might I trouble you to top off my water bottle with ice, please?" A faint radio station is playing golden oldies.

"Sure," says the waitress. "Where you from?"

"We only just left Washington this morning and are headed to Pittsburgh this evening. We're driving my friends to Tucson where they're taking up new residence."

"Pretty country out there. Hot and dry, though. You're smart to stay hydrated." She hands Cricket a full bottle and wishes him a good trip.

Bess listens to this brief, unexpectedly ordinary exchange and feels sad for some reason. Maybe because she sees Millie looking at the sign behind the waitress that reads "Home Is Where the Heart Is." She wants to comfort Millie, remind her not to put too much stock in pat, embroidered phrases. But the stupid sign is weighing on her, too. After this trip is over and she returns to D.C., will it feel as much like home without her grandparents there as it did before? "C'mon, Gram. Let's go. Cricket, we'll meet you outside."

She leaves Millie and Irv on a bench by the store while she drives the van over to the gas station across the lot. With a moment to herself she takes out her cell phone and listens to Maggie's message. She dials the New York number.

"Maggie?"

"Speaking."

"It's Bess Gray."

"Ah yes. How's the trip going?"

"It's been okay. I'm tired, and not a big fan of driving. But I think it'll be fine."

"I smash cars myself. It's a wonder I'm still alive."

And a wonder people like my dad are dead, Bess is thinking. What kind of person brags about smashing cars? "Are you in New York now?"

"In Seattle. I head back tomorrow."

"I see, so this is your cell phone." Bess sees Cricket motion to her to hurry it up. She waves and holds up a finger to say, *One minute*. "I don't have much time to talk. I just wanted to say thanks for returning my calls and understanding my situation. I was hoping we could meet sometime. I should be back from my trip in a few weeks. Any chance you'll be in New York . . . ?"

"Which way are you driving across?" Maggie interrupts.

"Through Chicago," says Bess, fumbling with her keys. "We should be there tomorrow night and then we're staying a few days. Why?"

"Perfect. I connect flights in Chicago. Can you meet me at the airport?"

Wow, thinks Bess. *She really wants to see me. But why? Is this a good thing?* "I can meet you there, sure, but it's just as easy to meet you in New—"

"Good. Done. I'll call you with flight info." She hangs up.

Bess hesitates before she tosses her phone onto her seat. Why is Maggie so eager to meet? Why didn't she ask anything about Rory like Carol did? Why did it sound as if Maggie just closed a deal? Bess entertains the idea of calling her back and backing out. *What do you think?* she says to Peace through the side window. Peace's dark eyes stare out toward the western horizon.

The highway dips and climbs through the Allegheny Mountains. Just beyond the sign marking the Mason-Dixon Line they see the gruesome remnants of a dead deer on the highway, the head and a leg. The van's passengers look on in silence. There's the God's Ark of Safety Church and whiskey barrels for sale and soon the sign for Fallingwater. They park, leave Cricket and

Stella and Peace, and walk to the octagonal outdoor reception area. It's elegantly designed and smells of cedar and honey. And it's quiet but for the insects and a handful of other tourists who will join Bess and her grandparents on their tour of the house, the last one of the day, which begins down a gravelly pathway that proves difficult for Millie and Irv. The guide warns them of the long walk and the steps, but they wave away her concerns. "We're fine, dear," says Millie, walking slowly, holding on to Irv's arm.

Bess observes her grandparents before she offers her help. They both look distinguished and adorable. She takes out her camera and snaps a photo. "Smile," she says, and they do. *Love each other and be happy*, she wants to add, as if their response could be just as easy and automatic.

The house over the waterfall is a dramatic sight. The tour guide tells them Frank Lloyd Wright designed it in 1935 for the Kaufmann family who owned a department store in Pittsburgh. Millie is impressed this belongs to a Jewish family, that they could afford it even though it went eight times over budget. She stops at the portrait of Mr. Kaufmann, a handsome, muscular man in elegant attire. His gaze captivates her, Bess notices. "Did you know him?" Bess asks, thinking maybe the Jewish/East Coast fashion industry was smaller than she first thought.

Millie does not answer right away. She looks wistful. "No, I didn't," she says, her voice seemingly heavy with a half century of unfulfilled dreams.

On guided tours, Bess likes to trail behind. She remembers her mom was the type to walk in front, wedging in extra questions to the guide, but Bess is innately averse to groups. Besides, everyone but her is part of a couple. She watches them, inventing their stories—the community college sweethearts with the gleaming white high-tops, married too soon, he in the military, away a lot, she gaining weight, too tied to her mother; the polite and plump West Virginia retirees, he barbecues and falls asleep in his La-Z-Boy, she cuts coupons and sings in the church choir and removes her husband's reading glasses and urges him to bed; the urban pair in faded jeans, she keeping her five-year-old's hands off the furniture, he with their sleeping second strapped to his back, their BlackBerrys in the SUV and their neighbor watching their dog and watering their deck plants.

"Excuse me," the little girl in the group singsongs as she wedges past Bess. Her dad smiles and nods, as if to say, *Sorry, but isn't she cute?* Bess offers a polite smile as she is hit with a little pang of jealousy: of a little girl who still has her dad; and of a guy who looks roughly her age who is lucky enough to have a daughter.

"Bess, where is your grandfather?" asks Millie. The group has walked up to the second tier of rooms. Bess is admiring the throw pillows when Millie approaches. With her arthritic hip, she looks like a puppet on strings coming up the stairs.

"I thought he was with you," says Bess. She takes her grandmother's arm and helps her up the last stair.

"He does this," says Millie, slightly out of breath but loud enough for the West Virginia retirees to glance their way. "He wanders off, forgets where he is. The old man, he'll be the death of me."

"Excuse me," says one of the retirees. "I think the gentleman you're looking for is out there." She points to one of several terraces that jut out from the rooms like concrete trays. Irv is standing alone, his hands clasped behind him, his body bent over a small algae-laden pool.

Millie turns abruptly and marches outside. She swings Irv around with a strong tug of his shirtsleeve. "What's wrong with you? Where did you go?" she screams.

"Nowhere! There was a bird. Look," he says, pointing with his eyes to the water.

"I don't care about a bird, Irving. You don't wander off at your age. You could have fallen off a cliff!"

The full tour group is now staring at them through an open doorway. Though her grandparents' voices are slightly muffled, Bess can hear them clearly, tuned as she is to their frequency of fury. The thought occurs to her to go to them, tell them to keep their voices down, be a buffer between them and defuse their argument. That's her usual role. But looking at them now, she feels a stronger impulse to disassociate herself from the spectacle. *Here, folks, you have the American marriage, circa 1940,* she imagines a tour guide saying. *Observe how the female of the species screeches and moves about. The male becomes passive and frightened.*

The tour guide begins to speak again and moves the group in the opposite direction. Bess hangs back and waits. But as she waits she notices that this fight of theirs sounds different than what she usually witnesses. Millie does sound angrier and Irv . . . why isn't he yelling back? She steps closer to the doorway. She sees Millie reach out and clench her hand around Irv's forearm. "Ow Mildred, you're hurting me," Irv is saying.

"Hey," says Bess, rushing outside. "What's going on?"

Millie releases Irv's arm, says *feh*, and turns away. "I'm going back to the tour, which way did they go?" She heads where Bess points.

Irv rubs the spot where Millie grabbed him.

"Did she hurt you?"

"I'm fine, Bessie."

"Let me see your arm."

"No. I'm okay. Your grandmother was just worried." Irv puts his hands in the pockets of his trousers. "Let's catch up. This is an interesting place, no?" Irv walks slowly in the direction of the group.

What just happened? Did Millie grab him too hard? Did she hurt him? A vision comes to Bess of the day her grandparents told her they were moving, when Irv stood in his undershirt by the window looking weak and wistful. Bess remembers the bruises on his arms. She had thought then that he was carelessly bumping into things, but now . . . could Millie be that angry? An eighty-two-year-old who all her life has encapsulated her anger in the robes of social etiquette and quiet despair? It could happen, Bess supposes. And despite her grandmother's size and age, she knows Millie has the strength to squeeze hard. She has felt it in the tight, bony grips of Millie's hugs, in the lingering pain of a pinched cheek. Is it suspect that Millie dresses Irv—as she always has, laying out his clothes for him on the bed in the morning—in long-sleeve shirts despite the heat?

Bess doesn't want to think about it. It's absurd, really, if you look at them, which Bess does now that they are seated for the video that will end their tour. Even though they are not holding hands or even sitting together, they are unmistakably a couple. Bess wants to hold them. She wants to tell them it's all going to be all right, this move, this slow dimming of their lives.

"So how was it?" says Cricket back at the van. He lowers his *O* magazine to his lap. Millie and Irv are walking toward them through the near-empty lot.

"Nice. Cricket, do you think my grandmother is capable of hurting my grandfather? I mean physically hurting him?" Bess is talking quickly while they are still alone.

"Millie, that sweet dove? Where did you get such a ridiculous idea?"

"I saw her grab him and I thought—" but here she stops. Millie and Irv are nearly upon them. "Never mind."

"Cricket, it was beautiful," says Millie. "You can see the waterfall from all the rooms through floor-to-ceiling windows." Millie gestures with her hand above her head to show how tall the windows were.

Irv steps quietly up into the van.

The traffic through the tunnel to Pittsburgh is thick with stickered cars showing their loyalty to the Steelers. Though it's not fully dark yet, Millie and Irv say they are tired and wouldn't mind ordering room service at the hotel, so they drop Cricket and Stella off at his friend's apartment and head for the Hilton. Bess kisses them good night after they check in and, exhausted herself, clicks her card key into her room and falls onto the bed.

She remains still for a while thinking of Millie. Her book

on Zen and karate talks about anger and its dismantling of
self-control. Anger as a feeling, the book says, is natural, but it
doesn't demand action. One doesn't want to be angry and thus
lose self-control in a sparring situation, but this is true for life,
too, no? Is Millie losing control?

After a time, her thoughts wind their way to Rory and then to
Maggie and Dao and the other wives. In some ways it feels like
they are traveling with her, ghosts in her suitcase that fly about
the room now that she's alone.

She turns on her laptop to check her e-mail. There is one from
Dao.

dear bess,

i commend your inquisitiveness. May you catch the
clouded leopard through the dripping vines. but be cautious.

i did not seek out rory's wives. my explorations then
were more inward and onward. if they were behind me, they
were through the labyrinth of my own origins, a wild overgrown jungle of tangled confusions. but i am older now and
i see the wisdom of exploring jungles other than one's own,
particularly if they help inform you of your own terrain. it is a
cushioned route to the truth, but i would have welcomed it.
i imagine i might not have been so raw.

but like you, two of rory's wives found me. you are like
the first, a voice from afar, welcome and unfeigned, though
she had already left this life behind. pam was her name,
the one before me. i saw her shadow on a full moon. she

dropped a rose petal on a caterpillar and said without words that marriage to rory would be like that. it made a difference to me.

but the other one i did not like. she stalked me. she called my house several times a day. she sent mail i would not read. i confronted her. she said she must warn me. she said I should leave rory while i still had my safety.

i threatened to file a restraining order and she did not bother me again. her name was lorraine, i believe. i do not think she should be among the ones you seek. the poisonous traps of a jungle are best left unsprung.

peace,
dao

Bess sends an instant message to Gabrielle, thankful to find her online.

Where are you?

Pittsburgh. I'm exhausted. How come you're not out? It's Saturday night.

Paul's coming over. I introduced him to my parents tonight.

Wow, that's huge for you. How did it go?

Big love fest.

You like him.

Kinda.

C'mon. You haven't introduced anyone to your parents since Jackson Kendall in the tenth grade. He could be the one.

Whatever.

Uh huh.

What?

I'm just saying.

What about you? Go all right with Rory?

We talked. Hard stuff. Hey, check your e-mail. I forwarded a response from Dao.

Hang on. (Pause.) Shit, that's fucked up. You totally have to find her.

Who, Lorraine? Don't think that's a good idea. She sounds unstable.

What, like Dao sounds stable?

But she's on e-mail, not face-to-face.

Or so she tells you. She could be stalking you for all you know.

Stop it. (Pause.) What do you think she means by a "cushioned route to the truth"?

No idea. Like I said, lunatic. She communicates with the dead, c'mon. I'll get on it, see what I can find. I may have a lead on Fawn. She's out West somewhere, so you have time. Will e-mail details. Gotta go.

Wait, Gabrielle? (Long pause.)

You okay?

Yeah, sorry. Have fun with Paul.

What she was about to write was that she was worried about her grandparents. Gabrielle has known them since eighth grade when Irv would drive the two girls home from lacrosse practice. Irv and Gabrielle have a tender fondness for each other, but Bess always thought Millie was a bit cold to Gabrielle. It was nothing overt—Millie was polite enough to offer treats and ask after her family, but there was never a follow-up question or a relaxed moment when Millie made an effort to get to know her. Bess suspects her grandmother is racist deep down, but she doesn't want to dwell there. Millie would never admit it anyway. Still, Bess wonders sometimes if Gabrielle has those same suspicions. It shames Bess. Gabrielle would listen to Bess's worries about Millie's anger and be supportive, no doubt, but Bess decides it isn't worth polluting the already tainted image Gabrielle has of Millie.

Instead, she calls Rory and is disappointed when she gets his voice mail. She imagines what he might be doing—laughing in a group at a pub, jamming with his friends. "Hey," she says at the beep. "I'm in Pittsburgh. I'm wiped. It's been a long day. Not a bad day, just a long day. Well, kind of bad. My grandparents are fighting of course, but I think it's gotten worse. They made a scene at Fallingwater. I'll tell you, I'm going to dread being with them in public for the rest of the trip. I wish you were home. I wish you had a damn cell phone. Call me when you get in, you can wake me up. I'll go to bed naked and it'll be like—" The beep cuts her off and leaves her in silence.

She turns on CNN headline news on mute and gets ready for bed. Before she shuts off her computer she types a response to Dao.

Dear Dao—

Thanks for the information about Lorraine. She does sound unstable, which is kind of the way Rory described her, though in a different way. When he was married to her, he said she was sweet and went to church and volunteered at lots of charities, that sort of thing.

Rory told you about his ex-wives before you were married, right? He didn't tell me until we were dating for three months, which was also pretty much at the same time he asked me to marry him. Bad idea, don't you think?

I guess what I really want to ask is: Why do you think your marriage to Rory didn't last? Was it because of his past marriages? Forgive me if I'm getting personal. My grandparents have been married sixty-five years and I'm beginning to think it was a mistake for them to have stayed together all that time. I wonder if my parents' marriage would have lasted, if my father had survived his car accident.

Anyway, thanks again for your responses, and your honesty.

—Bess

CHAPTER TWENTY-TWO

Bessie! Where you? Why aren't you in my bed! I took a cab home, I swear. Sean's fault. See what happens when you leave? I keep telling Sean we're meant to be. Are you naked? I want your titties! That was Vincent talking. Come here you naughty naughty! Also Vincent. I'll make you an offer you can't refuse. *Godfather*. Greatest movie ever. Sean can go suck my BLEEP! Seriously, you're not answering your phone. You left me message. Your grandparents are naked! Ha ha! Okay, not funny. I hope they are all right. At least they have each other. Hey, I played with Gerald this morning. Did you know he has a Bess beetle? You're much more attractive. Did you know you were Gerald's favorite? It's because you're young. You might have to marry him instead of me. He's a good guy. Listen, I'm sorry we had a fight. I love you, Bessie. You get me. You have a banjo. I'll be your family. Just give me a chance. I just farted! So Carol's happy? That's good. Maybe Carol found the right person. That's what it's all about right? Getting married for the right reasons. Do you think we're right, Bessie? Do you think I'm old? Did I tell you I saw Gerald? I like Gerald. Let's take him to a cloud forest, okay? When you get back. When are you getting back? At least you're not seeing my other ex-wives. Fuck 'em. Carol's not so bad. She would help my case. Case closed! Rory McMillan the perfect husband! Yeah, right. Who my kidding. A perfect fuckup. A perfectly fucked-up human being who any sane woman should run the hell away. Maybe I really can't do it. Maybe if I do do it I'll die. Kaput. Dead on arrival. That's a loaded question, Bessie. Should we go there? I don't know, Bessie. I don't know what I'm doing. We should talk. May be for the best. When are you coming back? Are you coming back? Shit, are you not coming back? Are you going to Vietnam? Great. You know what? All the women I know can go to fucking Vietnam and figure out their fucking identity and have a big fucking Vietnam stir-fry together and talk about Rory the fuckit and how they all got away. Never mind. Ignore me, Bessie. I don't know what I'm saying. Seriously, though. Don't go to Vietnam okay? And don't die. I love you.

CHAPTER TWENTY-THREE

Bess wakes up moody. She thinks maybe it's because the hotel's alarm clock went off an hour early to the undulating voice of a Sunday preacher. Or because the open curtains reveal a sad, misty morning as gray as smoke, a bad beginning for a tedious day-long drive straight through Ohio to Chicago. She brushes her teeth looking into the mirror. *What's your problem?* she asks aloud.

And then in the defiant eyes that stare back at her she sees her father, not in photographs as she has been wont to remember him but alive, looking at her mother across the dinner table. *What's your problem?* she could hear him say. She can see him slumped over his meal, unshaven, holding the newspaper in one hand.

Bess sits on the edge of the tub, startled. She had not thought of her father in this way before, as husband to her mother, as a man in his thirties not much older than she is now. His death must have buried these images under the more endearing ones of his loving side he saved for her, his young daughter.

She returns to the bedroom and stretches out on the floor for a few warm-up positions she's learned in karate. What was her

parents' marriage really like? she wonders. She had always assumed by her mom's grief that it was something worth missing.
The few times she tried to ask her mom more details about her
marriage, her mom became as vague as her grandparents on the
subject, focusing more on the shared sweet and gentle examples
of parental adoration for her.

She takes a deep breath and on the exhale is flooded with a
memory of Pete Seeger on stage singing "If I Had a Hammer,"
or not singing so much as calling out the lyrics a beat ahead so
the crowd could join him. Her dad sang loud; Bess tried to sing
louder. She sat on his shoulders so she could see over the crowd
and when the song was over she touched his mustache because
it tickled, flapped his ears because they were there, let go of her
hands because she knew her dad wouldn't let her fall. That was a
year before his death.

What are we going to do with the world, Bessie Girl? he used
to say. She would come up with all sorts of answers—*Toss it in
the air? Hide it? Lick it through to its bubblegum center?*—but she
knew it was just something he said to pass the time. And their
time together passed often at parks, coffeehouses, school gym-
nasiums—anywhere there was folk music playing he went and
took his Bessie Girl (why was her mom never included?). He
liked to inform people that she had the same name as the singer/
songwriter Bess Lomax Hawes, sister of Alan Lomax and daughter of John Lomax, all of them well-known American folklorists, making her name reason enough to draw her to her chosen
field.

Bess's leg cramps from staying in a spread-eagle stretch

too long, so she stands and prepares for a shower. Would she be
so much like her dad if he had been alive through her formative
years? Or would she be more like her mom, content with her
grocery checklists and cabinet of cleaning supplies and low-risk
mutual funds? She would have been named the very practical-
sounding Beatrice, she was told, had her mother gotten her way.
Would Beatrice have become an angst-ridden folklorist? And then
Bess has this startling thought as she drapes her towel over the
shower rod and tests the water: Had she become like her dad the
same way Cricket became like Darren, as a way of hanging on?
And if so, who is she *really*, underneath all that?

No, that's stupid. She was too young when he died. And what
does it matter how she ultimately got to where she is now in her
career and in her life?

That sounds like Rory. She stands in the shower, lathering the
soap, and wonders why Rory didn't call her back last night. Did
he even come home and get her message? Was he thinking of her
at all?

What would her dad advise her to do about Rory if he were
alive? She can't imagine, not having known him well enough.
And her mom? Don't do it, probably. Or maybe not. Maybe her
parents had a lousy marriage and would have been divorced. Or
maybe they would have had a rebirth and fallen in love all over
again and bought a little house in Bethesda that smelled of baking bread and sparkled with jolly Thanksgiving feasts.

Bess turns off the water and towels herself dry. Then she gets
dressed and checks her cell phone, which she hadn't realized was
turned off.

‧⟨══════⟩‧

I'll be right down," she says to Millie, who phoned her from the lobby. Bess wasn't running late until she listened to Rory's voice mail, and now she's stuffing her roller bag with forgotten items and rushing around her room feeling nervous, phrases running through her mind like *we should talk* and *maybe for the best* and *I don't know what I'm doing*. She knows she shouldn't put too much stock in drunken messages, but can't they be revealing, too? He said nice things, funny things, and they made her laugh, but he ended with a statement about Vietnam. Could he still be in love with Dao? Maybe she'll play it for Cricket, see what he thinks. Then she'd finally tell him about Rory's past.

"Good morning," she says to Irv. He is looking at the floor and lost in thought. Millie is standing near the reservation desk, arms crossed, watching a couple check out. They are both frowning. Millie turns to Bess as she approaches and her frown disappears.

"Good morning, dear." Millie walks over to give her a kiss. "How did you sleep?"

"Okay." Bess drops her bag by Irv's feet. She rubs away the throbbing in her cheek where Millie smacked her kiss. Bess had tried once to describe to Rory what Millie's kisses are like. She means to be affectionate, Bess had explained, but she's bony and surprisingly strong. *Feels like this*, she had said, poking her thumb into the hollow, soft spot of his cheek. *Ow*, he had cried out. *That's some kiss*.

"Gramp? You awake?" He is scratching at a small ink stain on his shirt. Bess notices it is a long-sleeved shirt again.

He looks up. His cheeks are sunken and stubbly. "Oh, yes. Morning, Bessie. Where's your friend?"

As if on cue, Cricket and his friend Sylvie walk in, laughing, engrossed in a conversation that continues even as they are standing in front of Bess and her grandparents for several moments. Bess notices an immediate difference in Cricket: his gait is relaxed and slow and he is genuinely laughing. She can't remember the last time she heard Cricket laugh. "Four in the morning," Sylvie is saying. "In a green apron stuck to the radiator. Don't tell me I don't remember."

"Morning," says Bess, more loudly than she intended. "You two are chipper."

"Hello, fellow travelers," says Cricket, bowing his head. "Ready for another adventure on the open road?" Sylvie's giggle at that comment sounds almost mean.

"I'll get the van," says Bess. Stella is outside on a leash tied to a railing. Bess unties her, gives her a hearty head rub. The inside of the van is muggy and smells of old coffee. Peace is still waving, still smiling and wide-eyed, though she has slipped half off her seat to lean sideways against the window. She looks as if she's on an acid trip enjoying a private joke. "Morning, Peace. Sleep well?" Bess adjusts her to sit upright, picks a bit of yarn out of her Afro, and adjusts her hand so it is no longer in a wave. She looks at Stella sitting in the passenger seat and then back at Peace. "Cricket's friend kind of looks like a ferret, don't you think?" *Oh, completely*, she answers for them.

Cricket's hug good-bye to Sylvie is heartfelt and long.

"How do you know her again?" says Bess as they pull out of the parking lot.

"We met at the DMV thirty years ago," he says, spraying Lysol on the dashboard. "Isn't she a doll?" Cricket talks about her for the next twenty minutes, how her husband left her for a nurse, how she practically built her new sunroom herself, how she was the top-ranked bowler in the county. It has started to drizzle, just enough to make the windshield wipers squeak every now and again and require continual readjustment. Bess loses her desire to share Rory's voice mail with him.

"Excuse me," Bess interrupts. "Do you all mind if we stop for coffee?"

"No dear," says Millie. "I'd like some, too."

"I could use a restroom," says Irv.

"We just left," snaps Millie.

"So what? I have to go again. You want me to go in the van?"

"Ech, don't be vulgar, Irving."

Hey," says Bess into her cell phone, "I got you." She is in the back of a gas station's convenience store, where the others can't see or hear her.

"Hi," says Rory. He sounds sleepy.

Bess feels awkward. "So where were you last night?"

"I met Sean out at Iota. One of his friends was in the band, sort of a rockabilly sound. Good crowd. We ended up going back to Sean's place to watch *The Godfather*."

"Oh. I tried to call you. Did you get my message?"

"I did. How was Fallingwater?"

"Beautiful."

"Hey, before I forget . . . what's Gabrielle's number? I left my running shoes at your place and she has my set of keys."

Bess gives him the information and thinks, *This is weird*. Why isn't he bringing up his message? Does he not remember making the call? Should she say something? "What time did you go to bed last night?"

"I don't know. Was late."

"You were drinking."

"I had a few."

"A few?"

"Why the inquisition?"

"Because you've had a problem in the past." This conversation isn't going at all the way she'd like it to.

Rory is quiet for a moment. "You're right. It's been a long time. I was upset that you left, but believe me, I won't be doing that again soon. Not given the way I feel now."

Now Bess is quiet. "So you hung out with Gerald."

"Yeah, he showed me his beetle collection and I met his mom. Wait, how did you know I saw Gerald?"

"You left me a voice mail."

"Oh no. Last night?"

"Yup.

"What did I say?"

"You said you wanted my titties."

Rory laughs. "Well, that's true."

"You were worried I went to Vietnam."

"Oh boy."

"You said, 'We have to talk.'"

"Bess, honey, I had too much to drink. I'm a babbling buffoon when I drink, I've told you that."

"Rory, are you still in love with Dao?"

"No. That's the truth."

Bess sees Cricket making a purchase at the counter. "I should go," she says.

"Where are you?"

"We just left Pittsburgh. I'm at a gas station."

"Oh," he says, and yawns. "Okay. Call me tonight. I'll be home."

At well past one o'clock, the travelers take a seat at a deli in the warehouse district of Toledo, Ohio. Stella is in view outside, lying under an awning.

Bess had hoped to see Toledo. She wanted to imagine Rory living there, married to his third wife, Lorraine. She knew only that it was an industrial city on the westernmost part of Lake Erie, a sprawl of factories and warehouses. It seemed a destination ripe with potential on a day filled almost entirely with sitting and thinking and conversing. Looking at her map, she drove downtown and urged everyone to join her on a walk before lunch along the Maumee River. They obliged her for an eighth of a mile until the droplets of rain felt heavier and threatened to trigger the pain in Millie's arthritic hip. They passed up the Kid McCoy's Tavern with the boxing gloves on the door for a restaurant called Grouchy's, because it looked filled with local lunchers, though Bess had a fleeting thought of it as a bad omen given Millie and Irv's propensity for public wrangling. It sets her on edge. They settle in and place their umbrellas under a wooden table.

"Speaking of names," says Millie, watching the busboy pour

her water, "how does someone get the name Cricket? It's un-usual, no?"

"My mother coined it. She said I was her moral conscience, like Jiminy Cricket."

"How interesting," says Millie. "What is your given name?"

"Walter."

Walter, thinks Bess. "You never told me that."

"You never asked."

"How come I always have to ask you to share things with me?" she snaps, scraping the chair aggressively against the floor, annoyed that it is slightly off-kilter and too low. "I bet Syl-vie knows your name. Did *she* ask?" Bess is careful not to raise her voice, but is cognizant of her petulant tone. She gives in to the chair by slapping her back against its seatback.

"What's wrong?" Cricket observes her above his reading glasses.

"Nothing," she says, quietly, examining her menu. "It's just . . . my parents are dead, my grandparents are moving away, and you're a stranger to me." *And who knows if Rory is in my future?* "Forget it," she adds, because what she just said aloud is too re-vealing, too raw to share before she's had time to mull over the feelings and manage their presentation.

Cricket fans his hand out on top of her menu and lowers it to the table. "Darling, look at me."

Bess obliges. She steals a glance at her grandparents, who are regarding her with heartbreaking pity.

"My name is Walter. My middle name is Clive. The men in my family used to call me Trey, because I was the third Walter

Clive. My stage name, should I ever need it, is Bambi Barker or Tinker Bell Moon, depending on which childhood pet and street I use. What else would you like to know?"

Bess relaxes her shoulders. Her eyes moisten, but she will not let herself cry. She half smiles at Cricket, loves him in this moment. "I'm good for now," she says. "Thanks."

A stalwart waitress takes a pen from behind her ear and says, "What'll it be today?"

Bess can see in the faces of her grandparents that they are distressed by what she revealed. From the moment the shock of their move wore off—just hours after they told her—Bess expressed her full support, claiming her only regret was that she wouldn't be close enough to look after them. When they admitted guilt for leaving her she told them time and again she'd be okay, that it's perfectly understandable what they're doing. Now she's blown her cover. "I think I'll get the Garbage Salad," she says, hoping to lighten the mood. "What are you going to get, Gramp?"

It doesn't work. Irv looks wilted. His legs are crossed as usual, but his body looks caved in, his shoulders slouched, the loose skin of his unshaven cheeks droop like Stella's jowls. His unseeing eyes are now cast downward at the table, but they rise to Bess's eyes and soften when he hears her question.

"He hasn't even looked at the menu," says Millie.

Irv waves her comment away. "I don't need a menu. I'll have a hot dog. I haven't had a good hot dog in years." He twirls the ice in his water glass with his straw.

"What are you talking about, Irving?" says Millie, rolling

her eyes. "You got one at the baseball game we went to with Bea and Harvey, and you said the same thing. And then you had gas pains all night."

"So that was a long time ago."

"It was last month," Millie says too loudly.

"So I like them, what's it to you?"

"Fine. You want to kill yourself, be my guest!"

"Mind your own business!"

"Mind your own business, he says! Your business is everyone else's business, mister, and always has been!"

"*Enough!*" Bess cries out to Millie at such a volume the diners at neighboring tables turn their heads. "My God, *leave him alone*! If he wants to have a hot dog, *that's his choice*!"

A fork clinks a plate, a child's leg swings.

"I think we need a few more minutes," Cricket says to the waitress, who nods slowly and says, "Take your time."

Bess can tell Millie is hurt. Millie is trying not to show it by remaining poised and smoothing out her napkin on her lap and looking everywhere but at Bess, who broke their unspoken contract. She didn't step in to keep the peace. She took sides.

"I'm sorry," says Bess, reaching her hands out to Millie across the table. So much for Zen and the art of self-control. "I shouldn't have said anything." Millie shrugs as if to say, *It's nothing*, or maybe, *I understand, we're all hurting*.

"I think I'll get a hot dog, too," says Cricket, eyeing Bess. "You and me, Irving. Hot dogs for the men."

The food arrives and they manage to move on to other topics, carried mostly by Cricket and Bess. Millie offers short answers to long questions and otherwise eats her salad quietly. Irv cuts his hot dog with a fork and knife and closes his eyes with each bite.

"Gramp. Who was a better cook, your mom or Gram?" Bess already knows the answer to this.

"Millie," says Irv, sipping his water.

Bess waits for him to elaborate. "Didn't I hear you say," she nudges, "that you never met anyone who could cook a brisket like Gram? And what about her banana bread?"

"Indeed," says Cricket. "Millie dear, your banana bread is pure heaven."

Bess pokes Cricket under the table, points her chin at Irv. "Gramp?" she says.

Irv wipes his chin. "Yes, Millie is talented in the kitchen. I've always told her that. It's one of the reasons I married her. She's fed me exceedingly well."

Bess eyes Millie as if to say, *Now it's your turn*.

"Thank you," says Millie. It looks like she is going to say something else, but then stops herself. She does this often, Bess notices.

"And," says Irv, quietly, "she used to enjoy a good hot dog, too, if I recall."

Toward the end of their meal while Cricket is recounting scenes from his mother's kitchen, Bess catches Irv cutting a small piece of his hot dog at the tip and slipping it onto Millie's plate. Millie ignores it at first. She lets it stay there for several minutes until she thinks no one is looking, most of all Irv, then places it in her mouth.

Bess feels as if she has glimpsed an angel.

They walk after lunch to digest. Stella pees on the sidewalk. Bess resigns herself to the fact that she cannot possibly get to know Toledo in a couple of hours. She tries to imagine a young Rory strolling down the sidewalk with his young, plump, churchgoing wife. Would he have held her hand? Raced her to the corner? What happened to turn her into a mad stalker?

Cricket calls to Millie to come see a window display and as she joins him, Irv sidles up to Bess. "So how is Rory?"

This catches Bess by surprise. "He's okay, Gramp."

"Good, good," he says, thoughtfully. He coughs into his fist. "He seems like a good man. Someone you can really depend on."

Bess knows what he's trying to say, that she's not alone in D.C. This is one of his life buoys. Why not let him think she'll be well looked after? She doesn't want her grandparents to know there is trouble with Rory. It is her life buoy to them. "He's a good guy," she says assuredly.

In the van, back on the highway, Irv discovers the banjo that Bess has all but forgotten. "Gramp, you play, right? Play for us," says Bess. Irv strums the strings. Millie opens her window and lets the noise of the traffic in. Bess, from her driver's vantage point, presses the button to close it.

Irv begins to play and sing and suddenly the van is filled with a noise akin to a squealing squirrel caught in reverberating power lines. Cricket cracks open his window. Bess follows suit and with a fleeting glance at Millie's smug stare, opens the back windows, too.

"Gramp," says Bess. "Gramp!"

Irv stops his playing.

Bess thinks to engage Irv in conversation as a distraction, at least until they stop for gas and she can place the banjo out of his reach. "Where did you learn to play?"

"I just picked it up."

Bess and Cricket exchange looks. "Just like that?" says Bess quickly. "From records? Or did you hang out in Georgetown?" Now a wealthy, well-kept section of the city, Georgetown was once the bohemian section of town in the late 1960s.

"No, that was your father who went there," says Millie. "Your grandfather went where the *shvartzes* went."

"I went where the music was, Mildred, so who cares who was there."

"All the time he went there, even after we moved."

"Moved where?" says Bess.

"Out of the city."

Bess is elated. She, again, has rolled up her window because finally, now, this conversation is why she is stuffed into this gold van driving a bland highway toward Middle America. "That was after the riots in '68, right?" Bess has read extensively about Martin Luther King Jr.'s assassination and its effects on D.C. Twenty thousand people raised hell until Lyndon Johnson called in the largest number of troops sent in for a U.S. disturbance since the Civil War. They arrested thousands. The inner city economy was devastated. Many moved out to the suburbs. "Do you remember what the riots were like?"

"Scary," says Millie.

"They had a right to be angry," says Irv.

"So that's why you moved out?"

"One reason," says Millie, quietly.

"What were the other reasons?" Bess asks, which prompts a look from Cricket that says, *Easy there, champ*.

Neither of her grandparents answers.

"Gramp," says Bess, trying again, "you went to those jazz clubs on U Street?"

"Oh sure. I started going when I was eighteen. We'd drive down from Baltimore to see Jelly Roll Morton play at the Jungle Inn."

"You never told me that." Bess tries to imagine Irv at eighteen, a small Jewish, out-of-town white boy trying to see over the all-black crowd at a time when blacks weren't allowed in many white clubs. "Your parents couldn't have been happy with that."

"He never told them," says Millie. "He didn't like to tell anyone where he was going. Could have been killed and no one would know."

"I just liked the music, that's all."

"There were record players, Irving."

"Not the same."

An unpleasant after-lunch odor fills the van. Bess looks accusingly at Cricket. *Wasn't me*, he mouths, discreetly cracking open his window. Bess continues. "Why are you saying he could have been killed? Gramp? Did you ever get in any trouble?"

"No, no trouble."

"What are you talking about?" Millie exclaims. "You had a black eye and fat lip at your daughter's bat mitzvah."

"That was an accident."

"Liar."

Bess looks at Peace. She is sitting directly behind Millie, her Afro framing Millie's tiny gray head. Did Irv talk to women like Peace at these clubs? Did he flirt with them? Bess is getting that familiar twinge of frustration that happens when her quest for answers results in hard-to-imagine scenes and more pertinent questions. "Gram, did you ever go with Gramp to the clubs?"

"No." Millie says this as if to a dog that's jumped up for table scraps.

"No, she never did," adds Irv.

Bess can't tell if he sounds angry or wistful, but she is sure there is something in their exchange of *no*'s that she's not getting. "Meaning what? Gram, you didn't like the music?"

"No."

"What kinds of things did you do instead?"

"We stayed home," she snaps dismissively, conversation over. "That's it. Your mother and I. We stayed home." Her voice trails off, her body turns to the world outside her window, flashing past and behind them.

Cricket pats the air near Bess as if to say, *That's enough for today*, and Bess nods. It is enough, at least, to ponder: her dad escaping to one part of town for the folk scene, her grandfather to another for jazz and the blues, her mom finding solace in staying at home with Millie, the two of them, mother and daughter, feeling abandoned and angry. In the rearview mirror, she sees the short-necked banjo leaning precariously next to Irv and has a sudden urge to protect it.

The hours pass, Cricket takes the wheel, and the van slows toward night to the pace of increasing traffic as they approach Chicago along Interstate 90. The weekenders are coming home. Bess watches a passing subway train to their left. She notices how high the streetlights hang overhead, how more of the radio stations are in Spanish. She finds comfort in the electronic signs projecting the time in minutes it will take to get downtown.

She digs through her purse just for something to do: through her kiwi-scented Chap Stick, cuticle cream, hand lotion, mirror, pen and pad, cell phone. There is only one message on her cell phone, but Bess plays it twice. It's from Gabrielle. "I found Lorraine Doyle," Gabrielle says. "You're going to see her in two days."

CHAPTER TWENTY-FOUR

Rory's cubicle walls are covered with overlapping charts, scribbled notes, printed e-mails, and other pieces of paper tacked haphazardly with pins in primary colors. Yellow sticky notes fan out around his computer and hang from the two shelves that hold all his reference books and product manuals. Unlike his colleagues, many of whom keep their surfaces clear and their family photos angled just so, his office makes him look busy and relied upon. Every few months, when a product or an update is due and the software development team is staying until midnight, Rory will be the one to order the pizza and give the pep talks. Otherwise, each morning at nine-thirty A.M. he enters the building, winks good morning to Kim the receptionist, and settles in at his desk with his headphones, bottle of water, and bag of pistachios, racking up vacation days he will soon lose if he doesn't use.

Today, though, he has decided to leave early to meet Gabrielle. He had called her yesterday about Bess's keys and they figured out that her Monday evening yoga class wasn't too far from his office. He could get the keys and bring them back to her by the time her class ended, she had said, or he could meet her afterward and they could go together to Bess's apartment. As he ate falafel for lunch and lamented, yet again, about his phone massage to Bess, he thought of a third option: taking the class with Gabrielle. It would be relaxing, he thought, he has clothes from his gym bag he could wear, and it might allow time for her to offer advice about Bess.

He turns off his computer, says good-bye to whoever is around, and strolls down K Street toward Foggy Bottom. The yoga studio is on the third floor of a new building near George Washington University hospital. Its lights inside are significantly dimmer than those in the building's hallway.

"You here for the class?" asks the young, fit woman behind a desk.

"Yes," says Rory. He peeks into the studio behind her and finds it empty. "Am I too late?"

"You're early, but that's good. First time?"

"I took yoga a year ago and embarrassed myself by knocking over the person next to me."

She laughs. "I meant new to this studio. But good to know. This is a class for all levels, but do take it easy."

"Thanks." Rory pays for the class, plus extra for use of a mat.

"You can go in," she says. "The class will start in about twenty minutes."

Rory enters the sparse studio and sets up his mat in the back corner by the window. There is a wall of cubbies behind him but he has nothing but his keys and wallet so he keeps them by his mat. The wallpaper on the front wall is of a pleasing bamboo forest. On a ledge by the stereo is a small Buddha, incense holder, and gong. He lies down, closes his eyes, and tries to meditate. Dao tried to teach him how to empty his mind and breathe deeply, focusing on tensing and releasing individual body parts while letting go of negative thoughts like bubbles floating up to the sky, but he never quite got it. He'd fall asleep, grow bored, or get frustrated that his negative thoughts kept coming back like a film of floating bubbles in reverse. The closest he came to understanding its relaxing powers wasn't with Dao (for she often unnerved him), but with Pam in Seattle. Life with Pam slowed to a calming pace: slow walks, long discussions, quiet afternoons watching the rain fall on the hospital grounds. Sometimes, when her pain was acute, Rory would tell her stories until her medication took hold and she fell asleep. Then he'd sit with her and take comfort in her breathing, letting his mind wander. He recalls wishing he had known her before she was in the later stages of cancer. How would they have met? Would she be so accepting of his past? Would he desire her? He thought so. On the night of their wedding in a downtown hotel room, they lay in each others' arms. She kissed him and he felt something. He gently massaged her body, lingering on the places she said felt good. Though she had too little strength by then to lift her own overnight bag, she was able to reach down and help him orgasm. They laughed afterward, and then they cried. It was in those moments that he started to crave a future with her while at the same time understanding to his core that it was not meant to be.

"Hey."

Rory opens his eyes and sees Gabrielle standing over him, her rolled yoga mat tucked under her muscular arm, her water bottle dangling from her finger. Her belly button is pierced with a tiny gold ring. Whereas Bess seems unaware of her own beauty, Gabrielle wears hers proudly.

"Hi," he says, sitting up slowly.

"You were snoring." She bends down and unrolls her mat next to his.

"I was? Sorry."

"You're taking the class?"

"Thought I might."

"You do yoga?"

"Not really."

"Didn't think so." Gabrielle sits and extends her long legs out straight, reaching over to wrap her hands around her toes. Rory tries the same move and can get no further than his fingers wiggling above his ankles.

"You're good at this," he says.

"I've been doing it for years. It helps if you commit to something and stick to it, know what I'm saying?"

She says this last bit looking directly at him with a few bobble-head bobs for emphasis and he knows instantly that Bess told her about his ex-wives. He thought he had detected something in her voice when they spoke on the phone. "Bess told you."

Gabrielle looks at him as if to say, *Duh*.

"Right," he says. The room is filling up with mats and limber bodies. Rory is starting to feel out of place. "C'mon then, you're supposed to be on my side."

"On your side?" she whispers.

He tries to whisper, too, but he's never been good at it. "You're the one who introduced us."

"Funny, you didn't mention your *harem* when we met."

"That's not fair."

Gabrielle loses her upright yoga posture when she waves away his comment with a dismissive flip of her hand. "Seriously," she says, a few notches above a whisper, "eight of them? What do you do when, like, you're up there and the priest or whatever says *until death do you part*? You just laugh?"

The woman on the purple mat in front of Rory shoots him and Gabrielle a look. Gabrielle apologizes. The woman who checked him in is now sitting cross-legged at the front of the room, welcoming everyone to her class with a warm smile and good eye contact.

Rory understands that he is not to speak anymore, though his thoughts are loud in his head as he follows the movements of the teacher, rolling his shoulders, reaching up, breathing in and letting it out. For the next hour he glimpses Gabrielle's positions: the hold on her down dog, the reach of her warrior. Rory feels like a Saint Bernard among statues. It doesn't help that he's having a hard time focusing on what he's doing, with thoughts of Bess and Gabrielle throwing him off-balance. Did Bess tell Gabrielle about his voice mail? That would be bad. He thinks back to when he and Gabrielle first met. He'll admit he was cagey about his past, since they quickly started talking about Bess's party and being single. Rory told her he was single because he hadn't met the right woman. That was true, wasn't it? Bess Gray, the woman Gabrielle wanted to fix him up with, the woman Gabrielle said was beautiful and smart and who loved foreign men and had killer abs and not a mean bone in her body, why was this woman still single? Rory wanted to know. Was she too picky? *Don't you watch* Sex and the City? Gabrielle had asked. He didn't. *Well it's the curse of our generation. And if you ask me, it's all your fault.* My fault? *Men like you, not having your shit together.*

"Psst," says Gabrielle to get his attention. Rory's head is buried under his hips, an awkward position he got into not without difficulty by lying on his back and swinging his legs up over his head. Everyone else is relaxing on their backs with their eyes closed.

"I can't get out of this," he says awkwardly to Gabrielle under the bunched fabric of his T-shirt and sweatpants.

"See now, that's just sad," she says quietly as she gets up, grabs his legs, and pushes them up over his head and back to the floor.

He sighs with relief. "Thanks."

She goes back to her own mat, fixing her towel for a headrest. "I should have left your sorry ass in the air."

"Admit it, it's a cute ass." Rory is smiling even though he's on his back supposedly relaxing.

"Yeah, well, somebody should kick it straight into the middle of next week if you ask me."

The teacher walks among them, spritzing something floral-smelling into the air. After a few minutes, she rings a gong three times signaling the class members to sit up, put their hands together, and say, *Namaste.*

"Namaste," he says to Gabrielle.

"Namaste," she repeats. People stand slowly and start to gather their things. She hands him a paper towel. He wipes his brow. "For your mat, Einstein," she says, handing him another. When Gabrielle's guard is up, Rory noticed tonight, Gabrielle moves like a lioness, confident in her skin, her dark eyes alert and on the offensive. The rest of the time, or at least most of the time Rory has spent with her, her confidence plays out in a penchant for teasing. He wipes down his mat, rolls it up, and returns it to the front room. He and Gabrielle retrieve their shoes among the dozen or so pairs at the entrance.

"I suppose you want these," she says, handing him a set of keys.

"Ah, thanks. How will I get them back to you?"

"You can keep those. I have another set. Bess said it was okay to give them to you. She said she's got nothing to hide." If Gabrielle had a signature look, it would be lips pursed and a slight tilt of her head downward so she's looking at you out of the top half of her eyes.

"I think you're enjoying this."

"Hey, you can thank Bess for that one."

The evening air outside is balmy but not hot. They decide to walk the extra blocks to catch the Red Line. Gabrielle leans to the left to offset the weight of the large striped canvas bag hanging off her right shoulder. Rory offers to carry it but she declines. "So," she says, "you been in touch with any of them?"

"Who?"

"The cast of *Lost*. Who do you think?"

"My ex-wives? No. Why?"

Gabrielle casually eyes a dress in a window display. "Just asking."

Rory suddenly feels suspicious. Bess must have told her about Carol.

They walk on for a block in silence. Rory is intimidated by Gabrielle, knowing that whatever impression he makes on her will now be communicated to Bess. He wants to ask her about Bess, but doesn't exactly know what or how to ask.

At the next corner they stop and wait for the light. "Do you know how we met?" says Gabrielle.

"You and Bess?" He's relieved that Gabrielle is guiding the conversation. "Didn't you go to school together?"

"Yeah, but that's not why we're friends. I got really sick when I was thirteen. I had meningitis, was home from school for, like, three weeks. Bess and I were in three of the same classes. We weren't friends, but we knew each other. She was the one who brought me the homework and helped me keep up with what we were learning. I was eight long blocks out of her way. Sometimes she stayed late, keeping me company, doing whatever. She knew I liked this boy in one of our classes, too, and she'd carry notes between us. My whole family loved her. She was shy, but she was a good sport about things. She played jump rope with my little sisters, listened to my brothers' records, helped my mom cook, asked a lot of questions. You know I think she came initially because she was kind, but I think she kept coming back because she craved a family. So it's life's cruel joke that she's still single into her thirties."

They reach the entrance to the Metro. "You're a good friend to her, Gabrielle."

"She brings it out in people."

"Can I ask . . . do you think she'll come around or am I a lost cause?"

"*Are* you a lost cause?"

"I truly hope not."

They head down the escalator and touch their SmarTrip cards to the turnstiles. Gabrielle turns to confront him. "Rory, let's say you guys get married. What are you going to do when the going gets tough, huh? What are you going to do when you find out she gets cranky if she doesn't get enough sleep? Or that she really doesn't like to watch sports, or she freaks out if you're late? Have you seen her wipe her nose on her sleeve? It's not pretty."

"Okay, okay," says Rory, holding his hand out to stop her. "I get it. She's not perfect, neither am I. Gabrielle, believe me. I'm serious about wanting this to work."

Gabrielle's look is hard to discern. She takes a few steps back and turns to face her destination. "Then really show her."

"How?"

"I don't know," she calls out as she walks away. "Figure it out."

CHAPTER TWENTY-FIVE

Bess walks into the afternoon sun shining off the shop windows along the Magnificent Mile. They've been in Chicago for two and a half days; it's Wednesday now. She and her grandparents are staying at a hotel on Michigan Avenue where she was able to get a discounted rate. Cricket found a place nearby that accepts dogs. Yesterday morning she joined her grandparents for brunch at Millie's sister's apartment in Lincoln Park. Bess's great-aunt Esther lives alone on the twenty-sixth floor of a forty-three-floor building overlooking Lake Michigan. Bess was perspiring looking out the floor-to-ceiling windows.

"Don't like heights, dear?" Esther had said, offering her a bowl of olives and miniature pickles.

"Not used to it. D.C. isn't allowed to have skyscrapers." Bess listened to their conversation about bunions and generic drugs and Esther's son's three children growing up so fast. She ate bagels and smoked salmon and cucumber salad doused in vinegar and some nice ripe melon her aunt was eager for her to eat. She touched the textures around the apartment—the lace doilies, the silk flowers, the porcelain figurines, the pastel frames of photos of distant family relations. There was one photo of her mom and Millie and Irv at some function. Millie and Irv were seated below her mom, their shoulders barely touching, their mouths closed in posed smiles. Bess's mom was leaning in between them, her smile broad as if she had been the one to say smile for the camera and had led by example.

"I wish—" Millie started to say, taking the photo from Bess.

Bess had waited for her to say more, but Millie was quiet. She remembered something Millie had said at her mom's funeral: *No mother should survive her child*. Bess wrapped her arm around her grandmother's shoulder. "I wish, too," she said.

"So tell me," Esther had interrupted, "why is a girl like you still not married, eh?"

This was Bess's cue to leave. She knew people were often thinking that around her, but hearing it voiced always made her feel lousy. Anyway, she knew they wouldn't discuss in front of her the more important topics of her grandparents' move, their finances, Esther's failing lungs. Would they talk about their feelings? Maybe. Bess guessed Millie and her sister would get to that while Irv took a nap on the couch.

An hour later, she met Cricket at a corner for a few hours of clothes shopping. Like a cow and a butterfly, Bess moved slowly, chewing her gum, making her way methodically along the sales racks while Cricket flitted about the interior of each store with outstretched arms and an eye for color. Outside, too, Bess liked to go up one side of the street and down the other; Cricket didn't see the logic of that when there was a store one absolutely must not miss right across the street.

In the evening, she checked her e-mail at the hotel and was heartened to find a message from Rory, even though it was short and simple: "My day," he wrote with a colon. "Worked late; cooked pancakes for dinner, half of which fell on the floor when I flipped them; called three cable companies; checked out new music software. James Bond has nothing on me. Hope you're having fun. I miss you. I love you." They had spoken twice in the last couple of days. He told her he was sore from his yoga class with Gabrielle; she told him more details about her grand-parents at Fallingwater. Mostly, though, they worked through some of what came up in his drunken voice mail. He allayed her fears that he might still be in love with Dao and she allayed his that she wasn't coming back. But the topic of marriage was still raw. *Could* he? *Should* she? Those were questions they couldn't yet answer and grew tired of thinking about after a while. No wonder his latest e-mail was innocuous, she thought. She had re-sponded in kind: "Dear 007," she wrote, "that's a movie I'd pay to see. Here was my (um . . . Lara Croft?) day: ate melon balls at my great-aunt's apartment; helped Cricket pick out a table runner; wolfed down two pieces of deep-dish pizza; wished you were here. I love you back."

Now she's walking along the lake by herself, watching the beachcombers and bathers, wondering why she hasn't yet gotten the guts to tell Cricket about Rory's ex-wives, or tell Rory about her search for the rest of them. In an hour she is reluctantly get-ting back in the van to meet Maggie at the airport. Tomorrow, she apparently has an appointment with Lorraine.

Gabrielle had hit the jackpot on the whereabouts of Lorraine

Doyle, Rory's third wife, thanks to Gabrielle's cousin, a cop, and a record of petty theft and violations of temporary restraining orders. Turns out she's a hairdresser in Joliet, Illinois, about an hour and twenty minutes south of Chicago. Gabrielle took the liberty of making an appointment for Bess for a cut and blow dry.

"That's not funny," said Bess.

"You have to do it. And take her picture. I want to see what this woman looks like. Oh, and by the way, I think Rory's last wife is back in D.C."

"Gloria? Did Rory tell you that?"

"No, I told you, he said he doesn't keep in touch with any of them so I didn't push it. I found her brother's name on a few 9/11 memorial Web sites where people can write comments about the victims. Gloria writes in every few months. Nothing major, just how much she misses him, but she happened to mention that she was back in the District where she first heard the news, and how strange that is. Last entry was in April. Want me to ask her to get in touch?"

"On the Web site? No, that's tacky. Let's leave it for now. Good work, though. I owe you."

Bess stops along her walk to admire a sailboat out on the lake. It's been over a year since she's been to Chicago, when she came to meet with the curators of the Polish Museum of America about a traveling exhibit. Early this morning she had coffee with the new head of the University of Chicago Folklore Society, but it was nothing official.

It's nice, this time alone. She sits on a stone wall, dangling her legs, and wonders what Michigan town is across the water that she can't see.

And then her thoughts turn to Maggie.

I'm outside baggage claim. United. Where are you?"

"Almost there," says Bess, following the road signs toward arrivals. She pulls up to the curb. Maggie had described herself as tall, thin, chin-length black hair, won't know what she's wearing but carrying a woven straw bag and maybe, if she remembers, a red scarf around her black roller bag. Bess sees the scarf and is immediately intimidated. Even the two gentlemen next to Maggie are checking out her figure in her black pencil skirt and sleeveless, racer-back white top. Her long legs are stunning in strappy sandals. Her toned biceps cascade down to chunky modern bracelets and shining red fingertips. Her bust is sizable and her neck is long and graceful, framed in a relaxed, layered bob, swept forward into her face so her casual gesture to brush hair out of her eyes looks sexy even from afar.

Bess parks the van and checks her teeth in the mirror. With her hair up in a halfhearted ponytail and mocha stains on her prairie skirt, Bess feels like Maggie's poor gofer. She walks to the curb. "Maggie? Hi. I'm Bess." She holds out her hand.

"Hello," says Maggie. "Of course, there's the gold van." Her handshake could hold a person hanging from a bridge.

"Should I park? I didn't know how much time you have." They had discussed having a drink in the airport, but Maggie never verified the arrangements.

"Change of plans. I'm staying overnight. Let's get out of here."

Rory was right, Maggie's green eyes are piercing. A dark freckle on her cheek looks like an accessory. She smells faintly, pleasingly of musky perfume.

"Friend of yours?" she says, pointing to Peace in the back-seat.

"It's my grandfather's." Bess had removed much of the bulky contents of the van, especially Gaia's box, in case she had to park it on the street. She kept Peace for company, and because a few days ago at a rest stop she had heard a little girl with a doll say, "Look, Mom, they have a grown-up's doll." Bess liked the idea of that, of having her own quiet, comforting protector with her.

"Take this exit!" Maggie points to what's immediately coming up so that Bess has to swerve across two lanes to catch it. She cuts off a taxi. The taxi driver honks. Maggie blows him a kiss. "Excellent," she says. "Now turn here."

"Where are we going?"

"I know a place. Best sausages in Chicago. Take the next right."

Maggie McCabe, gorgeous as ever!" A well-dressed man with the manner of the establishment's owner greets Maggie at the door. He embraces her, then makes a show of grabbing her ass. "What did you do with my little Irish girl, you corporate whore?"

"She's still here, Mick," says Maggie, pinching his cheek. "And she'll take a pint of Guinness. And one for my friend here."

Bess feels tiny. She hates Guinness. She doesn't even like beer all that much. "I'll just have a club soda, thanks. I'm driving."

Maggie and Mick are arm in arm, looking at her. "Mick," says Maggie, "this is Bess. She's dating my first love. Can you believe that? My first love!"

"Actually, he's my fiancé," says Bess, but she says it so meekly that neither Mick nor Maggie hear her over their conversation that has them laughing and patting each other on the back. She wonders why she even said that. She never said yes to his proposal, has never even said that word aloud.

Ceiling fans turn slowly over a black-and-white tiled floor and rounded red booths along the side wall. It's almost evening, when Bess assumes a piano player will start his shift and pull in more patrons than the seven or eight currently lounging about.

Maggie scoops Bess's elbow and steers her toward a private booth. "Mick, we're taking a table," she calls out.

The two of them slide in and stare at each other. "So tell me," they say together and look amused. "About Rory," Maggie finishes. "I want to know everything about him."

Has he aged well? Maggie wants to know. Is he gray? Is he handsome still, with that scrumptious smile? Did he quit smoking? Is he playing soccer? Is he still playing his fiddle? Where does he live? Is he happy? Does he ever talk about me? Does he still cross his eyes slightly when he comes? Ha! Tell me, does he not have the sexiest cock you've ever seen?

Maggie is soaking up Bess's information and firing more questions faster than Bess can answer, or wants to answer, or can't answer even if she had time. Is he happy? *Am I?* Rory suddenly seems like a stranger to her. How can it be that he liked someone like Maggie and now fancies someone like her? Does he have a type? Did he see similar traits in his wives or was he going for opposites? "You know what?" she says to a passing waitress. "I changed my mind. I'll have a cosmopolitan, please."

"Good for you," says Maggie. "So what about you?"

"What about me?"

"Ever been married?"

"No." Bess sees in Maggie a familiar expression she has grown to hate. "There's nothing wrong with me. I've just had bad luck, that's all."

"I didn't say anything."

"You didn't have to. Are *you* married?"

Maggie leans her head back on the seat. "I was. Divorce went through in May."

"I'm sorry. Is he the same man you left Rory for?"

Maggie looks up at Bess, puzzled. "The man I——? No. I met John a few years after I'd moved to New York."

"Oh." Bess tries to access what information Rory had told her about their breakup. Didn't she leave him for an attorney, someone who brought her to New York to be an actress? "Can I ask what happened?"

"Who's to say? Fatigue. Boredom. Depression. Infidelities." Maggie's voice gets softer with each vague, unattributed reason. She turns to the bar with her empty mug and signals for another beer. "How's Rory's family?"

"Fine, I think," says Bess, getting a little weary of Maggie's inquisition. "I mean, his mom passed away, and his brother did, too, before that. I can't remember his name."

"Eamonn," Maggie says softly. "That was a sad day when I heard the news."

"Did you know him? Well, I mean?"

"I did, yeah."

It is the way Maggie says *yeah* that makes Bess notice her vulnerability for the first time since they spoke on the phone days ago. It could even be that her brogue slipped out on that word, giving a glimpse behind her certitude of a young immigrant teenager, scared, but hell if she'd show it.

Mick delivers Bess's cosmopolitan. "Your drinks are on the house, ladies," he says. He is older, in his early sixties, Bess guesses. He carries his age well the way some gray men can, elegant and polished like a mid-twentieth-century movie star.

"Thanks," says Bess.

"Cheers," says Maggie. "To Rory." She clicks her mug to Bess's delicate cocktail glass and spills sticky pink liquid down Bess's wrist. "Mick, join us."

"For a quick minute," he says, slipping into the booth. "How're the kids?"

"Brats, every one of them. I hate the teenage years."

Mick laughs.

"You have kids?" asks Bess. For some reason, she hadn't thought of this possibility.

Maggie passes a photo from her wallet. "Erin's my oldest. Sixteen. Wants to be a pilot, though she says I'm ruining her dream by grounding her too often. She's funny. I hate her boyfriend. That's my middle one, Muriel, who thank God doesn't yet notice boys. She's too busy playing basketball and ruining my hardwood floors. And that's my baby, Caroline. Poor thing just got teased by her classmates and made me go shopping for a training bra."

"And they love New York, eh?"

"They love New York when they're with their father. He spoils them."

Bess looks hard at the photo. The three girls look alike, look like Maggie, even look like Rory perhaps, though Bess knows she's imagining that. Still, it's difficult to avoid the what-ifs with Rory's past. What if these were his girls? Would he be divorcing Maggie? Would they be happy?

"What I don't get," says Maggie to Bess, "is how Rory did it. I mean, forget the marriages. How did he go through a divorce so many times? The guy," she explains to Mick, "my first love I was telling you about . . . he's been married and divorced eight times."

Mick whistles. "No shit. I hope he's not picking up the alimony."

Maggie and Mick look at Bess. "I don't know," says Bess. "I don't think he did, or is." What an obvious question. How come she hasn't thought to ask him this?

"You know," says Maggie, "you would have looked at the two of us when we first came here and thought Rory was the one who would have settled down, had kids, and me, I would have been the one to keep shaming the priests."

"Excuse me," says Bess, lumbering off the low seat. "Can you tell me where the restroom is?" Mick points. She walks to where she can't see them behind the high, curved seatbacks of the booth and decides that it was a bad mistake to leave her bag. She needs her cell phone to call Cricket about dinner. She turns back to the booth, but something about the hushed, staccato nature of Mick and Maggie's private conversation—*Gerry's doing it. When? Next week. What's he saying? Reconciliation*—makes her retreat to the bathroom.

She returns to find Maggie sitting alone, rifling through her own purse. "God, I want a cigarette," says Maggie. After a few minutes she gives up her search with a disgruntled shove of her purse back into the corner. She looks at Bess. "What?"

"I didn't say anything."

Maggie drinks from her glass. She looks away.

"So," says Bess, "Rory said you wanted to be an actress."

"Didn't pan out."

Maggie mindlessly wipes the condensation off her mug with her forefingers. She seems young and old at the same time: sad, like a little girl who's dropped her favorite doll in a puddle but is too tired to pick it up and wipe off the mud. "I loved him, you know," she says.

Bess feels a nervous jolt in her chest. "Rory?"

"He couldn't let go and I didn't want him to. The phone would ring and I'd know it was him and I couldn't answer. Then the ring would stop and I'd feel like I was trapped under water." Maggie shifts in her seat after a moment and surfaces from her melancholy. "But that was a long time ago."

Could Maggie still be in love with Rory? Is that why she was so eager to meet Bess? To see her competition? Bess should ask this very question. But she is scared. She feels insignificant in

Rory's world, as if she is a Johnny-come-lately to a land already well settled.

Bess's dejection must be obvious for someone like Maggie to look at her the way she does now, her head cocked to the side. "Rory and I wouldn't have made it," she says. "We were too young. And now we're too old."

They sip their drinks. Two couples enter the bar and perch around the piano.

"They say," says Maggie, "you should never marry someone you wouldn't want to go through a divorce with. Damn good advice." She raises her glass. "To good advice and new beginnings." Bess clinks with her water this time, then gulps half of it down because it's not quite dark outside and she's feeling tipsy.

By the time Cricket joins them, Bess has had several cosmos and is drunk. "Cricket!" she exclaims, and then excuses herself to the restroom.

She splashes her face with cold water and wipes her neck with scented towelettes. She tries telling a woman coming out of a stall what she plans to say to Cricket. "There's a guy I know's been married eight times and he's my boyfriend and I'd be the ninth. Do you think that's funny?" The woman has her lipstick out and her lips puckered, leaning into the mirror. She looks at Bess's reflection and chuckles. Bess chuckles. The woman starts laughing so Bess starts laughing. Now they are laughing so hard the woman's face is wet and her mascara is running and Bess is leaning against the wall and snorting. "I know," says Bess, as if continuing some imaginary conversation. Then another woman comes in, sober apparently, and changes the mood.

The bar is more crowded than when she had first arrived. Where are Maggie and Cricket? she wonders. Her eyes follow the sound of the music. She notices two jolly people singing a duet around the piano. There is clapping.

"Cricket," she calls out, and waves. He sees her and makes his way to the booth.

"There you are," he says, reaching across to retrieve his martini glass.

"Do you know Maggie?" They glimpse Maggie still at the piano, singing over the shoulder of the piano player, who looks like Mickey Rooney.

"I do now," yells Cricket over the din.

Bess is confused. She can't read his countenance. She can't get her straw to her lips. "I have to tell you something," she says.

"Without spitting, if you please." Cricket wipes a napkin across his cheeks.

"Maggie is Rory's ex—" She stops to count with her fingers. "Ex-ex-ex-ex-ex-ex-ex-ex-wife."

"Yes, she told me who she was."

"When?"

"When you went to the loo."

"Did she tell you—"

"Yes, yes. I know all about Rory the octo-husband."

The disappointment Bess feels is oddly monumental. "But I was supposed to tell you."

"And yet you didn't."

"Are you mad?"

Cricket twiddles his fingertips at Maggie. "We'll talk about this tomorrow."

"But are you mad?"

"Encore!" Maggie yells, beckoning to Cricket. The few swaggering serenaders around the piano cheer him on.

"I'll be back. My public awaits."

Bess is ready to go. Cricket and Maggie are acting like new best friends, bringing Bess in as an insignificant third to their pronoun party—*You're a doll! He's a peach! She's a hoot! You're a blast! She's a ham!*—laughing at their antics. Cricket nonchalantly grabs her forearm like he had never heard of a germaphobe.

"Look," says Maggie, hanging on to Cricket's shoulder. "I think Bess is sulking."

"I'm not sulking," Bess slurs.

"Yes, you are." Maggie is laughing, circling her glass above her as if she were addressing an adoring audience. "You thought you'd get me to tell you something about Rory and all of us would suddenly make sense to you, isn't that true? Well let me tell you something, honey, life doesn't work that way."

"I'm leaving," says Bess, and walks out of the bar. Cricket finally takes pity on Bess and joins her in a cab back to the hotel. Bess won't remember the cab ride home, or Cricket putting her to sleep, or leaving the van at the bar, or how many drinks she had overall, and she won't remember earlier in the night inviting Cricket and Maggie to join her the next day to see Lorraine give her a haircut.

CHAPTER TWENTY-SIX

Rory had hopes of making it to Chicago in one day, but he got a late start this Wednesday morning and figures the best he can do is bed down for the night in Toledo. All things considered, he's impressed with himself at how quickly he pulled his trip together. It felt like old times. In less than forty-eight hours—from the time he had the idea of going after Bess (on his walk home from yoga on Monday) to the time he turned off the lights in his apartment just before noon today—he had wrapped things up at work, packed, mapped out a route, filled up his tank, and serviced his old Corolla, which took longer than expected.

What he would do once he got to Chicago was another story. He hadn't yet worked out all the details on that front. He had originally told Gabrielle he wanted to send flowers to Bess to let her know he was thinking of her. She gave him the name of the hotel where Bess was staying and said she'd be there until Friday. What he didn't share with Gabrielle is that he would deliver those flowers himself. At this rate, though, if he drove all the way through he'd arrive in the middle of the night and be

exhausted. Better to get a good night's sleep, shower, and be pre-
sentable when he arrived on Thursday. But that means he'll have
just one day with her before she's scheduled to head out. Maybe
she could postpone for a day or two. Maybe he could continue on
with them and pick up his car on the way back. Maybe he could
follow behind them, sharing the ride with Bess part of the time.
Or maybe this is another half-baked, impulsive, nut-job idea that
he should never have acted on.

He holds his map against the steering wheel. Forty more
miles to Toledo, he surmises. Too late to go back. Besides, he's
curious how Toledo has changed since he lived there. He never
really liked the city, truth be told. That could have had more to
do with his life with Lorraine and Eamonn's death than with the
city itself, but in his memory it's hard to separate it all.

Lorraine was strange. He should have known that from the
very first day they met. What was that pop song she liked? It
was by a male singer. Sting? No. Phil Collins. Lorraine loved
Phil Collins, whereas Rory—if he listened to pop music at all—
liked artists like Prince and David Bowie. How could he have
married someone who loved Phil Collins? How could he have
moved into that small apartment with her and all those stinking,
slobbering layabouts? He never told anyone, not even Sean, that
she liked to have sex from behind in a bathtub full of her stuffed
animals. He'd get distracted by the dogs scratching at the door or
the suspicious after-hours comings and goings at the car dealership he could see from the bathroom window. Sometimes he'd
have sex with Lorraine and think about Maggie, and feel guilty.

He pulls off the highway just as the rain starts. There are

signs for the Comfort Inn East and Rory decides that'll do. He's been driving for more than eight hours and it's getting dark. He checks in and drops his bag off in his room. Just out of curiosity he calls the local operator and asks for Lorraine Doyle. Not that he'd seek her out if she did still live in town, but he's relieved nevertheless that the operator has no listing.

Rather than dine alone at a sit-down restaurant, he decides to visit the White Castle he used to frequent and eat while driving around familiar streets. The rain has stopped. He drives past the building where he used to work, the field where he played rugby and the bar he and his teammates liked to go after games. He contemplates going in the bar for a drink, but rules against it. He's tired of driving, more tired than nostalgic.

Back in the hotel he sinks into the bed and turns on the TV. He wants to call Bess but is afraid he'll let slip a hint of his plans, so he refrains. He flips through the channels, lingering on an old episode of *M*A*S*H*, which always reminds him of Carol. Does it remind her of him? he wonders. He never understood what was so special about Toledo that made Klinger pine away for it in a dress.

He gets an early start in the morning, feeling refreshed and excited. According to his map it looks like it'll take just over four hours, which means he can make it before one. If Bess isn't at the hotel—and of course why would she be in the middle of the day?—he'll call her cell phone from the hotel and go meet her.

Once he's in the city he sees a florist and double parks, lucky not to get a ticket. The colorful bouquet he chooses is accented with red roses. He wolfs down a sandwich and reaches his destination in pretty good time. The air is crisp and clear, the sky above the lake is a feel-good blue, the tall buildings lining the river look regal. Rory pulls up his car and stops midway in the hotel's half-moon driveway, letting the bellhop know he'll be right out.

"Excuse me," he says to a woman in uniform at the front desk. "Good afternoon. I'm looking for Bess Gray, please."

The woman smiles and types at her computer. "Pretty flowers."

"Thanks."

She types some more. "I'm sorry, sir. I don't see her among our guests."

"That must be a mistake." Could Gabrielle have given him the wrong hotel? "What about Mildred and Irving Steinbloom?"

"No. Oh wait, I'm sorry." She reads from her screen. "Yes. They were guests. They checked out this morning."

Rory lowers his bouquet to the counter. "They left?"

"It appears that way, sir."

"Are you absolutely sure?"

"According to our records."

"What time did they check out?"

"About two hours ago." She looks at the flowers. "I'm so sorry."

He rubs his temples. *Shit.* This can't be. "Did they happen to say where they were going? If they were leaving town today?"

"I'm afraid I don't recall."

"Right," he says, because really . . . what more can he say or do? Bess said they'd go to Denver for Cricket so that's probably the direction they headed.

Shit, shit, shit, he says to himself. Should he try to catch up with her? How would he know exactly which way they went? He should call, find out where they are, why they left early, if everything's okay.

With his bouquet now hanging down by his leg, he looks out toward the lobby, wondering what he should do now. There are three people sitting in plush chairs near a fountain. The one closest to him is an attractive woman on her cell phone. She's looking at papers as she's talking. Possibly sensing that she's being watched, she looks up at Rory and it is in that moment that the world stops and time zigzags off track. Rory couldn't say who recognized whom first. "Maggie?" he says with utter astonishment.

The woman abruptly finishes her call. "Rory," she says.

CHAPTER TWENTY-SEVEN

W hat time is it?" yells Bess from the bathroom with immediate regret. Her voice is too piercing, her throat painfully dry. A slight rub of her foot on the porcelain tub roars like a ship's bullhorn, the flush of the toilet squalls like Niagara Falls. She curses the shiny, hard surfaces and keeps the lights low.

Just minutes ago, Cricket had smuggled Stella past the front desk, knocked loudly on Bess's door, and entered her room singing a badly remembered version of her dad's shout song. "Eight A.M.!" he yells. He pulls the curtains apart; Bess squints at the sunny day, snaps them shut again. He turns on the TV, she takes the remote and shuts it off.

"What's with you?" says Bess.

Cricket looks away dramatically, erectly, as if he were flashing his profile to a portrait artist. Suddenly, she understands. She sits down on the bed. "You're mad I didn't tell you about Rory."

Cricket relaxes out of his pose. "You got positively maniacal that I didn't tell you my real name, and yet here you are, keeping something like this from me. I had to hear it from a perfect stranger."

Bess curls into herself and tightens her robe. "I'm sorry. You're right. Even in my drunken stupor last night I knew I blew it."

He fingers a postcard on the desk. "You didn't *blow* it," he says. "Well all right, you did. But why? I'm hurt that you didn't think you could talk to me about that."

"I wanted to tell you. I just wasn't ready to endure any teasing."

"I wouldn't tease you about something this serious."

"Yes, you would. You can't help yourself. But that's why I love you. You make me laugh at my life, and thank God for that."

Cricket places his hand on his heart. "I can be serious, you know."

"I know." Bess rubs her temples. Is the trick to share everything you can with the important people in your life, or know that you can't sometimes and be forgiving when those closest to you can't, either? In so many ways Cricket is a mystery to her. So is Rory. So are her grandparents and her parents. Maybe she should be okay with that.

"Here," says Cricket, handing her two Advil. "Take these."

She reaches for her water glass. "Why aren't you hung over, too?"

"I ate a proper dinner. You, my dear, ate bar nuts."

Bess's stomach convulses at the thought.

"Come now. Let's get some coffee in you and you'll feel better. You can tell me the whole story of the wives."

"Okay, but I'm not going to meet Lorraine today. Especially not with Maggie. Besides, my grandparents told me last night they're ready to get going. Or at least my grandfather is. Aren't you?"

"I defer to the group, but I think you should meet this woman. Could be interesting."

Bess admits she is curious about Lorraine, about her marriage to Rory, her life since then and how crazy she's become, about why she stalked Dao. But as she thinks of Dao's e-mail, Bess asks herself: Does she *really* want to hear Lorraine's story? Would Lorraine even tell her the truth? Maybe she'd tell her life story like she was a character in a book, which is how Bess would rather hear it frankly, and she could make it any book, any story, any life lived that would sound better than what it was, and maybe still is: the basic personal ad of the human race—troubled, needy person seeks love and salvation.

Besides, Rory wouldn't want her to go. And after last night, she's not sure she wants to meet any more of his ex-wives. This isn't exactly a well-thought-out research project. What *could* she have learned from Maggie about marriage when her two marriages failed? What could the eighteen-year-old Rory really have taught her about the man he is nearly thirty years later? Maybe Rory was right. Maybe she's stirring up buried feelings Maggie has for Rory when she should just leave well enough alone. She pulls up her capris over a mysterious bruise on her hip and reminds herself to stay positive.

·⊂══⊃·

Bess and Cricket take a cab to the van, parked on a side street around the corner from last night's club. The street is empty, the bar closed and dark. Bess opens the door and finds Peace lying facedown on the floor. She props her back up and onto the seat.

Cricket coaxes Stella into her crate. "Why don't you leave the mannequin on the floor?"

Bess thinks about this. Indeed, why doesn't she? Why is she anthropomorphizing this plastic display pole with painted-on pupils and black lines where her limbs can be spun around and pulled off? "I don't know," says Bess. "She's just a *she* to me, not an *it*. And she has a name."

"Yes, but do you know her *real* name?"

"Funny," says Bess, but the question lingers in her imagination. It's possible that Peace is a replica of someone real, a specter of a buried secret. "Tell me," she says as Cricket takes the wheel. "Have you thought about why Peace is important to my grandfather?"

"I know why. She's one of the hundreds of lovers he had in his swinging days, only she was the rarest of pearls who loved him back and he has lived all the sorrowful days of his life with regret that he had to say good-bye to her forever."

Bess rolls her eyes. "You're reading romance novels again, you mush-brain." Though, she thinks, it would explain a lot about his fighting with Millie. "Let's say you're right. Why wouldn't my grandmother have tossed Peace out the window by now?"

Cricket parks in front of a diner where he can leave Stella in view, tied to a railing outside with a bowl of water. "Because Millie murdered the woman," he says, slamming his door. "She was never caught because she's good. She's CIA-trained, the little old lady thing is all an act. She made it look like a suicide. And so she feels guilty. It's her way of paying penance. I don't know why you're asking me this, it's all very clear."

"All right then," says Bess. *And you weren't going to poke fun at Rory's ex-wives? Right.*

They get a table and Bess nods an emphatic yes to the waitress who greets them with coffee. Cricket orders them both an egg-white omelet and whole wheat toast. Bess dumps more sugar than she's used to into her cup. The heat on her scratchy throat feels good. She watches Cricket inspect his glass for lipstick marks. She feels grateful that he's here with her on this trip.

"Cricket," she asks, "do you think Maggie could still be in love with Rory?"

"Irrelevant. He loves *you*, right?"

"I'm kind of insecure on that front."

"What a surprise."

Their breakfast comes. Cricket sprinkles salt into his palm, then pinches it onto his omelet. "So are you going to give me the unabridged story, or do I have to wait another three weeks?"

Bess tells him the full story of the wives as best she can the way Rory told it to her, then about Dao's e-mails and Carol's kitchen. Cricket listens and sips his second cup of coffee. "What do you think?" she asks, biting into a triangle of toast.

Cricket shakes his head.

"Now's the time you decide to keep quiet? Thanks."

"Sweetheart, look," he says, wiping the corners of his mouth with his napkin. "Do I think a marriage with him would last? I have my doubts. There, I said it. But marriage is always a risk. And so what if it doesn't work? Would that make you absolutely unhappy for the rest of your life? I would hope not."

Should she be going into a marriage contemplating how she'd be as a divorcée? Bess begins to respond and then stops when she hears Cricket's cell phone ring. He looks at the number and takes a deep breath before he answers.

"Hello?" he says. "Yes? What happened?" There is a long silence before he says, "I see." Another long silence, then "I'll be there. Thank you for calling."

"Who was that?" says Bess, though she already suspects she knows what it was about.

"That was Claus," he says, pushing his plate away. "Isabella passed away last night."

"Oh, Cricket."

Bess had called Millie and explained the situation and within two hours everyone was packed and ready to head off to Denver for Isabella's funeral on Sunday, three days from now. All are glum and eerily quiet, watching the waning view of the city skyline as they drive out of town. Cricket is especially languid, and Bess is tired and headachy, but Millie and Irv seem distracted, too, perhaps by hard farewells and fears of what lies ahead. Millie doesn't want to leave her sister. Bess knows this. Millie is thinking she might never see her again, despite Bess's assurances to the contrary. And even Irv is probably thinking in terms of never again, though Esther isn't one of his favorites. He is more than halfway to his new home and every mile must strike a death knell. Bess doesn't know if this is what's getting Irv down, but she thinks it's a good guess.

Cracker? she hints at Cricket, holding out a white bag of his favorite cheddar fish-shaped crisps she finds folded into the cup holder between them, but he declines with only the fleetingly gracious smile of the privately sad. He doesn't want to talk about Isabella and Bess is respecting that.

"I love you," she says into the space of the van. The words sound ethereal, like falling feathers.

No one responds. Millie's gaze is out the window to the left, Cricket's is to the right, his cheek pressed against his fist. Irv is staring at the seatback in front of him, his head bobbing from the bumps in the road.

Bess clears her throat. "I love you all, you know. I just want to say that."

"We love you, too, dear," says Millie, and that's all that is said.

Interstate 80 stretches across Iowa toward a big sky horizon that makes Bess feel like she's driving toward the edge of a flat earth. There is little in the scenery to lodge in the memory—a bland gray highway with trucks and cornfields and clusters of ignorable trees. Bess's mind wanders and comes back every now and again to the road, amazed that she can drive sixty-five miles an hour for this long without truly paying attention.

She puts in a CD of traditional folk songs, and her mind turns to Rory. Someday when things are good and steady, she thinks, she will tell him about Maggie and Dao.

Her mind then wanders to Gaia, wondering how she's doing.

They haven't spoken since Bess left D.C. And little Pearl. Sonny doesn't deserve a precious baby like that. Are they doing family things together?

Her cell phone rings and she checks to see who the caller is: Maggie. *Crap*. Cricket said she invited Maggie to go to Joliet to see Lorraine and now here they are, blowing her off. Bess makes a mental note to call Gabrielle and tell her to cancel the appointment with Lorraine. Oh well. She looks over at Cricket. Poor Cricket.

Her attention comes back to the road. She presses a button and shuts off the CD. "How about an episode of *The Shadow*?" she asks her fellow travelers. No answer. "I'll take that as a yes." *Who knows what evil lurks in the hearts of men?* inquires a foreboding male voice.

The best place to eat along Iowa's section of I–80, say the guidebooks, are any of the German-style restaurants in the Amana Colonies.

"Sounds touristy," says Irv.

"I'm not eating ham," says Millie.

Cricket uncharacteristically doesn't have an opinion.

"C'mon, the Amana Colonies are an historic landmark," says Bess. "One of the oldest communal living places in America."

"What does *communal* mean, they share toilets?" says Irv.

"Don't be stupid, Irving."

"They share property, Gramp, help each other out. Like the Amish. Let's try it."

Bess pulls into the largest of the seven villages, located in a river valley of quiet, rolling hills. Signs welcome them in German. Plank fences surround well-kept clapboard houses and shops selling antiques and wooden furniture and woolens. People strolling about look round and rosy-cheeked.

"Shalom, I want to say in a place like this," says Irv.

"You can," says Bess. "I don't think they'll mind."

They decide to take a look around before settling on a restaurant. Quickly enough, they get separated by the shops. When Bess tries to regroup, she can't find Cricket. She elicits Millie's help. "Wait here, Gramp, okay? We'll be right back." She leaves Irv to enjoy the scent of freshly baked bread in the bakery shop. "Go," he says. "I can stay here all day."

Bess calls Cricket's cell phone, but gets his voice mail. Millie and Bess search the craft shops and the general store. They search the Amana Meat Shop and Smokehouse, the Broom and Basket Shop, the Amana Wool Mill, and the Olde World Lace Shop. They stretch their necks around brick walls, down stairwells, in the middle of clustered leisure seekers with white sneakers and patriotic flag lapel pins. They wait outside a public restroom and ask a patron coming out if he's seen a large pink man with a floral shirt and diamond earring and he says no, he hasn't. *Cricket*, they yell. *Walter*. "Damn him!" Bess yells, and then looks down into the eyes of a pigeon-toed girl holding a red ball on her hip.

"Does your friend have a Shar-Pei?" The girl seems to be about ten years old, with thick purple-framed glasses and frogs on a charm bracelet.

"Yes, he does," says Bess. "How did you know?"

"How did I know you had a missing friend or how did I know he has a Shar-Pei?"

She is actually waiting for an answer. *Smart-ass kid.* "Both. Have you seen him?"

"I heard you ask about him, that's how. And I know what a Shar-Pei is because my stepmother has one. He's on the trail." She bounces her ball on the pavement.

"I'm sorry," says Bess, "he's where?"

"Over there." She points away from the shops to the edge of an acre of lawn.

"You go," says Millie. "I'll check on your grandfather."

Bess watches Millie walk away. Millie's arthritic hip makes her lean to the left and take lopsided steps, but she holds her head high like an injured marathon runner walking to the finish line.

Bess crosses the lawn. The damp grass tickles her ankles. Cricket is alone on a wooden bench with Stella at his heels. Bess sees him up close and her anger at his disappearance slips into empathy. She sits quietly next to him, letting the whispering wind in a chorus of leaves speak her concern.

Stella rises to a sitting position and rests her head on the bench between them. Bess reaches out to pet her at the same time Cricket's hand goes out. They touch and Cricket pulls back, but Bess doesn't let him. In a spontaneous gesture, she takes his hand in hers and squeezes it gently.

Cricket's eyes turn glassy. Bess watches his chest above his extended belly move up and down with his breath. She feels the weight of him, the pull of gravity on his head and shoulders. The thought of death makes it hard to have good posture. She remembers. "I'm so sorry, Cricket."

Bess tries to imagine Isabella. She tries to understand Cricket's pain, that shoulder-sloping hopelessness that news of death brings. In the quiet breeze and distant sounds of tourists' voices and birdsongs, Bess is flooded with memories of her mom's passing, when the doctor came down the hall of the hospital with that same tired, forlorn look. Millie had collapsed, wailing, so that the doctor had had to give her a sedative. Bess sat with her grandmother, watched her grandfather pace the hallway. She took them home, made them a pot of tea, put them to bed, and wrapped a thick blanket around herself and watched some old black-and-white movie on TV. It was hours before her body relaxed enough to let her cry. She stayed wrapped in her blanket well into the next day, when she should have been up, planning the funeral. But by that time, Millie could make the pot of tea, start the arrangements, and rock Bess in her arms.

"The least she could have done was wait for me," Cricket says, blowing his nose in his handkerchief. "That's so like her."

Bess rests her hand on his thigh. It's what her mother did when she first told Bess about her father's accident, sitting there on her twin bed covered in Snoopy sheets and a bunched yellow blanket. Bess had first met death then. She'd cursed it, thrown heavy objects at it, slammed doors on it, kicked it till it broke her toe, ignored it, talked to it about fairness and faith, even took stupid drunken risks a few times later on in her teens to try and understand it better, but she finally learned after her mom passed away that it helped most to just sit with it and feel the loving hands of the living.

Cricket looks down at his lap, wraps Stella's leash around his finger. "Claus said she was delirious last night. He said she was doped up and saying a lot of strange things, that she was sorry for burning the fried chicken. He wanted to know if I knew what she meant, because—" and he stops. "Because she hasn't cooked in years and hates fried chicken, so, he wanted to know, what was she talking about?"

Bess waits for him to continue. She swipes an ant from her ankle.

"Did I tell you about the last night of my marriage?"

"You didn't."

"Then I'll tell you a story."

"Tell me."

I was late for dinner. This was at the end of June 1969, in Knoxville. I was in a diner not far from our house, sipping coffee at the counter, when I overheard two men discussing the news they heard from up north, about a bar raid where the cops had managed to 'kill them some faggots.' I'd heard that kind of talk before and I'd learned the best thing to do was avert my eyes and walk away, lest they detect the secret life I'd finally allowed myself to have for the better part of two years.

"But they said something that caught my attention: the name of the bar I had visited on a business trip to New York, a bar in Greenwich Village. The Stonewall Inn. Heard of the Stonewall riots?

"I left the diner and found a pay phone to call a friend in New York. He told me how the cops had come later than usual, out of uniform, and unleashed their penis sticks on the crowd. He said those two vacuous vermin had gotten it wrong—some were injured but no one was killed. In fact, the truth was, we fought back! Such a monumental moment in history for so many of us. Leave it to Judy Garland to start the Gay Liberation Front with her suicide.

"I felt emboldened for the first time. It's difficult to explain. I don't mean I went home, flung open the door, and belted out 'Over the Rainbow,' thank you very much. But in a very small way, on the inside, I felt a tiny crevice open that let me breathe easier and . . . truer, for lack of a better word. I was thirty years old. I'd been married eight years. And there I was, standing on a street corner at a pay phone, scared and positively rhapsodic.

"I didn't know what to do with myself. I walked around the block. And then I realized the time so I got back in my car— a diamond green Ford Thunderbird, oh yes—and drove home. That's when I discovered my house was on fire. My kitchen, to be exact. Trucks with flashing lights and firemen with big hoses were all over my lawn. Smoke was coming out the front door and I panicked, looking around for Isabella. I called out for her, and one of the neighbors pointed to where she was standing with this blank look on her face. She was just standing there with her apron on, staring at the house.

"We had moved to Knoxville six months before so she could be nearer her sister while I was traveling. Her sister had three kids and Izzy, well . . . we didn't have any. She and her sister used to sit in their kitchen while they cooked for the kids, but she always hated our kitchen, claiming it wasn't 'functional.' It was certainly functional for me, I loved to cook, but she didn't want me to. Not manly enough, I suppose.

"*Izzy?* I said.

"*I was cooking fried chicken*, she said, not looking at me. *You love fried chicken.*

"She looked like the living dead, like I could wave my hand in front of her face and she wouldn't blink. I don't know what it was, but I just knew in that moment that our marriage was over. I knew it and she knew it, she knew the lie I'd been telling ever since we were kids. It's why I think I said what I did, right then, standing there helpless.

"*I'm homosexual*, I said.

"She kept staring at our house going up in flames. *How it burns*, she said."

Cricket pauses for what Bess suspects is dramatic effect. Did Isabella really say that? she wonders. Or has Cricket written the movie in his head? It shouldn't matter. Cricket's is a story of deep sadness and loss, and on some level Bess feels the sympathetic pangs of heartache. But she can't help thinking, too, about the facts. She has always been someone who craves historical accuracy, though the whole concept is inherently contradictory. One seeks facts, one gets versions of facts. She must be the only folklorist in America who has a problem with that. But maybe it's time for acceptance. She should stop asking for the *true story*, as she has so often with Rory. She should stop searching for it, feeling as if she has to uncover lies so as not to be needlessly ignorant of future pain and abandonment, for that's what it's about, isn't it? With Rory? To hell with it. Cricket's sharing intimate feelings just with her, on a bench, on a quiet trail many hundreds of miles from their everyday lives. She will not ask him the truth. She will only listen, and love him.

"Isabella decided that it was her fault, that she made me gay somehow," Cricket continues. "It made me so angry. And sad. When we first met in grammar school, I played with her because she had the most comprehensive doll collection of anyone I knew, rag to porcelain. I loved the sheer variety and artistry of them, their beautiful faces and delicate feet. But then over the years I spent time with her because of *her*, because in junior high school she drowned the dolls in chocolate pudding and called it 'Little People in Deep Shit: a Retrospective.' She had an uncle who was the devil incarnate, and between him and my daddy . . . well, we were just glad we had each other. Even through college I never found anyone who understood me the way she did. I grew to love her, but she was brought up a Southern minister's daughter. When the truth came out, she didn't *let* me love her. The more she said she could try harder to be a good wife, the more I turned away until I stopped talking to her altogether."

Cricket stops long enough for Bess to ask: "Until you saw Claus in the market?"

"No. Until Darren made me call her. He was into all this therapy about coming to terms with your past, and he sucked me into it. He convinced me that if she knew I was in a serious relationship with someone else, with him, she might come around. Especially after all those years."

"And did she?"

"Not really. I called, we talked. She was pleasant. I told her about Darren, she didn't really respond. She told me she had gotten married again. He was older, two grown boys. They had a good marriage until he passed away from a heart attack. His boys send her Christmas cards, she said, but that's about it."

"You make her sound lonely."

"Well, she was. Quite so. I called her when Darren died. She didn't say she was sorry for my loss or anything of the sort, but she listened and that was nice, I suppose. She said if I ever wanted to come visit, she'd enjoy the company."

"So you visited her?"

"Only when I heard she was sick a few months ago. She was in New York, seeing a specialist. I took the train up."

Bess puzzles over a new thought. "Was that the day after my party, when you were so mysterious about putting Stella on the bus?"

"I believe so."

"Why didn't you just tell me where you were going?"

Cricket looks at her, tilts his head. "We all have things we're reluctant to share."

Bess nods at his reference to her story of Rory's wives. It makes her think, too, of Rory's decision not to tell her up front about them. Maybe she should have been more sympathetic. How would she have reacted, she wonders, if he did tell her up front? She would have still been shocked, maybe even turned off from pursuing anything further, but she would have trusted him to tell her the truth about anything right from the start, no matter how difficult it is. How much is that worth in the portfolio of love?

"I'm still confused," she says. "If you had already been back in touch and had seen Isabella in New York, why was Claus chasing you that day in the market? That was a long time after the party."

"First of all, it's Claus we're talking about. I never liked that pebble-brained bully. He teased me relentlessly when we were children." Cricket picks at a tooth with his pinky. "But mostly I was avoiding them, both of them. I did see Isabella in New York, it's just . . . her fragility scared me. I could see how ill she was. I could see how much she needed someone. I didn't want to go through that again, not after Darren. A person withering is a terrible sight."

An image comes to Bess of her mother's arm, pale and thin by her side as she lay in her hospital bed, asking for a tissue or pitcher of water across the room, how it would rise unsteadily, arduously, from elbow to wrist to hand to finger, wavering and falling after only a moment's effort, a bird with broken wing. That same atrophied arm had once shoveled snow from their walkway, carried a sleeping child up to bed, had shot up over her head in triumph when the Baltimore Orioles won the pennant.

"So she went back to Denver and I didn't return her calls for a month," Cricket goes on. "Claus was right to yell at me. I was being a bastard. Which is why I wanted to make this trip. I wanted to make it up to her. I wanted to be there for her."

"You were. She knew you were coming." Bess wonders how

much of the bond that Cricket feels with Isabella was woven by marriage. Would he be here if they had remained simply childhood friends? And how much of that bond is patched with duty and guilt? *Who will be there for me when I die?* Bess has had this thought before, a single person's worry, but perhaps she's downplayed it too much. Perhaps it's the single most important reason why she wants not just present companionship, but someone to call her husband, her child, people who, even out of duty, would be there when she needs it most. No, that's stupid. There's no guarantee. Look at Rory, he's not going to be there for all his ex-wives. And it's selfish. What about being the one who's there for others? What about bucking up and being alone, so what? What about making younger friends? *What about just loving others and trusting in the world that it will return that love?* Bess shudders at this last thought, for its origin seems not from within but something foreign pulled magnetically from above. It is something her mom would have said.

"I miss him," says Cricket.

Him. Is that what he said? He's thinking of Darren. And why not . . . she's thinking of her mother. Isn't that what death does, makes you think of all death, past and future, even your own? And isn't the one that has hit the hardest the one that rises to the surface every time to let you know how little has healed? "I know you miss him," she says. Bess didn't really know Darren, but she remembers things about him: his sly laugh, his knowledge of wine and Shakespeare monologues, his affectionate towel snaps at Cricket.

Cricket says no more and she lets him be. If this is how their friendship deepens—with a simple phrase like *I miss him*—then so be it. It's a start.

"I need to check on my grandparents, see that they haven't beaten each other up. You okay here?"

"I'll come." Cricket pauses a beat, sighs deeply, and pushes himself up off the bench with great effort. Stella rises on her haunches, alert to new movement.

"We should eat," says Bess, readjusting the Velcro strap on her sandal before she stands. "We have a lot of distance to cover."

Before they leave the bench, before they come upon Millie standing by a lamppost in the shade like she's waiting for a bus and Irv bent over a nearby water fountain, sipping from a small arc of water, before they jointly point to a rectangular loaf of white bread on a wooden shelf and give exact change, adding to their basket hickory-smoked sausage and corn jelly and rhubarb pie, before they tug Stella away from the stump of a tree where her nose detects her predecessors, before they return to the van and gasp from the combustible heat of its interior and the burning vinyl seats that will stick to the flesh of their thighs, before all this—Cricket gives Bess's wrist a squeeze. "Thank you for listening," he says. "I don't know what I'd do without you."

They stay for a night in Omaha, sleep in, and get back on the road by lunchtime without much fanfare. The stately Great Plains absorb them indifferently, as sky to a bird or a placid lake to its trout—a straight shot through four hundred fifty miles of Nebraskan flatlands. They stop several times for Irv, who says his stomach is upset, but not too badly. Eventually, the sun sinks surreptitiously while their minds are elsewhere. The scattered livestock and vast wheat fields of the lone prairie fade into a sedate darkness like a dream, like sleep, like an end of a film where the road signs come and go like rolling credits. They stop for a tepid, tasteless buffet dinner with mashed potatoes and chicken wings in big tin trays. They stop again for coffee.

Bess and Cricket switch off driving every few hours until the Colorado border is upon them and they agree to push onward while Millie and Irv snore quietly in the back. They play Ghost and Twenty Questions. They play several CDs of *Pride and Prejudice*, repeating the name Mr. Darcy until they are satisfied with their British accents. They roll their necks and marvel at the endless black void beyond the edge of the road. Finally they arrive at a motel near the hospital where Isabella whispered her last words and only then, when Bess parks in the motel's lot and rolls the van door open to singsong "We're here" and ushers her grandparents to their room, does she notice Peace, the mannequin, is gone.

CHAPTER TWENTY-EIGHT

Maggie, what are you doing here?" Rory approaches slowly, trudging through a swamp of disbelief.

"I could ask the same of you," she says, rising from her chair. She looks sculpted and wealthy, a far cry from the sassy, mischievous girl he knew years ago, but she is still beautiful, still tall and lean and in shape. Her hair is shorter, but it's still thick and black. Her taut, V-necked shirt is showing enough cleavage to draw Rory's eyes to her breasts, which he can feel as she leans in to embrace him. His body remembers her.

"This is an unbelievable coincidence," he says. "I just drove up from D.C. to meet someone and here you are."

"Meeting your girlfriend?"

"My girlfriend, right, but I seem to have missed her. She already checked out." Up close, Rory can see the subtle creases around Maggie's green eyes, but the eyes themselves are still dancing the way they used to all those years ago when she found something to tease him about. He's starting to wonder: *Is this really a coincidence?* "How did you know I was meeting my girlfriend?"

Maggie looks down at the flowers in his hand.

"Of course."

"That, and I met her last night."

"I'm sorry, you what?"

"She didn't tell you?" Maggie is watching him closely.

"You met Bess? Last night?"

"We had a grand time. I'm guessing she had quite a hangover this morning."

"Bess? You've got the wrong woman. Bess hardly drinks."

Maggie smiles. She seems to be enjoying this. "Petite, dark shoulder-length hair, cute as a bear cub? She was there with her friend Cricket. *Loved* him."

Rory is furious. So Bess is out there looking up his other ex-wives? Why didn't she tell him about Maggie? Who else did she find? "Can I use your phone?"

"Sure." Maggie reaches down to the table and hands him her cell phone. He calls Bess; her phone rings several times and then goes into voice mail. He doesn't leave a message. "If it's any consolation," says Maggie, "she thinks it's me calling."

"Great. Why wouldn't she answer your call?"

"I don't know. Probably for the same reason she blew me off today."

"That's why you're here?"

"She invited me on an outing that piqued my interest. You know me, always up for an adventure. When she didn't show about an hour ago, I parked myself here to do some work. I don't know how you live without a cell phone." She stops and smiles, this time with more warmth than mischief. "It's really good to see you, Rory. You look good."

"Thanks," he says, somewhat distractedly. "You look pretty great yourself."

"Listen, I have an idea." She gathers up her papers, puts them neatly in a leather case and puts the case into her big straw bag. "You have a car, right?"

"Out front."

"Perfect. Wait here." She walks to the concierge station and talks to the person behind the desk. It looks like he's making a call for her. Rory lays the bouquet on the table and sits in her chair, plagued with indecision and mixed feelings. He looks over at Maggie. Her cropped white pants are attractively snug. He notices, too, how her gold metallic sandals harness the suggestive V of her toes. He sees the man at the desk watch her ass as she walks away. "Okay," she says. "Let's go for a drive."

"Where?"

"To find Bess. There's a possibility she kept her appointment."

"What appointment?"

"Just trust me."

Suddenly Rory is flooded with memories of their marriage: of Maggie's assertiveness, her spontaneity, her curiosity; of his passivity, his naïveté. And here they are again, together in an unfamiliar city, falling back into their old roles. *Wait here*, she commanded, as if decades hadn't gone by, as if Rory is still that scared young thing right off the boat. Years ago he would have followed her anywhere, her spell over him was that strong.

"Rory, c'mon," she says with affection, reaching out to gently squeeze his forearm. "I haven't seen you in all these years. We have so much to catch up on. And who knows," she says, letting go of his arm and adjusting her bag on her shoulder. "It might have been God's plan for us to meet like this." She smiles and winks.

Not long after his marriage to Maggie, Rory shed his Catholic responsibilities and turned agnostic. Over the years he's had spiritual longings, but they always stem more from nostalgia than a deep-rooted belief in a higher being. Maggie, on the other hand, rejected the Church even before they left Ireland.

"Sir?" says the bellhop. "I'm afraid you need to move your car. Would you like me to park it for you?"

"No, thank you," says Rory. "I'll move it." He turns back to Maggie. *What to do?* It's not like he has a better plan. And if Bess really is where Maggie thinks she is, why not show up with Maggie? After all, Bess was the one who conjured her up. "Excuse me," he calls out to the bellhop, catching him on his way back outside. "Do you have a girlfriend?"

"I do."

"Then please, give these to her." He hands over the flowers and the bellhop thanks him and bows. "So where to?" he says to Maggie.

Maggie smiles and slides her sunglasses on like a movie star. "You drive," she says. "I'll navigate."

The road out of the city is flat and in disrepair. "There are two seasons here, winter and construction," a gas station attendant had told Rory and he can see it now, two lanes being funneled into one past large machines and people in hard hats. They pass signs advertising wholesale mulch and discount tires. There is an industrial smell in the wind rustling the cornstalks and trucks behind and in front of them, going slower than Rory can tolerate, especially after all the driving he did this morning. Maggie apologizes for not knowing the trip would take this long, but she holds true to the secret of their destination.

"So what did you and Bess talk about last night?" says Rory. If she knows about his marriages, he figures, best to get it out of the way now.

"You, of course. Until the piano player sat down."

"You always loved to belt it out in public."

"Still do. We sang one Elton John song after another. You and I knew every word, remember? 'Pinball Wizard'? 'Rocket Man'?"

"'Don't Go Breaking My Heart'? 'The Bitch Is Back'?"

Maggie laughs. "Yeah, well. I may have been the first bitch in your life, but I hear I wasn't the last." She is flashing that impish smile again.

"Go ahead, say it."

"What?"

"My life. It's ridiculous."

"I would never say that." Rory looks at her askance. "I wouldn't. Though, you have to admit it's not exactly the norm, right? I mean, eight of them? Or eight of us, I should say? Just because you sleep with a girl doesn't mean you should marry her, you know."

"Funny. I did learn that lesson when you left me."

"Aw," she croons. "You still get that stubborn little boy look when you're mad, you know that?"

For the rest of the trip they catch up on the last few decades. She tells him about her work, her marriage and divorce, her children, her occasional longings to return to Dublin, to be closer to her father, now retired from a long and lustrous film production career and recovering from hip surgery. Would she really ever go back and live there? Rory wanted to know. Maybe, she says. She'd like her daughters to know Dublin, to have dual citizenship.

Maggie touches his hair. "Look at all that gray. Makes you look distinguished. God, I hate that about men."

They stop at a gas station so Maggie can get a soda. Rory eyes a bag of popcorn, which prompts the store's cashier, with a neck brace and gauze taped to his forehead, to inform him that popcorn is the state snack food of Illinois. Rory asks what the state bird is, to which the cashier says hell if he knows, he doesn't sell birds. Maggie and Rory laugh together on the way back to the car and for a moment Rory is back thirty years ago in Dublin, sharing an inside joke with a gorgeous, clever girl his age with long black hair who he could hardly believe chose a boy like him over all the others. He pops in a music tape.

"Is that you playing?"

"Me and Sean O'Leary. Remember Sean?"

"That flirt. God, he hated me for leaving you. You know I saw him not long after we split up and he threw a beer in my face."

"I can't believe that. You must have said something to provoke him."

"Me?" Rory looks at her long enough to see her wink at him.

They turn onto a small two-lane street and start to see signs of commerce. "Pull in here," says Maggie, pointing to a parking lot. The storefronts stretch half a block and include a post office, a hair salon, a drugstore, a candle store, and a fudge shop. Rory parks in an end spot in the shade and turns off the engine. He doesn't see Bess's minivan.

Maggie opens her door. "Just . . . keep an open mind, all right?" That was one of Maggie's stock phrases in their relationship, *keep an open mind*. He learned that good and well early on. If only he hadn't also learned to keep such an open heart.

The door to the Sunshine Hair Salon opens with a little bell's jingle overhead. The hairdresser closest to the front turns off her blower. "Can I help you?" she says, motioning with a round brush. Her client sitting below her looks up from her magazine. The fruity, chemical smell of hair products is overwhelming.

"I hope so," says Maggie. "Is Lorraine here?"

Lorraine? Did Rory hear her right?

"Lorraine!" the hairdresser yells. She looks like a former cheerleader who shows off her routines when she's drunk. The stylist next to her says something that makes her laugh.

Lorraine enters from the back room, shaking a bottle. Rory hardly recognizes her. She's so much larger, so much heavier, and tattooed all up and down her arms and calves and across her ample bosom. She seems to be straining to stay upright against the weight of her bust, made worse by her high-heeled wedges. Her hair is long and the unnatural color of a ripe cantaloupe. "Did someone call me?"

"You have visitors," says the cheerleading hairdresser, then to the side but loud enough for Rory to hear, "let's hope they're customers."

There is a moment before Lorraine sees Rory, a moment when he contemplates making a run for it. Where's Bess? Why did Maggie really bring him here? He finds himself furious again, at Bess and now at Maggie. Are they in cahoots? He looks over at Maggie, but all Maggie is doing is standing back, watching him, gauging his reaction. He would scream at Maggie if he could. How dare she get her kicks this way.

"Rory McMillan," says Lorraine, approaching cautiously. She walks around him, checking him out.

"Hi, Lorraine," says Rory tentatively, shifting his weight from foot to foot.

"So you're alive."

"You could say that." He can't look at her as she's circling. He looks, instead, at her silver ankle bracelets and toe rings and the rhinestones on the back pockets of her jean shorts.

"You aged pretty good."

"Thanks. You, too," he says, and happens to catch Maggie's eye. *Don't be mad*, she mouths.

"Who're you?" Lorraine says to Maggie. Even her voice, once ethereal in her church choir, has deepened to a smoker's rasp.

Rory has a mind to tell Lorraine exactly who Maggie is, if only to divert Lorraine's attention. If Lorraine had a fault years ago besides her strangeness, it was her jealousy. She wouldn't allow Rory to mention Maggie's name. He never knew what prompted that . . . a found letter perhaps? Spoken words in his sleep? It didn't matter. Lorraine had never met her or seen her and she preferred it that way.

"I'm his sister," Maggie says, ratcheting up her brogue.

"Mary?"

"Yes."

Suddenly Lorraine is more welcoming. She holds out her hand to Maggie. "Nice to meet you. You visiting from Ireland?"

"Yes."

"I'm saving up to go. Me and my guy. He's going to take me."

Lorraine shakes her bottle again. "So," she says to Rory. "You need a haircut or did you just come to reminisce about the good ol' days?"

Maggie lets out a laugh.

Lorraine punches Rory in the shoulder. "Laugh, McMillan. That was funny." A phone rings. Lorraine sashays awkwardly to the counter to answer it.

Rory shoots Maggie a look. "Can I speak to you for a minute, *sis*?" He holds the door for Maggie and follows her outside. He waits for the door to close behind them. "What the fuck was that?" he yells.

"Wow, you're really mad. I've never seen you like this. Good for you."

"Don't talk to me like a child. What are we doing here?"

"I thought Bess would be here."

"Bullshit."

"Okay, I admit, it was a longshot. But I also thought it might be cathartic for you to see Lorraine."

"Like hell you did. You just *love* drama, don't you. Can't get enough. How is it that I let you manipulate me *again*, after all this time?"

"Hey, Bess was the one who found her. I was just along for the ride."

"And yet I don't see Bess here. Do you?" he yells. He turns at that moment and sees Lorraine and her coworkers through the window watching them argue.

"Why waste an opportunity, is how I look at it," says Maggie as he grabs her elbow and pulls her toward the fudge shop.

"An opportunity for *what*?"

Maggie takes her elbow back and runs her fingers through her hair. "To say you're sorry."

Rory checks to see if they're still in the window and can't see them. He turns back to Maggie and takes a deep breath to calm himself down. He counts to ten the way Steven in Seattle had taught him to do when he couldn't think straight or felt angry or impulsive. "I don't hear *you* saying anything like that," he says.

For the first time today Maggie looks sad. She leans against the shop window and wraps her arms around her waist. Rory can tell he has finally pierced her tough exterior. Her fortress has a drawbridge and it's lowering before him. "I'm sorry," she says, softly. "I really am." It sounds like she's apologizing for bringing him here today, but he knows by her stare that it goes deeper than that.

His nod is subtle, enough to let her know his fury is abating. Is it his curse in life to be attracted to complicated women? "How do you know I have something to apologize for with Lorraine anyway?"

"She told me."

"Who, Bess?"

"No, Lorraine. She came looking for me right after you left her, only she was so high I was banking today on the fact that she wouldn't recognize me."

"What did she want?"

"Beats me. I think she thought you and I were getting back together."

"Jesus. I feel like I'm in a Dickens nightmare. *The Ghosts of Wives Past*." He rubs his face. "I wish I didn't feel obligated to stay now."

Maggie stands and motions toward the salon. "C'mon, Ebenezer. I think you could use a haircut."

"What, are you kidding? I'm not letting her get near me with a pair of scissors."

"Now who's being dramatic? I'm guessing she could use the business."

Rory reviews his options. He could try harder to reach Bess. He could drive back to the hotel and take a nap. He could tour Chicago. He could head home. *Bloody hell*, he thinks. *What am I doing here?* He doesn't know why, but he feels like staying. Maybe everything already seems so bizarre that he might as well finish out the day. Or maybe, now that he's seen Lorraine, he'd like to know what her life has been like the last two decades. "Fine," he says. "But you're paying."

Lorraine is blowing the hair off her chair and around her station with a hair dryer that she shuts off when Rory and Maggie walk back in.

"Everything all right?" she says.

"Yes, sorry about that. If you have time for a quick trim, that'd be great."

She holds her hand out triumphantly toward the back sink. "Have a seat."

Lorraine leans over to wash his hair so that he is inches from her bosom and can smell the familiar scent of her skin, can see that her tattoos are decorative butterflies and flowers. Whereas he remembers Maggie's whole body, how it fit with his, with Lorraine he remembers her meaty, malleable breasts and thighs. He is hyper aware and halfway turned on by the femaleness in the salon with all the exposed skin and curves around him.

"Too hot?" says Lorraine.

"Excuse me?"

"The water," she says, massaging his scalp slowly and deliberately.

"No, it feels good," he says with his eyes closed and then blushes when he hears her laugh and opens his eyes to see how close her face is to his. Her cheeks, he notices, are the texture and colors of an urban sidewalk. He clears his throat. "So you live around here?"

"Five minutes away. Remember my parents died, right? Well, my uncle got drunk one night and told me I was adopted. *No shit*, I said. So I went looking for my birth mother. Found her right here. I take care of her now. She introduced me to my boyfriend, Russ." She wipes her hands, walks to her station, and comes back with a frame holding two photos. "That's him." She holds it up so Rory can see. The photo on the left shows a large man in black leather on a motorcycle, a small American flag attached to the back. The one on the right shows a boy in his late teens with a cowboy hat riding a bull.

"Very nice. And who's that?"

"My son. He's down in Texas with his daddy."

"I see." Rory wipes suds from his eyelids. Lorraine is chattering on like all the hairdressers he's ever known and it's making him feel more at ease. Maybe this wasn't such a bad idea after all. He wants to ask about her son, but he opts for a topic of commonality. "You know," he says, "I was in Toledo yesterday."

"Oh really." Lorraine has been rinsing his hair but now lets the water rest on one spot.

"Yeah, you've been back?"

"Uh-huh." That doesn't sound to Rory like an answer. He wonders what exactly she seems to be remembering.

"What was that song you liked, that Phil Collins sang? The one you used to sing all the time?"

She shuts off the water and turns her back to him. "'You Can't Hurry Love.'"

"That's it." He sits up. She hands him a towel. Maggie is swiveling in Lorraine's chair, chatting with the other stylists. Rory and Lorraine seem to both take notice of her at the same time.

"Your sister's pretty, but she don't look like you."

"She looks like my dad's side," he manages to say.

"And this was her idea?"

"To come here? Yeah."

"How'd she find me?"

"You'll have to ask her."

She fixes her bra strap and walks toward Maggie. "Follow me," she says to Rory. Rory can't help noticing her laborious gait, how her weight, particularly her sizable rear end, shifts from side to side with each step. Maggie gets up and moves chairs. Lorraine takes a comb and scissors from her drawer and pumps up Rory's seat. She wraps him in a smock and Velcros the neck so that it's almost too tight. The other two hairdressers in the salon have finished with their clients and are up front, accepting payment.

"So," Lorraine says to Rory, "you married?"

"Nope."

"Really? That's not like you."

"What do you mean?"

"I mean, you like to be married, right?"

"Sure." Rory is trying to keep his eyes on the scissors, which she wields recklessly when she gestures.

"So it's kind of strange that you're not married again."

Again? Rory looks questioningly at Maggie. *Beats me what she knows*, her look says. Rory can see little pieces of his hair falling to the floor.

"Not really," he says. "Guys like their freedom, right?" He smiles to let her know he's just making small talk. The other clients leave and one of the hairdressers disappears into the back room. The other takes out a cigarette and steps outside.

"No," says Lorraine, tilting his head so she can get closer to his neck. "Not you. You like to be tied to a woman, don't you. Am I right, sis?"

"Right," says Maggie.

"Yeah, you like being married, but they just keep getting away."

What is she talking about? She is tugging a little harder on his hair with the comb. He finds the *snip snip* of the scissors unnerving. Maggie stands to survey Lorraine's work. She lets Rory know in the mirror that his hair is okay in back, not to worry.

"Women," Lorraine continues, "they just keep dying and moving away and going loco, don't they." At the word *loco* she circles her ear to show the common symbol for craziness, only she's circling the scissors in the air and it's making Rory nervous. "I mean," she says, back to cutting, "I wouldn't have left you. I don't do that. Give you an example, I had a boyfriend once. He cheated on me so bad, but I stuck with him. I knew he loved me, you know these things, even though he used his fist to show me, but he had a problem with his anger and I understood that. I stuck with him. Until he died. Then I buried him."

Rory's heart is racing, trying to watch the scissors. Why is Maggie being so quiet? She hasn't said two words since he sat down. *Calm down*, he says to himself. So Lorraine knows about his other ex-wives. Maybe Bess told her. After all, she told Maggie. "By any chance," says Rory as pleasantly as he can, "have you spoken with my girlfriend?"

Lorraine stops what she's doing. "You have a girlfriend? Why didn't you tell me? What's her name?"

"Holly," says Maggie before Rory can answer. "A very nice girl."

"She pretty?"

"*I* think so," says Rory.

"She pretty?" Lorraine asks Maggie.

"Sure," says Maggie.

Lorraine walks behind Rory and leans in toward his ear. "Does she like dogs?"

Okay, this is too much. Rory shifts in his seat. "Are you almost done?"

Lorraine runs her fingers through his hair. "Almost. I'm a perfectionist, I got to get it right."

"Okay," says Rory, breathing heavier. He admits, looking at his reflection, that the cut isn't bad. "It's just that we have to go pretty soon." He appeals to Maggie for help.

"Yes," says Maggie. "Rory and I have early dinner plans."

"I gotcha. Just want to see if it's all even." She takes a can out and sprays something musky on his hair. "So," she says, examining her work, "I didn't hear your answer. Does she like dogs?"

The memory of the first day they met is vivid in Rory's mind now. She was eerily persistent then, too, with her questions about dogs.

"I don't know," he says halfheartedly, then he senses that isn't the right answer. He's been looking at Lorraine's handbag hanging off her mirror like a dead raccoon, noticing something shiny and silver poking out. He is suddenly sure he knows what it is. "No, what am I saying, she loves dogs," he says, speaking quickly. "Of course she loves dogs."

Lorraine is brushing stray hairs off his shoulders and smock, tilting her head, almost lost in thought. "That's good," she muses. "Because the one in Colorado, the crazy one? She didn't like dogs. I think that's why she was crazy. You got to like dogs, right? The Asian chick, she liked cats but that's just not worthy of you, Rory. You're a dog lover."

Rory jumps up. He pulls the smock off. "Okay, great. Looks great. Thanks so much. Fantastic. How much do we owe you?" He walks toward the hairdresser at the front of the salon who has come in from her smoking break. *Human shield*, he's thinking.

Lorraine looks at him curiously. "Don't worry about it," she says. "On the house."

"No it ain't!" says the cheerleading hairdresser. She and the other woman have been hanging around the salon, pretending to be busy. "Man's haircut is twenty-five dollars."

"Don't you want me to dry it?" says Lorraine.

"Nope, I'm good, thanks. I love it just the way it is."

"Here," says Maggie, placing two twenties on the front counter.

"Right, then," says Rory, almost to the door. "Lorraine, good to see you. Take care. Say hi to your boyfriend, your son. Ladies," he says to the two other hairdressers who are now watching him, "thank you. Maggie? Let's go."

"Maggie?" says Lorraine, moving toward him.

"Shit," whispers Maggie behind him. "Mary," she says to him. "Mary."

"Mary, I'm sorry. Mary. Sorry." He feels like he's shouting. He is nearly out the door with Maggie right behind him, but he turns toward Lorraine and for an instant, for a quick moment he imagines her the way she was, the good parts anyway, the quiet, eager-to-please, charitable parts. "I'm sorry," he says. "For everything."

Calm down," says Maggie as Rory pulls out of the parking lot. "You're going the wrong way. Turn around up there."

Rory smacks the steering wheel with his palm. "How did she know their names? How did she know Dao had a cat? Can you tell me that? How could she possibly have known Olive Ann didn't like dogs?"

"I don't know. Stop yelling."

"Did you see what she had in her bag? A pistol, Maggie! A gun!"

"She had no such thing."

"I saw it. It was silver and shiny."

"That was a curling iron."

"No, you're wrong."

"Rory, I saw it. I know what it was."

"Did you hear what she said to me when she first saw me?"

"I don't remember."

"You're alive."

"It's something people say."

"I should call the police."

"And tell them what? A woman assaulted you with conditioner?"

"Maybe she killed her parents."

"Listen to yourself!"

Rory takes a deep breath. He counts to ten.

"That's better," says Maggie. The highway traffic heading

back to Chicago is slow-going. A truck in the next lane inches into their lane and moves ahead. "I can see," says Maggie calmly, "that she must have kept tabs on you, and that's pretty creepy. But I think she's ultimately harmless."

"Why would you think that?"

"I talked to the other girls when she was washing your hair. They seemed willing to talk about her behind her back. They don't like her boyfriend, said he's loud and obnoxious. They don't like how she tries to mother them. And they don't seem to think she's pulling her weight work-wise. But other than that, they say she's okay. She takes care of her mother. She bakes cookies."

"Yeah well," says Rory, running his hand through his newly cut hair. Lorraine didn't take too much off, but he could feel the difference. "Serial killers usually appear harmless."

Rory sprays wiper fluid onto his window to try and get the dead bugs off. The wipers swish several times and then stop. He feels Maggie's stare. "What?" he says, glancing at her.

"She gave you a pretty good haircut."

My God, he thinks, *am I dreaming?* He doesn't want to talk about his hair. Why did he listen to Maggie? Why did she get so quiet, watching him like a play? Why did she put him through that? He feels dirty. He wants to take a hot shower and crawl into bed and watch *M*A*S*H* or an old movie. He wants to talk to Bess. The sun is setting, the air is cooler, the day needs to end.

Rory and Maggie don't speak for a while. Rory counts to ten and ten again, letting his anger taper off into a pensive melancholy. The drive back into the city has given him time and space to start putting things into perspective. He didn't tell Lorraine where he was living, or Bess's real name. If she really is after him in some way, he supposes she would have acted by now. Maybe he'll still go to the police with something. He'd look up what to do online when he gets back home. He looks over at Maggie. She looks tired. She must be feeling lonely these days to do what she did today, he thinks.

Maggie returns his gaze. "What are you thinking about?" she says.

"I'm remembering how in Boston I often felt like your side-kick, like you kept me around just for your amusement. I felt that same way today."

Maggie leans back against the headrest. It appears as if she's giving his declaration serious consideration. "Did you ever wonder," she says, "what would have happened if we stayed in Dublin?"

"Not really." Had they had this conversation years ago or even on the drive down to Joliet, he might have told her the truth, that he used to think about it a lot. He used to imagine them still together with a couple of kids, visiting with the grandparents and cousins and uncles and aunts. But those imaginings were long ago, replaced with dreams of other women, other places, other lives. He doesn't want to wax nostalgic with Maggie any longer. "You know what the problem is?" he says. They are driving through the city now, almost at her hotel where she has asked to be dropped off. "You still need someone like me, or the way I used to be. You're a puppeteer, always looking for your puppet and an audience. But me? I don't need someone like you any-more. I need someone I can enjoy life *with*."

Maggie doesn't respond. He tries to gauge her reaction, but she has turned her body fully to the window so he can't see her face.

He pulls the car up in front of her hotel. It's been a long day. "I suppose you wouldn't want to come up for a drink, eh?" she says, still facing the window.

This time he doesn't respond.

"That's too bad," she says, holding on to her dignity with a smile and a deep breath. Her big straw bag is at her feet. She searches through it, takes out her wallet, and hands Rory her business card. "In case you change your mind."

"It was good to see you, Maggie." He kisses her on the cheek.

She steps out of the car. "Good luck, okay? I hope you find her."

Rory drives in the direction of downtown, not sure where he's headed. He's hungry. He finds a parking lot, pays the attendant, and ducks into a little Italian place under the el. He orders a hearty lasagna, then uses the pay phone by the restroom to call Bess. She doesn't answer and when the beep comes, he doesn't know what to say so he hesitates and then hangs up. He knows the area code will appear on her caller ID and he's not ready to tell her where he is. He needs time to think. Instead he calls Gabrielle and leaves her a message. "Hi Gabrielle, it's Rory," he says. "Long story, but I'm in Chicago. I came to find Bess, but she left the city this morning, a day early. I don't want her to know I'm here, I still want it to be a surprise, but I'm a little concerned. Have you heard anything? Don't tell her, okay? I'm still"—and here his mind races—"I'm still figuring out what to do. I don't know where I'm staying yet but I'll find a way to check my e-mail, so feel free to get in touch that way. Thanks."

He walks back to his table and indulges in a beer. His mind is swirling; he feels a little light-headed. What should he do now? Go home? Stay in Chicago? And do what? And then a thought comes to him: Cici. He could visit Cici.

CHAPTER TWENTY-NINE

G ood morning," says Rory, "where are you?"

"Hey there! I'm so glad you called!" Bess is empty-
ing the van of trash. She stops and leans against it. "We're in
Omaha. We're leaving soon to drive the rest of the way to Denver. I've been trying to reach you."

"Likewise. I've been having problems with my phone."

"What phone are you using now then? I don't recognize the
area code."

"I'm borrowing a friend's cell phone. So you left Chicago
early."

"How'd you know?"

"Gabrielle told me. I called her to make sure you were okay."

Bess is touched that he checked up on her, relieved that
they're finally connecting, overcome with love and excitement
just hearing his voice. "Cricket's ex-wife died. The funeral is
Sunday."

"Gabrielle told me. I'm sorry. Please pass along my condo-
lences, won't you?"

"Sure." She notices now that he doesn't sound like himself,

or at least there isn't the usual excitement behind his voice as there is with hers. "You sound down."

"A little," he says, and pauses. "So how was Chicago? What did you do?"

"Not much. I saw my great-aunt Esther, which was nice."

"I see."

Then he gets quiet. She's starting to feel nervous. "What's wrong?"

"I was thinking," he says, "why did you stop in Toledo?"

"It was on the way."

"You could have stopped anywhere. Why there?"

She bristles at his tone. "Like I said, it was on the way. The timing was right for lunch." And then she takes the first step. "And I wanted to see it, knowing you had lived there." She can hear him breathing.

"With Lorraine," he says flatly.

"What do you mean?" Is the anger behind his accusation so acute that he can't see the unlikelihood of Lorraine living in the same place? "She wasn't there," says Bess in a near whisper. Rory remains quiet. "I'm sorry," she continues. "But what's making you mad about that? Remind me. That I'm trying to understand you or that I'm not telling you what I'm doing?" Because, she is thinking, the latter can be rectified. *Please be open to what I have to tell you.*

"Both, Bess, good God. You're trying to understand someone who's not me anymore. And look who from. How would you like it if I searched out your ex-boyfriends, asked them if I should marry you?"

"I wouldn't like it at all," she says. She thinks of her ex-boyfriends, all of whom were before therapy, before karate, before anyone told her she sometimes had morning breath bad enough to kill a cat. No, she understands. She will stop. If she can't yet tell him about Maggie and Dao, she can at least assure him that the question of marriage is on her mind. "You know, I called you my fiancé once. It sounded strange, but kind of nice, too."

"I don't know what you're trying to say, Bess."

His tone has turned from tepid to cold and she feels the sting. She wants his warm flirtations back. But what *is* she trying to say? "I think about you all the time," she says. "I miss you. And I know this is awkward, that we haven't talked about your proposal hanging out there and maybe you even want to take it back." She pauses, hoping for an interruption. "I mean . . . do you?"

"Don't put this back on me. What . . . you want me to ask again? Or you want me to say I don't want to anymore, so it'll get you off the hook?"

"No, that's not—"

"Because I'm sitting here thinking I have to give you time to deal with my past. Okay. But then why aren't you coming to me for help? Why are you out there halfway across the country trying to figure out if you and I have a future?"

It's so logical, what he's saying. What has she really learned from Carol, from Maggie or Dao? She didn't know. She could scream from not knowing. "You're right. I should ask you more questions. I'm sorry."

"So ask."

"That's hard on the spot."

"Try."

"Okay, okay," she says. "Who was your best man at your weddings?"

"I told you about my friend Vijay in Seattle. We were each other's best men in our double wedding, when I married Pam. My brother stood next to me at my wedding with Maggie. None for the others."

"I see. Did you ever register?"

"For what? China? Steak knives? No."

"Ever pay alimony?"

"No. Most of them made more than me. C'mon, Bess. Ask me what you really want to ask me."

She imagines herself in a fetal position at the bottom of a rocking rowboat, the rowboat small and alone in miles of a dark, open sea. "Why do you think it's going to work with me, Rory? Why do you think I'm any different? Do you finally think I'm the one you're going to grow old with?"

He sighs. "I don't know that you are, Bess."

It is a punch to her gut. She feels frail, unhinged.

"I mean, I've done a lot of thinking. You can't go through what I've been through and be surprised anymore that things don't work out. But I have hope. And determination. And I love you."

"Why do you love me? Why am I different from the others?"

"Those are two different questions. I love you because you're smart and sexy and vulnerable. You're different because you're Bess Gray, and I'm in love with Bess Gray."

Bess feels tears well up. "Thank you," she whispers.

"What was that? It's hard to hear you."

"I said . . ." and here she pauses and looks up to the great expanse of a sky. "I love you, too. I really do."

CHAPTER THIRTY

dear bess,

here is a question for you: what can we truly know?

i knew much about rory's past before we were married, as much as he thought to tell me. and i believe rory would have honored his marriage vows to me. but i don't know if our marriage could have made me happy. i only know it didn't. rain that quenches and sustains life can also drown. or it can collect as rainwater and merely dry up in the sun. rory and i might have survived if we had a child, or we might never have had a first kiss had i found out who i was before i became who i was not.

my stepson speaks of living in america. he is only six. his teacher asked him what he might like to be when he gets older. he said a vietnamese american. he must have heard me label myself that way, but how did i say it? with pride? resentment? resignation?

i think the answers we seek—about ourselves and how we wish to live—are not preexisting. they don't lay dormant waiting to be found. they are little children who grow up and move away from the questions that brought them into the world, seeking out new questions to fall in love with. what funny games are they playing sending my stepson's imagination back to the place i escaped?

do you know about tet? it's our new year's celebration. we leave our cities and journey to our home villages with gifts for relatives and offerings to our ancestors. we buy new clothes and decorate our relatives' homes with flowering peach blossoms and mandarin orange trees in honor of the onset of spring. it is a beautiful time. but during my first year in saigon, i didn't see it as beautiful. tet was a sad and difficult occasion because i didn't have a village to go home to. now i visit with my husband's family and it is beautiful again, because his family is my family, that is the strength of our union.

i am sorry to hear that your father suffered an accident. i am also sorry that your elders are unmoored. i hope you can help them. i hope they can help you, too. may you each and together find your village.

peace,
dao

CHAPTER THIRTY-ONE

The paramedics in the parking lot of the McDonald's are scrambling. They push Bess aside to pull through their patient strapped to a stretcher with its squeaking wheels and accompanying contraptions: an orange trauma pack, an oxygen tank, a high-tech vital signs monitor like a toaster with tentacles. She sees parents gripping the shoulders of children to hold them in place, their eyes wide and alert. The exterior of the McDonald's in the dusk trumpets yellow and red, colors that make her think of sickly skin and blood. There is metal clanking, shuffling, bumping, words she can make out if she concentrates.

"Ma'am, are you a relation?" There are three attendants in blue uniforms. This tall one stands erect, his thumbs hooked on his belt, his gaze impenetrable behind his sunglasses, his thick, boomerang mustache a mask to his humanity. A small black box strapped to the top of his right shoulder burps static. He reaches up to bring it to his lips. "I got it," he says, then lowers his hand. "Ma'am?"

"That's my grandfather," she says through her fingers pressed to her lips. She and Millie had already told the other attendants who he was, had answered questions about his age, allergies, current medications.

Two men lift the stretcher into the back of the ambulance. She catches sight of Irv before the doors shut: his closed eyes, his face buried beneath an oxygen mask, his feet in white socks, his legs fanned out in a V. One attendant stays with him; the other helps Millie into the passenger seat. He pulls out the seat belt and makes sure she's strapped in before he circles the vehicle to the driver's side.

Bess—suddenly noticing that she is just standing there, paralyzed, watching the scene unfold—brushes past Pancho Villa toward the ambulance. She raps on Millie's window and Millie turns to her, scared and tiny with heavy red eyes and quivering lips. She motions for her to roll down the window, but Millie can't figure out how and is beginning to panic. "Stop," says Bess, her hand flat against the window. The glass feels the opposite of flesh. "It's okay, he'll be okay," she yells through the window. "I'll meet you at the hospital."

The driver starts the engine and the flashing lights begin to whirl. "Wait!" she yells. She circles the ambulance; he rolls down his window. His gray hair is parted prudently on the side, his shirt's silver buttons are gleaming and reflective. "I don't know where to go," she says. There is something deep and desperate in her words.

"Where's your car?" His voice is fatherly, like the head of a 1950s Midwestern television family.

"There," she points. "The van."

"Follow Herbert." He nods with his chin to the attendant still standing erect as if posing for a photo.

Herbert? she thinks. *Pancho Villa's name is Herbert?* "Didn't he come with you?"

"He's got his motorcycle."

The ambulance pulls out of the lot, leaving Bess several feet in front of Herbert. By the front door of the McDonald's, a cashier in a red baseball hat and a few remaining patrons linger to watch the ambulance depart. It is early evening and suddenly quiet enough to hear the scraping of a shoe on pebbles or the shaking of ice cubes in a paper cup.

"Interesting turn of events," says Herbert. He leans over and spits onto the pavement.

Bess follows Herbert's motorcycle out to the interstate. He obeys the speed limit in the right lane, unfazed, it seems, by the cars and trucks passing him by, turning his bulbous black helmet slowly from side to side like a gigantic carpenter ant. *Interesting turn of events.* What the hell does that mean?

The Rocky Mountains in the distance are pink in the waning daylight. She wonders for a moment where she is. Somewhere west of Denver. She dials Rory's home number, gets his voice mail. Now her tears come. She attempts to wipe them and notices there is blood on the sleeve of her tunic. The fatherly attendant had asked her about the blood. An elderly man collapses and bumps his head, not an unfamiliar occurrence he had hinted. But there's a scratch on his forearm. *I was outside*, she had said. *It's true*, the manager of the McDonald's confirmed, having given his statement to ensure his branch wasn't liable. *But her*, he had added, pointing at Millie. *She was here*.

Millie and Bess reunite outside Irv's hospital room and are told to have a seat in the waiting area. It is a windowless corner with rows of mauve seats facing different directions and end tables with scattered magazines boasting the best sex positions and light summer recipes. The only other person in the waiting area is a teenage boy, belching out a song lyric in a straining falsetto.

Bess looks over at Millie. It had been heart-wrenching to see her so scared, crying and wringing her hands and saying over and over, *He's going to be okay, isn't he going to be okay?* But now Bess feels familiar eruptions of anger and suspicion threatening the love and support she knows she should be bestowing. "Are you going to tell me what happened?" she says quietly into her lap, only half committed to the desire for an answer.

Millie brings her hand up to cover her lips and turns away from Bess. She breathes in two quick, congested breaths, as if holding back an outburst of tears.

Bess squeezes her grandmother's shoulder, then lets herself be distracted by the TV mounted high in the corner. She reads the subtitles unfolding in blinking misspelled words: something about the IRA renouncing violence. Next up: Larry King.

"Excuse me," says a weary man in a lab coat, standing in front of Bess and Millie, offering an outstretched hand. "My name is Dr. Higgins." He is balding, potbellied, and sad-eyed. His appearance is distinctly middle-aged with an emphasis on the old age he's headed into rather than the youth he left behind. He stoops like a beaten-down bureaucrat counting the days until retirement.

"Oh, Doctor," says Millie, standing with great urgency. "How is my husband?"

"We don't know yet, Mrs. Steinbloom. Please have a seat. I can assure you he is under the best of care. Ms. Gray?" he says, turning to Bess. "May I speak with you privately, please?"

Bess can feel her attitude toward Millie start to shift back to what it was in the parking lot. "Anything you have to say to me you can say to my grandmother."

Dr. Higgins hesitates. "You don't understand. I'm a staff psychologist with the hospital's social services division."

Bess nods. Millie looks down at the carpet.

Dr. Higgins removes his rimless glasses and uses them to point toward the corridor where he and Bess stroll out of sight of Millie. "Ms. Gray," he says gravely, "your grandfather has bruises on his arms and a fresh scratch, as if from a fingernail. There are witnesses who say they heard your grandparents arguing before he blacked out. Can you explain?"

"I'm . . . not sure."

He scratches his ear. "I'd like to speak to each of you. Separately. Do you think that's possible?"

"Of course."

"In your opinion, if I grant your grandmother's request to see your grandfather under supervision, she won't—"

"No! I swear. She loves him. I know that's not how it seems, but it's true."

"Okay. These situations are always complicated. I'm going to ask her into my office, and then I'll talk with you, all right?"

She accompanies the doctor back to her grandfather's room. Irv is asleep. Bess examines his aged, sagging, sweet face. She is hungry for answers and bloated with a fierce protectiveness. He had been awake, they told her, but was dizzy and dehydrated, so they had him drink water, take a pill, and stay still while they dressed his wounds and scanned his brain waves. Then they told him to relax, which sent him back into a soporific state. His heart, as it turns out, was intact, though they wanted to keep him overnight to make sure. She sits quietly by his side and thinks about frail marriages. *How did it come to this?*

A copy of *Coastal Living* magazine rests on the shelf by the window. On its cover are two empty deck chairs facing an endless, sunny future. "Tell him I'm here, okay?" she says to the nurse who has come in to close the blinds. "I mean, if he wakes up and I'm not in the room. Tell him he's not alone."

Bess stands in Dr. Higgins's office, a cluttered lair with shades drawn and a lamp lit in the corner. "So what did my grandmother say?" she asks.

"Let's you and I talk first, okay? Have a seat." He points to the couch and drops into a matching armchair. "Tell me what brought you from Washington."

Bess sits. She explains that they had driven into Denver late Thursday from Chicago; that *they* means her, her grandparents, her friend Cricket, and Cricket's dog; that Cricket's ex-wife had passed away and they had to make the funeral. "I slept until noon yesterday, and felt disoriented when I woke up. My grandparents haven't exactly been getting along and I get nervous leaving them alone for too long so that's the feeling I woke up with, like *Oh no, they're right next door and I don't hear them.*"

"What do you mean by not getting along?"

"They argue, they bicker. You know, like a typical old married couple."

"Is that a typical old married couple?"

"Look," says Bess, readjusting herself in her seat, "their bodies are failing them, their friends are dying off, they just sold their house where they've been living for over twenty years and are moving thousands of miles away from home. How do you think you'd be?"

Dr. Higgins shifts his weight to his other elbow resting on the arm of his chair. He lets silence ensue the way therapists do until it turns uncomfortable.

Bess doesn't care that it's all just paperwork to him. She wants to tell her story. "This was mostly for them, this trip," she continues. "But I guess I turned it into my trip, my needs, and Cricket's needs, too. Though he didn't know we'd have to rush to Denver for a funeral, and I didn't really think through what I was doing."

"What were you doing?"

"I was just looking for certain people. All I'll say is that I found some of them. And actually it was my grandfather who found one. That's where things started to go wrong."

Behind his glasses, Dr. Higgins's eyes look small and round and seem even closer together when filled with surprise. His eyebrows, arched up, look like little hats on round faces or circumflex accents on the letter O. "Go ahead," he says. "I'm listening."

CHAPTER THIRTY-TWO

See the plan was, Cricket and his dog would fly home from Denver, whereas my grandparents and I would spend a couple nights in Santa Fe, then head to Tucson to their new place, their *independent living* place the Web site calls it, right next to the *assisted living* apartments, which is next to a nursing home. I picture these places all in a row, the people just moving on down the line if they fail their checkup or something. You know, to *beyond assistance* and then to the *dying place*. There's probably a cemetery at the end of the street, making the whole thing oh so convenient.

Sorry. It's been a long day.

Anyway, like I said, I got up late yesterday. They were both in the room when I knocked. My grandmother was reading her book; my grandfather was resting on the bed. It felt too quiet, so I assumed they'd been arguing. I can usually tell. My grandfather does something with his lips, like this: sort of pushes his lower lip up, holds for a moment, then drops it, over and over again. Dead giveaway. My grandmother won't look at me. I asked what was the matter, but they didn't say anything.

It was nice out, so I suggested we go for a walk, which we did, and it *was* nice, until I yelled at a mime. You know the kind, with the baggy pants and suspenders and his face painted white? He was following people around, mimicking their mannerisms. We walked past him in a park and he sort of latched on to my grandparents. He . . . captured them perfectly. My grandfather's slow gait, his hands clasped behind him, his distant look, his sloped shoulders, his frown. I don't know, he seemed to encapsulate all the pain and sadness my grandfather is carrying around. And my grandmother's anger he nailed—her tight lips, her tense, proud walk, the way she clutches her bag to her side. He was going back and forth, first her, then him, and people stopped to watch and point and laugh. I couldn't stand it! So I screamed, *Stop it!* I remember the people who were laughing stopped laughing, and he backed off with the saddest expression, like he was so sorry for me. My grandparents didn't think much of it. They didn't see what he'd done; they only heard me yell and didn't ask. I'm not sure why they didn't ask, but they didn't.

And that's about it for yesterday. This morning my grandmother and I went with Cricket to Isabella's funeral. I told her she didn't need to, especially since neither of us had the right clothes. Cricket did, just in case. That surprised me, but I guess he's like that. He expects death. My grandfather didn't want to go and that was fine with us. So we went, and when we got back to the motel, my grandfather was missing.

We looked everywhere and were about to call the police when I found a note from him under my door. All it said was not to worry, he'd be back later. It didn't say where he was going.

The hotel clerk said he saw him earlier, sitting outside with one of the cleaning ladies. I knew the one—this nice Latina woman who liked to hum.

My grandmother was moving pretty slowly by now, so I let her rest in her room while I found another woman who told me she did see this Latina woman leave with an older gentleman. I knew that was my grandfather even before the nurse described him. I went back to their room, not knowing what to say to my grandmother, when I saw some of my papers I had left on their bed and I knew exactly where he had gone.

Let me back up, because this is important. There's this woman, Fawn Gilman. She's in her early seventies, and she lives not too far from here. I know her, or know of her, because she . . . knew my boyfriend. Actually, I don't think they knew each other all that well. They met in Las Vegas about twenty years ago, got completely blitzed one night and ended up getting married. And of course divorced the next day. Or something like that. It was a mistake, in other words. She was twice his age—a washed-up barfly, according to his version of the story. And that's kind of the amazing thing about different people's perspectives, because when my grandfather heard her name—I was talking about her with my friend Gabrielle back in D.C., on my cell phone, in the van on the way to Denver—when he heard her name, his eyes got all wide and animated. *Fawn Gilman?* he said with such reverence it made me stop talking mid-sentence. *Fawn Gilman, the dancer?*

Turns out, he was a big fan of hers back in the day. According to my grandfather, Fawn's mother was a Russian Jew and well-known dancer in the Ballets Russes in Paris and Monte Carlo. But she got pregnant with Fawn and had to drop out, ended up coming here, I think, in the mid-1930s. Somehow she got acquainted with Lincoln Kirstein—the guy who founded the New York City Ballet. He was the one who brought Balanchine over from Russia. My grandfather knew of the Kirstein family, either through the Jewish community or because Kirstein's father owned Filene's department store. My grandfather was in the dress business.

So Fawn, through her mother's connections, joined the New York City Ballet when it opened in '48; she was fifteen. My grandfather first noticed her when she followed another one of Balanchine's protégés to Philadelphia to start up the Pennsylvania Ballet in the '60s. He said she was a pretty Jewish girl with long legs that could stop a rocket. He'd take the train from Baltimore to go see her performances.

So here's what I'm getting at. Gabrielle sent me an e-mail that I printed out that had all this information on it, including the breaking news that Fawn lived not too far from Denver. See? The e-mail was missing. I had printed it out because I thought I might visit her, but then I decided that was a bad idea. But I knew my grandfather had taken the e-mail and sure enough, he got his cleaning lady friend to give him a lift out there. I didn't know for sure, I mean, I had a hunch and it just proved to be true. So I opened the e-mail again, got directions, and my grandmother and I went to find him.

Fawn's house was in this community of small stucco homes, which was surprising given that Rory—my boyfriend—had described her as being wealthy. We went to the main building, where there was a TV room and Ping-Pong table and coffee. It looked like a place where residents congregated so they wouldn't be lonely. That's where we found them, Fawn and my grandfather.

We heard a scratchy recording of a waltz, like a record playing on an actual turntable, and there they were, dancing, arm-in-arm, in the middle of the room. They looked beautiful, like a dying maple leaf falling from its branch, how it takes its time and twirls in the air. That's what they made me think of, or what Fawn made me think of, towering over him. I thought she was radiant, like a sunset: she wore orange pants, a burnt red sleeveless blouse, and a long crimson head scarf all shimmering and flowing about her. He looked more like a piece of bark that got stuck to her and was along for the ride, but he was happy. His smile was as wide as I've ever seen. I could have stood there and watched him for a long time, there with the sunlight streaming in.

Fawn had a body much younger than her age would let on, though you could see the truth if you looked closely enough at the veins in her skin or the gray at her roots. But it was mostly her face that gave her away. It was so wizened and pale, as if all she had endured in life was there in every crease and blemish and frown when she thought no one was looking. And those dark, sunken eyes of hers. It made me sad to see her eyes.

But I noticed all that later. When we first walked in the room Fawn and my grandfather were dancing and there were about a half dozen other folks sitting on the couches in a circle cheering them on. Someone yelled, *You show him how it's done, Fawn*, but my grandfather stopped when he saw us. He let go of Fawn and stood there encircling his hands one in the other.

I said hi to everyone. I didn't know what else to do. *Please don't stop on our account*, I said, but that came out petty, even though I didn't mean it that way. There was an awkward silence then when everyone was just looking at us so I started the introductions. Fawn came over and shook our hands and said she was very pleased to meet us. I realized that she and my grandfather had had a few hours at least to get to know each other and I wondered—How much did he share? Did he talk about my grandmother? Did he mention the e-mail, or that it was from me that he knew where to find Fawn?

The waltz on the stereo stopped and then started again from the beginning and Fawn said, *Mr. Steinbloom, you should dance with your wife.* He held out his hand and asked my grandmother to dance. It was such a little thing, a stupid invitation in a crowd of strangers in the middle of nowheresville, but it was so sincere even if it wasn't his idea and I almost cried seeing him there with his hand out to her. If I could have willed anything I would have closed my eyes and willed that dance to happen. It just seemed to me like everything would be okay, that all of this wouldn't have happened if they could have just danced a waltz in the sunlight. But she said no. *No, thank you*, she said, and he lowered his arm and the moment evaporated. That's when I saw Fawn's face. Really saw it; she was looking at me with such deep understanding that it gave me chills.

But Fawn changed the mood. She clapped her hands, went to a corner, and changed the music to salsa while she talked of the weather and welcomed them to take a seat. She did a little dance move on her way back to the couches. Then she plopped down on the couch next to an older gentleman, took off her shoes, and put her feet up on his lap. *Use the peppermint*, she said to him, pointing to a bottle of lotion on the table, and he squirted a dollop in his hand and began massaging her feet. I was fascinated by this minutia surrounding her *being*. She was one of those people whose *being* you noticed. She commanded that room. I could tell they all idolized her. Even my grandmother was somewhat mesmerized by her, though she tried not to be, looking away and down at her lap every now and again. I was surprised she even wanted to stay.

Fawn got everyone talking about all sorts of things, the kinds of things I tried to get my grandparents to talk about the whole drive out from Washington. Things from their childhoods, like visiting the candy stores and the Fireside Chats on the radio and the polio scare and how sad all the Jews were when Roosevelt died. I loved it. I asked questions and took notes. I couldn't write fast enough, spelling the names wrong, I'm sure—Milton Berle, Artie Shaw, Sid Caesar, Imogene Coca, Jack Barry. Fawn talked some about dancing, but she was more excited to talk about Loretta Young's dresses. I noticed she liked to say the phrase *P.S.* a lot, like she always had the last word. Someone would finish a story about Arthur Godfrey, for example, and she'd say, *P.S. he was the biggest goddamn anti-Semite in the whole country*. And then she'd make a joke. I got the feeling everyone there was Jewish and probably originally from the East Coast, that maybe that's the kind of community it was.

My grandfather was mostly having a great time, laughing and slapping his thigh, but my grandmother was pretty quiet. Though, I caught her smiling. I found myself hoping the place they're moving to has people like this that they can relate to.

Then things got serious.

Someone said something like *Those were the good ol' days*, that made everyone contemplative and despondent. Fawn broke the silence with an odd admission; she said, *I've been sober for eight years*. It was odd because no one had asked her, no one brought up the fact that they weren't all good ol' days, but she said it as if everyone was thinking it anyway and she needed to clear the air. The funny thing was, I really was thinking about it. The way Rory described her, she was an alcoholic and a coke addict back then and yeah, she seemed to be okay now so I wondered, health-wise, how she was doing.

I can't remember what caused the change. The music stopped, that's one thing. We were left listening to the sound of our own breathing, which, collectively, got to be loud in a room full of older folks. And then there was this woman, a huge, lumbering woman in the corner. She was mumbling things throughout the con-versation. They called her Agnes. I couldn't hear Agnes until ev-eryone stopped talking and then I could hear she was a little senile. Fawn yelled at her to shut up. I was taken aback, because Fawn had been so pleasant. I looked at my grandparents and they were surprised, too, as if we just glimpsed behind the curtain and every-thing up until then had been a mirage—the dancing, the laughing, the trip down memory lane. It got a little Twilight Zoney.

Somewhere in there, maybe to make polite conversation, my

grandfather asked Fawn how she knew Rory. She looked like she didn't have a clue about what he was talking about, so I offered a few details—his name, what he looked like, that she had met him at a bar in Las Vegas and what year that might have been. I didn't say they got married, mostly because I hadn't told my grandparents that he's been married before, but Fawn said it. Only, she said it as a joke. *Did I marry him?* She said it as if it was the most absurd thing in the world, and everyone laughed. Fawn laughed, too, and I could tell she really didn't remember. But then her smile waned just enough. Fawn gazed directly into my eyes. It was a look that lingered an extra second that made me think Fawn was reading my thoughts and understood on some level. And not only that, that she was sorry.

Then she said—and I memorized this—*A man iz voser iz, nit voser iz geven.* I asked her what it meant and my grandmother of all people was the one who translated. She said it was Yiddish for *A man is what he is, not what he has been.* I've been thinking about it ever since.

We left the group right after that. My grandmother asked in front of everyone if my grandfather had made arrangements to get home—she said *home* not back to the hotel. He said no and she said in her nasty way, *I didn't think so*, and it was at that point that I got up and corralled them into their good-byes and back into the van.

Right after we started driving, my grandmother said she had to go to the restroom. I stopped at the next bathroom I could find, which was that McDonald's. I waited in the car while they both went in.

This is going to sound strange, but I've never been in a McDonald's. My parents were into healthy food and never took me, and then, I don't know, it wasn't a principle so much as a challenge. But then this woman burst open the door and yelled at me to come inside. My grandmother must have told her I was outside. I ran in and found my grandfather on the floor. He was unconscious and folded up against the wall. My grandmother was on her knees, crying. This guy—I'm guessing he was probably the manager—he told me he had already called for help. He and I laid my grandfather out and I put a shirt or apron, something, under his head, all the time I was saying, *Shh, it's okay, it's okay* to my grandmother or maybe to myself, I don't know. I fixed his crooked glasses. He was breathing, I could tell that, but I couldn't get him to open his eyes. I kept asking what happened, but my grandmother was sobbing too loud for me to understand her and the few people standing around didn't know. The manager said he only heard a confrontation. There was a girl who was using the restroom. She said she heard my grandparents arguing but she couldn't say what the argument was about.

I held my grandmother, just so she'd stop shaking and crying. We sat at my grandfather's feet. I think I was in shock, because what kept going through my mind was: *So this is the inside of a McDonald's.*

We were sitting there and the girl said, *Guy his age, maybe he had a heart attack.* It made me think of Agnes and Fawn. Agnes mumbled about a lot of things, one of which was her cardiac muscle. She was going on and on about it until Fawn told her to shut up. *P.S.*, said Fawn, *it's called a heart, Agnes. Broken, bashed in, or ripped apart, it's still a human heart and it pumps until it doesn't. Look around you . . . we're all still pumping away.*

I don't know . . . sitting there on the floor of the McDonald's with my grandfather unconscious and my grandmother upset like that, I thought of that phrase, *pumping away*, and I heard it differently. I had this image of them rowing out from shore, pumping the oars, waving good-bye, turning their heads to the ocean and fading into the haze of the horizon. Images like that make me want to curl up in a corner and cry until I can't cry anymore.

And I do sometimes. Sometimes, I actually do.

CHAPTER THIRTY-THREE

Excuse me," says a nurse who has knocked on the door and poked her head in. "Your grandfather is awake. I'm sure he'd like to see you."

Bess looks around Dr. Higgins's office for the time and doesn't see it. She wonders how long she's been talking. "Where's my grandmother?" she asks the nurse.

"I sent her to get something to eat."

Bess follows the nurse to Irv's room. His breathing sounds labored through his open mouth. His skin is slightly gray, his eyes nearly unblinking as he stares at the window. Laid out on a bright white sheet in a hospital bed much too large for his slight frame, he has the look of a fresh trout on wax paper.

"Gramp? How are you feeling?"

He lifts a knee and turns to her. His gaze graduates from confusion to recognition to affection.

"Like a million bucks, Bessie dear." His voice is weak and strained.

"Inflation being what it is, we should be able to do better."

"Ech, your generation. You're all spoiled." His smile lasts only a second before he winces in pain at having tried to move.

"Easy," she says, adjusting his pillow. "Do you know where you are?"

"A Caribbean beach resort, I hope."

"Close."

Bess adjusts his pillow. "Gramp, what did the doctors, say? You all right?"

"I'm fine. They think I fell, bumped my head. Nothing to worry about."

"No heart attack? No concussion?"

"Your grandfather, he's a tough one," he says with his thumb pointed at his chest. "Takes more to beat me down than a fast-food joint."

"I see." Bess points to the gauze taped to his arm. "Does it hurt?"

"That? No. They go overboard, these doctors. It's enough already with the gauze, I told them." He avoids her gaze.

"Gramp. She can't be doing that to you."

"I got a little scratch this time. So what. She doesn't mean it."

"How do you know she doesn't mean it?"

He sighs and places his hand over his heart, perhaps uncon-sciously. "Because we never mean to hurt the ones we love most."

Bess feels her sadness like a tangible thing in her throat. "She has to stop, Gramp. It's not right."

"I told them: What's right or not right is between her and me."

Bess wants to ask him more questions, but he has closed his eyes as if he's ready to slip back into sleep.

She doesn't buy his last statement, but she is touched to find him loyal to Millie, as if by airing their domestic disputes to such a degree, they have pushed the emergency reset button that recalls a sixty-five-year-old partnership, turning them from foes to allies against the rest of the world. But she can't help wondering: Is he implying that he believes Millie has just cause? And how far back is he willing to give her to justify that cause?

Sometime between the start of her conversation with Dr. Higgins and now it has turned dark outside and she has been informed that visiting hours are coming to an end. She steps out of the room to make a call.

"Where have you been?" says Cricket.

"We're okay. Sort of." She relates the events of the afternoon in a more abridged version than she delivered to Dr. Higgins. It feels good to talk to Cricket. Unlike Dr. Higgins, Cricket syncopates her story with gratifying exclamations of shock and sympathy. She feels homesick hearing his voice.

"My Lord," says Cricket. "Well, it could have been much worse. At their age. Imagine. I'm glad Irving is okay. And Millie, she's holding up?"

Bess rubs her eyes. "I don't know. I hope so. I'm afraid of what the psychologist is going to say. Sometimes I think she doesn't know her own strength. You know how she pinches your cheek and can turn it black and blue? But then, I do think other times she knows exactly what she's doing and can't help herself. And I don't know why."

"Well, you're not going to get all the answers tonight, honey pie."

"I know. So how are you doing? We didn't get a chance to talk about the funeral. I thought it was very nice; everyone was particularly nice to you."

"Yes, that was a surprise. I didn't expect that from Isabella's family."

"What did you do afterwards?"

"I went back to her sister's place. Her son's pet tarantula escaped from its tank, I got a splinter in my big toe the size of a canoe, and I discovered butterscotch pudding gives me a rash. Lovely day. So have you talked to Rory?"

Bess is surprised and touched that he should think of asking that. "I called but no answer. Now I have to get my grandmother back to the motel."

"I'll wait up for you."

Millie returns from the cafeteria and Bess gives her a few moments with Irv. She watches Millie cautiously approach Irv's bed like a cat investigating a new food source. Fortunately, he is asleep; their first real encounter will have to wait until morning. Still, Millie stands close to him and cries, and maybe prays, too, though Bess can't tell for sure.

The door to Dr. Higgins's office is half ajar; Bess knocks gently. "Can I come in?"

Dr. Higgins stops writing, places his pen on his desk, and motions for her to enter.

"Visiting hours are over," she says. "You're working late."

He nods politely. "A lot to do."

"So we're free to go?"

"Have a seat," he says, taking off his glasses. She sits while he allows for the long pause one takes before saying something weighty. "I service four hospitals in the area and have seen hundreds of abuse cases over the years, particularly against elders. The system is currently overwrought. I'm treating a woman now whose nephew was charged with looking after her, but instead cashed her checks and ignored her. A neighbor found her in her wheelchair with severe bedsores and sitting in her own waste. The nephew is at large while she's fighting for her life." He fingers a silver insignia ring on his right hand. Bess finds herself staring intently at it. "So I'm not going to report this to protective services. They have enough to deal with. Nor do I wish to delay your arrival in Tucson, where your grandparents can begin to settle down and adjust to their new lives. But as I told your grandmother, she needs help dealing with her anger, immediately and regularly. That is of utmost importance. I'll write up my assessment and in the morning I'll contact the community they are moving to and see who they have on staff. I've spoken with the doctor here; he says he'll likely release your grandfather tomorrow to your care, provided you can safely transport him to Tucson."

What Bess mostly feels listening to Dr. Higgins is relief, for what comes through first and loudest, what is easiest for a taxed mind to understand is that they can leave, that no lawyers or cops will get involved and they can put this behind them. But she also knows there can be no more pretending that there isn't something serious going on that could get worse if unchecked. She knew this all along, deep down, and feels ashamed at the realization that she could have prevented all this somehow. "I should have talked to them," she says feebly.

"This isn't about blame. But yes, I think you might want to talk to your grandmother. At least I told her it was high time she talked to you."

Millie and Bess each kiss Irving on the cheek, thank Dr. Higgins for his time, and leave the hospital in silence. The darkness outside is crisp and quiet. The opening and closing of the van doors stop the clicking of the crickets. They put on their seat belts, Bess glances at the map, and with hardly a word they set off for the motel.

Bess looks over at Millie for a read on her state of mind, but Millie is staring straight ahead at the road with an impenetrable gaze. The collar of her shirt is tucked haphazardly under her pale blue cardigan, a detail she has never before let pass unnoticed or unfixed.

"Gram, I think we should talk."

Millie nods and looks down at her lap.

Bess's heart is racing. "I just think—"

"Yes," says Millie.

"What?"

"Yes, I think we should talk, dear."

Bess waits for her to say more, but Millie doesn't. Bess has learned through her studies how to encourage and record oral histories. Hours of interviews she has conducted or listened to— with immigrants and artists, border crossers and boxcar proselytizers. It's easier with the garrulous ones far removed from her own experience. Not so with the ones whose pauses quake with the possibility of life-altering truths.

On the dark highway there are few cars. Bess concentrates on holding her hand steady on the steering wheel and moving forward. "Gram," she says, slowly, deliberately, "what happened to Peace?"

"Who's Peace?"

"Gramp's mannequin."

"I left her in Iowa." Millie says this without looking at Bess.

"Why?"

Millie looks out the window. "That's a big why."

CHAPTER THIRTY-FOUR

There are things you don't know. Maybe it was a mistake you don't know. Maybe I should've told you these things. My family, we never shared. We didn't talk about the past. If you didn't talk about it, it would go away. That's it. That's how I was raised. So maybe that was wrong. Who's to say? We all make mistakes.

I couldn't conceive. It was my fault your grandfather and I couldn't have our own children, my broken uterus nobody could fix. May you never know such pain in the heart. Now you can't have babies, so what. They know what to do. Or you adopt, from everywhere you adopt. But you can't imagine how it was for me, for a new bride in 1940, big Jewish family always pinching your cheek, asking with a smirk and a wink what's taking so long, shtup, shtup, shtup and c'mon already with the grandchildren.

I stopped seeing our friends. They all had pink babies and perfect kitchens, that's the truth. Dinner parties were shameful, *shameful*. All that cooing and staring, you'd have thought they saw God in the damn diapers. Kid makes a stink and it's a miracle like you wouldn't believe. Kid burps and it's the funniest thing since Keaton and Arbuckle. We laughed until we cried. Or maybe only I was crying, I don't know. I stopped going. After a while, I didn't even leave the apartment.

It was hard on your grandfather, I know that. He liked to get dressed up, go out on the town. Boy, could he look sharp in his suit. He'd tip his fedora, call me babycakes.

He could make me laugh. He could always make me laugh.

Do you remember you asked me about a man in a photograph, when we were packing? Well that was Gerald's father. Good that you never met him. He was your grandfather's best friend, what could I do. They went to grade school together. Samuel, that was his name. What a schmuck. You know Vivian, Gerald's mother? She was religious back then, even. Kept kosher, never lifted a finger on Saturdays, waited on that putz hand and foot and he paid her back how? By cheating, that's how. With the goyim and the *shvartzes*.

So what happened? I'll tell you what happened. You hammer all those nails you split the wood. Colored girl comes to him, says she's pregnant. Poor girl, petite, pretty, skin like caramel, big eyes I never saw blink. She was a waitress at a diner on Rhode Island Avenue. Couldn't have been more than eighteen. She had mixed blood; her father was white. He was a schmuck, too, I heard. A cheater and a drunk. It's what she knew, I guess. Samuel offered her money to get rid of it, to go away, that's what he did, a real class act, but she wanted him to take the baby, give it a good home. She said she couldn't take care of it working like she was. Well you know your grandfather, can't leave well enough alone. *We'll take it*, he told them like he was ordering a sofa.

It was an equation to him, do you understand? An equation.

I didn't want any part of it. I said Samuel can go pish on his own feet. I said we had no business with a stranger, a colored girl and her colored baby, what would people say? My parents would have a heart attack right there on the spot.

But then the girl's water broke on my sidewalk. Right there in front of me when I was trying to shoo her away before the neighbors saw us talking. I got scared. Your grandfather laid her down in our bed and called for a midwife. Samuel didn't want her at the hospital, the cheap son of a bitch. *Oy*, all that pain hour after hour! The girl screamed so loud you wouldn't believe! I thought she was dying. I almost called the hospital myself. When it was over, I couldn't believe my eyes. There was your mother, a living, breathing, crying miracle of miracles and no darker than a pink cherry blossom.

The girl held her for a few moments, kissed the top of her tiny head, and said take her. Just like that.

All this time I thought your mother was a gift from God. But now I don't know. I think maybe it was a gift from that girl. The greatest gift. The greatest sacrifice.

Rose, that was the girl's name. I always thought that was a beautiful name.

But like I said, I was young then, not much older than Rose. I knew what your grandfather wanted me to do and I said to him where she couldn't hear, I said, *Irving, if we take this baby, the girl's out of the picture. It's our baby*, I said, *ours. She's got to go away like Samuel said*. I was quite adamant. I didn't like that girl, lying there in my bed. Not one bit. Don't ask me why, probably I was jealous. I wanted her out of my life forever. Besides, adoptions were hard enough in those days with all the hoops they made you go through, *oy gut*. And a colored baby? Never mind. Your mother didn't look colored, so no one had to know. Samuel of course was in favor of the whole thing and paid the girl to keep quiet. He and Irv did something, I don't know what. Fudged the paperwork, whatever it took, I didn't care. I had a baby. A stinking, burping miracle of my own and I can tell you all I did for years was stare at her beautiful, beautiful face. Sometimes I hugged her so hard I made her cry and we'd both cry and I would comfort her and say, *Mama's here*.

Rose? Rose went away and I never saw her again.

We moved into a new apartment to make a fresh start. I made your grandfather promise he wouldn't ever tell your mother she wasn't ours, you know, in *that* way. He didn't like it, not at all, but he promised. He did it for me. And oh God, did he love her. I don't think anyone loved a little girl as much as your grandfather did, same as he did with you. We were happy. Maybe the happiest we ever were. Every play we went to, every piano recital, every teacher conference and pediatrician appointment we went to together, *together*, and when your mother had nightmares, we let her sleep in our bed and I would fall in love with this, my family, again and again.

Samuel, in the meantime, was still a schmuck. He finally got his own wife pregnant, God bless. Vivian had several miscarriages, and then gave birth to Gerald in 1965. But there were complications. I don't even want to talk about it. He turned out to be a good boy, that's all that matters.

Samuel, he saw those medical bills, and that was it. He shook his fat pig head and walked backwards out the hospital doors and disappeared. What kind of a *shit* leaves his wife and newborn son in the hospital? Thank God she remarried Lou, the Orthodox Jew. He was a good stepfather to Gerald. He's deceased now.

Anyway one day, just after Gerald was born, your mother, oh she was, I want to say, sixteen? She comes to me and asks if she's adopted. Just like that! Like she's asking the time. I'll never forget it. Your grandfather was in Boston on business. We were on the stoop, banging the dust off our blankets, and I stopped cold. I was terrified if you want to know the truth. I wanted to know what made her ask. She says she overheard Vivian talking about her. Vivian always had a big mouth. What did Vivian say? I ask. She says, quote unquote, *That my birth father is a prick and my birth mother is a fool.* Well, I'll tell you . . . I didn't say a word. Not one word. What should I have said? I didn't even know if she knew what those words meant. And then a miracle. Your mother said she could understand why we didn't tell her. She thanked me for being her real mother and walked up to her room. That was it. Let her think we're the good ones, I said to myself. Weren't we?

I'll tell you something, your mother was always wise beyond her years, calm and determined. Not even the cancer slowed her down until the end, remember? It is what it is. That's what she used to say all the time, like your grandfather. *It is what it is.* And that was fine with me. You wouldn't believe how I feared a moment like that, her finding out, how it gave me nightmares! I thought if it ever happened she'd hate me for the rest of my life. Such good luck I felt. I didn't even tell your grandfather. Toast gets a little burned, you scrape off the black and no one has to know, it's good as new, so what.

It was your grandfather couldn't let well enough alone. He had had some sort of fight with Samuel before Samuel left. I don't know what it was about, he wouldn't tell me, but it upset him for weeks. He would pace the hallway, three, four in the morning. He wouldn't eat, not even my brisket and you know how much he loves my brisket.

Next thing you know he's going to look for Rose. I begged him not to, but you can't talk to him when he gets that way he gets. *Eingeshparht*, you know that word? Stubborn. That's your grandfather. He wouldn't tell your mother, he promised me that, but he had to do it for his own sake. That's what he said. I was terrified all over again, and so angry. He'd be out every night, God knows where. Twice I called the police I was so worried.

He found her all right, and I hated her all over again. I hated her for being a drunk. I hated her for taking advantage of my husband's pity. I hated her for stealing my husband every Sunday, every *goddamn* Sunday he'd visit her in her crummy apartment under a bridge and bring her challah and milk when he should have been home with me and your mother, reading the funnies or, or, or fixing the faucet. I hated her for ruining my marriage, my family.

Feh.

I hated her most of all for jumping off that bridge she lived under. Right onto a highway in rush hour. Stupid girl.

I hated her more than ever because I wasn't allowed to hate her anymore, do you understand? She returned my husband to me empty. He wouldn't laugh at the funnies, even though I put them right in his lap. He never had time to fix anything in the house because he was sleeping, why? Because he stayed out late, all the time with that music, that *shvartze* music he had no business listening to.

Maybe your grandfather told your mother about Rose, I don't know. He wouldn't tell me if he did. I hope he didn't. What did she need that pain for?

Maybe I should have left him. One time, I almost did. He started coming home with those mannequins, and boy I'll tell you. Such *chai kock* in my own basement. Who collects such things? I packed a suitcase and drove to my mother's apartment, but she ordered me to go back. *You make your marriage work*, she yelled at me. *That's what you do.* So I did. That's what we did in those days.

I always wondered whether my mother ever thought of leaving my father. I wondered what their marriage was like. Who knows. You never know. People lie anyway.

Why didn't your grandfather leave me? God knows I wasn't easy to live with. You'll have to ask him. I imagine it's for the same reason. Stay and survive. Find joy.

Find joy. There's a bit of wisdom from your grammy, *nu?* Get married, don't get married, it's all the same.

There was a time when I thought we could adopt another baby. Your mother brought us so much pleasure, I thought it could, I don't know, fix things. But I couldn't take the whole process. All that nosing around our personal lives, talking to neighbors, the surprise home inspections, the interviews, *oy gut*. They played God, those adoption people. I was told, the number one thing they wanted to know? If we had a happy marriage. How could they know that? What, a couple doesn't argue? He puts the toilet seat down? She cooks his dinner? What kind of *mishegoss* is that? Only you know if you're happy.

Sometimes I think it's how we remember things.

Lately, I don't know. I can't remember good things. It seems so hard, I don't know why. Your grandfather, he doesn't remember anything so there you go.

Where did the last forty years go, eh?

Do you remember your grandfather on the day of your mother's funeral? He sat on the edge of the bed, in his suit, limp like a wilted tulip. I said let's go, I'm here, we're *together*. You should have seen him, like I said a miracle. I'll never forget how he looked at me, the way he looked at me when we said our vows so long ago. He held me, kissed me, my husband with the sparkling eyes and dancing feet. We cried and cried, oh my God. For a few moments I let my mind drift to my wedding day, before your mother even came into the picture. I started humming our song. Do you know "Cheek to Cheek," that song? All these women wanted to dance with the groom and he only wanted to dance with me. Imagine that. Just with me.

He's a good man, your grandfather, a good man deep down.

I don't know what's with him and that mannequin. Maybe it looks like Rose, I wouldn't know. I never saw her after your mother was born. Maybe it looks like a woman he was futzing around with at those clubs. Maybe she's nobody. It doesn't matter anymore. It was too crowded. It's always been too crowded.

But I'm here now and I'm going to take care of him. Just me. Me and him, together.

End of story.

CHAPTER THIRTY-FIVE

Bess folds her grandfather's discharge papers into her bag as they wait for the nurse to usher his obligatory wheelchair out the door. "Now no more skiing, Mr. Steinbloom," says the attendant as he moves about the bed, stripping the sheets and spanking the pillows. "And no more of that hockey. I know how much you like hittin' them hockey pucks." He is shaking a finger at his patient, amusing himself.

Irv waves him away. "As long as I can still eat a hot dog. I can still do that, right?" He looks at Millie. Millie had cried at first seeing him. She had cupped his jowls with both hands and kissed him hard on the lips and whispered something in his ear that made him squeeze her shoulder. Now she sits politely in a chair with her ankles crossed, holding his sweater and sun hat. She meets his gaze and offers a knowing smile.

"Now *that* will surely kill you what with all that chemically nasty stuff," says the attendant, "but you do what you gotta do." He winks at Bess.

"She's coming," says Cricket, reentering their room. Cricket looks different, camouflaged and masculine. He's wearing jeans and a new, blue twill shirt with saddle stitching. Even his skin, ballooned at the chin, looks more tanned and tough.

"Is that a Velcro watch, Cricket?"

He flashes Bess a playful frown. "What's it to you?"

"Nothing. I didn't say anything Mr. Shoot-Me-Now-If-I-Ever-Wear-Velcro."

The stripes of sunlight beaming across the tile floor are bright and hot. Bess brought the van to a gas station this morning to fill up, check the oil, and get a general sense that there should be no problems on the road to Santa Fe and on into Tucson. It's time to bring her grandparents home.

"Let's give your grandparents some time alone, shall we?" Cricket whispers to Bess.

Bess has been watching her grandparents in these moments of their reconciliation. Irv relays a joke he heard one of the nurses tell and Millie flashes a coquettish grin. He reaches for a plastic cup and Millie jumps to his assistance. She insists he drink his water until the cup is empty, but she says so lovingly, encouragingly. When she reaches out to fix his collar, he reaches up to hold her hand.

Bess doesn't fully understand why forgiveness has come so easily to her grandfather, nor does she believe this is the end of their nasty outbursts and hurtful behaviors. But their endearments are bursting with hope for a new way of being together. She can feel their yearning to summon the best of their past and learn how to heal and move forward. She can do that, too. *Find joy.* Bess closes her eyes and makes a wish for Millie's advice to play out for them, may it be so for the rest of their lives.

"Bess, honey?"

Bess opens her eyes and nods to Cricket. "We're going to take a walk," she says to her grandparents. "We'll meet you in front."

The grounds around the hospital are peaceful and scenic. A dirt pathway winds around the building in partial shade past landscaped patches of shrubs and flowers, all labeled for visitors. Bess likes the simplicity of the Aspen daisies. Their flat white petals with yellow centers like sunbursts look like the kind of flowers kids first draw with crayons.

"Nice necklace," says Cricket, pointing to his birthday gift to her.

Bess smiles and rubs the silver pendant between her fingers. "Thanks."

"So how do you feel?"

"Tired. And strange."

"Well, that makes sense after what you've been through, darling. Have you thought any more about what Millie told you?"

"Of course. You know me, I can't stop thinking about it."

"Like what? What are you thinking?"

"I don't know." Bess removes a plastic candy wrapper from the dirt. "About everything. Like, Gerald's my mom's half brother. Does that make him my half uncle?" Cricket shrugs.

"I keep replaying all these memories I have of Gerald with this new spin on them," she continues. "And if that isn't freaky enough, I just found out I have black roots. Gabrielle will probably sign me up with the NAACP."

"Well, you knew your mother was adopted, and she had darkish skin you told me."

"I know, but I never thought I'd find out who her parents actually were. I mean, her father was my grandfather's best friend. I wish they were both still alive. I'd look for them."

"You would?"

"Maybe I wouldn't." Bess listens to the sound of their footsteps in the dirt, like the rubbing together of fine sandpaper. She feels far away from the urban click of heels on floorboards and closer to the earth. "What I still don't get is why my grandmother's so angry now when all of that was long ago."

"Look, give it time to sink in," says Cricket, pulling a leaf from Bess's hair. "And go easy on your grandmother. She did a very brave thing talking to you."

"True, but she's also hurting my grandfather."

"She'll get help. From what I saw in that room this morning, she wants to heal."

"No, you're right." She swats away an insect.

"Will you look at these," he says. He points to blooming prairie clover. "They look like little penises with purple pubies."

"Nice," says Bess. "Glad to hear you haven't changed that much."

"I haven't changed at all, what are you talking about?"

Bess pinches the sleeve of his shirt. "New duds, is all I'll say."

"You like this? I got it last night at Rockmount Ranch Wear, *yeehaw*."

"Didn't you have a shirt like that once? A black one?"

"That was ages ago, I'm surprised you remember."

A thought pops into Bess's head and she decides, looking at Cricket, to share. "You look like your old self, you know. The way you used to look when Darren was alive."

Cricket looks out toward the mountains. "Darren's with me."

Bess is struck by this sweet sentiment, rather unlike Cricket. She is moved by the depth of its meaning, for how true it is, the way we carry people with us. "He *is* with you," she says. "He'll always be with you, right here," she says, patting above her heart, "and I—"

"Stop! My Lord, I see you haven't changed, either. Bess, he's in my motel room. You know the white bag I took on the trip? The one I kept by my feet that I wouldn't let you near? It contains an urn."

"An urn."

"With his ashes. Which are now on the windowsill with a note to the cleaning staff saying please don't touch."

Bess is processing several new thoughts at once. "I don't understand."

"He had no family, remember, except for an elderly aunt, who gave me his ashes."

"Why did you . . ."

"Bring him along? Suffice it to say you weren't the only one who romanticized this road trip, my dear. I thought it was time to seek closure and I, well, I've seen one too many schmaltzy movies is what it comes down to. I thought I could drive out West and spread his ashes across the Rockies from the top of a cliff, something like that. Cue the orchestra, Max Steiner, and pass the box of tissues. Oh, but then I came to my senses. Darren was mildly agoraphobic, you know. He hated the dry air for puckering his skin, and spiders gave him nightmares. I don't know what I was thinking."

"Wow." Bess has stopped walking and is staring at him.

"What are you going to do? Bring him back to D.C.?" Is it appropriate to say *him?*

"I don't know what to do. I was so worried he'd spill all over the car mats every time we drove over a bump. I don't know if I can go through that again."

"Wouldn't you have a harder time taking his ashes on the plane?"

Cricket continues walking so Bess has no choice but to stay by his side. "I'm not flying back," he says. "I'm driving. With Claus."

She stops again. Did she hear him right? Claus, Isabella's brother? The irresponsible louse who let Cricket's dog escape? The albino maniac whom Cricket ran from at Eastern Market?

A sinister smile spreads across Cricket's face. "He's kind of cute, don't you think?"

Bess croaks a laugh. "No wonder he was so nice to you at the funeral."

"We spent all day Saturday together, and Saturday night."

Bess smiles broadly, but stops herself from teasing him. Last night was the night of Claus's sister's funeral. Something in Cricket's countenance confirms that this tryst of theirs was a comfort of many kinds. "Did you know he was gay?"

"Not when we were growing up, no. His father was a minister, if you recall; Claus was convinced that what he felt in adolescence was a terrible sin, beating me up for his guilt because he suspected I felt the same. He didn't come to his sister's wedding; he left home after he graduated high school to travel Asia and didn't return until a few years ago. It so happens he moved to

Washington and wanted my friendship, but Darren had just died so I wasn't too obliging. Plus, I couldn't forgive him for bullying me so viciously as children. I guess I'm suddenly in a forgiving mood."

Bess pinches a pebble out of her shoe. "Will the surprises never end," she says under her breath, and then sighs deeply.

"What? What's the matter?"

"Nothing. I'm happy for you."

"But?"

"No buts." She pauses. "Okay, one *but*. I wish I could reach Rory."

"Have you two spoken recently?"

"We had a hard conversation on Friday but haven't really connected since."

"I'm sure he'll call as soon as he's able."

"Maybe." She looks at her watch and points in the direction of the hospital's front door. "We should get back."

"I'll follow you."

"Cricket," she says, touching his arm. "I'm glad I have you to come home to."

He pats her hand. "And I you, my dear. And I you."

Bess and her grandparents drop Cricket off at the hotel and they hug him and pat a panting Stella good-bye. Millie and Irv extend an invitation to visit them in Tucson, and Cricket graciously accepts. "It has been a pleasure, Mr. and Mrs. Steinbloom. I promise to look after your granddaughter to the best of my ability."

"She'll be fine," says Millie. "Won't she, Irving?"

Irv advertises his feelings in his forehead. Bess can tell by his clenched or raised brow when he's relaxed, when he's frustrated, and especially when he's concerned, as he is now. His look is both deeply intimate and helplessly far away.

"Yes, I'll be fine," says Bess, wrapping her arm around her grandfather's shoulders.

"Au revoir," sings Cricket, blowing a kiss as the van pulls away.

The traffic on Interstate 25 is dense leaving Denver and thick again around Colorado Springs, but soon the four-lane highway opens up to skirt the Front Range of the Rocky Mountains with few cars and fewer rest stops. Irv sits in front with Bess, thinking. Millie knits in the back, evidently thinking, too.

At the state border a sign welcomes them to New Mexico, the "Land of Enchantment." Their ears pop through rolling pine forests. They turn west at Las Vegas, New Mexico, and by five P.M. they reach the outskirts of Santa Fe and stop at a tourist shop to pick up a sun hat for Millie. She chooses a wide brim with a small Kokopelli. "I forget what the guy with the flute symbolizes, do you know?" Bess asks the cashier. The cashier is absorbed in a Norman Mailer novel. She marks her page with a worn receipt, places the book to the side, and rings up the hat as if they just woke her from a nap. "Fertility God," she drones. Bess watches Millie put the hat on, fix her hair under it, and wear it proudly out of the store.

By the time they reach their hotel in the center of town, they are hungry and ready to be done with the van for the day. Irv needs to take his medicine, Millie and Bess need a restroom. They check in and agree to meet in a half hour for dinner. Bess has a fleeting thought that maybe she should separate them for the night or share a room with them, but she rules against it. Millie won't hurt him. Not tonight.

Bess lies down on her bed and surveys the room's decor—the geometric Navajo patterns on the quilt, the cowboy boot lamp, the color-enhanced photos of cacti and chili peppers. She unpacks her toiletries, washes up, and calls Rory. Again, he doesn't answer. What if Cricket is wrong? *What if he's given up on me?* She feels panicked. How could she have been so stupid, looking for his ex-wives?

By the next morning, Irv has his spring back in his step and a broad smile. There is a glint, too, in Millie's eyes beneath her new hat that betrays her amusement when she asks what the hell's gotten into him.

They peek in shop windows and point at straw appliqué crosses and oil paintings of wolves and warriors. They follow Millie into a store of scented soaps. She holds a few up to their noses smelling of rose water and sweet almond. Irv buys her a bar as a gift for their new home. Following the edifying advice on new home ownership from the young shop attendant, he also buys sage to bring them into balance and cleanse their minds and bodies of negative spirits and impurities. Bess likes the sentiment; Irv likes the smell. Millie thinks it's a bunch of baloney. By eleven A.M., Bess can tell Irv is feeling the effects of the altitude and the dry heat. They stop at a coffeehouse for a cool drink and a rest. "Ready to go?" Bess asks after a while, and they nod yes. *Yes*, they say, *we're ready*.

Arizona greets them with postcard images: a blinding sun on a surging, liquid highway; snakeweed and ocotillos and wind-blown dust devils across fifty miles of a hot, bleak desert; a soaring turkey vulture circling over a dead jackrabbit in a dry riverbed; a fiery sunset over the darkening valley. They arrive into Tucson with a smattering of smudged bugs on the wind-shield. They crane their necks to see a passing graveyard of old fighter planes, and finally, just before nightfall, reach Millie's sis-ter's house where they will stay until their furniture arrives from back East. Slowly they emerge from the van exhausted and hun-gry for the quesadillas she serves them for dinner, mesmerized by the drone of the after-dinner TV crime show. Bess excuses herself to take a hot shower and turn in early.

Sometime during the middle of the night when Millie must think Bess is asleep on the couch, she stands by the bay window in the living room, looking out toward the Catalina Mountains. Bess glimpses the thin, gnarled, naked silhouette of her grand-mother beneath her nightgown made sheer in the moonlight. She closes her eyes and dreams of infants in wooden cradles and sun-flowers poking through fog.

In the morning, Bess unloads the van into the empty two-bedroom apartment and they discuss design options. Bess in-vestigates the mental health facility across the street and ensures her grandparents are on their radar. Then they get a tour of the synagogue and the main building for the assisted living folks and neighboring inhabitants. A large quilt hangs in the lobby with Hebrew letters sewn in at the top, a saying, they're told, that means "From Generation to Generation." In the dining room, elderly Jews are doing jigsaw puzzles and playing dominoes and visiting with grandkids. It smells like popcorn and cleaning fluid. On a cluttered bulletin board in the hallway there are flyers for ice cream socials and tai chi classes. There are sign-up sheets for special events: Ludy on the Piano, Pokeno with Roger, Reading with Dell, Crafts with Linda, Cards at the Café, Bingo with Joan.

Millie picks up the schedule for the bridge club and chats up one of the residents sitting in his wheelchair while Irv wanders out to the courtyard and eases into a bench in the shade. Bess follows him. She's been looking for an opportunity to speak with him alone ever since her illuminating car ride with Millie, though, given the number of enlightening conversations she's had over the last couple of days, she's beginning to feel talked out. Why did all this stuff have to surface at the end of the trip, when she'd been wanting it all along?

"I know about Rose," she says, taking a seat next to Irv. "Did Gram tell you she told me?"

"She did."

Well, that's progress, thinks Bess. She wonders what their conversation was like.

A lizard hurries behind a flower pot. The heat of the midday sun is ponderous. "Did Rose look like Peace, your mannequin? Is that why you brought her along?"

"Oh, I don't think so," says Irv. "I liked the look of her, that's all. But it's best she's gone."

Does he not comprehend the inner workings of his thoughts and feelings, Bess wonders, or is he hiding something? "It was you, wasn't it?" she says.

Bess watches her grandfather's reaction for indications that she figured out the truth, that she had mulled over Millie's story umpteen times trying to fill in the gaps, to make sense of statements that seemed slightly off for reasons she couldn't explain. "I figure," she says, and then runs her version by him: that he was the one sleeping with Rose, that he got Rose pregnant and didn't want Millie to know, so he asked his best friend to say it was his. Irv could then look like the good guy in Millie's eyes and she'd be more likely to accept the baby. Sam then threatened to expose the truth, causing their big fight right before he left Gerald in the hospital. Irv never told Millie the truth, but he told Bess's mom that, biologically, he was her father. Which means, Bess continues, he is her biological grandfather, her heritage.

Irv wipes the sweat from his forehead with his handkerchief, then puts it back into his pocket. He looks off into the distance, blankly, as if he didn't hear what she had just said and was enjoying the quiet. "Your mother was a beautiful baby, did you know that?" he says after a long minute. "A beautiful, beautiful baby."

When is the keeping of secrets an inviolable right, and when is it a cop-out? Bess wonders. When does one have the right to try to expose someone else's secrets? If the sun wasn't stifling; if she hadn't packed up everything to be on her way to California; if she could just press a button in front of a big-screen TV and watch the life of her grandfather through from the beginning, maybe she'd understand his actions, his justifications, his wrongdoings and righteous acts the way they really happened.

Maybe she'd understand the ways he loved. Maybe she could find out the truth. *How much can we truly know?*

Millie opens the door, sees them, and retreats slowly, letting the door shut on its own. In the blinding sun outside, it appears as if she disappears into blackness.

"Gramp," says Bess, "if you had to do it all over again, would you? Get married, I mean?" Bess wants, once and for all, the definitive answer she so craves about marriage, about life, about choices and happiness. She doesn't want him to sugarcoat their sixty-five years together, to inaccurately tally the good and the bad and lump his whole lifetime into a general feeling of remorse or contentment. She wants him to *think*, to think *hard*. She wants to hear the truth. But the question slipped out and she knows what she's going to hear.

"Yes," he says, "I would do it all over again."

The end. Irv says this wistfully and it makes Millie mad. They have all elongated their good-byes with clinging hugs and choked-back tears and they are standing now by the driver's side of the van in the parking lot of the synagogue, immobilized and fidgety. *What are you talking about? This isn't the end,* Millie snaps with the familiar vestiges of anger in her voice. She is sad and stressed, Bess allows. He has reverted to his woebegone, past tense mindset. It was bound to come out. It is time to leave and trust they'll find their balance. *I'll call you later,* she says. *Don't hurt each other anymore. I love you very much.*

In front of the synagogue, a large desert agave fans out its succulent, fleshy, pointed green leaves, and from its leaves, a single asparagus-like stalk sprouts straight up into the air for a good fifteen feet. According to the man Millie was talking to, the plant, called a century plant, is old. The agaves grow their stalks only when they're ready to die. The stalk blooms for the first and last time at its tip in yellow, waxy flowers, then one day the stalk falls over. The green leaves start to shrivel. Bess sees the agave in her rearview mirror as she departs. It will be gone soon, removed from the premises and planted over. But this morning it stands tall, taller than the nearby trees, thicker than the street-light, sharp-edged and stubborn, reaching to the sky in a burst of color.

CHAPTER THIRTY-SIX

Here," says Cici, "take these and I'll meet you outside." She hands Rory two tumblers of San Pellegrino and points him toward the French doors that lead out to the pool. She is house-sitting in Berkeley for a professor who married the daughter of a Texas oil tycoon. It's a sprawling Mediterranean-style home in a quiet cul-de-sac with soaring ceilings and views of the Golden Gate Bridge and Mount Tamalpais. The floors, Cici had told Rory on her tour of the house this morning, are Brazilian cherrywood. Rory has never seen anything like it— the massive fireplace in the family room, the contemporary art, an elevator! "Bloody hell," he had said when he first stepped onto the terrace overlooking the garden. "I could use a tiny cottage like this."

Cici was delighted at his proposal to come visit. Knowing him the way she did, she wasn't at all surprised by his call, or that he was already halfway across the country without a plan, concocting one as he went. She *was* surprised, instead, that his old Corolla had enough life in it to make the trip. *This might be her last*, Rory admitted.

It took him three days to drive from Chicago; he arrived late, got a good night's sleep, woke to the smell of fresh coffee, and went for an invigorating four-mile run before breakfast. Now he's lounging by the pool, where Cici joins him carrying two towels. Rory is struck by how much she looks like Olive Ann. She's twenty-five now, and for the last seven years, every time Rory has seen Cici he's been in awe of her girl-to-woman trans-formation. How did she get to be a beautiful, six-foot gazelle of a creature? How did she emerge from those hard years with her mother and the Alaskan winters to be a strong woman of inde-pendent means? Rory is full of pride. "Please," she says, point-ing her chin to a couple of lounge chairs. "Have a seat."

"So how's school?" he says. "You're on break now?"

"It's going well. I'm taking one summer course, and working at the library."

She turns to sit and Rory catches sight of a wide V-shaped tattoo on her lower back just above her bikini bottom. "Business, right?" he says.

"I'm actually going for a dual MPH/MBA."

"What's MPH? Miles per hour? You out to change the speed limit?"

Cici smiles. "Master's in public health. I think I want to do something with health care policy. Who knows, maybe I'll get a job in Washington."

"Oh now, don't be getting my hopes up unless you mean it. You tell me what I can do to tip the scales and I'll get right on it."

"All right, I'll keep you posted." She scratches the scar on her knee. Rory had taken her to the hospital for at least one of her knee surgeries when she tore her ACL riding a dirt bike on a treacherous mountain trail. She learned to love riding motorcycles in Alaska. Rory thought maybe her need for speed was one of the ways she pushed herself to overcome her panic attacks.

Rory lathers sunscreen onto his face and neck. The sun is high and bright, though the air feels cooler and less humid than what it typically is in D.C. this time of year. "And your mom?" he says. "Where is she living?"

"She's in Salt Lake City. When she's on her meds, she functions well enough. She's still painting, so that's something." She takes a sip of her drink. "She does look really old, though, but I guess illness does that."

To the untrained ear, Cici has all but gotten rid of her stutter through modification therapy, but he can still detect a hesitation here and there or a slight prolonging of certain vowels. She has developed maneuvers to help disguise these remnants of troubled speech, like raising a glass to her lips and drinking. He detects it mostly when she speaks of her mom.

"What else? What about your dating life?"

"Don't have one."

"Why not? Attractive girl like you?"

"I didn't say I wasn't sleeping with someone, I said I don't date. I'm too young for that, don't you think?"

"I do," he says, acknowledging that he'd been married three times by the time he was her age.

"So," she says, leaning back in her chair like a sunbather. "Your turn. You haven't told me yet why you're on another road odyssey."

"Right," he says, also settling in. "It's a story."

"Of course it is."

Over the years, Rory's role in Cici's life has shifted from something like a stepfather to more of a friend. That has partly been due to Cici warming to her own father, a gruff, albeit big-hearted fisherman who tried to be there for her when Olive Ann couldn't be. But Rory suspects it's also due to their personalities: Cici grew up fast into a worldly sophisticate, while Rory moved from coast to coast, hardly ever fancying himself a good enough parental role model. So she talked to him about stocks and film and sports and men (always men, not guys) and he asked her for relationship advice.

He had told her about Bess when he and Bess first started dating, and now he brings her up to speed: about his marriage proposal; telling Bess about his ex-wives; chasing her to Chicago; his encounter with Lorraine; his trust in Bess plunging when she had the opportunity to tell him about Maggie and didn't.

Cici listens without interruption. "Hm," she says when he's through.

"Hm," he says.

She sits up. "Let me ponder this." She dives into the pool.

Rory didn't think to bring a bathing suit so he is wearing one of the professor's. The waistband is loose, making him cautious about diving into the water. But the water looks inviting, so he sits at the edge, dangling his legs, which are tired from his run.

"I'll tell you," says Cici, treading water, "I never thought you and Dao were well matched."

"Really? You never told me that."

"I'm telling you now, probably because it's occurring to me in hindsight."

"Why weren't we well matched?"

"She was too, what's the word . . . I don't know . . . intense. Too serious."

"Huh. What about Gloria?"

"Too young." Cici does a slow sidestroke to the end of the pool and back.

A cloud covers the sun. Rory scoops water with his palms and watches it trickle through his fingers. "I have a confession. I saw Gloria at Bess's party and I never told her."

"What party? Never told who?"

"Bess. You know, that singles party at her apartment where I met her. I was there and I saw Gloria walk in, or at least some woman who looked like Gloria, I didn't really get a good look. She was pregnant. I kind of panicked and left."

Cici does another lap. "Did Gloria see you?"

"I don't think so. At least she never said anything to Bess."

"Why didn't you just stay and say hi?"

"I'm telling you, I don't know. I think maybe because she was having a baby, like she moved on with her life and I didn't want to deal with that."

"Why didn't you tell Bess?"

"I just . . . I thought she might think I still had feelings for Gloria."

"Do you?"

"No. Not in that way. I agree, we were a mistake."

Cici swims over to him and rests her arms on the side of the pool next to where he's sitting. She looks at home in luxury, Rory thinks. Maybe this is the kind of life she'll end up with. "From what you've told me," she says, "Bess seems like a keeper. She seems good for you. So stop screwing it up and keeping secrets."

"But she——"

"Stop. If you ask me, you're the one who started it by not telling her up front about your past."

"She probably wouldn't have stuck around."

"You needed to take that risk."

"Yeah," says Rory. "Well, now she's seeking out my ex-wives behind my back. Talk about trust breakers."

Cici hops up out of the water and takes a seat. She runs her fingers through her hair and shakes it out. "Rory," she says, "you need to forgive her. And you need to forgive yourself."

Rory looks out toward the mountain. *Forgive myself.* For a quick moment he wonders what she means, wonders what he has to forgive himself for, but he knows, deep down he knows he has never been able to rid himself of the shame of his failed marriages, a deep shame that began the day Maggie walked out and has grown stronger ever since.

Suddenly a memory comes to him of his brother Eamonn playing poker with some of the local boys in the back of a warehouse. Rory stumbled upon them one night; Eamonn let him stay provided he kept his mouth shut. Eamonn had put a big chunk of what money he had left on a bluff that Rory exposed with a poorly timed gasp. Eamonn lost. But instead of beating Rory to a pulp the way his friends' older brothers would have done, Eamonn kept silent. He wouldn't talk to Rory and that was a worse fate. Rory followed him all over town. *I'm sorry*, he'd say, over and over again until one day Eamonn turned to him. *Did y' learn somethin', Rory? Tell me that, did y' learn somethin' that night?* Rory said he learned to keep quiet so he could keep on learning. *Then stop apologizing*, Eamonn had said.

Rory looks over at Cici. Wouldn't it be wonderful, he thought, if Cici lived in D.C. and could come over for dinner now and again to a home he shares with Bess?

"I love you, you know." He sticks his finger in her ear the way he used to do when she was a kid because it tickled her.

"I know," she says, batting him away, smiling. "I love you, too."

A large cloud slides by and lets the bright sun shine down on them again.

"So you going to invite me to the wedding this time?" says Cici.

Rory smiles.

"Good," she says, "let's shake on it." He extends his hand and she pulls him into the pool.

CHAPTER THIRTY-SEVEN

The palm trees are dancing in the breeze, the saguaros on the sidelines are raising their arms and cheering. The Union Pacific train pulls ahead with its fastened loads of logs and crates, leading the way. It's hot and dry on the split highway cutting its way westward through miles of flat desert. Signs warn of "Blowing Dust Areas." The parched mountains toward the horizon look like dung piles. Off in the distance an oil refinery stands alert, a state prison lies low, two sheriffs' cars idle side by side on a cattle guard while their drivers chat. The distance between haciendas grows and then there is nothing but sky and sand and brush.

Bored and tingling from exhaustion, Bess follows the phone lines and changes lanes to stay awake. On the border into Pacific Time there are no working radio stations, no cell phone coverage, no rest stops or gas stations for forty-mile stretches, and for the first time today she looks at the empty seats surrounding her in the van and the big sky outside and feels utterly alone. But it's not a bad feeling, she takes note—this being alone. She feels calmed by the solitude, comfortable even with her own company.

Still . . . what does one do when there's so much aloneness? *The desert needs show tunes*, she can hear Cricket say like some modern-day Fitzcarraldo. *Sing, darling*.

What is Cricket doing now? she wonders. Is he laughing at something Claus has said? Is he feeling at peace? She hopes so. She hopes he finds a place to leave Darren's ashes behind. She never made much of an effort to get to know Darren, but she will with Claus, if he becomes important to Cricket.

Hours ago, just after she offered her version of the past to Irv and Irv stayed annoyingly silent on the subject, she imagined asking him to undergo a DNA test, to see if they really are biologically connected as she still suspects, but now she feels differently. How wonderful to feel differently, it suddenly occurs to her. She doesn't need to know. Doesn't want to know, even. *Why not?* a tiny voice inside her yelps. "Don't know, don't care," she says, smacking her hands on the steering wheel.

But this new attitude seems more suited to her mother's strict, incurious ways than to her own, and the feeling doesn't last. Bess admits she does want to know more about her grandfather, and more about Rose, her *biological grandmother*, a term that sounds like it's from a foreign language. Did Rose regret giving up her child to a woman so stubborn she still says the word *shvartze* not thinking it might apply to her own daughter and granddaughter?

Why and when Millie fights her battles is a mystery to Bess. Why didn't she take her stand early with Peace, for example, before they left Maryland, rather than disposing of her surreptitiously in Iowa? Maybe it was to allay her guilt for bruising him. And why *was* she hurting him? Was it selling the house that started it all or made it worse? Is this what we become when death is around the corner?

Bess is feeling the heat. She closes her window and turns up the AC. Well into California now, past Joshua Tree National Park, the air is hazier. Temperatures have to be in the high nineties. Hundreds of white windmills like airplane propellers are spinning madly amid rolling green farmland. She sees signs for a casino and bowling lanes.

She takes a swig of water and thinks back to the time before Rory. She remembers the dread of having a singles party. She thinks of Harry the divorcé who left a card on her pillow, of Sonny and other blip boys, of the depth of her loneliness and despair at being single in a spouse's world. But now that she thinks of it, Rory's ex-wives all found themselves a spouse at one time or another and are they any happier than she in the end? Lorraine, Maggie, Fawn? Carol seems happy, but that was true before she and Ina were married. Maybe Dao's the happiest of all. But then Millie's right . . . how can anyone know for sure who's really happy?

Where is Rory? She calls him again, and again her call goes straight to voice mail.

She pictures him nude. He looks great nude. And how adorable is he playing his fiddle? And his accent, his humming in the shower. He really is a nice guy—someone who picks up the Indian takeout and helps with the dishes and holds doors open and wants to hold hands. Bess's mind starts montaging the course of their courtship and can't stop—images of Rory sitting, standing, sleeping, snoring, watching TV, making love. Her favorite time

to observe Rory is during their morning routines, when she feels
the power and intimacy of being a couple—watching him spit
toothpaste into the sink, glide on deodorant, snap on his boxers,
look around for his wallet. It's when she feels most in the present.
Nighttime, just after they turn off the light and kiss good night,
is when she allows herself to imagine their future—shopping at
Home Depot, visiting Ireland, decorating a nursery.

Please, she thinks, *please don't be breaking up with me. Please
give me a chance.*

According to Gaia's latest e-mail, she, Sonny, and Pearl moved
into the suburban ranch house of Sonny's uncle in Riverside,
California. Bess's plan was to stop there for a quick visit to drop
off Gaia's box on her way to her friend's place in Los Angeles, but
she got a late start. So instead, she apologized to her friend and
had called Gaia to ask if she could spend the night.

She follows Gaia's directions and finds the house in the dark,
driving the quiet backstreets, squinting to read numbers on
houses. She parks along the curb and turns off the engine, figuring the house is one of the three on the other side of the street.
She shuts the van door slowly, but it still crashes down on the
silence of the neighborhood. She looks for a sudden light in an
upper window, but nothing happens.

It's hard to see. The nearest streetlamp doesn't seem to be
working and the lights in the houses are all off. She walks up the
driveway of one and sees it is the wrong one, so she heads to the
house next door. The number matches, but it's difficult to discern which is the front entrance. The door facing the street has a

walkway leading up to it, but the door itself looks unusable. The handle is duct-taped to the siding and the screen is barricaded in front with big boxes and a set of golf clubs. The door facing the side of the neighbor's house has a small awning, two potted plants on either side, and a stroller a few feet away.

Bess approaches the side door. The darkness is so consuming she's scared of it. She thinks she hears leaves rustling. "Hello?" she says, looking behind her. Nothing. She opens the screen door and raps lightly. "Anybody home?" She raises her fist to knock again when she hears a footstep from behind and when she whips around she sees a figure in the shadows coming toward her quickly, now nearly upon her, his hair hiding his face, a weapon in his hand, a tall frame, a threatening build, "*No!*" she yells, and with every ounce of her body, with every thought in her head from every self defense class she ever took in her karate school, she tightens into a machine of self-protection, yells, "*Groin!*" and snaps a hard kick to her attacker's balls.

She hears a sucking in of breath and then, "*Ow! Fuck*! Motherfucking *shit*!"

A light turns on inside the house, a dog barks down the street. The door opens and the light spills out onto her attacker lying on the ground, wincing, clutching himself. Bess looks up to see Gaia in the doorway. "Sonny?" says Gaia.

"Baby," Sonny whines from the ground. He is barefoot and has on black sweatpants and a black T-shirt. "Jesus Christ, Bess."

Gaia opens the door and joins them outside. "Bess, hi. You made it. Sonny, what are you doing on the ground?"

"Hell, Gaia. She yells *groin* like she's yelling halfway to China and I'm lying here holding my dick, what do you think happened? Jesus Christ, motherfucker."

"Stop saying Jesus Christ like that," says Gaia. "You know your uncle doesn't like it."

"Yeah, well he ain't here and I got me balls gonna swell up like fucking pumpkins."

"I'm sorry," says Bess, coming out of her daze, looking from one to the other. She's still shaking from what happened, though from being attacked or successfully striking out at her attacker she can't tell. *I struck an attacker*, is one of the thoughts. *I did it.* And, too, she is now admitting to herself how good it just felt to hit Sonny of all people, the noncommittal ex-boyfriend and abandoner of his pregnant girlfriend. "Sonny, what did you think I'd do, coming at me like that, in the dark, holding—"

"A balloon, for Christ's sake!" He points to a long, blue balloon nestled at the foot of a nearby bush. "The tail of this damn dog a clown made for my daughter."

"Well, I didn't know that. You came at me with it."

"I was playing. I saw you drive up, thought I'd have some fun."

"That's how you play?"

"Sonny, you need help?" says Gaia.

"No, just let me be for a while. Go on inside." He pulls himself up to a seated position.

"Sonny, I said I was sorry," says Bess. She notices his hemp bracelet and the length of his hair, which is thick and black and down to his shoulders. She has always liked long hair on Asian men.

"Sounds like you should apologize to Bess, too, Sonny," says Gaia.

Sonny picks his head up. "I apologize for making you kick me in the balls."

"Apology accepted." Bess smiles.

"Yeah, yeah," says Sonny, waving her away. "Good thing you don't know karate."

Bess follows Gaia inside.

The house is baby blue. The walls are blue, the counters are blue, the rug and couch and ceramic figurines on the shelves in the living room are all shades of pale blue and old-fashioned. Gaia has Bess take off her shoes.

"Sonny's uncle is hardly ever here," says Gaia, picking up bottles and stuffed animals as she walks Bess through the house, her breasts swinging freely beneath her oversized T-shirt. "Since Sonny's aunt died, his uncle doesn't like to be in this house, he likes his other one in Florida better, which is good for us." She brings Bess to the kitchen. "Would you like some tea?"

"I'd love some."

"How's the trip been?"

"Okay, I guess. Glad it's almost over. How's Pearl?"

Gaia takes dirty cups from the counter and places them in the sink. She tells Bess about Pearl and Bess elaborates on some of the details of her journey, especially about Cricket and his ex-wife, since Gaia had met him. She doesn't talk about Rory; she couldn't remember if she even told Gaia about him. Nevertheless, Bess thought maybe Gaia would take one look at her and understand her emotional turmoil as she used to be able to do, but the luminescence that once surrounded Gaia has faded with fatigue. Bess can see the way her shoulders slope and her feet drag, but she is still beautiful. Her skin is smooth, her red hair long and lush.

Sonny comes inside and announces he's exhausted, that he's going off to sleep. He kisses Gaia on the forehead, tells her he fixed the latch on the garbage so the critters shouldn't get in any-more. "Bess," he says, "you're welcome in our home anytime. I look forward to catching up in the morning." He sounds sincere.

"Thanks, Sonny."

"Hey," says Gaia, waiting until Sonny is out of sight. "Do you have the box I gave you?"

"It's in the van. You never told me what's in it."

"I'll show you." They retrieve the box and Bess's overnight bag and place them in the living room. Gaia runs a knife along the box top and cracks open the four cardboard folds. She opens the box with such excitement that she temporarily seems to re-gain her old fiery aura.

"Clothes?" says Bess, watching her take out pants and shirts. "I don't understand."

"Not just clothes," Gaia says, making a pile at her feet. "This." She pulls from a box within the box a white wedding dress. It is one of the most elaborate wedding dresses Bess has ever seen, with little buttons and beads and lace and embroidery. "It was my grandmother's. I didn't want Sonny to get nosy about it. You think he'll like it?"

"You're getting married?"

"Yes," Gaia says from the kitchen, attending to the kettle. "Didn't I tell you?"

Of course you are, thinks Bess. *Of course I drove your wedding dress across the country.* She asks Gaia questions about the wedding to be polite and when they finish sipping their tea, Bess announces she is exhausted and, not to be rude, but she'd like to get to bed after a quick peek in on Pearl. Gaia gives her sheets for the couch and a towel. She guides Bess to Pearl's room where healthy green plants surround a rocking chair and a crib on a yellow shag throw rug. Over the crib is a mobile of exotic animals, and in the crib, sleeping soundly, is Pearl, as wondrous as her name implies. Standing there alone with Pearl, Bess is overcome with a strange, calm feeling, a sort of love for all the innocent people of the world. She blows Pearl a kiss. She closes her eyes and makes a wish: *May you be happy, little one, in your family of three. May your mommy and daddy stay alive, may they stay happily married into old age.* Bess opens her eyes. "And if they don't," she whispers, "call me."

Bess is nearly ready for bed. Gaia has said good night and has slipped into what Bess assumes is their bedroom. Does Sonny still snore? She doesn't hear anything. She wants to ask him what got into him, leaving Gaia at the hospital, but she won't. It's not her business. Sonny was never really her business even when they were dating, he had made that clear. Anyway, it's all better this way. She rubs lotion into her hands and as she is about to turn off the light in the bathroom she stops abruptly in front of a shelf of photos. She had noticed the photos before—the bathroom seemed an odd place for them—but she hadn't looked closely. Most of them are of Pearl, and of Sonny and Gaia with Pearl, but some are of Sonny or Gaia with people she doesn't recognize. One of them, taken on a city block somewhere, is of Gaia and a group of six others laughing and making faces. This one shows a guy on the end holding a bottle of beer, staring flirtatiously at the photographer, a guy whom Bess recognizes without a doubt—now that she has it in her hand and is studying it up close—is Rory.

She moves to bring the photo closer to the light, but bumps her elbow and accidentally drops it, shattering the glass in the frame. She bends to pick it up and bangs her forehead on the shelf and two more photos crash onto the tile floor. Gaia rushes into the bathroom. "You okay?"

"I'm so sorry," breathes Bess. "Don't come in, you have bare feet."

"So do you. Don't move, I'll be right back." Gaia returns with slippers, a plastic bag, and a brush and dustbin.

"I hope I didn't wake up Pearl."

"When she's asleep, she sleeps through everything. Like her daddy. Listen, I shouldn't have put photos there. Sonny told me they were in the way."

"No, no, it's my fault," says Bess, picking up the larger pieces of glass. "I'm so clumsy." She searches the floor for glass shards and holds the bag open for Gaia as she empties the dustbin. They concentrate on cleaning up and being quiet until they survey the bathroom and conclude they got all they could get. For those few minutes Bess is shaking from nerves and theories. She hands

Gaia the photos from the broken frames and points to Rory. "Can I ask you . . . do you know him?"

Gaia takes the photo. She looks at it, then at Bess, and smiles. "I forgot that photo was there. I do know him. That's Rory Mc-Millan."

Bess is breathing quickly. "How do you know him?"

Gaia is looking at her intently. "We were married."

Bess feels attacked for the second time tonight. She braces herself against the wall, trying to make sense of Gaia's declaration. Did Rory not tell her about Gaia? Were there nine wives? That doesn't make sense. "When were you married? Like, how long ago?"

"Right after 9/11. Didn't last very long, and I haven't seen him for a couple of years."

Bess's mind is spinning. "*You're* Gloria?"

"I *was* Gloria."

There are too many questions, too many facts she's trying to conjure up about Gloria that Rory told her, too many leaps she's trying to make from the Gloria she heard of to the woman standing in front of her. "When did you change your name?"

"About two years ago, on the anniversary of my brother's death." Gaia points to a photo on the shelf of her and her brother as teenagers. "I don't know why, it was kind of a whim that stuck. My brother's name was Ray so I combined our names into one, to keep him close. Gaia's the goddess of the earth, and I kind of dug that."

"So wait . . . did you see Rory at my party, the night we met?"

"Rory was there? No, I didn't. I was sort of busy."

Bess slides down the wall of the hallway until she is sitting with her knees bent and her head in her hands. She is thinking about her singles party. She is thinking about talking to Rory then, about Gaia and Sonny's arrival, about taking Gaia through the party into her bedroom, about coming out to her main room to find Rory had left. *Did he see her? Is that why he left the party?*

"Bess?" Gaia whispers, squatting next to her.

Bess slides her fingers down her face and sighs. "I told you I was dating this guy, but I didn't tell you much about him. Well . . . it's Rory I'm dating."

Gaia sits and hugs her legs. Bess notices Gaia is now looking at her the way she used to do, as if she is seeing into the depths of Bess's soul.

"Isn't that a really bizarre coincidence?" says Bess, trying to coax a reaction.

"I don't believe in coincidences."

There's the Gaia I know. "So let me ask you, did it bother you how many times he'd been married?"

"Of course."

"But you married him anyway."

"I did."

"And it was inevitable that it would end, right?"

"I don't think so."

"GOD!" says Bess too loudly and then apologizes, looking over toward Pearl's room. "This is so frustrating. I wish someone would just give me a straight answer. Tell me eight marriages doesn't mean shit. Tell me eight marriages is sick and I should stay away. Tell me Rory is a psychopath and I'll be dead in a year if I stay with him. Or . . . or tell me he's the greatest guy on the planet and how lucky I am that eight women like you let him slip through their fingers and I'd be the biggest idiot to let him go. Just please tell me *something*."

Gaia rests her chin on her knees and watches Bess.

"Oh, don't do that," says Bess. "I hate that, that silent stuff therapists do. Okay, fine. At least tell me why you and Rory split up. Tell me why you think you have a better chance with Sonny, and don't say it's because of Pearl because I don't believe that."

Gaia stretches her toes. "I think marriage is what you make of it and what I made of it with Rory I didn't much care for. With Sonny, I think I can make something beautiful."

Bess is getting a headache. "Why couldn't you make something beautiful with Rory?"

"It wasn't beauty I was after. I wanted our marriage to help me survive, to take my pain away, and fear, and loneliness when I lost Ray. And it didn't in the end. I think for either of us. It's not that I don't feel all that at times with Sonny, it's just that I don't expect him to save me."

"But couldn't you have changed your expectations of Rory? Couldn't you have realized he wasn't going to save you and made it work? Isn't that how marriages last?"

"I could have. But I didn't want to. We were both meant for someone else."

In the middle of the night it is quiet enough for Bess to hear herself swallow. In the quiet middle of the night in this stranger's house on the other side of the country, Bess feels thousands of miles off course from where she should be, from where she knows herself.

"He asked me to marry him, too, but I'm not even sure he still wants that," Bess says softly. "I haven't been able to reach him, and he hasn't called me in five days."

"Maybe that's because he's coming to get you."

Bess looks into Gaia's eyes. The empty rings to his home number, the calls from strange area codes. *Could it be?* Oh, strange, clairvoyant Gaia, she thinks, *I hope you're right.*

CHAPTER THIRTY-EIGHT

There he is, waiting for her atop the roof of the Griffith Park Observatory on Mount Hollywood, where she had asked that he be. She studies him before she comes into his view, trying to memorize the very details of him—his attire (steel-colored cargo shorts, white button-down shirt, leather sandals, black sunglasses), his body (lean, muscular legs, not too hairy, slightly sunburned; broad shoulders; hair cut short since she's seen him last), the casual way he's leaning on the ledge (one leg taut, the other slack; the weight on his elbows; his hands clasped, a small bag at his feet). He's perfect, she thinks, he's handsome, he's *mine*. She wants to soak in this image until it lives inside her.

He has come for her, all this way.

My husband, she whispers. *Please let it be until death do us part.*

It was Gabrielle who orchestrated their coming together, in the beginning and now today. When Bess left Gaia and Sonny's house the next morning, she headed to UCLA to visit her grad school friend. There she called Gabrielle and cajoled her into

revealing what she knew, that Rory had just missed her in Chicago, that he went to visit Cici, that he was on his way to California. Rory wanted his arrival to be a surprise and was relying
on Gabrielle to find someplace he could meet Bess and figure out
how to get her there.

But once Bess knew, she wanted to choose the place. The
real proposal was coming, she could feel it: the one she had been
dreaming about since she was a little girl. Hell if she wasn't going
to get her Hollywood ending. *Tell him to go to the observatory at
noon*, she told Gabrielle. *I'll be there.*

And now here she is, there he is, on a cloudless day with a
small breeze and a beautiful view out beyond the lawn of the
observatory, to the hills and the famous Hollywood sign. She
hurries toward him, imagining what the two of them could look
like from the outside: a woman calling out to her lover, jumping
into his arms, he smiling and laughing and swinging her around
while they kiss.

"Rory!" she calls out.

Rory turns and suddenly looks alarmed. "Bess! What? What
happened?" She arrives in front of him with open arms. He grips
her shoulders. "Are you all right?"

She doesn't understand. "Yes. Of course I'm all right.
What—."

"Oh, thank God. The way you were running, I don't know. I
thought someone was chasing you."

Bess loosens herself from him, curls a lone bit of hair behind
her ear, smooths out her sundress. "No, sorry. I just . . . saw you
there and . . ." She clears her throat. "It's good to see you."

Rory leans in slightly, perhaps to kiss her, she thinks, but then pulls back. "It's good to see you, too." He wipes away a drip of sweat from his temple.

"How are your grandparents?" he says.

Bess feels something inside her start to unhinge. She doesn't know what to do with her hands. Her heart rate is accelerating too fast. She clings to small talk as if she were holding sight of the horizon on rough seas. "They're okay. Thanks. I mean, I think they'll be okay."

"Good." Rory takes a deep breath and looks out to the hills. "Bess, you must be wondering—" and then he stops.

Bess is crying. Hard. Big wet sobs she can't control.

"Oh, Bess. Honey." Rory wraps her in his arms.

She doesn't even know why she's crying. Her emotions have taken over like a big swirling hurricane and all she can do is let them come. It's been such a long journey. "I'm sorry," she gasps. "I love you. I shouldn't have looked for your ex-wives. I should have talked to you. I should have trusted you. I do trust you."

"No," he says, kissing her cheek, her forehead, her lips. "It's my fault. I'm so sorry I didn't tell you everything the day we met."

"Rory, ask me again," she says.

"Are you sure? We don't have to—"

"Ask me. Please. Won't you? I mean, will you?"

He bends down to the bag at his feet and pulls from it a director's clapboard he must have bought at a tourist shop. He steps back, holds it out, and says, "Bess and Rory, Marriage Proposal, Take Two," then cracks the clapstick. He moves toward her, bends down on his knee, and opens a blue velvet box to present an elegant, modest silver ring with a tiny ruby, because he remembered from one of their conversations about marriage in general that she didn't want a diamond. "Will you marry me, Bess Gray?"

What a sight she must be with bleary eyes and her nose running. But she doesn't care. She doesn't care that his clapping a clapstick and getting down on one knee might be corny. She doesn't even care that he may have been that corny eight times before. She loves his corniness. He took a risk coming out to California. She can take a risk, too. "Yes. Yes, I will marry you, Rory McMillan."

They kiss and she cries a little more and even he tears up and an older couple nearby claps for them, apologizing that they overheard but, *Oh*, they say, *how romantic.*

Down in the parking lot, after an hour of strolling and holding hands and catching up on the days they missed and talking about some of the hard secrets they've kept (promising never more to keep the important stuff from each other), and thinking about the future in giddy spurts of ideas (even the possibility of a family), they come to the van. While they wait for the air-conditioning to kick in, Bess looks out toward the Hollywood sign. "We'll make it, right?" she says. "I mean, you think we have a good chance?"

He reaches out and brushes her cheek with his fingers. "I think we have a very good chance," he says.

CHAPTER THIRTY-NINE

For God's sake, woman, don't keep me waiting . . . how is post-proposal bliss? How was L.A.? You haven't called me in days." In his voice mail from somewhere in Middle America, Cricket sounds like he's yelling into his cell phone. Gabrielle's message, the other reason Bess's phone light is blinking, is of a similar urgency, only hers has a bonus threat. "I'm so excited I'm peeing. If you don't call me the second you walk in that door, if you're even listening to my message without having dialed my number I'm never going to speak to you again. I want details."

Bess doesn't need to be admonished. Now that she's back home, she's excited to call Millie and Irv and her friends and finds them all equally excited to hear her news. She is less eager to tell Gerald, knowing that will be a tough subject, but she nevertheless wants to see him, to see how he is doing without her grandparents and reassure him of her devotion. She speaks to Vivian and makes plans to visit them later in the week.

After several extraordinary days together tossing out ideas for a wedding and living arrangements and other logistics,

Bess asks Rory for some time to herself and Rory thankfully understands. She wants to be in her apartment uninterrupted, to sit with her things and reacquaint herself with herself. And she wants to be in Washington, to know what it's like without her grandparents nearby, to know it'll be okay. She cleans the upper half of a closet, buys fresh goat cheese from a market, takes from her shelf a book on Mexican folklore that she'd begun but set aside and begins again. She makes notes about where she might start digging up information on Rose, should she feel like doing that, and as soon as she can she attends a Tae Kwon Do class at the dojo where her fellow students welcome her back, a nice reminder that she's part of that community. She suspects she'll be sore after the class, having been away from it for a couple of weeks, but even that will feel good. *Nice power, good eye contact*, her sensei says during one of the drills, and then compliments her again at the end of class on the confidence she projected during forms.

One afternoon, twirling her engagement ring and feeling like a fiancée, she walks down to the shops below Dupont Circle and tries on a new dress, thigh-length and off-the-shoulder. As she comes out of the dressing room, she looks up and sees her reflection in a round mirror, a distorted image showing her head much larger than the rest of her, her feet the smallest of all. It strikes her at first that maybe she is glimpsing who she really is inside. Journey or no journey, ring or no ring, she is someone who can't get away from her big thinking, worrying head, too heavy for such little feet to get her anywhere. *Here*, says the saleswoman, pointing her to a full-length mirror on a far wall, *you can see your-*

self better. This time, Bess looks at her reflection and sees herself proportioned and whole and imagines she is looking at a stranger in many ways, but someone she would like to get to know better, someone she could trust. *You like it?* asks the saleswoman. *I do*, says Bess. *I'll take it.*

That evening, she settles into her apartment with a mix CD she made for herself before her trip with some of her mellow favorites: Kate Rusby, the Decemberists, Nanci Griffith, Tom Waits. In her living room, she closes her curtains and something tickles her hand. On the window ledge she notices the fir tree Gaia had given her on the evening of her birthday. *It's just a baby*, Gaia had said. And it is, its little branches only a foot high, its pine needles an inch long at most. But under Bess's care, and Gabrielle's care while she was away, it had grown. Or maybe it hadn't grown so much as it filled out, its branches thicker, its needles greener, its stem sturdier and smooth. *When you're ready, you can choose its home outside and plant it in the ground*, Gaia had said.

Bess steps outside and chooses a spot to plant the tree in front of her building, just below her window. She digs at the dirt with her hands, enjoying the feel of it on her palms. She's hit with a warm memory of repotting plants with her mom when she was little: her mom explaining how she was giving each plant a new home to grow. It was then Bess's job to nourish their transition with her water can and cooing assurances.

She hears a siren and looks for the source down Eighteenth Street. She notices the gay couple across the way are unlocking their door, having just come home from some activity that has them in a good mood. They wave to her, and then to another neighbor down the street, an older woman who waddles and carries her groceries home in a cart. The woman makes way for a Chinese food delivery man who has double-parked his vehicle, rings a bell, and transacts with a teenager who has run down to collect her dinner in her ballet outfit.

Is there anything more alive than a city at dusk?

Bess turns back to her baby fir, now planted in D.C.'s soil. There is an old, majestic oak on the other side of the building's entrance that Bess imagines will watch over her little tree. Gaia once said that old trees have the best stories, we just have to learn how to listen. Bess touches the trunk of the old oak. It probably does know this city better than anyone, beyond its politics and museums, its crime rates and torchlike summers. It's probably dropped leaves on all kinds of people, immigrants and soldiers and society wives alike. But it's silent and still and that's what Bess loves about trees, a reprieve from the world's stories. Still, when she heads over to Rory's tonight, relaxes into his embrace and eases into sleep, she might dream of her own stories she could tell an old tree, sweet ones and sad ones that she knows have never been told, and maybe even ones that have yet to be.

Acknowledgments

I owe a great deal of thanks to a great many people, many of whom I will thank here and some I won't, because I'll forget. I'll forget because I feel much older than when I started this book a gazillion years ago and because I'm a mom to a two-year-old, which means these days I'm more likely to remember the name of Elmo's goldfish than, say, where I parked my car. Please forgive me.

First off, thanks to my good friend and ghost-agent, Alex Glass, for accompanying me through the whole journey—for brainstorming ideas, reading a draft that was way too long, offering smart suggestions, and for his sound advice and encouragement on everything that has happened since. Thanks to Carolyn Parkhurst, Leslie Pietrzyk, C. M. Mayo, Kitty Davis, Ann McLaughlin, E. J. Levy, Susan Coll, Paula Whyman, Paulette Beete, Leslie Schwartz, and Keith Donohue for their support and thorough reading of chapters hot off the press or early full drafts. I can't imagine the unwieldy beast this would have been without their red marks, question marks, and big Xs, kindly offered.

Thanks to my wonderful and attentive agent, Marly Rusoff, for making possible new beginnings and new endings. Thanks to my editor, Claire Wachtel, whose good counsel (I can finally admit) made this a much better book. Thanks to Richard Peabody for first publishing an excerpt from this novel in the anthology *Electric Grace*.

Thanks to my teachers and fellow students at the D.C. Self Defense Karate Association for their inspiration, to the gals who drove with me in a minivan to Fallingwater and Pittsburgh for research and homemade margaritas, and to the awesome folks who came to my singles' party years ago and made me feel a little less lonely.

Thanks to my dear friend Jen Brickman who came in at the twenty-fifth hour and gave me a *schmeckle*. I am deeply grateful for her superb editing skills and words of encouragement when I needed them most. Thanks to the McNeels for giving me a place to think.

A loving thanks to my mom, who passed on to me her passion for reading and thirst for good books, and my dad, a talented banjo and hammered dulcimer player who introduced me to Irish music. Loving thanks, too, to my family—my husband, Alex, and son, Eli, for their hugs and laughter and for putting up with me yelling downstairs from my writing nook, "give me just five more minutes!" and then taking twenty.

Finally, thanks to the city of Washington, D.C., and all its interesting and friendly citizens. I'm proud to call it home.